ULTIMATE SECRETS

Game On!
S.K. Lundberg

Also by S.K. Lundberg

THE ULTIMATE SACRIFICE: THE DEAD OF WINTER

ULTIMATE SECRETS

SCAVENGER HUNT

S.K. LUNDBERG

Cedarside Publishing

Ultimate Secrets: Scavenger Hunt is a work of fiction. Names, characters, places, and incidents are a product of the author's imagination or are used fictitiously. Any resemblance to actual event, locales, businesses, or persons, living or dead, is entirely coincidental.

Published in the United States by Cedarside Publishing.

Library of Congress Cataloging-in-Publication Data is available.
ISBN: 978-1-7373341-0-1
eBook ISBN: 978-1-7373341-1-8
Cover design and photography: S.K. Lundberg

Printed in the United States of America

This will always and forever be for the boys and their families. One day, justice will be served.

ACKNOWLEDGEMENTS

A big thanks to my editing crew: Sara, Jordan, and Bruce. Your eyes are swifter and more cunning than mine will ever be. I couldn't have done it without you. You're awesome!

Huge props to all the armchair detectives out there still searching for the truth. Keep sharing your knowledge and insight with the world. Together we will solve this mystery.

Thank you to all the Payton fans who fell in love with her and her quirky way. I appreciate your patience and your never-ending support. You guys rock!

For everyone who stopped by my booth at the markets to chat and purchase a signed copy of my books, it was great to meet you. Hope to see you all again soon.

PREFACE

Since 1997, a strange phenomenon called the Smiley Face Murders has plagued the Midwest, the Northeast, Portland, Australia, and the United Kingdom. For some strange reason, this flies under the radar of most of the media and local law enforcement. Here is a brief summary: Smart, popular, athletic, young men continue to vanish after a night out with their friends. Days, weeks, or even months go by before their lifeless bodies are discovered in a river, pond, or other water source. The Smiley Face name caught on because a smiley face or other sigils are found near or next to many of the bodies. Some of the boys are never found at all, leaving their families and friends still looking for answers. Why are so many people in authority looking the other way? What is really going on here?

In 2006, I joined the countless armchair detectives exploring the theories floating around the globe. After watching a local news anchor from the Midwest report yet another young man disappearing during the dead of winter, I figured it was time to start my own research on the subject. So, I did.

A few years later, I decided to take all the theories surrounding the Smiley Face Murders and weave them into a crime fiction novel. This is my creative way to share this strange phenomenon with the world. I wanted to do something different than report a list of the boys and where they were found. My goal is to get more people talking about it. The Ultimate Sacrifice: The Dead of Winter, for obvious reason, is set in the fictitious small town in the Northwoods called River Bend. A cast of unforgettable characters were created for their fate to be revealed in a suspenseful storyline. Payton, a tenacious college student, leads her friends on an investigative journey to try to solve the mystery when someone they all know becomes a victim.

This second book in the series will hopefully keep people talking. Ultimate Secrets: Scavenger Hunt is set in the fictitious spring break paradise of Port Cristibel Island. Payton and her friends will reunite with the infamous Smiley and the murderous games will continue.

May your awareness bring us all one step closer to the truth and one day justice will be served. In the meantime, enjoy Payton's bumpy ride.

CHAPTER ONE

The intense blistering rays of the sun sizzled across my bare skin while a tiny bead of perspiration trickled down between my breasts. I took a sip of my margarita before I rolled over on my beach towel in my favorite blue thong bikini. I untied my top, letting the straps slide across my glistening skin.

The pure white sand that surrounds my towel is ridiculously hot. But not as hot as the two lifeguards, Hector and Luis, who are about to rub oil on every inch of my perfectly sun-kissed body. Apparently, three really is a magical number.

Relax. It's more of a massage á trois than a ménage á trois. Are you waiting for me to wake up from a dream? Psych. I am awake and loving every minute of this.

Hi, my name is Payton M. Richardson. Usually the "M" in my name stands for mischief, mayhem, and murder. So far today, it just stands for Marie.

What can I say? Life has been outstanding lately. My slight, temporary incline has spiked to an all-time high, and now I am comfortably resting on a blissful plateau. Presently, I am celebrating the fact that it has been forty-one days since anyone has tried to kill me. This just happens to be my new personal best.

On the downside, however, it also means that it has been forty-one days since I have tried to kill anyone. This fact is a little troubling to me. In my defense though, I was having an extremely shitty week when I stabbed the creep. I know. My bad. Enough said. Let's move on, shall we?

According to my math that would make today, March 13. You know what that means. Tomorrow, my secret mission to catch the River Bend killer continues. It is the day I stop running from danger; and instead, meet it head-on at the universal (3-14) Pi Day Festival.

Personally, I prefer to enjoy my Pi Day alamode, without the sinister scoops of murder and mayhem. Unfortunately, fate is a vile bitch with a dark sense of humor. She isn't about to let that happen.

For approximately four days, Port Christibel Island will be teaming with evil scientists, wicked witches, mind-bending enthusiasts, and an abundance of drunken unsuspecting partygoers. I am predicting a catastrophe of epic proportions. Just kidding, we have a plan. The bad guys will go to jail for a long, long, long time. If only it could be that easy.

I almost forgot. My parents will be there too. Janna's uncanny psychic ability and Stan's demand for family bonding time will certainly challenge my schemes and push my creative lying to an unhealthy level. Trying to keep my mission a secret from them will be damn near impossible. Wait. I've changed my mind. This does have disaster written all over it. Wish me luck. I would love to tell you more about my plan, but I need to finish my margarita and my massage. Then I have a plane to catch.

* * *

IN THE MIND OF A MURDERER

Did you miss me? Of course, you did. I am evil. I am brilliant. I am absolutely unforgettable. Admit it—you are an addict. You need me. I am under your skin like a needle full of that juice. I am the fix pulling you back into my game. You want more. You cannot deny it. I am the itch you cannot scratch. You need to know who I am.

Let me bask in the glory of being me for a second ... There. That is better. Life as it should be—me first. Do not worry, I will not be losing my head over my newfound fame, but somebody might. It is all part of the plan.

Today, will be like a day at the beach. Sun and fun for everyone until the waves come crashing down, and the party is ruined. My prediction: You will know the floater and you will hate me for it. That is just a little teaser to get you salivating for more. You know you want it all: the dark, the disturbing, the grotesque. And you shall have it but be patient. It is almost time.

As for Payton, she already hates me. When she finds out who I really am, she is going to wish we were both dead. It will be a fun ride until then. As always, pay close attention. Secrets will spill out when I want you to know them, not before. That is all you need to know. So grab a beer and join the party. It is spring break on Port Christibel Island. The sand is hot. The water is wet. It is time for someone to die. Shall we play a game? Curtain please.

***

Just before sunrise, I received a text from an unknown number:

Meet me downstairs in the outside pool area at 8 a.m. Sit up at the Tiki bar. I will find you. It is a matter of life or death. Tell no one. You MUST come alone.

This was most unfortunate. I sent back a quick reply:

K

Yeah, I know. My blissful incline just took a freaking nosedive. I put on my favorite thong bikini and said a little prayer kissing my ass good-bye. My tramp stamp and I hit the Port Christibel beach early to start our secret mission.

I walked through the propped open access door leading to the outdoor pool area. Spring break was definitely in the air. And so were a few of the girls without their bikini tops. They were riding their boyfriends' shoulders in the pool, playing a game of chicken. In a sense, so was I. At some point today, I was bound to fall off and get a face full of something unwanted. Ugh!

The pool area was already a party pandemonium. It was either leftover partiers from last night or a fresh batch of new recruits. It didn't really matter. A sea of gyrating half-naked college students, doing body shots off each other, filled the tiled patio and spilled onto the beachfront beyond the pool.

To my left, a group of shirtless semi-steamy guys were playing hacky sack. They yelled, "Show us your tits," as I passed by.

It's going to be a long four days. "Guys, I'm already in a thong bikini. Do you mind if I pace myself for a while? Besides, I never show my boobs before my first breakfast beer."

Every male within earshot held out their glass of beer, offering it to me.

Oh brother. "No thanks, guys. I can buy my own beer," I said.

After I shot them down, a few of the boys said, "Aw, man." They looked disappointed.

"But round two is on you," I joked.

The boys went wild with high fives, fist pumps, and body slams. Guys are so easy and predictable. I wasn't sure how I was going to talk my way out of this. The next female contestant through the door was my best bet and my new best friend. I would gladly buy her whatever she wants to take my place in the titty parade. Maybe my first breakfast beer will inspire me.

I made my way through the crowd of rowdy adolescent angst to the Tiki Bar on the edge of the sand. The only seat left was on the side of the bar closest to the beach. The seat was made of wicker. I wrinkled up my nose. It was not thong friendly. I found a spare towel on the bar top and placed it under my exposed behind.

There was a ruckus in the doorway. As soon as I recognized them, I hid my face behind a bar menu. It was Teagan and Lily. Teagan, my slutty friend, confidently strutted through the doorway in her neon orange and hot pink striped bikini. Without anyone asking her, Teagan proudly showed off what Mother Nature had given her and proceeded to the beach. The expected hoots filled the air. I was off the hook and it didn't cost me a dime. Thanks, Teagan.

On her way by a group of virile lads, Teagan put her arm around the only blond in the group, kidnapping him away from his friends. He was her flavor of the day, or maybe, the hour. It was clear to everyone that this weekend Teagan's idea of a committed relationship was a box of condoms and an alibi.

Next, the crowd of boys looked at Lily, my brother's Goth girlfriend, who was in a black and white skull and crossbones beach cover-up and dark sunglasses. Her dyed black hair covered by a black floppy beach hat. There was nothing sexy going on with her outfit, but that's Lily. She gave them the finger, waving it around for all to see when asked the less than delicate question about showing us her goods. I chuckled at her behavior. Her spunky dark side was showing. I love that about her.

The boys turned into an angry protesting mob. Lily hit a few of them with her oversized beach bag as she walked by. Three or four of them fell into the pool. When she was done making a scene, Lily stomped her way in my direction. I ducked under the bar, bending over like I had dropped something. I was hiding because I was told to come alone.

She stopped at the corner of the bar. I could see Lily's black and white self-pedicure and black, two-dollar flip-flops. From where I was hiding, I could tell she was talking to the bartender. I could see his feet too. They were having a private, whispered conversation that I couldn't quite make out. Lily took a large cyclonic-shaped drink from him. He slipped an envelope into her beach bag.

Lily seemed to be on a secret mission of her own today. For now, I had to let her go. I would catch up to her and my brother later. She walked to the edge of the tile and looked around. When she stepped onto the sand, Lily disappeared into the massive crowd of people.

I popped up to find myself face-to-face with my mid-twentysomething bearded bartender. He smiled a toothy grin at me. His eyes were hidden behind a pair of mirrored sunglasses. Dark brown hair hung out from underneath his backwards baseball cap, fringing his face. His red and white striped work polo shirt and faded blue jean cargo shorts hung loosely on his thin frame. Tattoo sleeves crept up both arms, disappearing under the cuff of his short-sleeved shirt.

"What?" I asked, as he continued to stare. "I suppose you want to see my boobs too?"

He laughed. "Maybe later, Payton. Right now, you look thirsty," he said in a voice an octave lower than I expected.

I felt my eyes widen from behind my expensive sunglasses. He knew me. I was at a definite disadvantage. Okay, I'll play along.

He filled a plastic to-go cup with an ice-cold breakfast beer and sat it down in front of me. "I'm Jeremy, by the way." He laughed again.

"Is something funny?" I asked. He was being borderline creepy.

"Definitely not." He looked down at my beer.

That was a little suspicious. I picked up my beer and took a sip. It was an acceptable Midwestern brand. I nodded my approval. When I glanced down at the napkin, there was a note:

Meet me over by the wooden fence in five minutes.

After I read it, the bartender grabbed it, put it in the ashtray, and set it on fire with his cigarette. We both stopped for a brief second to watch it transform to ash.

I pulled a crisp fifty out of my beach bag. "Thanks."

"No problem. See you around."

As I pushed my barstool back, a perfectly bronzed, blond-haired surfer with dreadlocks rammed into me. He was obviously loaded. I fell onto the sand in a heap.

He hopped up on my vacant seat without noticing that he had knocked me over. "Give me the daily special," he rudely demanded.

"With pleasure," said Jeremy without missing a beat.

I picked myself off the ground, brushing away the sand from my skin. Bloody surfers! They think they own the beach. Without looking back, I strolled through the sand until I found a secluded spot by the gray sun-damaged fence. From here, I spotted Lily down the beach past the lifeguard station. She was talking to a dark-haired girl. It was Stephani Waters.

Here's the thing about Stephani; she is not my friend nor is she a frenemy. I would categorize her as my foe in training, more about that later. Currently, I'm trying to figure out her and Lily's connection.

The two of them were having an intense conversation. Stephani grabbed Lily's beach bag. Lily shoved her backwards into a nearby sand dune. I chuckled to myself. They weren't having a friendly chat. They were fighting. I expected Stephani and her gym toned biceps to retaliate. Instead, Stephani got up and brushed the sand off her bulging thighs and broad shoulders. She scowled at Lily and walked down the beach. I didn't blame her. Lily could be a scary Goth girl when she wanted to be.

I took two slow steps contemplating if I should go talk to Lily or follow Stephani.

"Psst, Payton, over here," whispered Jeremy.

Duty awaits. My attention immediately shifted. I needed to deal with this first. He was hiding behind a large plastic banner advertising tonight's drink specials at the Chaos beach bar. He motioned me over with a hand gesture. I did my best to inconspicuously meet him over there. It was broad daylight. We weren't really fooling anyone with our overt stealthiness.

"I don't usually get involved in other people's business," started Jeremy. "If Brent didn't show up for his shift, I was supposed to give you this." He reached under his shirt and took a white envelope from the waistband of his shorts. He handed it to me on the down low. "Seeing as how you gave me the fifty, I figured I should fulfill my end of the bargain."

I looked around to see if anyone was watching us. They weren't. The flap of the envelope was stuck shut, stopping anyone from reading its contents. I ripped off the end and pulled out the note inside: know are I to the through other B.

I looked at Jeremy. "What the hell does that mean?"

"I have no idea. This is all too cryptic for me. I'm out. I hope Brent isn't in any kind of trouble."

I held up another fifty. "Are you sure you don't know anything else."

He took the bill from my hand. "See that girl down the beach in the skull and crossbones?"

I didn't have to look. "Yeah, I know her."

"She has the other note."

"That's it?" I asked, feeling a bit shortchanged.

"Sorry, I'm out. My rent is due so…" Jeremy slinked away.

Not money well spent. At least it's not as bad as bribing a tow truck driver with my mother's diamond earrings that were worth six-grand. Yeah, I actually did that for Dylan, a boy I was in love with, so Vivian, his stepmom who is also my housekeeper, wouldn't be angry. I know, it's a bit complicated. My life always is. In my defense, the boy was smoking hot. I would do it again in a heartbeat. The downside: I still need to creatively explain to my mother what happened to her earrings. I sighed and walked in Lily's direction. I made my way through the crowd, walking up behind Lily.

"Hey," I said, grabbing her by the shoulder.

Lily spun around. "Geez, Payton. You almost gave me a heart attack."

"You seem a bit on edge," I said as we continued to stroll down the beach.

"I am," she said, confiding in me. "Have you seen your brother Luke?"

"No. Why?" I was genuinely concerned, especially after Brent's weird message.

"Luke couldn't sleep last night. He went for a walk on the beach early this morning. I haven't been able to get ahold of him."

"Why am I just hearing about this now?"

"Sorry, I've been trying to get in contact with Brent too. Something is wrong. I can feel it."

"Lily, let me see the note Jeremy gave you."

"What note? I have no idea—"

"Cut the crap. Jeremy told me he gave it to you."

"Fine. Here." She handed me the envelope that was in her bag.

I opened the envelope. Her note read: They we here had go with plan.

"Your note doesn't make any sense either," I said exasperated.

"Let me see yours," said Lily, holding out her hand.

I gave it to her. She held them up together.

"Oh shit," said Lily in a distressed tone. She looked at me.

"What does it say?" I begged for her to tell me what she knew.

"He split the message into two notes." She read the message out loud: "They know we are here. I had to go with other plan B."

"Plan B? We don't have a plan B. What is he talking about?"

Lily shrugged her shoulders at my questions.

A woman's blood-curdling scream echoed across the beach. I looked north towards the jetty. A group of roughly twenty frantic bystanders stood on the jetty pointing at something in the water.

Our eyeballs simultaneously widened to their limits. The intense feeling of dread that plagued me for months was back. I quickly chugged the last of my breakfast beer and followed the stampede of people working their way towards the jetty.

I followed Lily as she pushed her way through the crowd, hoping for the best but fearing the worst. Lily reached the circle of panicked onlookers first. She shoved her way into the center by the water's edge.

I stopped short on purpose. This was just too much for me. The blackness was creeping back in. That little voice was echoing in my head again. Please no, not him.

Lily's agonizing scream confirmed what I already knew. I fell to me knees cursing and pleading to the heavens. "Why him?"

***

I do enjoy a good plan B.

CHAPTER TWO

The crowd was closing in on me. Claustrophobia is the tale-tell beginning of a panic attack for me. To fight it off, I jumped up and joined Lily at the water's edge. The stunned crowd gave way with little resistance.

Oh god, it was worse than I thought. The headless male's body, dressed in jeans and a familiar t-shirt, bobbed in the waves. With each pulse of the current, the body slammed into the jagged rocks of the jetty. His arms and torso looked like they had been burned with a blowtorch. His hands and feet severed and missing. It was a gruesome sight that I was not prepared to see.

Dread and relief filled my head again. My prayer had been answered only to have it shoved back in my face with another heart wrenching outcome. The body wasn't my brother Luke. It was Brent Biggerton.

Brent was the third cog in the wheel of our plan. Lily, Brent, and I had come up with a scheme to flush out the killer. This wasn't it. Our plan was simple. Brent, who was Lily's friend and tattoo artist, gave me a tramp stamp that would attract members of a certain witchy group, if you know what I mean. From there, we were going to surveil and hopefully infiltrate the group. This was horrible. Brent was the brains behind it all.

Brent was invaluable because he knew so much about the occult. I still had so many unanswered questions. His death changed everything.

Just when life couldn't possibly get any worse, it did. A large, gray shark showed up. It grabbed Brent by the leg. It thrashed in the water as its teeth tore through his flesh. There were audible gasps from the crowd and a woman screamed in horror.

"That's it, Julie. I'm outta here. I'm going home," said a girl that I did not recognize.

"But you're my maid of honor," said a distraught Julie Pederson.

Julie, the bride to be, was my ex-best friend. She is currently engaged to my ex-fiancé Brad Thomas. That simple fact explains a lot, I'm sure. Clearly, my life is more complicated than it needs to be.

Julie ran over to her unhappy maid of honor, while Brad, our town's police lieutenant, walked over to Lily and me.

"Any idea who the stiff is?" asked Brad with a raised eyebrow.

"Shut up, you ass!" cried Lily. "Brent is … was my friend." It was obvious to everyone that Lily was terribly upset.

"Brent Biggerton?" Brad asked slowly like he didn't really want to know the answer.

"Yes, you ass. Now. Go. Away." Lily's voice was filled with intense anger and grief.

Brad gave up trying to get more information out of Lily. He turned to me. "Payton, what's going on?"

I put my hands on my hips in a confrontational manner. "You tell me, Brad. You guys are getting married … here? … now?"

"Relax! It's just the rehearsal. Julie thought it would be romantic to get married out here on the jetty."

"Not very romantic today, is it?"

"No shit," he answered back. "I better go find my dad and tell him his girlfriend's son is dead."

I grabbed him by the arm to stop him. "You're joking, right?"

"Afraid not," he said, pulling away from me.

I had to ask one more time to make sure I heard him right. "Your dad and Big Bad Nancy Biggerton are dating?"

He turned around just long enough to comment, "Afraid so." Brad continued on his way to locate his father, Richard Thomas, aka the Chief.

This was epically unfortunate for me. The two nemesis in my life have joined forces and they are cahooting, cohorting, whatever. It's just bad.

Let me try to explain this in the simplest way possible. First, the Chief hates me because I dumped his son Brad at the altar. Nancy hates me and my family because my mom won the lottery. My mom got to retire from the hospital in grand fashion while Nancy is still stuck working on the nightshift. Now Nancy's son is dead. They are going to blame me for this and make my life a living hell.

"Payton Marie Richardson," boomed from the Chief's throat, "are you standing over another dead body?"

I immediately swung around. Our eyes met head-on. It was profound.

"I'm so sorry, Brent was a nice kid," slipped out of my mouth before I could stop myself.

The Chief went from pale to purple with anger in record time. Nancy's eyes widened. Two seconds later, she fainted. The Chief jumped to her side. He looked up at Brad who was walking up to them. "Get what's left of Nancy's son the hell out of the water." Brad ran towards the hotel pool to try to find something to fish Brent's body out of the surf.

The Chief helped Nancy to her feet. He put his arm around her to help escort her towards the hotel. Before Brad could get back with a lifeguard pole, another shark grabbed Brent's arm and pulled his body underwater. It never resurfaced.

"That was wicked," said a familiar voice in the crowd.

It was Chameleon. I turned around to find eight local X-Box gamers from River Bend standing on the jetty with us.

This group of high school students rent the upstairs apartment over my parents' restaurant for their gaming tournaments. They prefer to go by their gamer tags instead of their real names. Actually, I don't even know their real names. The rest of the gang is Blond Ambition, The Singe and his older brother Thirteen, Feed Bag, and Wolfman who is the leader of the group. They added two new recruits to the group, who I did not recognize.

"What are you guys doing here?" I asked. I was honestly shocked to see them this far from home.

"Chameleon's dad is our science teacher. He drove us down here in one of the school buses for the science convention," said Blond Ambition.

"This isn't a safe place for you boys to be," I said in protest. "You boys should go home immediately."

"Relax, Payton," said Chameleon. "my dad has us doing daily projects to keep us out of trouble."

"Today's project is to pick up the trash on the beach," said Feed Bag.

"And then to write a group paper on beach conservation and the impact spring break has on our ecosystem," added The Singe.

"Let's get back at it," said Wolfman, pushing his thick brown mane back off his forehead. "If we are done by 2:00p.m., Chameleon's dad is buying us pizza for supper."

The boys all waved good-bye before they disappeared back into the crowd. This was going to be an impossible mission to keep everyone I know safe. As the crowd started to disperse, Luke emerged with a large coffee in his hand. Lily ran over to him, threw her arms around him, and planted a big kiss on his lips.

"I was so worried. Where have you been?" she asked, starting to cry again.

"I went for a walk and a coffee. Jeez. None of the shops on the beach had soy milk, so I had to walk into town."

Lily punched him out of grief and anger. "Call me next time, okay?" Lily grabbed Luke by the hand. "Let's go back to our room. I need to lay down. You can help me fix my racoon eyes from crying." The two of them walked away hand in hand.

I had never seen Lily so vulnerable before. She usually has this thick candy shell that hides her emotions. It generally goes well with her whole Goth girl persona. Brent's death must have really gotten to her. Maybe she has never lost anyone close to her until now.

Brad finally showed up with the lifeguard pole. He looked in the water. "That's just great. My dad is going to be pissed."

"So who is going to investigate what happened to Brent?" I asked.

"Kind of hard to do that without a body, Payton. You or Lily will have to fill out a police report that states you identified the body and that's all I know for now."

Julie walked up as I was about to leave. I was hoping to make a clean getaway. Things were still a little hanky between us.

"Payton, I, … we, … need a huge favor from you," said Julie in a super sweet syrupy tone.

"O … kay?" This is bound to be painful.

"Will you be our maid of honor tomorrow? Sheila is on her way to the airport, so we can't get married without you." She gave me a big pleading smile. "Pleeeeease?"

This is so beyond twisted. Julie was my maid of honor when I was marrying Brad. And now Brad gave her my old engagement ring when he proposed to HER. Yep, twisted like a big, salty pretzel. What do I do? Maybe I'm not ready for them to get married yet. This is all happening so fast. I thought I was going to have more time to process this.

Ugh! I sighed. They both stared at me waiting for an answer. "Okay, I'll do it."

Julie screamed and hugged me. Brad nodded his silent, thankful approval.

I must be crazy. "I need a beer." That thought was supposed to stay in my head, but it came flying out.

"Don't forget to pick up your dress today at Family Bridal. It's downtown," said Julie beaming with joy.

"I have to pay for my dress?" Another thought that just slipped out.

"And any last-minute alterations. I'd probably go soon. You and Sheila are NOT the same size. Thanks, Payton. You're the best." She was positively radiant which was making this even harder to swallow.

"So, who am I standing up with? Anyone cute?" I had to ask, right? I had to throw her off my inner turmoil.

"You remember Nick from the police force?" said Brad. "He's my best man."

"Yes, I remember him." How could I forget creepy Nick? "When did you two get so chummy?"

"After the unfortunate incident when Tim died, my dad made Nick my partner. We hit it off. He's a great guy. Do you want me to put in a good word for you?"

"Ew. No. I'll pass." Well, that came out harsher than it should have. "I guess I will see you guys tomorrow then." I gave them both two thumbs up. I don't know why. It was totally lame.

"The ceremony is at 10:00 a.m. sharp," said Julie. "Meet us down here at quarter to 10:00."

I ran away as fast as I could in search of a beer. After that, I will file a report, and no doubt buy the most expensive ugly-ass bridesmaid's dress in history. How do I get talked into these things?

***

Well, that was fun to watch.

***

Before I headed to the police station, I stopped at a food truck on the beach for the special of the day. It was a beer burrito combo. It hit the spot and managed to chisel away some of my anxiety from the earlier shitshow. From my seat at the picnic table, I spotted a local store that carried beach attire. The smart-ass in me decided to buy a mesh coverup with a smiley face emoji motif. You know what they say: If you can't join them, just piss them off. I was trying to get noticed in a sea of people. Trolling for my enemy was my new obsession.

Feeling like a determined badass, I turned the corner to the left, heading away from the beach and into town. It was about a three-block walk to the police station from here. I did my best to get all the beer belches and gassy business out of my system before I stepped inside the precinct.

The clerk behind the counter gave me a slight eye roll due to my minty barley breath. I composed myself as best as I could with my crazy tale from earlier this morning. I don't think Wes, badge number 8475, believed my shark tale, but we both signed the death certificate at the bottom. It was official. The deed was done. Brent was gone in real life and on paper.

I stepped back out into the light of day. Boy, was it steamy with the sun beating down directly overhead. The GPS on my phone showed that Family Bridal was two blocks up and two blocks over. I decided to take a short cut through the shaded parking garage.

The shade of the garage was welcoming. There was a slight breeze that blew through the cement pillars. It was refreshing. That feeling faded away fast when I noticed a person had followed me in here. He or she was lurking behind a few of the cars.

My phone rang, saving the day. It was investigative reporter and news anchor, Crystal Pierce. She and Special Agent Smith of the FBI were helping me solve the case of the drowning boys of the Northwoods. They were obviously down here in Port Christibel somewhere ready to come to my rescue when needed.

"Hello," I said, happy to finally touch base with her.

"Hey, Payton, are you alone right now? Can you talk?"

"Mostly. Why?" I looked back to see if my stalker was still there. I didn't see anyone.

"We need to meet up in private. Agent Smith and I agree that you need a tracking device, so we can tell where you are at all times."

"Is that really necessary?"

"We heard about your friend. This is for your own safety."

"All right," I said giving in. I nervously looked over my shoulder again. It was hard to stand still. I felt like I was being watched already. "Meet me in the parking garage on corner of Fifth Street and Crescent Avenue."

"Okay, I'll be there in less than ten minutes."

"Can you try to hurry? I think I'm being followed. I'll do my best to lose them."

"Hang tight, Payton. I'll be there as fast as I can," she commented before she hung up.

I stopped behind the next large cement pillar. With my eyes closed and my back pressed against it, I exhale and inhaled slowly to try to calm myself down. Get it together, Payton. Don't be such a wussy, I told myself. The sound of footsteps echoed on the hollow cement floor. Whoever they were, they were getting closer. What should I do? It was time to dig deep and find badass Payton. My badass inner ego just happens to be an eighty-year-old woman. Together we handle stuff fairly well.

I slowly counted to three in my head. One, I grabbed my periwinkle Prada purse handle with both hands. Two, swung it backwards over my shoulder. Three, stepped out from behind the pillar and hit the person right in the face.

Whack! My purse made excellent dead center contact.

"Sonovabitch, Payton!"

I looked at the person standing in front of me. "Tim?" I stared at the man in the baseball cap, sunglasses, and dark beard.

"No, It's still me … Nick." He put his hand up to his face. "Jeez, Payton, I think you broke my nose,"

Wowza, he still looked so much like my deceased cop friend, Tim, even with the beard. Sadly, Tim passed away trying to help me catch the killers. My psychiatrist, Dr. Parks, told me I would stop hallucinating soon and stop seeing him. It has been a month and a half. Enough already.

"Nick, why are you stalking me? What's with the disguise?"

Nick took off his hat and sunglasses. "I'm not wearing a disguise. I'm freaking sunburned." He paused and made a face.

"Wait. What? Stalking you? I was on my way to pick up my tuxedo. Brad told me you were in the wedding now. I saw you walk in here. I thought we could walk over together and get reacquainted."

"Sorry, I have to make a pitstop first, so you can go on ahead. I'll meet you there. It will be fun." I smiled, trying to seem sincere.

"Sure," he said, clearly unconvinced by my rambling on. "I'll see you there, maybe."

As soon as he was out of sight, I started to loudly whisper her name. "Crystal. Crystal. Crystaaaaal."

"Over here behind the white minivan," she whispered back.

"Don't you mean the serial killer van?"

"Ha Ha, very funny, Payton. Nice touch with the smiley face coverup though."

"Thanks. And I wasn't joking. You know people have reported seeing it lurking around when the boys go missing."

She gave me the stop wasting my time look. "Quick, give me your purse before someone spots us," demanded Crystal.

Crystal hadn't changed much since she and Agent Smith drove me to the airport forty-two days ago. She was still monochromatic with her clothing selection. Today, her pink blouse matched her pink skirt, pink sandals, and pink clutch purse. That amount of dedication to fashion would be exhausting.

"Here, take it," I said, handing over one of my prized possessions. "Be gentle with her."

"Nice bag. You have good taste," She made a teeny tiny slit in the satin lining before placing the monitoring device inside.

"Why didn't you just use one of the pockets?"

"Pockets are for amateurs. We'll be in touch soon. Stick to the plan," she said before disappearing around the corner of the van.

***

Locator devices are for amateurs. I will always know exactly where you are. I will be watching your every move.

***

As soon as I stepped into the bridal shop, I was met with arrogant stares and pompous disapproving looks. I won't take it personally. It was most likely my choice of beach attire. Anyway, that's my story and I'm sticking to it.

"Hi, I'm here to pick up the bridesmaid's dress for the Thomas wedding."

"Of course, you are," said a skinny middle-aged blond woman who looked like she had put her makeup on with a shovel. "Have a seat in our waiting room while I check our inventory in the back."

There was no sign of Nick which was a relief. I had enough random creepy stuff for one day. I found a seat by two dark-haired girls. They were whispering and elbowing each other. Yes, sometimes I have that effect on people.

"Nice coverup," said the girl with the ponytail to break the ice.

"Thanks," I said back, trying to be nice.

"Bride?" asked the other girl with curly hair.

"No." I shook my head. "Absolutely not."

The clerk came out of the backroom and stood impatiently at the counter. I got up and met her. She held up a hideous, three quarter length, green and pink flowered monstrosity with lace around the sleeves and hem. The dress was in a large plastic bag. It could stay in there forever as far as I was concerned. I checked the tag. Great, the P.O.S. was slightly undersized and way overpriced. I sighed before handing over my credit card.

"Any chance this dress can be altered by tomorrow? Size? Color? Style? Price?"

She gave me an icy stare. "I'm afraid not." She handed me back my credit card and my receipt.

The ungrateful shrew didn't even say thank you. When I turned to leave, the two girls from earlier cornered me by the door.

"Nice tattoo," said Ponytail, inching closer to me.

She was referring to my tramp stamp that Brent had artfully given me to help lure the science loving witchy group out into the open. The tattoo we designed had three upside-down triangles (the symbol for water) and three roses with dates when three of the victims died. There was also a phrase in an ancient language that Brent added. We have no idea what it means. Probably not the best thing to have permanently tattooed on your body. It seemed like a good idea at the time.

"Thanks," I tried my best to be calm, "a good friend gave me that." This was all for Brent. He will not die in vain.

"Would you be interested in coming to a private party put on by Chaos tonight?" asked Curls in a tone I knew better than refuse.

"Sure," I said in a confident pitch. "Where and when?"

"Meet us past the last sand dune just after dark," said Ponytail, like a cat that was ready to purr.

"Don't forget your cloak," added Curls.

Jackpot. I'm in. "The airline lost one of my suitcases. You wouldn't happen to know where I can get another one?"

The two girls looked at each other. I might have just blown it.

"I should have one you can borrow. Meet us at 10:00p.m. sharp. You can't get in without it."

"Great. Thanks. I'm Payton, by the way."

"See you tonight, Payton." They said in unison.

Creepy much? They weren't about to tell me their names, unfortunately. Of course, I have a bad feeling about this but at least I made contact.

On my way back through the parking garage, I dialed Dr. Parks. I needed her daily reassurance that I wasn't losing it.

"Hello, Payton. How are you today?"

She sounded in good spirits. Dr. Parks was probably sitting at her desk, looking fabulous in a designer outfit that complemented her slim build and long sleek black hair.

"I'm doing rather well considering how my day is going." I took a second to look around the dimly lit garage to make sure I was still alone. "I thought I saw Tim again. You told me this would stop after a few months."

"Payton, it is normal for this to happen when we lose someone close to us. Our mind wants to see them again. Does this happen often?"

Before answering her, I stopped briefly because I thought I heard footsteps again. I crouched down to look under the cars for feet.

"Payton, are you still there?" asked Dr. Parks.

I stood back up and continued walking. "Yeah, sorry. I thought maybe I was being followed. I'm fine."

"Oh dear. You don't sound fine. How long have you been seeing people?"

"It's not people. It's just Tim. It hasn't happened for a while, then bam, Nick shows up here looking likc Tim, and my anxiety is back. And to top it all off, one of my good friends was eaten this morning by—"

Flashes of fabric and skin surround me as three bodies jump out from behind one of the larger pillars.

"Surprise!" They yelled.

I fell backwards on my butt on the hard-concrete floor. Hysterical laughter ensued on their part.

"Dang it, you guys. You have to stop doing this to me. Now I know why I self-medicate." I got to my hands and knees and stood up.

"Payton? … Payton? … Payton? What is happening? Are you all right?" blared from my phone.

"I'm okay, Dr. Parks. It was just my three friends from college trying to scare me. I'll call you back later."

"But, Payton?"

"Bye, Dr. Parks." I disconnected our call.

"You three are in big trouble. What are you doing down here?"

"Seriously? It's spring break," said Amber Reynolds, who is my smart, logical red-headed friend.

"I'm just here for the boys and the booze," stated Teagan Green, my free-spirited, moderately slutty friend.

"I came to surf and run in the Pi Day Marathon this afternoon," said Lisa Wilson, my sporty, health-conscious friend.

"It is really great to see all of you," I said, giving them all a big group hug. I know I saw Teagan this morning, but I really didn't want to get into why I didn't say hi earlier. I was in my secret mission mode. They really don't need to be involved in my plan.

"What's with the fugly old-lady dress?" asked Teagan in her usual crass demeanor.

"I've been drafted as the maid of honor for Brad and Julie's wedding tomorrow at 10:00 sharp on the jetty. I humbly request your presence for moral support."

"Holy shit, Payton," said Amber. "Are you okay with this?"

"I guess I have to be. It's not like I'm going to win him back wearing this … thing," I said sadly.

"Can I bring a date?" asked Teagan, with a smirk. "I'm trying to keep all my options open."

"Sure, why not? Brad and his father are flexible, fun-loving people."

We all laughed. They definitely are not.

"Come shopping with us, Payton," said Amber. "After that, we are going to Lisa's race. Then … cocktails with all the boys on the island," practically sang from her mouth.

"Sorry, guys, as tempting as that sounds, I can't. I have to do 'family time' with Stan and Janna tonight. Besides, Lily is still upset about losing her friend on the beach today. I need to check on her. But tomorrow, we will hang and get crazy."

"Okay, we will give you a pass for tonight," said Teagan. "Tomorrow, we will conquer the party universe. Woo-hoo!" She held her arms over her head in victory.

"Sounds like an awesome plan. See you guys in the morning."

I walked off with my geriatric gown and bag draped over my right shoulder. Lying to my friends was the absolute worst. I'm just glad they will be there tomorrow for support. There was still the big question: Should I speak up tomorrow when they ask if anyone objects to this union? I guess I have to live through tonight first.

***

Will Payton be the life or the death of the party?

CHAPTER THREE

The elevator doors opened to my family's penthouse suite on the top of the Carlton Hotel. Not too shabby for Payton. This is what winning the lottery buys: high ceilings, low floors, lots of marble stuff, expensive puffy furniture, a gourmet kitchen, private baths with jacuzzi tubs, and four-poster beds in every bedroom, and a huge balcony overlooking the beach. This clearly beats the fifth floor in the psych ward where I have also stayed, unfortunately.

With my hideous dress hidden in the hall closet, I began my search for friendly faces. I found my parents in the kitchen making homemade pizzas.

Stan looked up from his ball of dough he was kneading, "There's my girl." He beamed a mile-wide smile at me. "You got in late last night."

"Yes, I did," I said, giving him a huge hug. After we parted, I brushed the flour from his apron off my beach coverup.

Janna glanced over her shoulder as she gracefully stirred the Italian sausage that was browning in the cast iron skillet. She moved the meat around carefully so not to get any grease on her designer top and shorts. "Hello, my adventurous daughter."

"Hi, Mom. You know they deliver pizza down here, right?" I asked in a joking manner.

"Your father and I are working on a pizza recipe for the restaurant."

"Cool. I think that is a great idea. The customers will eat it up. Ha Ha."

I started to walk over to give her a hug too, when I realized that my tramp stamp tattoo was visible through my beach coverup. Janna would strongly disapprove. To avoid the awkward confrontation, I backed my way out of the kitchen.

"I'm going to jump in the shower quick to get all the beach off of me. Can't wait to taste it." I gave them a smile and two thumbs up before leaving the kitchen. Good grief, is the thumb thing my nervous "I'm lying" tell. I need to stop doing that immediately.

***

Payton the Beach Slut was safely washed down the shower drain before I joined my family for supper. A white tank top and a pair of black and white athletic shorts seemed to be appropriate for our dining experience.

Lily stayed in her room during supper. Luke brought her a piece of pizza, but she declined to eat it. She wasn't missing much. The pizza toppings, sauce, and cheese were good. The crust was too chewy and a tad over baked. My parents needed to play around with that part of the recipe. I scarfed it down with a smile on my face to make them happy. About an hour later, I was quietly reaching for some antacid tablets.

I went out onto the balcony so I could burp and fart in private while I drank my beer and watched the sunset. There was nothing girly about what was coming out of my body. It was disgusting. My eyes were burning.

From up here on the tenth floor, I could see the beach below. The guy passed out on the lounge chair looked familiar. A pair of binoculars were on the table. Let's take a slightly less than stalking gander around the property. I put the spy glasses up to my eyes. Yep, just what I thought. It was the rude surfer that knocked me out of my chair this morning. He doesn't look so good. Wait. What is this? Oh, snap. Is that Curls and Ponytail trying to pick him up and carry him off?

I refocused the eye piece until they came in clear view. It was them all right. This just got interesting. The sound of the patio door opening drew my attention away from the beach.

"Are you ready for the movie?" asked my father.

I set the binoculars back on the table. "You know, Dad, I think I'm just going to go to bed." I yawned for effect.

"It's only 9:00p.m." He was shocked because I was normally a night owl.

"It has been a long day with all the sun and fun. Then I have that wedding in the morning. Sorry." I gave him my best pouty face.

"Okay, kiddo. You probably have jetlag. See you in the morning."

"Night," I replied as I headed towards my room. Once I was safely inside my room, I closed the door. Now to devise a plan to sneak out without getting caught.

Before leaving my room right before 10:00 p.m., I made a fake Payton out of pillows just in case someone decided to check on me. As I passed by the living room, the booming noise from the surround sound covered up my footsteps in the hall and the creak of the front door. The feeling of relief drifted over me when I quietly inched the door closed. My breathing was slow and steady as I tiptoed to the elevator.

My anxiety increased while I waited impatiently for the elevator door to open. At any moment, someone could pop their head out and see me. The elevator dinged, letting me and everyone within earshot know that it had arrived. I panicked. I jumped in and pressed the Lobby button a gazillion times hoping it would close faster. It didn't. When I reached the ground floor, I jumped out and ran like a purse snatcher through the lobby and ducked out the back door that led to the beach.

Once I was outside, I slowed down a bit to look around for Curls and Ponytail. They weren't hard to spot by the last dune in their black cloaks. They both smiled when they saw me coming.

"Hi, guys. Great night for a party. The moon is stunning, don't you think?" I was trying to schmooze them.

"You're late," said Ponytail, being abrasive.

"Put this on," insisted Curls. She handed me her spare cloak.

I grabbed it from her and slipped it over my head. They glared at me with their arms crossed over their chest in a disapproving manner.

"What?" I asked, waiting for an explanation.

"We don't wear clothes under our cloaks," said Curls.

"Oh, sorry. I forgot." I reached up under my cloak and inched out of my athletic shorts. "So where are you guys from?" I asked, trying to make this striptease less awkward.

"Illinois," said Ponytail.

That was all I was going to get out of her. "That's nice. I'm from Wisconsin." I pulled my arms out of the cloak sleeves, pulled my arms out of my tank top, put my arms back in my cloak sleeves, and pulled the tank top over my head. I threw them both behind a nearby bush.

"The underwear too, Payton," demanded Curls.

I did what they said. I placed my bra and underwear with my other clothes. "Anything else? Are we good?"

"Let's go or we'll miss the ceremony," said Ponytail.

Our cloaks billowed in the breeze coming off the water. We walked down the beach in the glorious light of the full moon. Being in commando mode was oddly refreshing and invigorating. I felt empowered by my newfound freedom.

My thoughts drifted to Streak, a clothing challenged gamer, that drowned mysteriously in the river behind my parents' house this past January. This crazy thing I was about to do was for him and the other boys sucked into this vortex of evil.

As we approached the party, I heard hoots and hollers on the other side of the dunes ahead. It sounded massive. What have I gotten myself into? Maybe I shouldn't have tried to go it alone. I was seriously regretting my purse sitting on my dresser. Crystal and Smith had no idea where I was. There was no one to come to my rescue.

The music blared across the water and sand. I was expecting Stairway to Hell instead of an annoying pop princess being their jam of choice. When we got closer, I could see the DJ, the food, the booze, and the mass of people. I was seriously getting cold feet. The hamster was on the wheel in my brain, desperate to come up with a plan to get me out of this. First, I needed to lose these two.

"I'm going to grab some food and a drink," said Ponytail.

"Me too," said Curls.

"I'll stay right here," I said to distance myself.

"Don't be silly, come on," said Ponytail, pulling me by the arm.

I felt like a pig being led to the slaughter. My breathing was becoming erratic. Shit. No. No. No. I took a deep cleansing breath as they pulled me through the crowd. I was surrounded by a sea of cloaks and unknown faces. We stopped by a ten-foot by ten-foot tent next to the food and drink trucks. A group of picnic tables for dining were to our right.

"I'll hold our spot and grab a table while you guys get some food. Can you guys grab me a beer?" I asked.

"Sure, we'll be right back."

I scanned the crowd for a familiar face. The only person a recognized was the rude surfer. He was lying motionless in the center of the party on top of a table. No one seemed to care or notice him. Talk about the life of the party. Or was he the death of the party? I had no idea what to expect. Was this for real or just a moon lovers spring break bash?

Out of nowhere, I felt someone place their hand over my mouth and yank me backwards. He or she pulled me inside the tent. It was pitch black inside the nylon walls without the light of the moon. I struggled to get away. My elbow slammed into their stomach. They let go of me temporarily. Then they grabbed me again. I was about to scream for help when I heard my name.

"Payton, calm down. It's me."

"What the heck, Lily." I shoved her off me. "What are you doing here?"

"Apparently, I'm saving you from those two wicked witches," she whispered loudly because of the music. "What are you doing here? This solo shit wasn't part of the plan."

I grabbed the sleeve of her cloak. "I guess I could ask you the same thing," I stated in a judgmental tone.

"Look, I was on the balcony trying to sneak a cigarette, mourning my dead friend, when I see a girl spastically run through the pool area and down the beach. So of course, I followed you," she said in her defense.

"What about the cloak? Where did you get it?"

"Really … we're doing this right now?" Lily jabbed back.

"Yes," I crossed my arms defiantly over my chest in the dark. Lily couldn't see it but whatever. I was standing my ground.

"Fine. While you were pulling your underwear out your arm hole, I snuck passed you guys in the bushes. I borrowed a cloak from someone who left it outside the port-o-potty. Are we done with the stupid questions?"

"Let's just say that I believe you." I could feel Lily's eye roll.

"We need to get out of here before your new friends find us."

"But we are so close," I said in protest.

"So close to death. They do not tolerate outsiders well. Look what happened to Brent."

"I'm sure the killer is here." I didn't want to give up yet.

"That's an even better reason to leave. Did you see the size of the crowd? There is at least a hundred hooded moon loving people out there. How are you going to find him or her?"

The music suddenly stopped. A man's voice welcomed the crowd.

"Gather around my children," he said. "Tonight, we celebrate her, our shining goddess of the sky."

"Blessed be," repeated the crowd in unison.

"Creepy," I whispered

"Can one of my special children retrieve my sacred book and potions from my tent?"

"Oh. Shit." Said Lily. "We're making a break for it right now." Lily grabbed my arm, leading me out of the tent. We didn't look back. The two of us headed straight for the water's edge.

Lily dropped her cloak and ran into the surf. "I hope you can swim, Payton."

I was waste deep in water when my clothing predicament happened. The cloak was tangled around my legs. I stepped on the front of the cloak and ended up with a face full of salty water.

Lily turned around in the water to see what was taking me so long. "Ditch the cloak, Payton or you'll drown."

"But I'm …"

"The fish don't care. Hurry."

I ditched the cloak and caught up to her. We swam away from the shore just out far enough for it to be over our heads. Then we headed down the shore towards our hotel. I was falling behind Lily with each pathetic stroke.

"Hurry up, Payton." She looked back over her shoulder at me.

"Geez, what's the rush. We're not being followed."

"There are guys with gray suits on out here." Lily treaded water so I could catch up.

"What? You are not making any sense."

"The full moon is the perfect time for predators to hunt."

I caught up with her. We were both treading water. "Why does that matter?"

"Don't make me say the 'S' word, Payton."

"Oh … Oooooh!" Just as I said that I felt something large and dark bump into my body. "Shit, something just touched my leg."

Lily and I stared at each other wide-eyed for a brief second. It swam between us near the surface. Lily and I kicked, punched, and screamed causing a flurry of water to splash about. Whatever it was disappeared under the surface. We vigorously swam to shore like maniacs. The two of us crawled out of the raging surf exhausted. We flopped down on the sand like washed-up fish.

"That was loads of fun," I said sarcastically, happy to be alive. "Any idea how we are going to sneak back into the hotel buck naked?"

"I'm thinking we borrow a sign, a tree branch, a pool toy, basically anything we can find," instructed Lily.

We crawled and hid behind bushes, fences, palm trees, and beach chairs. It all felt very "Double-O" until we encountered a man walking his dog. Nothing brings you back to reality like getting your butt sniffed and almost getting peed on. Ugh!

From there, we ran by the pool area and hid by the maintenance shed. It just happened to be next to the hot tub. A young oblivious couple was in the tub making out. We spotted their towels hanging on the fence. Lily nudged me. I nodded in agreement. I was okay if we borrowed them tonight and brought them back tomorrow. Here we go, another diabolical turn in my personality due to survival mode. Just to be clear, survival is not my favorite kind of mode.

We wrapped the towels around us and headed for the lobby. The elevator that caused me anxiety earlier was a beacon in the storm now. The elevator door closed. To break the awkward silence, I just had to ask, "So did it hurt when you had your nipples pierced?"

"Not as much as you would think. The stud in my—" she started.

I held up my hand signaling that I had heard enough.

"—hurt worse," she finished.

"Good to know." Lily's dark Gothic habits were a little too much for me to handle.

"This adventure stays between us, right?" asked Lily. "Luke is not to know anything."

"No problem, I'd like to forget it ever happened."

When the elevator door opened, my mother was standing there. It's like she's psychic. She's not, but her instincts are uncanny.

"Girls?" my mother asked with an authoritarian tone.

"Late night swim," I added, which wasn't a lie.

"I'm exhausted," said Lily. She yawned.

"Good night to all," I said, heading directly to my room before anything else could possibly go wrong.

***

Someone else is about to get cold feet. Do you think I mean that figuratively or literally? I will let you mull that over while I stalk my prey. Enough said.

There you are without a care in the world. I am about to change that. The moon shines brightly overhead as you wade in the surf. Sneaking up behind you will be masterful but not necessary. We have met before. Do you fear me? I am thinking, not yet. Believe me when I say that you should, and you will.

The darkness that comes from within me is unpredictable. I can feel it bubbling to the surface. There is no turning back now, the uprising has started. The evil oozes out of my pores and mixes with the salty night air. The need to see the fear in your eyes gets me going. Sensing your racing pulse always brings the evil back to life.

Tonight, you will fill my need because you have broken my rules. Soon, you will die an excruciating watery death. I will not stand and watch from the shadows. It is time to get my hands dirty. A little "wet work" is in order. This is what you have all been waiting for. You want to watch as I steal the colors from their eyes. I dare you to look away. I dare you to turn the page like you are above all the depravity. Nice … You are all still here … so I will continue. Curtain please.

It is time to enter your world and play my game. I will call this one Truth or Die. The "or" is there to give you false hope, there is no hope, just death.

I watch as you skip stones and shells into the ocean at the water's perimeter. I scan the beach for spectators. We are all alone. It is just you and me and the goddess above in the sky as my witness. She will approve of me restoring the balance of nature: righting the wrong that you have committed.

As I walk up behind you, I reach down and pick up a rock. The raging surf muffles my approaching footsteps. With the rock still in my hand, I pull my arm back and flex my muscles. The rock leaves my hand from an underhanded toss. It skips across the surface of the water three times before going under. Your head swings around. Our eyes meet. You give me a welcoming smile. My game just keeps getting better. I wave at you and walk towards you with extreme confidence. I am now completely enveloped with the darkness that consumes me. You have mere seconds to live; only a few wholesome breaths before fear takes over.

I lead you playfully into the surf. This is still just a game, is it not? You splash me and smile. I splash back once to initiate the game and play along. We walk further into the surf. You splash me one more time. The darkness takes over. You think I am still in a playful mood. I am not.

So much for asking the truth question that I had intended. I grab you by the back of the head and shove your face into the water before you realize what is happening and can fight back. I come around behind you with lightning speed and wrap my other arm around your waist to help hold you under the water. Leverage works to my advantage. I can feel the resistance. It is glorious. You are trying to pull away from me and stand up. You slap and claw at my arms with your hands frantically. I let you come up for one quick spastic breath before I shove your head back under. Shame on me for wanting this euphoria to last. I let you come back up one more time. "Where are they?" I demand an answer.

"At the hotel," blurted out of your mouth along with water and vomit.

Shame on you for thinking that I was going to let you live. The truth equals death. I push your head back under the water. You try to wiggle loose but my need to kill you is greater than your will to live. You claw at me and the surface of the water trying to find anything to grab ahold of. You are failing miserably. I can feel your struggle to live lessen. Any second you will lose the fight and take a breath. When you do, it is all over for you. Water will race into your lungs; the convulsions will start.

I feel your lungs expand as you take your last breath. I hold on tighter. You thrash in the water with one last effort to save yourself. Denied. The water fills your lungs. The rhythmic convulsions start. I can feel them against my chest and stomach. Then I feel nothing physically or emotionally. The seal breaks. Your essence flies free. You are gone from this earth.

I roll you over in the water to check your eyes. They are gray and fixed. My game isn't over. I have one more house call to make before the sun rises.

CHAPTER FOUR

My eyes flicked open with the buzz from my phone. Beams of light enter my squinted eye sockets. Nothing like a predawn text from reporter Crystal Pierce and Secret Agent Smith to jump start my day. They wanted to meet up with me in five minutes. I tried to set my phone down on the nightstand next to my bed, but it wasn't there. My phone dropped into the sand. Yes, the sand.

Uh-oh. I'm not dreaming. I am wide awake and lying on a lounge chair down on the beach. Sleepwalking? Well, that's a new one. I jumped to my feet and decided not to give it another thought. Today was a HUGE day and thinking would just wreck it. I grabbed my purse that was next to my lounge chair and did the walk of shame to the lobby in search of Crystal and Smith.

They weren't in the lobby or anywhere on the hotel grounds. My purse and I decided to head to the coffee shop downtown. They can follow my signal and catch up to me there.

I went inside the shop and ordered myself a Grande iced coffee with whipped cream and sprinkles. It was all part of my cover story. When I turned around from the counter, I saw

Crystal and Smith at a corner table. The table next to them was open. It was time to think outside the box.

Instead of sitting down, I took my coffee and headed for the ladies' room. Just as I expected, Crystal followed me. Inside the bathroom we checked under the stalls to make sure we were alone.

"Any luck making contact yet?" Crystal asked after taking a sip of her coffee.

"I met two girls yesterday, but I failed to extract any new information," I said. That was the sugar-coated version. "I'll see if I can find them on the beach after lunch."

"Stick to the plan, Payton."

"I'll do my best," I answered back without missing a beat.

The look she gave me did not exude confidence in my ability to complete my end of the bargain. I had faith and that is all that matters.

I left the bathroom and headed back to the hotel. About a block from the beach, a school bus pulled up next to the sidewalk in my vicinity. The door opened and a group of familiar teenage faces greeted me. It was the same group of video gamers from back home that I saw on the jetty yesterday. They helped me investigate their friend Streak's mysterious drowning death more than forty days ago. It was blamed on Rod Huntley and Kurt Meriwether, who are both dead, but I still believe the real killer is still out there.

"Good morning. How goes it?" I asked.

Chameleon stepped off the bus first and gave me a hug. It's okay. He hugs everyone. It's his thing. "Today is going to be a great day." He sounded extremely cheerful.

"Why is that?" I asked, to play along.

"Because today is marine biology day," said Blond Ambition as he walked down the steps of the bus.

"No picking up trash for us. We'll be down at the beach in style today checking out—" started The Singe.

"The girls … all the girls," finished one of the gamers that I hadn't been introduced to yet.

They all laughed. He had to be the new comedian of the bunch.

He looked me up and down from his window perch. The word ish came to mind.

"Hi, I'm Gluteus Maximus. My friends call me Max for short."

Good grief, he is a bit full of himself. "Nice to meet you, Max."

He smiled back a crooked, cocky smirk.

"I'm hungry," said Feed Bag, sticking his head out of one of the back windows.

"So what else is new?" asked Wolfman. He ran his fingers through his thick mane of sandy brown hair to fix his beastly bedhead.

"Seriously, guys. I'm withering," urged Feed Bag.

"Shoes, you and Thirteen take Feed Bag to find food," instructed Wolfman. "We'll meet you by where we were fishing yesterday. Bring enough back for everyone."

"Okay," said Thirteen.

They headed towards the beach.

"I'll see you guys around."

"See you at the bar later," said Blond Ambition, showing his fake ID.

"Oh…no. Give me that," I said, taking it from him.

"We all have them," said Chameleon.

"I have two," said The Singe, aka the boy who loses everything.

"You boys behave. I mean it," I said with a finger point and a stern look before heading to my hotel.

"Bye, Payton," they said in unison.

***

Who doesn't love a good scavenger hunt? I have added some dangerous twists to keep the game interesting.

***

An hour was not enough time to make myself look good in this hideous dress. I tried my hair up, down, side pony, and single braid. My locks would have none of it. I grabbed my straightener and went with chic, brown nothingness which seemed to pair well with the curtain-like fabric.

Maybe I needed a little pizazz. I grabbed the silver and diamond winged-shaped earrings Rose had given me. Nope. They were too much.

Lily's voice boomed from the hall outside my room. I opened up the door. "Help me, please. I can't get this damn thing zipped," I said, referring to the dress.

Lily stepped inside the bathroom. She grimaced at the sight of me. "How about we just burn it?"

I wish. It's for Brad and Julie's wedding today. I'm the maid of honor."

My mother walked around the corner just in time to hear the good news.

Lily burst out laughing. "Why are you torturing yourself?"

"I'm with Lily, dear. You owe them nothing," stated my mother.

It's too late for that. I need to be on the beach in ten minutes for the ceremony. Help me wedge myself into this god forsaken thing."

My brother Luke walked by while Lily pulled the fabric around the zipper together and my mother inched it upwards.

"Suck it in!" shouted Lily.

"I am." I protested.

My brother shook his head and kept on walking.

"Done. Go," said my mother.

I grabbed my purse that was on the bathroom counter and ran. In the elevator, I began to ponder speaking up in protest. Was it the classy thing to do? Definitely not. Was it the right thing to do? Maybe. It all depended on the connection in Brad's eyes when we saw each other. Then I would know for sure.

Down by the jetty, I found Julie standing by herself. She looked fabulous in her beach-appropriate white lace dress. It made me feel a little bad for what I was about to do. Crap!

I walked up to her. "Look at you. You look beautiful."

Julie smiled back at me.

"I'd hug you, but I'm afraid I'll split open my dress."

"Thank you again for doing this, Payton."

"You're welcome." I was starting to feel really bad because she was being so nice. "So where is everyone?"

"My parents should be down in a minute. They will be bringing down the rest of my family. I'm just too antsy to be up there. The Chief went to take Nancy to the airport. I think he's coming back."

"Where's Brad?" I blurted out not really thinking.

She gave me a concerned look. "I just sent Nick up to look for him. He's not answering my calls or text messages."

"Why don't I try." I took my phone out of my purse and dialed his number. It rang four times before going to voicemail. "Sorry, he didn't answer me either." I was secretly hoping he would have picked up for me.

Julie was visibly upset now. Tears were starting to form. I put my arm on her shoulder trying to comfort her.

"I think I need a few minutes alone, Payton, if you don't mind." She walked away from me, heading towards the jetty.

I watched her walk across the sand. About a minute later, Teagan, Amber, and Lisa came up from behind me.

"Where's the party?" asked Teagan.

I turned around to face my friends. They already had beers in their hands.

"Anywhere but here at the moment," I answered back.

"Yikes," said Amber. "That dress isn't any better ON you."

"Thanks," I sighed. I knew it was true.

I grabbed her beer and took a huge swallow. Lily and Luke were making their way through the crowd. I waved them over. They weren't exactly dressed for a wedding, more like beach casual. But they were here for support.

“Thanks for coming you two.” I said to Lily and my brother.

“I wouldn’t miss this for anything,” said Lily. She was almost giddy.

“She made me come,” stated Luke. He was the opposite of giddy.

I gave him a sour look. When I glanced over my shoulder at the chairs and trellis altar, people were starting to gather and take their seats. Oh boy, we were running out of time for Brad to show up.

Teagan, Amber, and Lisa had found the snack and beverage table. They were comfortably grazing on veggies, cheese, and small sandwiches. On the other side of the girls, I saw Feed Bag and Thirteen filling their plates. I’m sure the rest of the boys weren’t far behind.

The gift table was located next to the snack table. Boxes and cards were already starting to pile up. That sick feeling poked at the pit of my stomach when I suddenly realized that the maid of honor, me, had not gotten them anything. The palm of my hand slapped my forehead showing my disgust with myself.

“What did you get the happy couple?” asked Blond Ambition.

“Nothing. I’m the worst friend ever.” Remorse was setting in.

“But we saw your name on one of the big boxes,” said The Singe. “We figured you probably got them something really cool like a puppy.”

“Or a karaoke machine,” added Shoes. He busted out with a few bars of his favorite rap artist.

“Which box? Show me.” I said anxiously.

We all moved over to the far side of the gift table. There it was … the mystery box. The two-foot by two-foot box was wrapped in smiley face paper.

“Maybe it’s a new X-Box,” said Max. He looked at the small tag attached to the gift. Max read the tag: “Who wants to play a game?”

I looked over his shoulder. Sure enough, it had my name on it, right next to the cryptic message. I signaled Lily, Luke, Amber and the girls, the rest of the gamer boys, and Julie with a wave and a solemn intense wide-eyed stare.

I moved the box to the ground and carefully started ripping at the paper.

"You're supposed to read the card first," commented Max.

He had no idea what kind of sick game was about to unfold. I didn't need to read the card; I knew who it was from.

Julie walked up. I stopped tearing at the paper and opened the card like Max suggested.

It was a cheap blue card with silver wedding bells on it. Best wishes to the Mr. and Mrs. was on the front of the card. I opened the card. There was a personal inscription on the inside. I read it for everyone: "This is your gift, Payton. Solve the puzzles to find your groom. You have until midnight tonight if you want to see Brad alive."

I looked over at Julie. She slowly sank to the ground and started to cry.

Suddenly, I realized I was doing the same thing. The thought of never seeing Brad again hit me harder than expected. To cover, I grabbed Julie's hand in support, letting her know I was there for her.

I finished reading the rest to the group. The note at the bottom was clear: "Absolutely no cops. If I see you talk to anyone in law enforcement, it's GAME OVER!"

This serious message made me jump back to my feet in a hurry. Julie slowly made it to her feet as well. I closed the card and looked around the circle. "Does everyone understand? You can't back out. You're in this until midnight. Agreed?"

They all nodded in agreement.

"Open the box," said Chameleon.

The rest of the paper came off the box slow and easy. I was being extremely cautious under the circumstances. Everyone moved closer as I lifted off the top of the box. Inside was a white envelope with, "First Riddle" written on the outside, along with what I guessed to be Brad's boutonniere.

The plain, white, folded card had nothing written on the outside. I flipped it open to reveal the riddle: "What is dark, light, then dark again?" After I read it to the group, everyone was quiet.

"The sun?" blurted Blond Ambition.

"Leave it to the bride to start opening the presents early," said Nick from behind us.

Our eyes all got huge. The note had said, "No cops."

"Julie really wanted a new toaster," I said jokingly to throw him off. "Any luck finding Brad?"

"Sorry, I couldn't find him," answered Nick. "I searched the hotel and the grounds."

"My grandma told me I could open this one early seeing as how she couldn't make it down here," Julie added, trying to cover up what was going on.

Julie started to cry. "It's no use. He's not coming. Nick, could you please go tell all the guests that the wedding has been postponed and thank them for coming. I just can't face them right now. I'm humiliated." She sobbed harder. "I can't believe he stood me up."

"Sure. No problem. I'll take care of it," he said, looking truly upset.

"Thank you. Tell my family that I'm ok. I just need some alone time to process this."

He walked away to address the crowd.

"Let's make a break for it before people start asking questions." I demanded.

"We can all pile in the school bus," offered Chameleon.

I turned to face him. "Where's your dad?" I asked. "He shouldn't be involved."

"Don't worry," said Wolfman. "He ate some nasty beach burrito last night that gave him diarrhea. We are on our own today."

"Super," I said. What a relief. "To the Bat Bus."

The bus was parked on the second floor of the parking ramp. We were almost to the bus when we got a strong whiff of rotting flesh.

Julie ran forward. "Brad! Brad!" she screamed.

The rest of us approached cautiously. A car parked in the vicinity of the bus was the culprit of the ghastly smell. No doubt it was the killer's public 'don't F with me' neon sign. Lily and I looked at each other.

The two victims were in the front seat of a bright yellow sports car. I didn't notice the make or model. I was too busy staring at their hair and blueish flesh, their faces twisted in agony. It was Curls and Ponytail.

"Do these two girls look familiar to anyone?" asked Julie.

My eyes begged Lily to stay quiet. She did. Everyone shook their heads.

"Let's get the heck out of here before the cops come," I said.

We quickly piled into the bus. Chameleon decided to drive because his dad had borrowed the bus in the first place.

"Dude," Blond Ambition said to Feed Bag while waving his hand in front of his face. "Can I change my answer to 'what's dark, light, then dark again?' from 'the sun' to Feed Bag's underwear?" jabbed Blond Ambition. "My eyes are burning back here."

"Sorry. I've never seen a dead body before," said Feed Bag.

The bus filled with laughter and an unfriendly gas. We all opened our windows for some fresh air.

***

Outsiders are not tolerated. What happens in the circle, stays in the circle. I taught those two girls a lesson they will take into the afterlife.

CHAPTER FIVE

"Guys, we need to get serious about this riddle," said Chameleon. "I can't keep driving in circles."

Teagan rested her crossed arms on the back of the bench seat in front of her. "We should head back towards the beach," she suggested.

"I think she's right," said Max. "From what I've been told about Streak, this killer has a hard-on for water."

Everyone nodded in agreement. Chameleon took a right at the next corner, heading back towards the sand and surf.

"Can I see the riddle card?" asked Amber.

I passed it back to her.

She opened it and read it out loud slowly, "What is dark … light … then dark again?"

"I feel like there is a passing of time," suggested Shoes.

"That's why I thought it was like the sun and the moon," said Blond Ambition. He took a drink from his mystery cup.

"Hmm. What turns on and off?" asked Lisa. She sighed and stared out the window deep in thought.

"The light in a refrigerator," said Feed Bag.

"That light never shuts off because you never close the door," laughed Wolfman.

Right after we passed a large road sign for Bulivan Point, Chameleon slammed on the brakes and pulled over on the shoulder.

"Did you guys see that sign?" asked Chameleon. After he put the bus in park, he turned around to face us. We gave him a blank stare waiting for him to elaborate.

"Bulivan Point. The lighthouse. It's a dang lighthouse. The rhythmically flashing lamp rotates to signal approaching vessels."

"It gets light and dark," said Luke.

"That makes sense," I said. "Let's go."

Chameleon turned around in the driver's seat. He cranked the wheel and punched the gas. The bus swung around so fast that most of us fell out of our seats, landing in the aisle.

***

The Bulivan Point Lighthouse was only two miles away from where Chameleon pulled over. The way Chameleon was driving, we were there in a matter of minutes. We all piled out of the bus anxious to search for the next clue.

The hundred-foot, dark brown, metal lighthouse towered over us. It was nothing fancy as far as lighthouses go. At the base was a small shed, and on the other side, a living quarters.

"I want to sound the foghorn," said Max with a determined grin.

"Absolutely not," I said, pointing at the "NOT OPEN TO THE PUBLIC" sign.

"Now what do we do?" asked Julie. She was still visibly upset. "We need to find him."

"We will. We will. I promise," I said, making eye contact with her.

The boys headed over to check out the living quarters. We all followed behind them.

Wolfman stopped walking and turned around. "We should split up," he recommended.

"Okay, we will check out the shed and the door to the lighthouse," I agreed. I abruptly turned around and headed back the other way.

The boys continued to follow Chameleon and Wolfman. The girls came with me. We went to the wooden shed first. Of course, the door was locked. I tried rattling the doorknob and kicking the door with my foot like in the movies. The door didn't budge.

"That was great," said Lily in a smart-ass tone. "Let me try."

I moved to the side. "By all means, be my guest."

Lily dug around in her purse before pulling out some small metal tools.

"I'm about to 'borrow' access to this shed. If you want to claim plausible deniability, I suggest you leave or turn around."

We all stayed to watch her do her thing.

"Okay, then here we go," breathed Lily just above a whisper.

She inserted a narrow, pointed, lock picking tool into the keyhole. Lily wiggled it around until she heard the lock give way.

"Ready?" Lily asked with a huge smile.

We all took a few steps back for safety purposes. Lily turned the knob and pushed the door open. Lily stood her ground. The group shuffled forward to gawk at what was inside. I found myself tiptoeing between Teagan and Lisa to get a better look. We were all sadly disappointed. The shed was empty, completely freaking empty.

"Why the hell would you lock it if there is nothing to steal?" asked Lily in an unhappy tone.

Julie stepped inside for a quick inspection before she walked out and slammed the door. "Ugh! What if we're wrong and we're wasting time?" She was brewing with anger.

"Maybe the boys are having better luck," I said to ease her distress. "Let's go see if we can get into the lighthouse."

As we walked over to the lighthouse, we could see the boys peering in the windows of the living quarters. I was wondering if Lily should give them some assistance. So far, it didn't look like they were having any luck either.

At the lighthouse door, I paused briefly to read the sign: "First built in 1852 to guide the ships into the port."

While I was trying to read about its reconstruction, Amber started screaming. "A note. A note. I found a note."

Julie removed the note that was stuck halfway under the door. She opened it carefully.

"Guys, we found something," I yelled and waved for them to come over.

Julie read the note: "Try again. You are getting closer."

The note was quickly passed around the group. When it got to me, I looked inside the note, there was a smiley face drawn in red marker or pen. Underneath the smiley face was the comment Julie had read out loud.

"Getting closer? What the fudge nuggets is that supposed to mean?" Julie asked. Her voice cracked halfway through the sentence. Julie was losing it.

Wolfman stepped in with his calm demeanor to try to settle her down. "The good news: we are on the right track," he said confidently.

"Maybe we are at the wrong lighthouse," suggested The Singe.

We all stared at him in wonderment for having such a logical thought.

"Hey, what are you kids doing?" boomed through the air.

We turned to see an old man in his seventies emerge from the living quarters.

"Back to the bus," yelled Wolfman.

"Max, Google lighthouses in Port Christabel and find us directions on your phone," Chameleon ordered as we scrambled to get away.

"Will do," said Max, who happened to be the second one on the bus after Chameleon.

We all crammed back on the bus and found our seats. The gang was ready to head to our next destination before the caretaker could rat us out to the police. I watched him fade into the distance and disappear when we went over a hill. For Brad's sake, I really hope he didn't get our license plate or bus number.

Max gazed at his phone screen. "Do you want the good news or the bad news?"

"The good. Definitely the good," I said. I crossed my fingers and gave him a hopeful look.

He looked up from his screen and smiled back. "There are only two other lighthouses on the island."

"The bad?" I asked with an apprehensive grimace. I held my breath waiting for his reply.

"They both close soon," he said with a troubled look.

"Which one is closer?" asked Wolfman. He walked to the front of the bus to give him guidance.

"Port Christabel Lighthouse is the closest," said Max.

"That is where we are going then," instructed Wolfman, looking over the crowd. "Does everyone agree?"

We all looked at Julie. She nodded, so we all nodded in agreement. It was unanimous.

"Chameleon, take a quick right up ahead," said Max, trying to guide him through the heavy traffic.

Everyone braced themselves this time for the sudden turn. I looked over at Julie. She was clearly coming apart. Her blank lifeless stare had me concerned. She wasn't coping well with the whole situation. I had faith we would get there in time, but was it the right lighthouse?

The Port Christabel Lighthouse wasn't as tall as the first one. The white stone cylindrical tower was topped off with a black metal lantern room. It stood majestically at the water's edge. A long cement sidewalk led up to a staircase of at least sixteen steps. The top of the long staircase led to a smaller metal set of steps with a railing that went right up to the door of the lighthouse. For it being almost closing time, there were still plenty of inquiring visitors waiting to get in. This might be a problem.

We climbed part way up the steps and got in line like civilized adults. After about two minutes, I said, "Screw this," and pushed my way to the front of the line. The rest of the bunch followed behind me like I was their fearless leader. At the moment—I was.

"Excuse me. Pardon me. Coming through," I informed the crowd of unhappy lighthouse lovers. At the front of the line, I really turned it on. "I promised my brother, Luke, that as his last dying wish, we would visit as many lighthouses across Texas as we could."

I gave Luke "the look" to play along. He coughed twice and limped up to where I was standing. Luke hunched his shoulders over and weaved a bit like he could pass out. Braaaaavo! My brother was a quick study.

Everyone else moved out of our way and let us inside. I should really feel bad about being despicable and underhanded. I don't in the slightest. Does that make me a horrible person? Probably. I'm choosing not to care at the moment.

Once we were all inside, we decided it was best to split up. We divided into small groups of three and four to speed things along. Lily, Luke, and Max were with me.

"Where should we start?" asked Luke, continuing to cough excessively into his elbow.

Good boy, I thought. "I say we head to the penthouse." I pointed up to the lantern room. The other groups checked around the lower level for a clue or a note.

The stairs up to the lantern room were narrow and steep. The metal spiral staircase was more than I bargained for. I stubbed my toe because of my flip flops and took a small chunk out of my shin trying to hurry. No doubt my penance for my earlier bad behavior.

"Sonavabitch, that hurt," I yelped.

"Easy, potty mouth," joked Luke. "you'll get us kicked out of here."

I gave him a sisterly glare.

When we reached the top of the stairs, the red metal door to the lantern room was locked. "Crap!" I frantically twisted the handle. The sign on the door read: "Authorized Personnel Only."

"How do you know we need to go up there?" asked Max. He pushed his blond curly hair out of his eyes.

"I could say it is just a hunch, but hey, why not check out the big bulb that gets light, dark, and light again, right?" I do realize I'm being a bit of a sarcastic bitch. My story is the hideous dress made me do it.

Max just rolled his eyes at my rebellious comment without saying anything in return.

There was a small window next to the door that led outside. From this spot, I could see the lower of the two black, metal balconies that surrounded the lantern room. On the railing outside the window was a small red smiley face with an arrow pointing towards the sky.

"Check it out," I said, pointing to the symbol out the window. To me it was a big, red "come get me" sign. This was not my first serial killer rodeo. I tried to open the door. "It's locked too."

"Block me," said Lily while she worked her lockpicking magic on the door leading out to the balcony.

We transformed ourselves into a human wall and one-by-one snuck out the door to search for the clue that was undoubtably there.

The four of us walked all the way around the first level of the lantern room balcony.

"It's not here," said Luke. "I give up."

"We can't give up," I demanded. "Look harder. It has to be here."

I felt something plop onto my shoulder and ooze down my back. When I looked up, I saw a seagull staring at me from the railing of the second balcony.

"Did you just shit on me?" I already knew the answer before I asked it. The beady-eyed little bastard had violated me good and scarred me for life.

My revenge instincts won out over my survival instincts. My flip flops were off my feet within seconds. I grabbed one of the metal support bars for the balcony above us with both hands. I used it to climb up onto the railing of our balcony.

While standing on top of the railing, I leaned forward and placed one hand on the black metal outside wall of the lighthouse. My other hand was swatting in the direction of THAT bird.

Luke looked up trying to shield his eyes from the sun with his hands. "Jeez, Payton," said Luke. "You are going to kill yourself."

"Payton, get down before you fall!" yelled Lily. She nervously paced around the balcony.

I suddenly froze with both hands on the black metal wall in front of me after almost losing my balance. Next, I made the mistake of looking down. My eyes slammed shut. I took a deep breath and exhaled. This was no time for an anxiety attack.

"Oh my god, Payton, look up," said Max. "There's something up there."

"I can't," I screamed back. I was frozen spread eagle on the railing. My mind wouldn't let me move my body.

"Stay where you are, Miss," yelled someone from below.

Luke moved over closer to me on the balcony. "Payton," said Luke, "it's a security guard. He's coming up here. You have to grab it."

"I can't. I'm scared," I pleaded.

"You can," said Max, trying to give me courage.

Lily moved over so she was next to Luke. They were both looking up at me. "Do it for Brad, Payton," insisted Lily.

"All right," I agreed. "That man is going to owe me big time."

"Hurry." Luke ordered.

Slow and steady was my motto. My hands and feet inched their way over. I reached out my hand and carefully pulled the note from the second level railing. Max slid over and was right beneath me. "I'm dropping the note. Someone catch it."

A gust of wind blew the note. Luckily, Lily reached out and caught it with both hands before it flew over the railing. She shoved it into her pocket.

"Now climb down, Payton. We'll catch you if you fall," said Luke.

"You better," I yelled back.

I took a deep breath, prayed a little, and stopped myself. "I can't do it."

"Payton, the wind has started to shift to the north, so in about two seconds, everyone on the ground will be able to see your underwear," said Lily.

"I can already see stuff," said Max. "Are you wearing a thong?"

"Jeez, thanks Payton. I'm officially blind," said Luke. He stared down at the ground below to avoid having to scratch his eyes out.

That was the inspiration I needed, "Here I come. On the count of three," I instructed.

"One … two … three." I let go. There was some screaming, not all mine, by the way. They caught me. We all landed in a heap of elbows and assholes on the metal walkway. Lily was the first to be back on her feet. She held the door open for the rest of us. Soon after we were back inside, the guards tried to chase us, but we lost them in the crowd.

Downstairs, we found the rest of the group. We signaled them to run to the bus ASAP. Two guards chased the bus on foot for half a block before they gave up.

Everyone on the bus, except Chameleon who was driving, gathered around Lily as she pulled the holy grail out of her pocket. She flipped the paper open.

Lily read it: "Well, Hell's Bells. The third one is the charm." She grimaced and then looked sad. I knew why—it was Brent. He loved the number three.

"Can we make it to the next lighthouse in time?" I asked.

"We have fifteen minutes," stated Max.

"Where is the next lighthouse?" I asked.

"Halfmoon Lighthouse is up the shore to the East," said Wolfman. I turned and looked at Lily. Our eyes met; we both knew this was the right one.

"Drive as fast as you can without killing us," I said to Chameleon.

***

We pulled up to the Halfmoon Sandbar building, and I do mean building. It didn't look like a typical lighthouse at all. The one-story, white vinyl-sided, hexagonal architecture was topped with a two-story lantern room. This was disturbing and disappointing on so many levels. The lighthouse was closed already.

After reading the sign posted by the front steps, it cleared up why the lighthouse was on a grassy knoll on a corner lot in the city, instead of on the water. It was retired in 1942 and moved here.

A raised white wooden deck surrounded all six sides. There was only one main staircase containing 5 steps leading up to the main door. Three flags waved proudly on their own flagpoles located to the left of the building. Black cast-iron bells surrounded by pink and red flowers lined the deck, making it feel homier and less industrial. The lawn looked recently mowed. Maybe someone lived inside.

Most of us walked up the stairs and across the deck. Looking in the windows like a Peeping Tom seemed to be the thing to do. Chameleon and Julie took the front door. Me, Lily, Luke, Feed Bag, Amber, Blond Ambition, and Thirteen split up between the windows on either side of the front door. Everyone else was looking around the yard.

"All I see is the entryway," said Julie. "There is a wooden bench and a yellow raincoat hanging on a wooden coat rack."

"The door is locked," said Chameleon, trying to turn the handle.

"Nice kitchen. I wonder if there's anything in the refrigerator," said Feed Bag. "I'm hungry."

"Maybe there's beer in there," said Blond Ambition. A smile formed on his face.

"I can see the dining room," I said. "Oh my god, is that Brad's tuxedo jacket?"

"We need to get in there now," insisted Julie. She shoved Chameleon out of the way and spastically tried her best to pry the door open.

"Hey guys, I found something," said The Singe.

We ignored him while we all tried to open the windows and beat down the front door.

"See, look," said The Singe. He held the square metal Jack-in-the-Box toy out away from his body with both hands like it was a bomb. "Who wants to turn the crank?"

We all stopped what we were doing and approached him.

"Where did you find that?" asked Chameleon.

"In the largest of the three bells," said The Singe. "The riddle said: 'Hell's Bells', so I figured, look in the bells."

"This has to be the clue," said Amber. "What should we do?"

"Can someone turn the crank? My arms are getting tired," said The Singe. We all looked at each other with apprehension.

"I'll do it," blurted Julie. Julie walked over to where The Singe was standing. She reached out and grabbed the crank. The music started the "Pop Goes the Weasel" theme song.

Da dunt, da dunt, da da da da dunt. Da dunt, da dunt, da daaaaa dunt. Da dunt, da dunt, da da da da dunt…

"Pop! Goes the weasel," sang the boys as the creepy, blue-and-white polka-dotted clown flew out from under the metal flap. Taped to the clown's hand was a key.

Julie grabbed it and ran for the door. It worked. We all ran inside to the kitchen.

"Brad! Brad! Are you in here?" she yelled.

We all took turns opening all the closet and cupboard doors. Luke even looked under the bed. There was no sign of Brad except for his jacket. I started rummaging through the pockets. In the inside chest pocket, I found a note. It read: "Try your luck at darts. You only get one shot, make it count."

"Who wants the honors?" I asked.

"Finders keepers," said Luke.

"I'll do it," offered Blond Ambition. "I'm a great darts player. I almost always hit the bullseye." He picked up the one dart from the table and stood at the line drawn on the floor. We all looked at the dart board that was filled with tiny pieces of folded paper. No doubt another piece of this crazy puzzle.

Blond Ambition let the dart fly. It hit the bullseye. We all cheered for some reason. The whole crew walked up to the dart board to watch him retrieve the paper prize on the board. He pulled the dart out and opened the piece of paper. There was one word: "Parasailing."

"Parasailing?" I furrowed my brow. "At least it didn't say skydiving."

"I bet they all say parasailing," scoffed Luke as he walked up to the board.

"Don't, Luke," I begged.

"Shhh! The killer could be listening," said Lisa.

Luke grabbed a slip of paper before I could stop him. He read it out loud: "Amateur." He grabbed another, read it, and turned pale. He looked at us in disbelief.

"What does it say?" I asked.

"You are next, Dead Boy."

"Let's get out of here," I said, pushing him towards the door.

***

What could possibly go wrong with Payton flying over open water like a kite? I hope she can swim. She looks more like bait to me.

CHAPTER SIX

In the bus, Wolfman checked out our parasailing options in the area. There was only one—Paradise Parasailing and Boat Rental. It was only two miles down the beach. Wolfman dialed the number.

"Hi, I would like to make a reservation for today," inquired Wolfman. He paused to listen. He put his phone against his leg so the party on the other end couldn't hear him. "Who should I make the reservation for?" he asked.

"Go ahead and make one in my name," I told him.

"It's for Payton Richardson." He paused to listen again.

"You already have a reservation for two at one o'clock, and it's already paid for. Super. See you then." Wolfman hung up.

"Great, how bad could this be." I rested my forehead on the palm of my hand. "Who's brave enough to go up with me?" Things got really quiet on the bus. Everyone was doing some serious soul-searching.

"Fine. I'll go up by myself." I looked around the crowd for a pity partner in crime.

"I'll go," Chameleon volunteered. "I've done this once before when I was nine. It will be just like riding a bike."

"Well, the last time I rode my bike, I broke my arm," I said super sassy. "I'm hoping for a better outcome this time."

"Me too," agreed Chameleon. He parked the bus and handed the keys to Wolfman. "Just in case I don't make it back," he said in a serious tone.

I thought that was a bit much. "Are you guys staying here?" I asked the rest of the gang before getting off the bus.

"Are you kidding me? We're not missing any of this," joked Blond Ambition.

I looked at Chameleon. "Let's go, before I change my mind," I said.

Chameleon and I went inside Paradise Parasailing while everyone else waited outside by the food truck to grab some lunch.

"Do you guys want anything?" asked my brother.

Chameleon said, "Order me two corndogs. I can eat that on-the-go."

"You're not supposed to eat before you swim," I stated.

"Payton, you go from the boat, to floating in the air, to back on the boat," said Chameleon. "You won't even get your toes wet."

"We'll just see about that," I said. "Things don't always go well for me."

Inside the store, a cheery, sun-tanned man in his mid-fifties stood behind the counter.

"Are you Payton?" He asked while checking his schedule.

"Yes," I said. "And this is…"

"My friends call me Chameleon." He smirked at the fact that I still don't know his real name.

"I'm Paul, the owner. Hey, Justin, get your butt out here." A few seconds later, a young dark-haired kid in his late teens came out of the back room. "And this is my nephew Justin."

"Hi, nice to meet you," he said. He approached the counter with an honest and wholesome resolution.

My fears subsided a little because of their friendly demeanor. Paul handed us each a life jacket. We put them on.

Paul reached in one of the top drawers. He pulled out two pieces of paper. "Before we go out on the water, I need to have you read this waiver over and sign it at the bottom."

It seemed to be a simple form stating that he was not responsible for anything going wrong and we understand the risks involved. Yay! I'm feeling so much better about this whole thing. We both signed it and handed them back.

"Any questions before we head to the boat?" asked Paul, reaching for his boat keys.

"This might seem weird," Chameleon started, "but can you tell us who paid for the parasailing today?"

Paul opened his scheduling book and stared at the page. His finger ran down the column until he found our reservation. "It just says, 'paid in full' by Payton Richardson." His eyes left the page and looked back up at us.

We stared back at him in disbelief. Chameleon and I looked at each other with bewilderment and shrugged our shoulders. This kept getting weirder by the minute.

"Can you tell me when the reservation was made?" I inquired, trying to get more answers.

Paul looked down at his scheduling book again. "It looks like it was made about two weeks ago. Does that help?"

"Not really," I said, making a disappointed face.

"Let's go," suggested Chameleon, "my corndogs are probably getting cold. No one likes cold dogs."

Justin laughed at Chameleon's joke. "Always say no to cold wieners," he said with an immature giggle.

We both looked at each other again and decided to leave that one alone.

"I almost forgot," Paul reached under the counter. "There is a note in the ledger to give you this." He pulled out an envelope.

I'm sure my eyes lit up. "Did someone drop it off?" I asked eagerly.

"No, I found it in the mailbox with the rest of the mail," said Justin. "Sorry that I can't tell you more than that."

That information was of little help to me. I opened the envelope to find another clue/mystery to solve. The note read: "You cannot see what you are not looking for."

"Deep," said Chameleon. He was internally analyzing the clue.

"Is this one of those prank shows?" asked Justin, reaching for his sunscreen that was on the counter.

"No, it's more of a scavenger hunt," I answered back on the way to the door. But what the hell was I looking for?

***

Before starting the engine, Paul and Justin had us securely strapped into the double harness at the stern of the boat. I inspected the black polyester harness with stainless steel buckles. It seemed safe. The rest of the gang waved from the shore as we were heading away from the dock.

Chameleon seemed happy with his double-fisted corn dog feast. "Payton, do you want one of these? You look pale. Maybe you should eat something."

"My stomach doesn't feel that great. It's probably better if I don't eat anything."

"Okay," he said. "I tried to be a gentleman." He stuck the ketchup-covered corndog in his mouth and pulled an empty stick back out. It reminded me of a piranha leaving nothing but a boney skeleton behind. He smiled from ear-to-ear as he chewed and finally swallowed.

"Hang on. Here we go," Paul yelled back to us.

"It's just like flying a kite," said Chameleon as we were jerked backwards. "Except we're the kite." As we jerked back, I heard a rip. I was hoping it was just the zipper of my overly tight dress.

Our feet left the deck of the boat. Justin kept cranking, letting out more of the tow rope. Before I knew it, we were three hundred feet in the air.

"Are you still doing okay, Payton?" asked Chameleon with concern in his voice.

"Peachy," I answered back, tucking my dress between my knees. "It's pretty cool up here, actually."

"We'll be fine up here as long as the boat maintains a fifteen-to-thirty mile per hour pace," stated Chameleon.

"What happens if we don't?" I asked with genuine concern.

He looked at me, making a whistling noise while pointing down at the water. I felt my eyes widen and my heart race. I needed to concentrate at the task at hand to calm myself down. The boat was heading back towards the area of Paul's shop. We waved to our ant-sized friends below.

I was doing my best to scour the land in search of a clue. "Do you see anything yet?" I asked.

"Not yet," he said, looking around at the beach-front properties and down at the water. He pulled a small pair of binoculars out of his oversized fannypack.

"Are those for parasailing?"

"For viewing the ladies," he answered back with a silly smirk.

"Ah, I see. Do you have anything else useful in there?" I asked, pointing at his pack. "Maybe something medicinal?"

"Alcoholic or herbal? He asked with a raised eyebrow.

"Just alcoholic, please. No one needs to see herbal Payton."

He laughed. "I would like to fly high with herbal Payton someday. In the meantime, I think I have an emergency tiny bottle of liquid courage in the form of tequila."

I immediately perked up. "That sounds like my kind of medicine." I held out my hand ready to accept my complimentary inflight cocktail.

"I'm DD today, so it's yours." He handed over the tiny bottle.

I twisted off the top and emptied the bottle in one swig. "Not quite the same without a lime chaser."

"Thirsty?" He asked and snickered.

"You have no idea," I shot back. "What else do you have in there?"

"Yesterday, as a group project for my dad, we made homemade shark repellent with sunscreen."

"Sweet. I'll take some of that, please." I held out my hand, waiting for a squirt. He pulled out a tube and squirted a large dollop into my palm. I rubbed my hands together, then rubbed it on my face, neck, chest, and arms.

"What's the SPF factor?" I inquired as I finished rubbing in the lotion.

"I'm not exactly sure. We were supposed to test it down at the beach today before we ran into you. We talked Feed Bag into laying on a raft out by the jetty to see how it worked against the sun and the sharks." He grabbed the tube and began rubbing copious amounts on his exposed skin.

"Hey, look," I said pointing to the shore, five or six shops down from Paul's. "Is that a huge smiley face drawn in the sand?"

"I think you're right." Chameleon vigorously squirted the lotion on the top of his head and rubbed it in his hair.

I gave him an ominous look. "What the heck are you doing?"

He pointed below us to the boat. It was slowing down.

"Oh no," I said, seeing the smoke coming out of the engine. "What can we do?" I asked urgently. Paul was checking out the engine. Justin frantically ran around the deck getting Paul the tools that he needed. By their hurried actions, we could tell it wasn't good.

"The way I see it, we have two choices," said Chameleon. "One: we do nothing, hit the water…hard…and swim for shore…that's if we survive the fall and the sharks. Two: I cut the tow rope and I try to steer this thing in the direction of the shore. Hopefully, we land in the sand."

"Cut the rope! Cut the rope!" I screamed. Chameleon pulled his knife out of his pack. It was a sexy three-and-a-half-inch blade, folding knife.

"Nice knife," I said, admiring the black Cerakote blade finish, fluid lines, and fancy gray handle. The butterfly on the blade was a nice touch.

"It's a Benchmore Geek," He proclaimed right before he cut us loose.

The tow rope dropped away, falling into the water. The wind immediately lifted the parasail and pushed us backward away from the boat, which turned out to be a good thing. Baroooomph! The boat exploded into a ball of fire.

"Oh my god, did you see that? Paul! Justin!" I screamed. "We need to do something."

"It's too late. Lean towards me, Payton. Now!" yelled Chameleon. "I'm trying to steer us away from the flames and closer to shore." The blast of exploding gases worked to our advantage. It pushed the parasail towards the shore.

"Can you steer us closer to the smiley face in the sand?"

"How about I get us anywhere on land, so we don't have to see if the shark repellent works?"

"It was just a suggestion," I said, trying to make amends for my stupid request.

"You're forgiven. Now, lean the other way." Chameleon said in a slightly calmer voice.

"Why?" I blurted out, needing an answer.

"I'm trying to find us a pocket of air, like a Jetstream."

I did what I was told. "I don't think it's working," I said.

"It's not. Damn it!" he said out of frustration. "I don't think we are going to make the beach. We're descending too fast."

"Look," I said, pointing at the two jet skis coming our way. It was Wolfman and Blond Ambition to the rescue.

"Lean towards me again," he instructed.

"I'm trying my best." This was so nerve racking. "Oh shit, is that a dorsal fin?"

"Maybe it's just a dolphin," he said to make me feel better.

"Sure, it is," I said. "Because everything always works out for me."

"Are you being sarcastic right now?"

"Yes, yes I am. What should I do?"

"Don't scream. Keep calm. When we hit the water, the parachute should land in front of us. Tread water slowly to conserve your energy. Don't spaz out and panic. It will attract the sharks. The boys will get to us as soon as they can."

"Why are you so dang calm?" I asked.

"Because I'm an Eagle Scout . . . and I might be herbily enhanced."

I punched him in the arm. "Oh my god, we're gonna freaking die." I sighed and rolled my eyes. I took a deep breath just before we hit the water. I popped up out of the water first. The surface was choppy. I frantically searched the surf for Chameleon. Wolfman and Blond Ambition pulled up, instantly slowing their engines. I swam over to Wolfman. With his help, I climbed aboard his craft.

"Help me find Chameleon," I begged. He didn't resurface. We all frantically searched the water. The boys slowly idled in small circles looking for him.

Finally, Chameleon's head broke the surface. "There he is!" I yelled. "Over there!" I pointed to the edge of the parachute. He had somehow gotten trapped underneath when he tried to come up for air.

Blond Ambition zipped over there and pulled him up onto his jet ski. Once he was safely onboard, we all headed back to Paul's Paradise Parasailing to return the jet skis.

"I don't think that was an accident," I stated.

"Me either," said Chameleon.

"What do we do now?" asked Wolfman as he got off his jet ski.

"We get the hell out of here," I said. "No cops, remember? Thanks for saving me by the way."

"No problem. You're part of the team," said Wolfman.

***

Paul and Justin heard my voice. They had to die. Find the clue and solve for ____.

CHAPTER SEVEN

The group stood around the edges of the large smiley face drawn in the sand. We all looked at each other for a suggestion of what to do next.

Teagan nudged me with her elbow and handed me a blended icy, boozy concoction. It was red, my second favorite flavor. My favorite flavor has always been green in the form of a margarita, of course.

"Let's bow our heads," said Chameleon. "I propose a moment of silence for Paul and Justin. They took one for the team. For that, we will be eternally grateful." I felt horrible that this had to happen to them. Evil will not prevail over justice.

After a respectful amount of quiet reflection, Julie spoke up. "What now? What do we do now?"

"Does it bother anyone else that there are zero footprints around the rock that's supposed to be the nose in the center of the smiley face?" asked Thirteen. "How did it get there?" Thirteen's OCD wheels were turning. He made an excellent point.

"Maybe it was already here, and they drew the smiley face around it," I suggested.

"Someone would have moved it if that's true. It hasn't been there for long," said Amber.

"Someone could have thrown it in the middle," suggested Julie.

"There's no roll marks around the rock," said Chameleon, disproving her theory.

"Then, what?" Julie asked. "I'm out of suggestions."

"Guys, I think we are missing the point." I stated. "I think the alcohol was getting the cogs in my brain to start turning. "Smiley faces don't have noses." I stepped into the circle.

"Payton, stop!" shouted Lisa.

"Yeah, there could be a landmine or something," said Max.

"I think you've played one too many video games," I said, heading further inside the circle.

"The boat blew up, Payton," said Lily, concerned for my safety.

"Death wish, much," said Luke. "You are such a drama queen."

"I am not," I insisted, picking the six-inch roundish rock up in my hands. Half of the crew dove into the sand. "Seriously," I said, making a mental note of the brave souls that were still standing. I flipped the rock over to find a note written on the bottom with white paint. It was addressed to me. Big surprise there.

I read the note to everyone: "Payton, solve for Pi. Find the radius of the circle."

"Okay mathletes, this one is for you. I'm out," I said. "I'm willing to supervise." I walked back out of the circle to let the gifted and talented go to work.

Chameleon, Max, Amber, and Lily stepped up to the challenge. "Lily," I said, "you know math?" I was shocked.

Lily got in my face. "In a former life, I was a nerd, Payton. Do you have a problem with that?"

"Not at all," I replied. "Carry on." I crossed my arms over my chest, waiting for someone to amaze me.

The four brainiacs stood in a small group to discuss their strategy. "So how do we measure the diameter of the circle?" asked Amber.

"What's the formula?" asked Max.

"Pi equals the circumference divided by the diameter," said Chameleon. "Did you also know that 22/7 is closer to Pi than writing 3.14? Circumference equals 2Pir. The radius is half of the diameter."

We were all stupefied by his knowledge of Pi and math facts. Speaking of pie, I was getting hungry.

"I've got it," said Blond Ambition, joining the group. "We can measure the diameter of the circle with that cement block over there,"

"How? Why?" asked Lily with a gruff tone to her voice. She put her hands on her hips to display her impatience.

"My dad is in construction, right? I've had to help him lay block. Each cement block is 8x8x16 inches. We can use it as a unit of measurement."

"That's brilliant," said Max. He ran over to the block and carried it over to the circle and began measuring across it. After he worked his way from one side of the smiley face to the other, he said, "It's twenty feet across the circle."

My brain was getting fuzzy from the sun, booze, and lack of food in my stomach. I looked past the circle and thought I saw a mirage standing by the edge of the café. It looked like Dylan, my hot ex-boyfriend. (We were a thing for two glorious days. He was the love of my life before he mysteriously dumped me roughly forty days ago.) I didn't say anything to anybody just in case I was dreaming. The earth moved and butterflies were flapping their wings again. My heart was racing like crazy as I walked in his direction. His dark wavy hair and muscular build was making me sweaty. His sizzling, raw sexuality was breathtaking. His shirt and pants were tight in all the right places. Oh my. Someone throw a bucket of water on me quick before my lady parts catch on fire.

The lightbulb fought its way through the brain fog as I got closer to Dylan and the café. The sign in the café window said: "Free ice cream with your slice of Pi." Duh, it was a Pi celebration joke. The smiley face was a clue and a distraction. Sometimes, my stomach is smarter than my brain.

I looked down at myself. Yikes! Disaster a la mode was my fashion statement. My ugly dress was ripped and soaking wet, my shin was missing skin, and the remnants of sunscreen made my hair look overly moussed and greasy. What was I worried about? The man has seen me in the ER covered in puke, hovering over a biohazard garbage can without pants. I am good to go.

"Hi." I gave him an eye twinkling grin. It was awesome to see him again.

"Hi, yourself," he said in his smooth, angelic voice. "Should I ask why you look like that?"

"Probably best if you don't," I answered back. Never have I uttered a truer statement.

Apparently, there was no time for more idle chit chat. He grabbed my arm and gently escorted me inside the café. I felt the spark again when he touched me. I was warm and tingly all over. It was awesome. Inside the café, we found a booth way in the back for privacy. He took a seat across from me.

"It's still not safe for us to be around each other," he said. He slid an envelope across the table at me. "This came to me last week. The note said that I was supposed to bring it down to you here, today. I was instructed to stand in front of this café around noon, hand you the note, and leave."

"Thanks for still being here." I reached for the note, brushing his hand with my finger. There were sparks. All the old feelings came rushing back. Was this good or bad?

"I shouldn't be here. What sick game have I been pulled into this time?"

I grabbed Dylan's hand. "I'm sorry. Brad is missing. People are dying. You should probably go before you get hurt too." I gave him a sad look then sighed. He needed to go, but I really wanted him to stay. Getting lost in his dreamy emerald, green eyes was not an option right now. I needed to be strong. It was time to open the clue and get on with solving this puzzle. I let go of his hand and opened the envelope.

The clue read: "You're red hot. Choose your favorite." Oh crap! Did they mean Brad or Dylan? I continued to stare at the note with ideas running rampant through my brain.

"What does the clue mean?" asked Dylan.

I waved the waitress over. "It means, I hope you're hungry."

A young blond-haired waitress in her early twenties came over to our table. If her nametag was correct, her name was Sabrina. "Can I get you something?" she asked.

"Yes, I would like all of your raspberry rhubarb pies, please."

"All?" She asked, questioning my motive. "We have like ten pies."

"Yes, I'll take them all." I gave Sabrina a mile-wide smile. I was excited for some pie.

Sabrina blew a large obnoxious bubble with her gum and popped it before speaking. "Do you want ice cream with your order?"

"No thanks, just the pies will be great. Oh, and we will need two forks."

Sabrina nodded and walked back to the kitchen to fetch our pies.

Dylan shook his head at my request. "What are you doing, Payton?"

"I think the next clue is baked into one of those pies." I answered with confidence.

"That's crazy," he said, not wanting to believe me.

I looked directly into his sparking green eyes to convince him that I was right. "The clue said to choose my favorite. Raspberry rhubarb is my favorite."

"Oh shit," he said, ducking under the table.

I ducked too, out of instinct. "What's wrong?" I asked in an anxious tone.

"Stephani just walked by the window. She must have followed me down here."

"I saw her yesterday fighting with Lily. What is her deal?"

"It's still complicated. She won't leave me alone. I wish I could tell you more, but I can't for your safety."

I gave him a disappointed look as we both hid under the table. My hand touched his face. It was electric. "You should probably sneak out the back door while you can still get away," I said with a heavy heart. I wanted him to stay.

"Bye, Payton. Good luck." He kissed me quick on the lips, then disappeared down the back hallway leading to the bathrooms.

I sighed. The kiss, not wanting him to leave, and the eye candy as he walked away. Dang it, that man got under my skin again. I continued to stare in his direction after he was gone.

I climbed out from under the table and took my seat again.

"There you are," said Julie as she approached the table. "We thought we lost you."

I looked over to find the rest of the gang staring at me. Sabrina walked over with two trays full of pies, setting them on the table in front of me.

"We're gonna need more forks," I told her.

"Sure thing," said Sabrina. "Be right back."

Teagan walked up to the table. "Spill, Payton. What's this?" she asked. "You're hiding something, I can tell. You look all glowy. Did you have sex?"

"No. But I wish." I was telling her the truth.

Lily, Luke, and Julie sat with me at the booth. Max and Chameleon each pulled one of the tables over next to the booth. Everyone else grabbed a chair to sit down.

"Chameleon, how did the math problem turn out?" I asked.

"It didn't," answered Chameleon.

"The math got fuzzy, so we decided to take a break and come in here," said Lily.

"What's with all the pies?" asked Max.

I couldn't tell them about the note from Dylan, that was my little secret. "I had a hunch. The clue said: "Payton solve for Pi." My stomach led me in here. Everybody dig in. I think the clue we are looking for might be in one of these pies."

We all grabbed a fork, no plates, and dug in.

"Can I have some ice cream?" asked Feed Bag.

"Shut up and eat," said Blond Ambition. Feed Bag gave him a sour look.

It was extremely quiet for about five minutes while we stuffed our faces and searched through each pie plate. After we were all stuffed, we continued to pick around the crust and filling.

"There's nothing here," said Lisa.

"There has to be." I was extremely disappointed. I put my elbows on the table, resting my face in my hands. One of my elbows slipped and bumped the tray. One of the aluminum pie plates hit the floor. It landed upside down with a plop.

"Hey, you're wasting good pie," bitched Feed Bag.

"Don't eat anymore pie, Feed Bag. You're gonna get the shits," declared Wolfman.

"Hey, look there's the clue," said The Singe. He pointed at the floor. We all craned our necks to look over the side of the table. The clue was written on the bottom of the pie plate with a red, permanent marker. It was meant for us for sure because a smiley face was drawn below the letters.

The Singe read it out loud: "lunaga radem hiplond aby."

"Check the rest of the pie plates," Luke instructed. The boys flung pie and plates around the table. To say they made a mess would have been an understatement.

"There's nothing else written on these," said Chameleon.

"I guess that's our only clue," said Shoes. He looked down in horror when he saw a glop of raspberry rhubarb on his fancy new shoes. He quickly wiped it off by using the cuff of his sweatshirt.

"What does it mean?" asked Julie. She bent over and picked up the plate, staring at the groups of letters.

Thirteen walked up from behind us. He must have been in the bathroom. "I love that place. Dolphins are the best." We all turned around with raised eyebrows.

"What place?" I asked eagerly.

"Laguna Madre Dolphin Bay. Are we going there?" Reading mixed-up messages must be Thirteen's superpower. "Yes, yes we are," I said happily.

"To the bus," said Chameleon, waving everyone to come on.

Sabrina showed up at our table with the bill. She did not look happy when she saw the mess.

"Does a fifty percent tip work for you?" I asked.

"Make it seventy-five," she demanded. I painfully gave her my card. Overpaying is the worst.

Luke and Lily looked over at me. "Mom's going to be pissed," said Luke.

I rolled my eyes. "What else is new?" I asked as sarcastically as I possibly could. "Lately, I can't do anything right."

On the way to the bus, my phone rang. It was my mother. From across the island, she had felt the unfortunate shift in my bank account. Yes, my mother is that good.

***

Slackers! They gave up too easy. The answer: the circumference was 62.8. The diameter 20. The radius 10. Congrats to Payton for finding her pie and solving the puzzle. But did she really choose her favorite? Now, off to the water park. Soon you will find out why they call me "The Pusher."

CHAPTER EIGHT

Do I answer it? Do I really have a choice in the matter? Probably not, I thought as I climbed on the bus.

"Hi, Mom, how are things?" I was trying to act casual like nothing was wrong.

"Things? Things? Things are not great, Payton. This trip was supposed to be about family time, not galivanting around the island with your booze-soaked friends." My mother was on one of her tirades.

"Mom, calm down. You are going to give yourself an aneurism. There is no soaking going on," I stated, while watching Teagan let Max do a belly shot off her abdomen. I took off one of my flip flops and threw it at her. After I got her attention, I mouthed the word NO at her.

"Don't lie to me, Payton. I know how Spring Break works," said my mother with conviction.

"Seriously, Mom, I'm consoling Julie. She's devastated. Getting left at the altar is brutal." I looked over at Julie who was sitting across the aisle from me.

Julie shot me an evil glare that narrowed her eyes, furrowed her brow, and did unflattering things to her mouth. I know I was being a liar and a hypocrite because I did the same thing to Brad when I ditch him at the altar.

"Your father and I demand that you, Luke, and Lily play a round of golf with us today. We have our standard 3:00 p.m. tee time at the country club. Be there."

She meant it. "Okay, Mom, we will be there." It wasn't hard to get Luke's attention; he was hanging on every word. I pointed at him, Lily, and myself then did a golf swing with my arm that wasn't holding my phone. Luke shook his head no. "Luke says he can't wait," I said lying my butt off again. Now Luke was glaring at me.

"This isn't a request, Payton. See you at 3:00 sharp. We'll bring your clubs," she said in a very stern voice and hung up.

My mother meant business. I sighed. I've been doing that a lot lately. "Any chance the dolphin park is by the country club?" I asked to anyone who was listening.

"Let me check the GPS," said Wolfman. He flipped through a few screens and said, "It's your lucky day. The country club is right down the block."

"Swell," I said with heavy sarcasm. "Ain't life grand?"

***

We pulled up to the entrance of Dolphin Bay. Chameleon shut off the engine. He reached into the glove box, grabbing a roll of black electrical tape.

As I was exiting the bus, I asked, "What are you going to do with that?"

He got up from the driver's seat. He grabbed his backpack from the floor of the bus. "I'm going to change the bus number from 334 to 884."

"That is a smart idea. We are probably on the police's radar by now."

Outside the bus, Chameleon used his knife to cut the tape and changed the numbers by the door.

"Don't forget the top and back numbers on the bus," suggested Max, trying to be thorough.

Feed Bag and Blond Ambition approached us. "While you guys are doing that, Feed Bag and myself will go check out the price of admission." The boys walked towards the front gate.

Chameleon crawled up on the roof of the bus while Max took care of the numbers on the back. Chameleon jumped down. "We are officially undercover."

"Sweet," said The Singe. "We are in incognito mode."

The boys came running back. "You are not going to believe this," said Blond Ambition.

"It's only five dollars apiece to get in," added Feed Bag.

"I guess we are all going in. Is everyone okay with that?" I looked around the group. My scan stopped at a disgruntled face.

"Fish freak me out," blurted The Singe. "I can feel their beady little eyes staring at me through the glass. It's like they can see through my soul. Can I stay behind and keep an eye on the bus?"

I did my best to contain my laughter. His fish phobia was news to me.

"Sure," said Chameleon, handing over the keys to The Singe. "If the cops come, stay cool. Got it?"

He nodded back. "Got it. I can be chill."

Again, I paid for the entire group with plastic. Gail, the middle-aged women behind the counter, gave me a pamphlet along with tickets for everyone.

I leaned in close to Gail. "Did anyone happen to leave a note or a package for Payton Richardson?"

"Let me check," said Gail. She bent down. Her head was under the counter while she searched. I heard the rustling of papers. She briefly popped her head up over the counter. "I didn't see a note or an envelope. There is one more cabinet I can check." She moved over to another spot under an adjacent counter. "Found it," she said in an excited tone. She stood up and placed a gray and white stuffed dolphin on the counter. It had an envelope attached.

"Great. Thank you," I said with a smile before walking away with our newest clue.

"Hey," said Luke, "aren't you going to ask her what the person looked like who left it?"

"No," said Chameleon in a stern voice. "Last time we did that, they blew up."

"All right then," answered Luke, "don't ask too many questions is how we are playing it."

We stopped by a palm tree on our way into the park to read the clue. Everyone gathered around me. I handed the stuffed animal to Julie before opening the small envelope. The note read: "A pirate's dream."

"This clue is easy," said Blond Ambition. "The answer is rum."

All the boys laughed at his joke.

Teagan cleared her throat to get everyone's attention. "Don't be dumb," she said making a face at him. "The answer is sex." Teagan flipped her hair in a sensual way.

The boys gawked at her in a sick, puppy-love fetish way. Ew!

Teagan continued with her commentary. "Haven't you boys ever seen 'A Pirate's Dream' on Skinflix? The treasure map is on his—"

"For the love of all humanity, Teagan, stop talking," I demanded.

"What?" she asked with a coy smile. Teagan twirled a lock of her long blond hair.

No more booze for Teagan. She was wearing her slutty friend badge with distinct honor today. Some of the boys appeared to be stunned by her behavior. They turned red and did their best to hold back their laughter and comments. Max seemed to be very intrigued. I smelled trouble.

"I've got it," declared Amber. She was beyond excited. "I know the answer."

"So, what is it?" asked Wolfman.

The entire group looked at Amber for her response.

"The answer is treasure," said Amber. "That is what every pirate wants. You know like gold doubloons and pieces of eight."

"Yo, ho, blow the man down," sang Teagan. "That's in the movie too, by the way."

My hand smacked my forehead after her comment. "Let's keep this PG, please." I shot her an unhappy glare.

Teagan's silent comeback was more hair twirling, trying her best to play innocent or dumb. I knew better. It was her signature move.

Julie started walking forward into the park. "Let's go find the treasure." She was trying to move the group forward.

"Where is the dolphin tank?" I asked, following Julie. I looked around. "Does this park have one of those big, mallmanac thingies? Never mind." I felt stupid. "I have the map Gail gave me."

"Um … Payton," stammered Julie. "Look at the stuffed animal again." She held it up for everyone to see. "It has big teeth."

The whole group said, "Oh shit," in unison.

The stuffed animal Julie was holding in her hand was a shark, not a dolphin.

I looked back at Chameleon. "Do you have more of that shark repellent?"

"Most definitely," he said patting his backpack.

"I have a feeling we are going to need it." My knees suddenly felt weak. I sat down on one of the wooden benches next to the stone path that led into the park. I put my face in my hands and leaned forward. My head was whirling in circles again. I hated to have the kids see me like this. I needed to keep it together and try to be their fearless leader. Breathe slowly ran through my head repeatedly. I felt a hand on my back. It brought me back out of my breathing exercise.

It was Feed Bag. "Don't worry, Payton, we won't let the shark eat you."

For some reason I found this hilarious. It was just what I needed to hear. "Thank you, Feed Bag. That's the nicest thing I've heard all day." I stood up, I felt better.

"Payton, let's go," insisted Julie. She was getting antsy.

"Yes, let's tackle this shark head on," I said. I opened the map to the park. We needed to speed things along. I couldn't be late for the family golf outing. It is a sad day when your mother scares you more than a man-eating shark and a serial killer.

I pointed to the spot on the map where we needed to go. "Shark's Cove. That sounds safe. Maybe it's just a baby shark."

We followed the path to the left. It led us right to the shark tank. The group stood with their noses pressed against the glass. The tank was large and quite deep to house its star attraction. We all watched the eight-foot tiger shark swim around majestically in its watery domain. It glided near the sandy bottom. Its snaggle toothed grin was horrifying as it approached the glass to get a better look at us. Our eyes met as it swam by. I felt it look into my soul. The Singe's fish phobia was now fact based. The fear was real. It shook me to my core. Was it too late to run away? Yes, yes it was.

"I wonder if they can sense fear?" asked Luke.

Lily hit him in the arm.

Luke shook his head. "Hey, I was speaking in general," he explained.

"Are the other fish in there its food?" asked Shoes. "That's disgusting that they are trapped, waiting to be eaten."

"I don't think so," said Lisa. "The sign over there to our right says: 'Shark feedings at noon and 4:00 p.m.' "

Thirteen tapped on the glass with his index finger. He was pointing at something. "There it is," he said with excitement. "I see the treasure chest."

Thirteen was right. The rectangular wooden chest was nestled amongst the green vegetation and the gray rocks on the bottom.

"I'll do it," said Shoes, volunteering himself. "I have some diving experience."

I walked over to him. "I can't let you do that," I insisted.

Lily came over to where we were standing. "Maybe you should listen to him, Payton," she said. "Your luck sucks. Let him do it."

She had me there. "Unluckiest girl in the universe, right here," I said, pointing at myself.

"Here, Sharkie, Sharkie," said Feed Bag. His voice sounded muffled and far away.

I looked up through the water to the surface of the tank. Faint ripples were forming and then a splash.

"Oh my god!" I yelled. I pointed towards the surface. "Feed Bag is up there. What if he fell in?"

The shark's attention was immediately drawn to the surface. Its calm, graceful, horizontal swim abruptly turned vertical. The shark was headed to the surface to check it out.

The entire group ran along the incline ramp that led to the surface. As we ran up the ramp that circled the tank, I prayed for a miracle. There was a lot of pushing and shoving as we all scrambled to reach the surface first.

Everyone came to a screeching halt when the top of the tank was in view. Our heads swung around frantically in all directions looking for Feed Bag. There was no sign of him.

"Help! Help!" shrieked Feed Bag. "Get me out of here."

We all rushed to the side of the tank. Feed Bag was clawing at the glass, wildly trying to pull himself up.

"Guys, hurry. Help me. I don't want to die." He yelled in a frenzied voice.

"Stay calm," said Chameleon. "Try not to splash. You'll provoke the shark."

The shark was circling dangerously close to Feed Bag. At one point, Feed Bag reached out and pushed the shark away with his hand.

"Somebody do something!" shouted Thirteen. "Our buddy is about to get eaten alive."

Chameleon grabbed the metal lifeguard pole that was hanging on the wall behind us. He poked at the shark whenever it tried to get close to Feed Bag.

"I have an idea," said Luke. He ran over to the opposite side of the tank. Lily followed him. They began splashing at the surface of the water with branches they pulled off the surrounding bushes. Blond Ambition and Max joined them to help distract the shark. The boys started pounding on the side of the tank. It was working. The shark immediately left the area by Feed Bag. Its predatory instincts took over. It went to search for the fish in distress.

Chameleon quickly moved the pole over next to Feed Bag so he could grab it. "Hang on. We're going to try to pull you up."

"What can I do?" asked Wolfman, eager to lend a hand.

"Here, take my knife," instructed Chameleon. "Cut off enough velvet rope from the post over there by the entrance of the 3-D theater. We might need it to pull him out of the water."

Wolfman grabbed the knife from his hand. "Will do, I'll be right back."

"Julie, Payton, Shoes, help me pull him up," instructed Chameleon. "I'm not strong enough to do it by myself."

We all grabbed the pole and pulled as hard as we could. The angle was all wrong. It didn't work. Feed Bag dropped back into the water with a splash.

"Guys. Hurry. Please! The shark might come back," yelled Feed Bag. He was frantic.

A small crowd had started to form. Stealthy and inconspicuous was off the table. Saving our friend was more important. Wolfman came back with the rope just in time. The shark was bored with the branches and all the splashing. It was coming back. Maybe the shark smelled Feed Bag's fear. Feed Bag became even more restless in the water. He panicked and thrashed about in the water.

Wolfman threw the rope into the water for Feed Bag to grab. "Everyone grab ahold and pull," he demanded.

Julie, Shoes, and I let go of the pole and grabbed the thick velvet rope. Chameleon held onto the pole to defend against the shark. Two bystanders grabbed the rope too to help us pull him out of the water. The shark was closing in.

"Hurry, the shark is coming closer," I screamed.

"Pull," instructed Wolfman.

Feed Bag looked over his shoulder as he was being hoisted up and out. The shark's dorsal fin cut through the surface of the water. He looked back at us with pleading eyes. The shark was coming for blood this time.

We all wrenched back as hard as we could. This was life or death. Feed Bag reached up with his left hand to grab the edge of the tank. He was trying desperately to help us lift him out. Unfortunately, at this point, his legs were still dangling beneath the surface. The shark was headed straight for them. Chameleon used the pole one more time to try to deter the shark.

Chameleon poked at the shark as hard as he could. "I see something," he said. "Get Feedbag out of the water. I'll get it, just get him out."

"One more time, guys," I said. "We got this. One, two, three, puuull."

We pulled so hard, Feed Bag rolled over the top of the protective glass partition, landing on top of us. We fell into a heap on the floor. Before we could stand up to see what was going on, we heard violent thrashing in the water. Right after that, something thumped against the glass wall of the tank. Was it the shark?

"Got it," shouted Chameleon. "Victory is mine." He put his arms in the air to celebrate.

All of us jumped to our feet in time to see the shark swim to the bottom of the tank. Whatever just happened, the shark chose to leave. The rest of the group came running over from the other side of the tank.

"What is it? What did you find?" asked an exhilarated Max.

Chameleon held up a small cylindrical capsule. "This must have fallen off the shark when I accidentally hooked its tail. Lucky for us it floats," said Chameleon. "I scooped it out of the water with this net." He held up the net end of the lifeguard pole.

"Open it," demanded Julie.

"Yeah, let's see what it says," insisted Lisa.

"That's not treasure." Teagan was disappointed. "Where is all the gold?"

"Stop," I said, noticing the growing crowd that was gathering around us. "We should do this somewhere else."

"You're right," said Chameleon. He put the capsule in his backpack.

Our group quickly left Shark's Cove. We headed farther into the park.

"Can we go to the food court?" asked Feed Bag. "I'm starving after all that exercise."

"I thought you bought a foot-long hot dog on your way in?" inquired Blond Ambition.

"I did, but when I was trying to feed some to the shark, someone pushed me into the water."

"You are sure someone pushed you in?" asked Wolfman.

"Positive," answered Feed Bag as he tried his best to wring the water out of his shirt and shorts.

This was huge. The killer was here somewhere. "What did they look like?" I asked, looking around the crowd.

"All I saw was someone in a black hooded sweatshirt running away," said Feed Bag. "Sorry I can't tell you more."

"Looks like we have ourselves a 'Pusher'," commented Chameleon.

"Great, a new twist to the game," I said out loud. That was supposed to stay in my head. Everyone got real quiet. It was time to lighten the mood a little. "Who wants nachos?" Nachos fix darn near everything. It was unanimous. We continued to follow the path to the food court in search of cheesy comfort food to stuff our faces with. After we are all fat and happy, we will read the next clue.

***

Your lackeys should not be doing your dirty work for you, Payton. That is going to cost you in the next round. Who will I push over the edge next?

CHAPTER NINE

Chameleon unscrewed the top of the small vial. He tapped the vial upside down on the table a few times to help dislodge the tiny piece of paper. Once it fell out into his hand, he carefully unrolled it. The entire group crowded around him looking over his shoulder while he read the note: "I can see you."

We all looked around, examining every face in the crowd.

"Who doesn't love to be spied on?" Julie joked.

"Is someone really watching us?" asked Lisa. "Maybe we should go check out the crowd." Lisa took one brave step away from the group.

I grabbed Lisa's arm. "Yes, someone is watching. Stay here. Don't provoke them. We need to stay calm and act normal."

Chameleon began to read the rest of the note: "A real pirate's dream: a sunken chest and a large booty."

"See?" said Teagan flipping her hair again. "Tits and ass." She smirked at her own joke.

There were a few snickers before Chameleon finished reading the clue: "Digging for treasure is your duty."

"Cool, it rhymes," said Feed Bag, eating a chip dripping with cheese and meat.

"Hang on," said Chameleon. "I'm not done yet."

"Everyone be quiet and let him finish it," urged Julie. She put her hand on his shoulder. "Go ahead, we are all listening."

"The box you seek is on dry land. Begin your search in the ____. Chameleon flipped the small piece of paper over. "That's it. They didn't finish the sentence."

"Fill in the blank maybe," suggested Lily. She threw her hands in the air out of frustration. "It could be anything, anywhere."

"I bet it has to rhyme," said Feed Bag, feeling good about his deductive reasoning skills.

Blond Ambition started blurting out words in alphabetical order: and, band, canned, fanned, hand —"

Luke blew out a big sigh. "The word you are looking for is sand. It's the only one that makes sense."

"Crap," said Max. "Do you guys realize how much sand is at the beach? This is impossible."

"Maybe we need to go back to the smiley face and dig," suggested Amber.

"Does anyone have a better idea?" asked Wolfman. "If you do, speak up now. We are wasting time."

I looked at the time on my phone. It was almost 2:00 p.m. That only left a little over an hour before the golf outing with my parents.

"Let's head to the beach," said Julie to get us all moving. "We need to find Brad, or has everyone forgotten about that?" Julie had that look.

All righty then. We took her comment as "move your asses" and our cue to head out of the park. Everyone was pretty quiet and subdued after Julie threw her mini hissy fit. On the way to the main doors, I saw a young boy, maybe four years old, being pulled by his mother through the crowd. He was kicking and screaming, "I want to go back to the Dinosaur Sandbox. I didn't find the bone."

I stopped in my tracks and turned to the group. "Did you guys hear that? The Dinosaur SANDbox."

I ran after the woman and her small child. "Excuse me," I said to her. I grabbed her shoulder to get her attention. "Can you tell me where the sandbox is located?"

The woman gave me a tired, aggravated look. She pointed down the hall. "It's all the way down there at the far end."

"Thank you," I said. "You've been very helpful." Out of nowhere, the angry little boy kicked me in the shin. The same shin that was already missing skin. "Ow!" I glared at the little turd. I was hoping his mother would have given him a spanking or made him apologize. Nope. She pulled him to the door with him making a "ha ha" face at me. I was tempted to show him one of my fingers, but I was sure he would show me his in return. "Ugh! I'm never having kids."

I ran back over to the group. "New plan: We need to head down the hall over there and check out the Dinosaur Sandbox." I waved with my arm to follow me as I started to jog. "Come on, we need to hurry. We have less than an hour to find the next clue before Luke, Lily, and I have to leave."

"If we split up and spread out, we can do this," said Luke.

"Cool, dinosaurs rock," said Feedbag.

"I like them because they are big and gnarly," said Max.

"I like them because they are extinct and can't eat me," added Feed Bag.

"Same," I said agreeing with them all.

***

With our admission, which I paid for, we each received a shovel, a plastic pail with a handle, and a treasure map. Money well spent.

Zac, the sixteen-year-old guy behind the counter, gave us the "you're too old" look. "Maybe you should stick to something more age appropriate like the shark feeding," he said. "That starts in five minutes."

"No thanks," said Feed Bag. "Someone already tried to feed me to the shark."

Zac gave him a weird look. "Sure, they did." He wasn't buying his story.

"Truth," said Chameleon, giving Feedbag a high-five.

"Do you have a package or an envelope for a 'Payton Richardson'?" I asked nicely with a smile.

"Nope. There's nothing here," he said without emotion.

The boys approached the counter. "Aren't you going to look?" asked Shoes.

"Nope," he replied without making eye contact.

The overactive crowd of youngsters pushed us forward without Zac complying to our request.

"C'mon, guys. We're on our own," I said.

Julie and her snow-white dress pushed back through the crowd. She grabbed Zac by the collar of his green polo shirt and got in his face. "See this dress. It's a bride's dress. You know who's missing? That's right, the groom," she said answering her own question. Chameleon and the boys stood behind her as backup. "And you're gonna help us locate him." Zac nodded.

Oh boy, Julie was on her way to crazy town. I smacked my forehead with my hand. This wasn't good for all involved. Any second, he could call security. The killer must be watching and rolling right now. Julie has been pushed over the edge.

Julie let go of Zac's collar. "Now bend over and look under the counter for a package for Payton." She gave him the "do it or die" death glare.

"Nice," said Chameleon, approving of her "getting it done" tactics.

Zac did as he was told. He came up empty handed. "Sorry, there is nothing here."

Zac's boss, a middle-aged man, approached the counter. "Is there a problem here?"

"Yeah," said Zac. "I'm not getting paid enough to deal with crazy customers. I quit." He handed his boss his work vest and left.

His boss looked at Julie. "How can I improve your digging experience today at the Dinosaur Sandbox?" he asked with his fake corporate smile.

Before Julie could start in, Chameleon grabbed her by the arm. "My lady friend didn't get her shovel. Could you please get her one?" Chameleon asked, trying to defuse the situation.

I made my way back over there to help nudge her away from the counter.

"Sure thing." He handed Julie another shovel.

"Thank you." I smiled at him for some reason. It was my "trying to stay out of jail" smile. I grabbed Julie's other arm and we escorted her away from the counter. Dang that was close.

***

Well. Well. I poke the bear and the kitty cat comes out to play. It is two for the price of one today. I do love a good bargain. Julie and the kid behind the counter lost it. Who will be next? I can see the cracks forming in Payton's armor. Can she be drawn over to the dark side?

***

"Come on, guys. Apparently, there isn't another clue." Everyone followed me. We stopped just inside the digging area to figure out where to start. I flipped open my treasure map to take a look at our options. The sandbox was divided into areas: Pterodactyl Playland, Camp Cretaceous, Stegosaurus School Yard, Gallimimus Dino Graveyard, and Tyrannosaurus Rest Stop.

The Pterodactyl Playland was basically swing sets, slides, and jungle gyms surrounded by sand. The metal poles used were painted a variety of green shades to look like dinosaur scales. Orange slides and swing seats added a pop of color. Black and blue climbing toys accented the area.

Camp Cretaceous had random nylon A-frame tents and fire pits with fake flames spread out in the sand. Six-foot high dinosaur statues were scattered around in between the tents. There was also a small kiddy pool/pond full of sand where the kids could pan for gold.

The Raptor Ranch was cowboy-meets-caveman. The back wall of the area had six small cave entrances. In front of that were three wooden ranch-style playhouses. Fenced in areas containing dinosaurs displayed like cattle were next to the play-houses. This seemed like a violation of the dinosaur's rights, but yeehaw, that's a fight for another day. In the center of the ranch was a large five-foot boot where people could pose for pictures. Why not capture this family moment on film? And of course, there was sand everywhere.

The Stegosaurus Schoolyard had brightly colored, oversized letters and numbers dispersed throughout the sand. The extra space was filled with child-sized desks and worktables for hands-on learning projects. Big black standing chalkboards were in front of the desks for playing school fun. I wondered if we would be using those to do more math problems. Ugh! Here's to wiping that slate clean.

Gallimimus Dino Graveyard had a three-foot high black metal fence surrounding the tombstones. The gated entrance was guarded by a six-foot Gallimimus on each side. The grave-yard was a large sandbox where kids could dig for realistic look-ing dinosaur bones to keep. Limit three per customer accord-ing to the sign by the gate.

Last, but not least, was the Tyrannosaurus Rest Stop. This was the food court for the kids filled with small tables and chairs. The menu included: slurpies, mac and cheese, chicken nuggets in the shape of dinosaurs, carrots and ranch dip, and chocolate chip cookies for dessert.

If I were four, this would be like Disneyland. My parents would have to drag me out of here kicking and screaming. Yes, I do get the irony of the little turd from earlier. Seeing as how I am twenty-four, this was lame as shit with lamer clues to fig-ure out. The decision on where to start was hard. It was time to let fate chose for me. I closed my eyes and randomly placed my finger on an area of the map. I opened my eyes to find my finger on Raptor Ranch.

"I'm heading over to the Raptor Ranch. Everyone spread out and try to solve the riddle. Holler if you find something." The gang had lost its mojo. They aimlessly meandered around in the sand.

I walked around the ranch and thoroughly inspected each fenced-in dinosaur. Yippee ki yay, sand lovers. There was nothing to see here. The dinosaur movies sucked all the prehistoric fun out of this for me. Raptors were no longer my favorite. Being hunted by a pack of anything would be beyond frightening.

It was time to check out the playhouses. Each one-story, twelve-foot by twelve-foot, wooden structure had a door and windows with shutters that opened and closed. On the inside, they had kid-friendly furnishings. There was a play kitchen set with a table and chairs in one corner. The living room area on the other side of the room had kid-sized couches and chairs. A TV played nonstop dinosaur cartoons and educational programs. I walked through each tiny house uninspired. There had to be a clue here somewhere. Nothing jumped out at me. This seemed hopeless.

Before I headed over to the caves, I looked around the sandbox. Everyone else from our group was digging, except Blond Ambition. He was headed in my direction. He stumped through the sand to get to me. I could tell there was something wrong by the distressed look on his face.

"Payton, some little brat just wiped his juicy, green booger on my arm," he said frantically. "What should I do?"

"Oh geez," I replied with a "sucks for you" expression on my face. "Go find a bathroom and wash it off immediately. And come right back. It is not safe for you to be wondering around alone."

He took off running to the restrooms by the T. Rest Stop. That had me thinking about The Singe. We hadn't heard from him since we left him alone with the bus. I found Max nearby hanging out with Teagan. This looked like more trouble brewing.

"Max, can you call The Singe and check on him? Get back to me ASAP. I'm heading over to the caves."

"You can count on me, Payton," he answered back.

Teagan gave me a strained look for interrupting her fun. I ignored her childish behavior. On the way back over to the

Raptor Ranch, I saw Amber, Lisa, Chameleon, and Wolfman taking selfies by the big boot.

"Guys, focus and dig please," I told them. It was time to get out of here soon. Even I was turning lame and too adult like. I rolled my eyes at myself for being a boring pain in the butt.

The six caves stood before me. Which one do I pick? They all looked dark and creepy. Screeching bat noises echoed inside the fake stone walls. I must be out of my mind to check these out by myself. Well, it won't be the first or last time I did something incredibly stupid.

Without warning, a small boy ran past me crying. He pointed at the third cave entrance from the left. "Mommy, there's a boogie monster in that cave." He was genuinely terrified, but his mother didn't seem to care.

"How about some ice cream?" she asked. That seemed to calm him down. They walked off together to find a stand.

This left me perplexed. I wondered if I should venture into the cave of possible doom or join the mother and son for a cold, creamy bowl of ice cream. My brain was feeling lactose intolerant and epically heroic. I would like to order two scoops of bravery sprinkled with stupidity please. It appeared to be the special of the day.

The cave felt oddly damp and realistic. It was dimly lit by torches sporadically placed on the simulated stone walls. There was a scent in the air that was familiar to me, a mix of fear and aftershave. Someone was definitely in here with me.

"Okay, you can come out now. I know you're here," I said in a stern, convincing voice.

My feet shuffled forward slowly in the sand that dusted the cave floor.

"I mean it. Show yourself." The tone of my voice was rigid. I demanded an answer.

My hand was reaching for my phone when someone reached out of the darkness. I tried to scream, but their hand was already over my mouth. The fight to save myself was purposeless and ineffective. He was just too big. I was overpowered.

“I am going to take my hand off your mouth. Do not scream,” he instructed.

I could feel his hot breath on the back of my neck.

“If you understand me, nod your head,” he whispered in my ear.

There was no reason to play the hero at the moment. I nodded my head like a good girl. He let me go.

“Damn it, Agent Smith. You scared the crap out of me. What are you doing in here lurking around in the dark?"

"I was waiting for you, Payton. We need to talk. Our mission has been compromised.”

“Yeah, I noticed that.” I agreed with his comment. “Brad is missing now, and someone pushed Feed Bag into the shark tank.”

“That is unfortunate.”

“Someone has interjected themselves into our game. What do you want me to do?” I asked, hoping he already had a new plan.

“Continue as planned. The clues should be simple enough to solve. They should expose our person of interest soon.”

“Okay, I’ll try. I can tell that some of these clues aren’t ours. This game could get deadly.”

“My advice to you is to be careful. Do not put yourself in harm’s way. And do not let on to anyone that you are involved.”

“That is not going to be easy. I would feel better if someone else, like one of my friends, knew what was going on.”

“Absolutely not. Trust no one. We have no idea who all is involved at this point.”

“Okay, I will keep the secret.” I changed the subject. “Where is Crystal? Is she with you?”

“No, Miss Pierce isn’t with me. A double surveillance detail was unnecessary. We split up to cover all options.”

“Is there anything else I need to know before someone from my group comes looking for me?”

“No. Just go with it. I will be watching.”

"Maybe we should have a signal," I suggested. "If I start rubbing my nose, come in guns blazing."

He chuckled.

I was serious. Dead serious. "Did anyone see you come in here?"

"No, I've been waiting for you for over an hour," he explained.

"Good. I don't want anyone asking questions."

When the daylight outside the cave hit me, I was temporarily blinded. As my eyes adjusted, I spotted most of the gang taking selfies and sitting on the large boot. They were laughing and making faces. Ugh! They should be digging around for the buried treasure. We were running out of time.

I walked over to the group. They stopped having fun immediately. Oh, great. I have officially become the fun-sucking patriarch of the bunch. "Guys, I'm sorry, but we need to get back to work," I suggested, trying not to be such a buzz kill. "Max, did you ever get ahold of The Singe?"

"Arg! You heard the lady, Matey. Get your bums off the booty," said Max in a pretty good pirate impersonation. "Sorry, Payton, The Singe never answered my call. He must be b—"

"That's it," said Lily, interrupting us. "The large boot or booty, like in the riddle about the pirate's dream."

"That's stupid," scoffed Chameleon.

"Do you have a better idea, smart guy?" she asked.

Chameleon threw a tiny fit and turned his back on Lily to ignore her.

It was time for me to step in and take charge. "Okay, everyone grab your shovel and start digging by the boot."

Everyone spread out around the large, brown, fiberglass cowboy boot. Dirt and sand flew everywhere as the group dug in like gophers.

"Jackpot!" yelled Wolfman as his shovel made contact with an object in the sand.

Everyone else stopped digging and gathered around him as he uncovered what he had found. Wolfman brushed the sand off the top with his hand. Then he carefully cleared the sand

and debris away from the sides. With his fingers outstretched, he reached underneath the six-inch by twelve-inch box and pulled it out of the hole.

Out of the corner of my eye, I saw a group of security guards running our way. "Guys, it's time to scram," I said in a hurried voice. Everyone ran away from the guards. Unfortunately, it wasn't toward an exit. We could easily be trapped with no way out.

***

You can run but you cannot hide. Death will always find you.

CHAPTER TEN

Getting arrested and thrown in jail was not an option. We desperately needed to continue with the game and find Brad. We were all running through the crowd like a wild herd, which wasn't a good idea. "Stop," I shouted at the group. We briefly ducked into a store front. "We need to split up if we are going to outsmart security. Wolfman, you and Chameleon guard the box and make sure it stays in your possession. Everyone else meet back at our Carlton penthouse suite at 5:30 p.m. We'll have pizza and open the box then." I looked around the group. "Where's Blond Ambition?" I asked, looking at the boys. They shrugged their shoulders. "Find him, please."

"You can count on us, Payton," replied Wolfman. He and Chameleon split off from the rest of the group, heading towards one of the side hallways.

The rest of the group dispersed into the crowd. They were doing their best to blend in and disappear. I was weaving my way through the crowd when someone grabbed my arm.

"Payton, wait up," demanded Julie.

"You can follow me if you want, but I'm not slowing down." I glanced over my shoulder briefly. The guards were still coming. Julie suddenly pulled me behind a vender kiosk.

The guards ignored our whereabouts and ran by. They headed towards a large gathering of people by the Dolphin Lagoon.

"Looks like something is going on up there, Payton. We should go check it out."

"Not interested. I think we should get out of here while the guards are distracted."

We came out of our hiding space just in time to see two paramedics pass by wheeling a gurney covered with a black body bag. The paramedic at the back of the gurney said, "What do you mean the body is standing upright in the water?"

"That's not good," I said. "I've changed my mind." I had a bad feeling. You know the one I'm talking about. It's the feeling that crawls up the back of your neck and whispers oh shit! in your ear. It also makes you look under your bed and in your back seat. Yeah, that one … the one that gives you nightmares. "C'mon," I said, pulling Julie in the direction of danger.

As we got closer, I saw a familiar face in the crowd. It was too late to duck. She had already made eye contact with me. Julie and I continued to walk in her direction. My instincts told me to run the other way.

"Payton, what are you two doing here?" asked my mother in a stern tone. She was already dressed for our golf outing. My mother had hit-up the Pro Shop for a salmon-colored golf skirt and matching sleeveless golf top.

"What are you doing here?" I asked her back, trying to avoid lying to her.

"Stop deflecting, Payton. Have you seen your brother and Lily?

"Yes, they are here somewhere. I'm not sure where they went." That was the honest truth.

My mother looked at our clothes. "Why are you two all dirty and full of sand?" She reached out and touched my dress. "Payton, your dress is damp and ripped. Is that fruit stuck to the front of your dress? What have you two been up to?" She seemed very suspicious. She had that look in her eye that always makes me spill my guts and tell the truth. There was no getting out of it.

"We've been busy seeing the sites around the island. We went to the lighthouses, the beach, parasailing, stopped for pie, fed the shark, and dug for treasure in the Dinosaur Sandbox." I smiled at her hoping to melt off a chunk of the iceberg. Julie nodded in agreement.

"I hope my daughter has been able to cheer you up, my dear. There are other fish in the sea. Forget about Brad. You will be better off."

And there it was, my mother's icy dagger planted in Julie's chest. Julie's face turned grim and deflated.

"I know," said my mother sparked by an idea. "Julie should join us for golf." My mother turned to look at me. "That's a great idea, right, Payton?"

"Sure," I agreed. "She can ride in the cart with me."

"I think it would be fun to mix things up today," suggested my mother. "Lily can ride with you, Payton. Julie can ride with Luke."

Good grief. Was my mother really playing matchmaker on Julie's epic fail of a wedding day? The answer is most likely yes. She generally gets her way.

"You two will have to stop off at the Pro Shop first before our round and find golf appropriate attire. You two look hideous."

"Thanks, Mom," I said sarcastically. Another dagger for Julie as she stood before us in her wedding dress and me in the dress Julie had picked out. "I get that we are dirty ... but seriously, Mom." Julie had a shocked look on her face. She hadn't seen Janna in action since her pocketbook had expanded. My mother was a bit of a snob these days and I resented her for it.

My father walked out of the busy crowd of lurkers and joined us. He too was ready for golf in his collared blue and black shirt and black golf shorts. I was anxious to figure out a way to ditch my mother and go see what all the commotion was about. I still had that uneasy feeling.

"Such a shame," my father said, shaking his head.

"What happened?" I blurted out, demanding an answer.

"It looks like some young man drowned in the lazy river that was under construction. The grand opening was supposed to be tomorrow. They were about to pull him out when I walked away."

"Did you see who it was?" asked Julie with extreme urgency.

Julie was thinking the same thing I was. "Dad, what was he wearing?" I asked with the same urgency as Julie.

"What has gotten into you girls?" my father asked with a befuddled look on his face.

We weren't getting the answers we so desperately needed. Julie bolted first and I followed her. She was headed towards the paramedics.

"Payton, we have a tee time," shouted my mother.

We ignored her comment. Julie pushed her way through the crowd. I followed in her wake. We quickly made our way up to the spot where they were loading the body onto the gurney. Luke and Lily were already there. Lily looked back at me with a petrified stare.

Julie pushed her way to the front of the crowd. We got up in front just in time to see them close and zip the bag. I saw enough of the hair and facial features to recognize who it was. Julie stood there motionless. She was trying to process what she had seen. Julie was in a state of suspended relief. The victim ended up being the rude beach bum from the hotel's Tiki bar and the same person Lily and I saw lying on the table unconscious at the Chaos party. It was also the same guy I saw Curls and Ponytail move from the lounge chair at my hotel. They are all dead now, no more loose ends. This was another public message to follow the rules of the game.

Lily and Luke walked over to us. "I heard one of the paramedics say that he was completely drained of blood."

"Accidental drowning my ass," added Luke.

I watched the paramedics wheel his body past us. "Is this the part where we don't joke about vampires ever?" I asked Lily.

Lily looked at me with a serious expression. "You are catching on, Payton."

"Don't you want to know what happened to all his blood?" asked Luke.

"Ish. No. I don't think I do," I answered back.

"Who is he?" asked Julie. The initial shock had subsided.

"As far as I know, he was just a local beach bum. He was at the wrong place at the right time. We need to get going," I said to the group.

My mom and dad found us in the crowd. "Luke, Lily, Payton, and Julie, the limo is waiting," begged my father. My mother pointed towards the front door. We obeyed and went willingly.

***

This was all for you, Payton. The bum got what he deserved.

***

The limo was parked next to the curb, not far from the front door. We all climbed in and got comfortable in the back. I reached for a bottle of dark colored liquor. My mother shot me the "No" look like I was two again. I obeyed. I sat back in my seat knowing that there would be a beer cart on the golf course with my name on it. On our way through the parking lot, we passed by what was left of a burning school bus. Smoke billowed out of the windows. The inside was trashed. The seats were black and charred down to the metal in some places. So much for changing the bus number, it was now retired for good. Part of me wondered if the lack of Mountain Dew to put out the fire was the main reason the bus didn't survive the wrath of The Singe. This would no doubt be an interesting tale. Not far from the scene, we passed by a soot-covered Singe, along with Max, Feed Bag, Thirteen, and Blond Ambition, which was a relief. How were the boys going to get home? And what were they going to tell Chameleon's dad?

***

It is time for me to play through again. The game of golf is to die four. Get it? I just kill me, lol. After this round, someone will be removed from the leader board.

CHAPTER ELEVEN

It felt great to change out of my sea-soaked, sand-covered, ugly-as-sin bridesmaid's dress. In the Pro Shop, I found a cute lilac golf skirt with a matching light and dark purple paisley print tank top.

Julie reluctantly traded her slightly used bridal gown for a pair of dark blue shorts and a nice looking turquoise and blue polo shirt. She rented a set of golf clubs and a pair of golf shoes.

Lily was oddly okay with my mom's golf cart musical chairs suggestion. Now that's a strong, trusting relationship. My mom, dad, Luke and Julie would play together in a foursome. Lily and I would follow behind them at a safe distance.

Lily and I quietly watched everyone tee off. Julie did very well for not playing much. She managed to hit the ball long and straight down the fairway. Was she trying to show off for my brother?

As soon as their carts pulled away, Lily started in. "Spill it, Payton. I saw you go into the cave." She held her driver in a semi-confrontational manner.

"What do you mean? I was looking for clues," I said in my best convincing voice.

"Fine," she said in frustration. "Don't tell me." She walked up to the tee box to hit her first drive over a small pond.

It was time to even the score and poke for answers. She was about to hit her ball and was in the middle of her backswing. "I saw you fight with Stephani on the beach. What was that about?" I dug around in my golf bag for a tee and a suitable ball.

"That was nothing," she remarked after her follow through. Lily blasted the ball straight down the fairway.

"Nice shot," I remarked. "It didn't look like nothing." I walked up to the tee box.

"She made a snide remark about Luke. She pissed me off, so I shoved her. End of story."

I bent over to put my tee in the ground. So we each had a story to tell that was simple on the surface and more complicated underneath. I approached the ball. My stance was good. Now for the waggle to get set, perfect backswing, with a graceful follow through. Not. I ended up topping the ball. It hopped into the water. I threw my club towards my golf bag.

"Nice shot, Payton," said Lily, mocking me. She snickered.

"Shut up." I leered at her then started laughing. "I'm glad you are my only witness. This is going to be a tough round. Let's try to find my ball. This pond doesn't look very deep. Maybe I can fish it out with one of my irons.

"Remember where you are, Payton." She sat in the cart while I walked towards the water.

"Why?" I said, poking my club around in the water. "My sand wedge is the perfect scooping tool."

"Forget the darn ball before you get eaten by an alligator."

"Oh crap." I jumped back from the water's edge. "I forgot about those." I ran over to the golf cart and got in. We motored away from the water. "Stop. Here is a good place for me to take a drop." I took out another ball and dropped it on the ground. My swing was solid this time, but I shanked it into the trees.

Lily snickered again and didn't do a good job of hiding it either.

"Pull up over there by that bush. My ball should be near the edge of the tree line if it didn't ricochet off of a tree. Hopefully nothing will try to eat me in the woods."

"No guarantees on that." Lily sat safely in the cart while I searched for my ball.

I used my seven iron to move the underbrush out of my way. "Oh, thank god," I said relieved.

"Did you find your ball?"

"No." I pointed out into the fairway. "I see the beer cart coming."

I walked out of the trees. Lily and I did our best to flag down the girl behind the wheel. The girl driving the cart made a sharp turn to change directions. She cut across the fairway and pulled up next to our cart.

"I'll take two beers. Do you want anything, Lily?" I looked at her while she decided.

"Make me two vodka lemonades," she told the female bartender.

She handed us our drinks. I took a long chug of the cold, crisp liquid, burped, and said, "Ah."

While we were digging for cash, I decided to ask her a question. "My ball went into the woods. We're not from Texas. Will anything eat me in there?"

The girl laughed. "Probably not in the daytime."

"Good to know." We each gave her a healthy tip and she left.

"Okay, I guess I'm going back in."

Lily and I looked around the golf course. There was no one behind us at the moment. There was a foursome on the next fairway directly over from ours. "Go ahead and look for your ball. I'll stay here and enjoy my cocktail," said Lily.

"Like hell you will. Grab your drink and help me."

Lily reluctantly followed me into the thick vegetation. We spent about five minutes pushing brush around with our irons.

"This is dumb," said Lily. "We should sneak back to the clubhouse and wait for them."

"Absolutely not. This little white ball will not beat me today. I'm going to be a good sport and drop another ball." The response from Lily was an eye roll.

We carefully walked out of the overgrown brush. I threw down a third ball and crushed it with my hybrid. "See. All I needed was a beer." I threw the empty can in the back of the golf cart. There is literally no littering in the game of golf. We both got back in the cart. Lily drove us up the fairway to our balls.

"Hey, Payton. Did you just see that?" She pointed to the brush on the left side of the fairway.

"Yeah. Was that a person in a black hoodie? Head over there so we can check it out."

Lily pushed down hard on the gas. My head whipped backwards and then forwards. I was going to feel that in the morning if I lived. Seriously, I need to stop saying that. There was no time for complaining. We were both anxious to investigate. Lily and I were like two slightly buzzed bloodhounds, hot on the trail with our noses to the ground. Lily found an extra gear. The cart flew across the fresh cut grass with extreme precision. She was like a race car driver.

"There are more layers to you than I was aware of," I said to Lily about her driving skills.

"We'll have a chat about that sometime. For now, keep an eye on our drinks so they don't spill. Where'd the hooded person go?"

"Roger that." I pointed and she followed. We left the evenly cut grass and entered the weedy rough. Lily shot straight across the woods headed for the next fairway. The small trees shot by us in a blur. We were hot on his tail.

Our cart popped out of the trees about thirty feet between my mother making her chip shot and my brother and Julie who were already on the green.

"Hi, Mom," I shouted as we sped past in hot pursuit.

My family, obviously in shock, watched us chase after the person in the black hoodie. They all picked up their balls and followed behind us. The hooded person cut to the right, trying to lose us in the trees. Lily didn't slow down. She managed to pick a path barely wide enough for the cart to pass through the trees. I might have briefly closed my eyes. In the past, this has never turned out well for me.

I opened my eyes just in time. Lily made a sharp left turn to avoid hitting a tree. Part of my body left the cart. My butt was airborne. Luckily, both hands were hanging onto to something sturdier than my cocktail at the time.

At the moment, the hooded person was running away from just Lily and me. We had lost my family somewhere along the way. All of a sudden, Luke and Julie came out of nowhere. They shot out of the bushes, heading him off with their cart. The hooded person immediately changed directions. He was running straight towards us.

"Look out," I screamed. It echoed across the whole golf course for sure. So much for a quiet game of golf today.

Lily didn't slow down. The hooded person abruptly made a ninety-degree change of direction to avoid us.

"Hang on, Payton," yelled Lily as she attempted to follow him.

"I freaking am," I shouted back. My left hand gripped the dash. My right hand hung onto the roof top handle. My butt was airborne again as we made the sharp turn. Lily gripped the steering wheel with all of her might to keep herself inside the cart. We both let out a simultaneous scream. "Shiiiiit!"

"Get him," shouted Julie from behind us. She and my brother were doing their best to keep up with Lily's fast and furious driving. My parents' cart was nowhere in sight which was a blessing. They didn't need to witness any of this.

We passed through tall weeds that were over our heads before hitting a clearing next to a purely aesthetic small pond with a dock. Lily came to a screeching halt. She cranked the wheel hard to the left. The back end of the cart swung around hard to the right. You can probably guess what was about to happen. I wasn't prepared. I rolled out onto the grass.

The hooded person ran down the dock. It was their only escape. I jumped up and followed. I heard Julie and Luke pull up as I ran down the dock. The hooded person jumped into the water trying to get away from me. I was about to jump into the water when I heard Lily yell.

"Payton, don't do it. Remember the alligators."

I managed to stop myself in time thanks to my golf cleats. The hooded person resurfaced. Their hood had slipped down exposing their identity.

"Alligators?" he asked, clearly in panic mode.

It was the bartender from the beach. "Jeremy?" I was shocked. "What the hell?"

We made eye contact with each other briefly. He was about to say something when we both noticed movement under the surface of the water. His eyelids expanded with fear.

"Swim to me," I demanded.

Instead of trying to get away, he changed directions in the water. His quick swimming strokes headed towards me on the dock. I was focused on Jeremy. I didn't turn around when I heard Luke, Lily and Julie's footsteps echo on the weathered wood behind me.

Without hesitation, I knelt on the dock and extended my arms. "Grab onto me. We'll pull you out."

He reached up and grabbed my hands in his. Our eyes met again. All I saw was pure terror in his eyes.

"Why?" I asked, gripping his hands tightly in mine. I was trying my best to pull him out.

"I can't say. They will kill me," was all he said before the alligator lunged and attacked.

I felt the warmth of his blood spray across my face before the scaly green beast pulled him under the surface.

"Payton … Payton … you need to let go, sweetie," said my mother.

I looked up at her and then down at my hands in a dream-like fog. My eyes followed my hands to another set of hands that were attached to tattooed arms … that were attached to nothing … nothing but bloody stubs. When I looked down at my lap, I saw Jeremy's severed head next to my knees on the dock. There was blood everywhere. I immediately let go. Jeremy's arms fell into the water. The next thing I knew, I was standing by my golf cart. Talk about a brain wipe for my own sanity and survival.

"Who wants pizza?" asked my brother Luke, mocking my grotesque appearance.

***

Walk it off, Payton. I am not finished with you yet. There are riddles left to solve. As for Jeremy, he is collateral damage. I could no longer trust him. He had to go. I said heads were going to roll. Mother Nature did me a favor and took care of it. Funny how that works. The survival of the fittest can be a real bitch sometimes. Hint: Four will be tonight's magic number.

CHAPTER TWELVE

If you thought I was a mess before, you should see me now. Jeremy's dried blood spray was still on my face, in my hair, mixed in with the paisleys on my shirt, and spattered across my light purple golf skirt. Dried streaks of blood ran down my legs from kneeling in the pool of his red head juice. Rumor has it, Jeremy's head rolled across on my lap. I'm okay that I don't remember any of it. A shower with a bottle of bleach and some kind of alcohol was in my future.

Normally, my parents would have called the police. To avoid any scandal on the island, we left the country club quick and quiet. After all, it was just an accident. Jeremy's unfortunate demise will be attributed to an accidental alligator attack. It will be reported by one of the unlucky greenskeepers that stumbles upon what is left of him on the dock.

The ride in the limo was like a slow-motion silent movie. I couldn't tell if my mother was mad because our family outing was ruined, or she was upset with genuine concern for my state of mental health.

I reached for the bottle of brown liquor. My mother handed me a glass with ice and got one for herself. After she filled our glasses, the questions started.

"Why were you chasing that boy?"

Lily jumped to my defense. "He was lurking around trying to take stuff out of our cart."

She was lying for us. Why? I'm not complaining, mind you. "We just wanted to talk to him," I added. That part was the truth. I took a long drink from my glass. Some of the stress melted away.

"It looked more like you two were trying to run him over," joked my brother.

My mother shot him one of her disapproving glares. She picked up her phone and tapped on one of her contacts. Next, she handed the phone to me.

I gave her a weird look. "Hello," I said, not knowing who to expect on the other end of the line.

"Hello, Payton," said Dr. Parks. "It's nice to hear from you again. Is everything okay? This is your mother's line."

"She thought I should talk to you." I sighed and gave my mother an exhausted look.

"What happened, Payton? It must have been devastating for her to call me," she inquired.

"I don't want to make a big deal out of this, okay?" I looked over at my brother and Lily who were having their own whispered conversation. Julie was in her own little world staring out the car window. I finished my drink before I started my story.

"You know, Payton, like I have recommended before, self-medication is not the answer," said Dr. Parks.

She must have heard my ice cubes bounce around in the bottom of my empty glass. "Sorry, Dr. Parks, but it's not every day that someone gets eaten right in front of me. I'm still wearing his bodily fluids like warpaint."

"Don't forget about Brent," said Lily, interrupting me.

"Let me correct myself, this is the second person that's been eaten in front of me today. I think a drink is called for." I held out my glass for more of the brown liquid. My mother shook her head no.

"Oh my. I'm sorry to hear that. Did you know these people?" asked my doctor.

"The first one, yes. Brent's dead body was eaten by a shark. The second guy, no. An alligator bit off his head and it pretty much fell in my lap, apparently. I don't remember it."

"Oh dear. How does that make you feel?"

"I'm sad that they are both dead. I'm grossed out that I have blood all over me. And I'm angry as hell that this is now my life."

"Those are all healthy emotions, Payton. As far as I'm concerned, you seem to be well adjusted to the new tragic events in your life."

The limo pulled up to the curb of the Carlton Hotel.

"Good to know. Dr. Parks, can we be done now? I'm all talked out. Here, talk to my mom. I'm heading upstairs to take a shower."

"I'll call you tomorrow to see how you are doing."

"Sure."

My mother graciously took her phone back. The rest of us stepped out of the limo and headed inside the building. Inside the lobby, next to the bank of elevator doors, sat the entire group of rowdy gamers. They took one look at me and their immediate reaction was dead silence.

"How was golf?" asked Chameleon with a raised eyebrow.

"Brutal," I answered back.

"We should see the other guy," he added.

"Something like that," I said. "Alligator attack."

They all nodded like they understood.

"You guys coming upstairs?" asked Luke. "I'm ordering pizza."

The group jumped to their feet and got in line for the next elevator. Amber, Lisa, and Teagan entered stage left from the bathroom and joined us.

The girls stared at me.

I held up my hand for them not to comment. "Seriously, I'm fine." I looked at Chameleon and Wolfman. "Do you guys still have the box?"

Chameleon patted his backpack. "Yep. Just waiting for you so we can open it."

"By the way," said Julie, "what happen to the bus exactly?"

Blond Ambition laughed. "The Singe plus fireworks equals spontaneous combustion."

They all laughed.

"Hey, it was an accident," stated The Singe, trying to defend himself.

"It's always an accident," added Feed Bag. "Can we go have pizza now? I'm hungry."

"You're always hungry," said The Singe.

I'm glad to see everyone is still getting along. The rest of the night was going to be a challenge.

***

Something unexpected happened to me in the shower. As I was washing the death cooties out of my hair for the fourth time, my anger and disgust turned to sadness. A wave of grief from the day hit me like a Mack truck. Was it something Dr. Parks had said to me, or was it all my emotions finally bubbling up to the surface?

My back slid down the slippery tile wall of the massive free-standing shower stall. I curled up in a tight ball with my knees up to my chest. The hot water continued to flow down my back as the tears rolled down my cheeks. I hoped the sound of the water coming out of the three spray heads was enough to drown out my heaving sobs.

Okay, Payton, that's enough of this shit, said the little voice in my head. I generally listen and do what I'm told. The grief lifted enough for me to make it back to my feet. I can do this. I have to do this. I heard a noise outside the shower stall. I froze in place. Someone was in here with me.

"Hello, is anyone there?" I heard the bathroom door shut. I peeked out the glass shower door. I was hoping to find an empty toilet seat. To my amazement, it wasn't empty. There was an ice-cold beer sitting on the toilet lid. Sweet. Someone knows me too well, which I decided wasn't a bad thing at the moment. I grabbed it and hopped back in the shower. The hot water poured over my head as the ice-cold brew flowed down my throat. Badass Payton was back. She just needed the right fuel. I finished my beer and my biohazard sterilization of my body. I stepped out of the shower ready and revved up for round two.

***

The group had dived headfirst into the pizzas before I arrived in the kitchen. There was almost an entire sausage-mushroom-green olive left, which is my favorite. I took this as a good sign that things were going to go okay tonight. Shut up. Stop laughing. Let me have this moment before everything goes to hell.

I grabbed two pieces and filled a glass with root beer to wash them down. I looked around the kitchen. "Luke, where's Mom and Dad?"

He shoved the last bite of his pizza in his mouth. "They're getting ready to go back to the country club. Dad said something about a dinner/ball thing."

Well that explains their hasty retreat earlier. They didn't want to be linked to anything scandalous if they were planning on returning tonight. My mother's morals were on hiatus.

"That's good," I answered back. "They'll be out of our hair for the rest of the evening, so we can finish the game."

"What game?" asked my father from the doorway of the kitchen.

"Just a friendly game of Pictionary, Sir," voiced Max just in time to save my butt.

"Are you guys hanging out here, then?" asked my father.

"Not sure," added Luke with a smile. He was trying to leave our options wide open.

My mother poked her head in the kitchen. "Just make sure you clean up your mess."

That was when I saw them. My mother was wearing the wing-shaped diamond earrings Rose had given me. I needed to do something quick.

"Mom, you're wearing my earrings." My voice skipped an octave.

"Don't worry, Payton. I won't lose them. Let's go, Stan. We are already late."

Before I could say or do anything, my mother, dressed in a full-length black evening gown, and my father, who was all decked out in a black tuxedo, were out the door. It felt like a rock was in the pit of my stomach. This wasn't good. I could feel this earring thing with my mother already biting me in the ass.

As soon as the door closed, Chameleon pulled the box from his backpack. He placed it on the counter.

"Did you guys look inside the box?" Julie asked on her way over to the counter.

"No," said Wolfman. "Like we said before, we were waiting for us all to be together."

We were all crowded around the box as Chameleon lifted the lid.

There was a knock on the door. We all scanned the circle. Everyone was here. Chameleon closed the lid.

"I'll get it," I said, heading towards the door. Before opening the door, I looked through the peephole. What was she doing here? This was going to be trouble.

I opened the door a crack. Without saying hello or being invited in, Crystal burst through the door looking all disheveled. Her royal blue pantsuit was all wrinkled and missing a button on the jacket. Her blond hair was falling out of a bun. Crystal also had a faint smug of dirt on her cheek.

"Welcome to the party. Where's Smith?" I asked her out of concern.

"That's why I'm here. He's not answering me." She seemed genuinely upset.

"That's not good, not good at all." I turned around to see the group standing by the door to the kitchen. No one knew that I was secretly working with Crystal and Smith and I wanted to keep it that way. I was trying to keep that cat in the proverbial bag, but that darn cat was now on my doorstep with its ratted fur hanging out for all to see. It wouldn't take a genius to figure this out.

"I heard you were dead," Chameleon said to Crystal.

"You can't believe everything you hear," she said back. "What is going on here, Payton?"

"Guys, we might as well tell her. Maybe she can help us," offered Julie.

Crystal looked back at the group waiting for an answer.

Chameleon stepped forward. "We are about to open a potentially lethal puzzle box. You in, or out?" he asked. Chameleon seemed to be the one running the show now.

She looked around the room. "Of course, I'm in," assured Crystal.

The group flowed back into the kitchen. "There is no turning back for anyone, understand?" Chameleon had a serious look on his face. We all nodded in agreement. Chameleon flipped the lid of the box open again. He reached in and pulled out a note.

The note read: "You have until 10:00 p.m. to solve the four puzzles and save your friend. I dare you to find us."

Lily smiled when she heard Chameleon say the number four, which is her favorite number.

"That's it?" asked Julie with a raised voice. She took the card from him and read it to herself.

"Let's see the puzzles," said Luke. He pulled them out of the box. He carefully laid each clue out on the kitchen counter.

Clue one: a small plastic bag filled with Scrabble tiles. Clue two: a Rider Waite tarot card. Clue three: a bottle rocket. Clue four: a sticker of a blue ghost.

"This is impossible," said Julie, resting her head on the counter. "Brad is as good as dead."

"No, he's not," I insisted. "We'll split into groups and solve the puzzles to save time." I wrote everyone's name down on small pieces of paper, put them in a bowl to keep it fair, and picked them out one by one.

"The group for clue one is Crystal, Lily, Teagan, and Max." Teagan and Max looked at each other and smiled. I saw trouble. Lily and Crystal looked at each other and grimaced. I saw trouble again. I sighed. It is what it is.

"The group for clue two is Feed Bag, Thirteen, Luke, and Amber." I really didn't perceive there to be an issue with this group other than frequent food stops.

"The group for clue three is The Singe, Shoes, me, and Lisa." I felt okay with keeping an eye on The Singe. I must be losing my mind. I sighed again silently.

"The group for clue four is Wolfman, Julie, Blond Ambition, and Chameleon." Great, Chameleon can keep Julie together if she comes unglued. I was okay with this too.

"Everyone needs to stay with their group. This is absolutely imperative if we are going to pull this off," I said as a final note.

"Should each group have a leader to keep the order?" asked Lily.

"I was hoping that it wouldn't be necessary, but how about Teagan, Amber, myself, and Julie. Is everyone okay with that?" I asked.

Everyone seemed to agree except maybe Lily and Crystal.

"It's almost 6:00 p.m., that gives us four hours to solve four puzzles. Use your time wisely. Remember, this isn't about us. It's about saving Brad. Good luck, guys."

Lily walked past me. "Good luck with The Singe. Maybe you should keep a fire extinguisher handy." She joked.

"Good luck with Crystal. Try not to kill her." I whispered back.

***

Bravo for making it this far, Payton. Spoiler alert: No one gets a trophy. The scavenger hunt will continue. People will die. You know it is true. They were dead the day they met you. It was only a matter of time.

My games have consequences. I am sure you know that by now. If you don't follow the rules, I will not be merciful. I will torture, maim, pillage, and plunder until I get what I want.

What do I want? I want to finish the game. I want you to know who I am. The thing I want the most is to see the anguish when you realize who I am and the depth of my depravity. The second you see it, you cannot unknow it. Secrets will be revealed. I will watch you squirm when the truth is too much to handle. Call me sick and twisted. Call me morally corrupt. Then look in the mirror and tell me what you see. That is what I thought.

Everyone has a dark side. Everyone will fight to survive. That is what I am counting on. This game will be twisted, so trust no one, except me. I am the only predictable one in the bunch. I am afraid that does not say much about most of your friends. It is human nature to destroy yourself. Good luck with that.

When will I show you my true colors and my identity? All in due time. You will get what you are waiting for. I promise. If you follow my clues and my puzzles it will lead you to the truth. Play like your lives depend on it … because they do. That is all. Now back to the game

CHAPTER THIRTEEN

GROUP ONE: SCRABBLE TILES

Crystal, Lily, Teagan, and Max stopped at a small, round table in the lobby of the hotel. Max dumped the Scrabble tiles out of the clear, plastic bag. They bounced across the table. He flipped each of the square, wooden letters upright and placed them in a row. The letters were: U, R, M, L, A, L, N, E, B, I.

"We need to start brainstorming," said Max as he took a seat at the table to study the letters.

The other three sat down. All four were quiet, deep in thought. All of a sudden, Max started firing off random words.

"Bra, bean, rum, lamb, barn, brain," he blurted.

"Bar, rail," said Teagan. "Dang, I must be thirsty. Mall, mine, men, man." She gave Max a sexy grin. "I must be real thirsty."

"Stop!" demanded Crystal.

"There's no 's' in the puzzle," said Teagan.

"No," said Crystal. "I meant stop it, as in knock it off!"

Teagan was clearly upset by Crystal's scolding. Lily chuckled to herself because she found it all to be hilarious.

"Maybe the letters don't mean anything," suggested Lily. "Maybe we need to go to the actual tile store or something."

"That's retarded," jabbed Teagan.

"Not as retarded as you," Lily jabbed back in a raised voice.

The girls both stood up ready to duke it out.

"Whoa, whoa, whoa. Calm down," said Max. He was ready to get in-between the girls if need be.

One of the female front desk managers named Joan approached their table. She was dressed in a dark blue pantsuit and white blouse. A red scarf was tied around her neck. Joan looked more like a flight attendant instead of a desk clerk.

"I'm sorry, but I am going to have to ask you to leave. You are disturbing the other guests."

"See what you did, dumbass," said Lily.

"Now, please," said Joan in a nice, but firm manner.

They all got up and walked out the front doors before they were thrown out. At the curb, they paused.

"Where to?" asked Crystal. She looked up and down the street for options.

"I could use that drink now," said Teagan, pointing at the Blue Marlin bar across the street.

"I'm in," said Max in agreement.

"I'd like to see your ID," said Lily. "You are not old enough."

Max reached in the back pocket of his beige cargo shorts, flipped open his wallet, and proudly displayed his Illinois driver's license for them all to see.

"What planet is that from?" scoffed Lily, obviously pointing out his fake identification.

"It's from earth," stated Max in a sassy tone. He got in Lily's face.

"Well, it might as well be from Uranu—" said Lily, not backing down.

"Guys! Stop!" yelled Crystal. "We need to get along and solve this. Remember what Payton said? All in favor of going across the street to the bar?"

"Fine," said Max with a sneer.

"Fine," said Lily, giving in with a gothic, extra black eyeliner eyeroll.

"Yay!" said Teagan, clapping because she was getting her way. She bounced up and down in her blue jean miniskirt and low-cut tank top.

Max's sneer turned into a smile.

At the door, Crystal stopped. "Try to blend in. We look like something out of the *Breakfast Club.*"

Lily looked everyone over. "The rich girl, the misfit, the jock, and the slut."

"There wasn't a slut in the *Breakfast Club,*" said Teagan.

"You don't say," laughed Lily. "After you, Molly," Lily said to Crystal, signaling her to open the door and go in.

The retro atmosphere inside the bar was relaxing. A mix of sixties colors and styles blended with a beach motif. Colorful Tiki bar garden patio lights helped to set the carefree mood. Fake palm trees were placed between the Tiki bar tables. Realistic-looking stuffed fish, beach signs and anchors, along with round flotation devices decorated the walls. It had a solid nighttime TV *Brady Bunch* in Hawaii meets *Gilligan's Island* vibe.

The group walked up to the bar to place their drink orders.

"We should order something exotic," suggested Teagan. "Like a Mai Tai or a Bahama Mama."

The all studied the drink menu up on the wall. The fifty-something-year-old bartender came over to take their order.

"Hi, I'm Todd. What can I get for you?" he asked.

"I'll take a Dark 'N' Stormy," said Lily. Max snickered at her request.

"I like dark rum, okay?" Lily said, defending her choice.

"A Blue Lagoon for me," said Teagan happily. She was looking forward to her blue concoction containing blue colored rum and tequila.

"I'll have the same," said Crystal. "Can you add a little extra pineapple juice to mine?"

"Sure thing," said Todd. He turned his attention to Max.

"What IPA's do you have on tap?" asked Max, trying to act like an avid drinker.

"I need to see your identification," he said in an authoritative voice.

Max reached for his wallet and showed his driver's license to Todd.

Todd gave it back. "I have a special one that just came in last week. It's called Rubber Goose."

"I'll take a frosty mug of that," said Max. He placed money on the bar for our drinks.

Todd poured Max his beer from the tap and walked back down to the group. Lily noticed Todd's gold watch.

"Wait a second," demanded Lily. "I know you. You're that campus Rent-a-Cop from Clearwater Falls, Wisconsin. You helped Payton and I find her missing boyfriend. What are you doing here?"

Todd looked surprised at first. "Oh yeah, I remember you and your friend. She was the tenacious 'do it now' girl. I retired, moved down here, and bought this bar shortly after that."

"Good for you," said Teagan, interjecting herself into the conversation.

"Excuse me, duty calls," said Todd before he walked down the bar to take more drink orders.

Max looked at Lily. "See, I told you. This thing is legit," said Max about his fake ID.

"Let's move to a table, so we can talk in private," said Crystal. "That table over in the corner looks good."

At the table, Max dumped the tiles on the wooden surface. They stared at the letters: B, E, N, M, L, A, U, R, L, I.

"There are 10 letters. This has to be two or three words, tops," stated Crystal using her logic.

"Maybe if we move the tiles around, it will spark something," said Teagan, taking a long drink from the straw in her Blue Lagoon.

"That's a great idea," said Max just before he belched from his beer.

"Gross," said Lily reacting to the smell of his beer burp. She waved her hand around to disperse the foul odor of the rotten beer stench. "That might actually work," she reluctantly agreed.

Max started moving the letters around.

ULMAL BRNEI

"The consonants can't be bunched together. Let me try," insisted Lily.

RAN LUB MILE

"I need another drink. I'll be right back," said Teagan.

"Let me try something," said Crystal as she swapped the words and letters around.

LAB RUN MILE

"It's words, but what does that mean?" asked Max.

"Is there another running event in town?" asked Crystal.

Max started Googling races on his phone.

Teagan walked back to the table holding a large fishbowl containing a sky-blue liquid. She set it on the table. "I ordered the drink special of the day."

"What's it called, a Brain Flush?" joked Lily.

"No, it's a Blue Marlin," she said, taking a huge sip. "It's yummy. Todd suggested it."

Crystal and Lily looked over Max's shoulder while he typed into his phone. Teagan drank her drink and played with the letters.

"Shit, I can't find a single race in the area anywhere," said Max.

Teagan stared down at the letters as she mixed them around. BLU…

"What if it's an animal shelter? Try that," said Crystal. Max started typing and searching sites on his phone.

"Guys, I think I solved it," said Teagan in an excited tone.

They looked over at the table. Teagan's drink was half gone already.

"How ironic, huh?" said Teagan showing off the letters proudly. "Just like the drink and the bar!"

BLUE MARLIN

"How did we miss that?" said Crystal.

"Because you can't see what you aren't looking for," said Max.

"We still don't know what that means," said Lily, taking a seat back at the table.

"Maybe we should ask the big blue fishy," slurred Teagan as she staggered over to it to have a conversation. They watched her pull a chair over and climb up on it so she could get eye-level with the fish.

"Is that—?" asked Crystal.

"Yeah, it is," said Max. "It's a blue marlin."

"Hey, look, there's something in the fish's mouth," said Teagan.

"Unbelievable," Lily said, mocking Teagan's lucky guess.

"It's a piece of paper," said Teagan, as she drunkenly waved it around.

Lily, Crystal, and Max ran over to Teagan to help her down and to retrieve the note. Teagan gave Max a hug. Crystal held out her hand to see the note.

"I don't think so," she told Crystal. "Payton put me in charge." She opened the note. "And just for the record, I don't trust either of you bitches." She slurred her words and pointed at the two girls with her index finger.

"Oh, but you trust him?" asked Lily. "The guy who just got added to the group yesterday?"

"The feeling is mutual," said Crystal. "Now, shut up and read the note."

Teagan taunted her in a drunken, clumsy manner before she started: "Row, row, row your boat, gently down the stream. They're all tied up, you better hurry. Brad's about to scream."

"Oh god, I think I'm gonna be sick," said Teagan. Her face had a greenish tinge.

"It's not that bad," said Max.

Teagan put her hand over her mouth and headed for the bathroom.

"Who's they?" asked Crystal. She looked over at Lily.

Lily shrugged. "I better call Payton." Lily grabbed her phone from her pocket.

Max took out his phone first and looked at the screen. "I think we should just meet Payton," he said holding up his phone. "I don't wanna miss a second of this."

CHAPTER FOURTEEN

GROUP TWO: THE RIDER WAITE TAROT CARD

"But I don't understand why we have to be in a rib joint. We just had pizza," said Amber, trying to figure out boy logic.

Thirteen and Luke pointed at Feed Bag. "Ask the bottomless pit," said Luke with a chuckle.

"Hey, it's not my fault we ran out of pizza," said Feed Bag in his defense.

"Let's grab a table so we can work on our clue while he eats," said Amber, clearly taking her leadership role seriously.

The four sat in a booth in the back of the Country Style Steak and Rib House. Amber and Luke sat on one side, Feed Bag and Thirteen on the other.

Sabrina, the waitress from the Pie Café, walked over to their table. The second she recognized them, she turned around and headed back towards the kitchen.

"Wait," said Luke. He stood up. "Come back. I'm a big tipper," he added, remembering how his sister won her over earlier in the day.

She stopped and turned back around. "How much are we talking about?" She was definitely interested.

"Bring me a pitcher of beer, four glasses—"

“Three glasses.” Amber interrupted, knowing full well that Feed Bag was underage.

“Three glasses,” said Luke correcting himself, “a rack of ribs with all the fixings, and a platter of chicken wings. If you do that, there is an easy hundred in it for you,”

“Deal,” she said immediately. She disappeared into the kitchen to place their order.

Amber opened her purse and placed the rectangular tarot card on the table. The card’s central focus seemed to be a knight in full black armor with a skeleton face. The knighted skeleton was riding a white horse. In his left hand, the skeleton was holding a black banner flag. On the flag was a white Tudor Rose with five ears of corn spread out evenly around its pedals. In the left upper corner of the flag was the number thirteen written out in Roman numerals.

In the foreground of the card, by the front hooves of the white horse, there was a dead king lying on his back on the ground. His golden crown laid in the mud under the horse’s feet. On the right foreground of the card, in front of the horse, there was a kneeling maiden in a white gown, a kneeling small boy dressed in blue, and a standing priest praying in a gold-colored robe. In the background, there was a ship on the river, a blue waterfall, and a golden rising or setting sun between two white towers. The word beneath the whole cryptic scene was DEATH.

“I just lost my appetite,” said Amber.

“More food for me,” laughed Feed Bag.

“Lily should be here to help us with this,” said Luke. “She loves all this dark stuff.”

“There is a fortune teller down the block next to the corn dog stand,” suggested Feed Bag. “Maybe she can help us.”

Amber sat up straight in her seat. “Are you positive?” she asked.

“Oh, he’s sure,” said Thirteen. “If it has anything to do with food, he knows about it.”

Sabrina walked up to the table carrying a pitcher of beer and three glasses.

"Sorry, we have to cancel our order," said Luke. He threw down two hundreds on the table. This should cover it."

"What about my ribs?" asked a disappointed Feed Bag.

"I'll buy you a bouquet of corn dogs," said Luke, standing up from the booth. "Let's go."

The four left the rib joint, heading down the block adjacent to the water. They stopped at Corny's Dog Stand and went inside the self-serve restaurant.

"I am a man of my word," said Luke. "Order what you want."

Feed Bag and Thirteen approached the counter to order. "I'll take a dozen corn dog supremes to go," said Feed bag.

"I'll take the Dynamic Corn Duo to go, please," said Thirteen.

Amber and Luke watched Feed Bag slop sauces and fixings on his pile of dogs. Thirteen meticulously put each sauce in its rightful place on each dog, followed by a precise amount of onion, pickle, cheese, and cashews.

Amber cringed at the sight of their creations.

Thirteen looked at the group. "Cashews add texture. I'm such a foodie."

Amber made a horrified look that wrinkled up her nose.

"Don't knock it until you've tried it." Thirteen held out one of his corn dogs for Amber to try."

She put up her hand and said, "No thank you."

***

The group stood outside Sadie The Sorceress' shop. The sign read: "Hours 10 a.m.-7 p.m."

"Hurry up and eat, guys," said Luke. "Her light is still on. Maybe she is still there."

"Should I knock?" asked Amber as she approached the door.

"Is it locked?" asked Luke.

She turned the antique, metal doorknob. "No, it's not," she replied.

"Let's go in," said Luke. He looked at Thirteen and Feed Bag. "You boys coming in?" He held the door open for them. They quickly scarfed the rest of their last corn dogs and followed Amber inside.

The front parlor looked like something out of an old horror movie. Dark red velvet wallpaper covered the walls. A red and brown tapestry patterned area rug covered the wooden plank floor. Two brown velveteen-covered chairs were separated by a round, antique end table that displayed a glass hurricane lamp from the 1940s. Old portraits in heavy, dark frames covered the walls.

Feed Bag looked around the room. "I've changed my mind. I'll wait outside."

"Don't be such a chicken," said Luke.

Amber approached the burgundy velvet curtain in the doorway to the next room. "Hello," she called out.

A short, dark-haired gypsy-looking woman emerged from between the folds of cloth. "We're closed," she said in a deep, gravelly voice.

Feedbag, Thirteen, and Amber were immediately startled by her presence in the room. Luke pulled out a fifty and showed it to her.

"It appears we are still open. How can I be of service?" she asked.

Amber held up the card. "What can you tell us about this?"

"Follow me into the reading room," she said. She held the curtain back for them to enter.

When Luke passed through the curtain, she took the fifty, her fingers brushed against his hand. "Wait, I'm getting something." She paused for effect. "You are in grave danger."

Luke laughed as he walked through the curtain and entered the reading room.

"You laugh at my talent?" she asked.

"Sadie, I see you are giving me my money's worth," said Luke. "Awesome parlor trick."

"We are all in danger," said Amber. "That's why we are here."

"My comment was directed at him, not you." Sadie said, pointing at Luke.

Luke blew Sadie off as a quack. "Thanks for the warning. Now, what can you tell us about this card?"

Sadie twirled around in her purple and black flowing skirt. "Sit. Please. I'll explain."

Each of the four took a seat at the table covered with a large, dark green, silk, fringed scarf. In the center of the table was an eight-inch crystal ball on a black circular stand.

Feed Bag reached out and touched the crystal ball out of curiosity.

"And you, you will have high cholesterol," Sadie smiled. "No one touches my orb."

Feed Bag pulled his hand away like a frightened child.

"Show me this card again," instructed Sadie. She waited patiently while Amber searched her purse for it again.

Amber placed it on the table, so it was right side up in front of the empty chair. Sadie took a seat.

"This is The Death Card. It will cost you extra," she said.

"Of course," Luke said, rolling his eyes. He placed another fifty on the table.

"My vision is much clearer now." Sadie looked at Amber. "I see a lot of cats in your future." Luke started laughing.

Amber shot him a look. "Hey, I have a brain. I don't have to dress like a floozie to get through life. I'm not going to die old and alone." She looked down at her sensible longer cotton shorts, and generic button-down cotton short-sleeved shirt. "Besides, I'm self-conscious about my bullet wound scar on my shoulder."

"That's cool. Can we see it?" Thirteen inquired.

Amber wrinkled up her nose. "Nooooo!" She pointed at the card. "What can you tell us about the skeleton riding the horse?" Amber was anxious to change the subject.

After Amber yelled at Thirteen, he was avoiding eye contact by focusing on the scarf and its fringe.

"First of all," Sadie started, "this is a Rider-Waite-Smith Death Card."

"There's a difference?" asked Amber, still very curious.

"Yes, the pictures and symbolism vary. This death card has to do with transformation and new life, not just death," Sadie looked around the circle. "It is about interpretation and timing, death and rebirth, but I will tell you a brief summary if that is what you are looking for."

"It is," said Amber. "Please continue."

"The skeleton skull represents consciousness. The skeleton is all that is left when consciousness dies. Some believe this represents the Grim Reaper."

"I'd believe that," said Luke with a slight chuckle.

"We see what we want to see," said Sadie. "It's all about interpretation."

"Why is he wearing armor?" asked Amber, needing more information.

Sadie continued, "The armor symbolizes invincibility."

"No one can escape death," said Thirteen, deciding to join in on the discussion.

"That is exactly correct," Sadie said to Thirteen. "You are more perceptive than the rest of your friends. You have great insight and clear potential."

"Thirteen counts the meat on his pizza." Even Feed Bag was skeptical.

"And puts it into groups," stated Luke.

"Whatever you are looking for could be about the tiniest detail. Never scoff at another's wisdom," Sadie said clearly. "You wouldn't be here if you weren't seeking knowledge."

Sadie's comment seemed to pacify their rebellion against Thirteen.

"Why is the skeleton knight Grim Reaper dude riding a horse?" asked Luke, trying to get back to the matter at hand.

"The white horse represents purity. Death is the great purifier that cleanses the soul. The white rose on the black flag also represents purity and new life. The corn represents seeds and new life. Others say the flag represents the taking of souls. On some cards, there is a sickle instead of a flag."

"Like the Grim Reaper with a sickle in scary movies," said Feed Bag.

"The horse also represents the horsemen of the apocalypse which is a scary story in itself," said Sadie.

"Why is there a thirteen on the flag? Could this be about me somehow?" inquired Thirteen with a trembling voice. "Am I going to die?"

"Yes," said Sadie, "but not today. The thirteen is the number of the card. In this deck, it is the fourteenth card because the numbers start at zero. The number thirteen symbolizes stability and strength."

"That makes me feel better," Thirteen said with relief in his voice.

"It also has to do with superstition, obviously," added Sadie.

"Oh, that's probably not a good thing," said Luke.

"Probably not," said Sadie, being purposefully vague.

"What can you tell us about the rest of the card?" asked Amber. She wanted more information.

"The boat you see in the river is traveling towards the north. If the sun is rising, then death is moving to the south."

"Does the river have a name?" asked Luke.

"The river Styx is where the dead souls travel to get to the underworld," said Sadie.

"Sorry I asked," commented Luke. "What about the four people?"

"The dead king, the praying priest, the maiden, and the young child all represent that no matter what stage of life or vocation, you cannot cheat death," said Sadie.

"Does it bother the rest of you that there are four people on the card and one of them is dead?" said Luke, looking around the group. "Is this some kind of omen?"

"The card is very open to interpretation," commented Sadie.

"Actually, there are five if you count the Grim Reaper," said Amber, correcting Luke.

"Interpretation," said Luke smugly. "There are five of us in the room right now. Is one of us going to die?"

Feed Bag and Thirteen had freaked out looks on their faces.

"Stop scaring them," said Amber. "Sadie, please continue."

"The pillars on either side of the sun could represent the gates of a city, the light at the end of a tunnel, or new beginnings. It is possible that the sun behind the pillars of Boaz and Joachim could mean the pursuit of immortality and sacred knowledge. The quest to be immortal is real."

"Like a vampire?" asked Feed Bag, clearly shaken. He stood up, ready to leave.

"It's more like the fire of our spirit lives on forever," said Sadie.

"Is there anything else you need to tell us about the card?" asked Luke.

"I believe I covered everything," said Sadie.

The rest of the group stood up, ready to leave. Amber grabbed the card and put it back in her purse. They pushed their chairs in and exited the room. Before they reached the front door, Sadie gave them one final message: "May the tarot card gods shine on your souls. Blessed be."

"Bye," said Amber before walking out.

Once they were outside, they all breathed a sigh of relief.

"That was weird," said Feed Bag. He pulled a candy bar out of his pocket and unwrapped it.

"Now where do we go?" asked Luke. "The sun is going down; we're running out of time."

"Remember what Sadie said about the boat and the sun?" asked Thirteen. "If the sun is setting, move towards the north."

"North it is," said Luke.

"Look for a sign," said Amber.

After walking a couple blocks, Thirteen pointed at the skyline. "Look, two towers in the direction of the setting sun."

"I'll get us an Uber," said Luke.

"I'll call Payton and let her know what's going on," said Amber.

"Don't bother," said Feed Bag, holding up his phone to show them the picture. "I know exactly where to find them."

CHAPTER FIFTEEN

GROUP THREE: FIREWORKS

I exited the back door of the Carlton Hotel with The Singe, Shoes, and Lisa following close behind me to the parking lot. "Let me see the firecracker," I told The Singe.

"It's a miniature skyrocket," said The Singe, correcting me. He took out a lighter from his pocket. The Singe was about to send the six-inch rocket on a stick into outer space.

I took the lighter away from him. "Don't you dare," I said in protest.

Shoes pulled a small lighter out of a side pocket on his sneaker and handed it to The Singe. "Spark it," he said. I was not shy about showing my astonished look.

The flame ignited. The Singe touched the fuse attached to the rocket before I could stop him. The flame crawled up the fuse at a steady pace. I knocked the mini rocket out of his hand. It landed on the blacktop by Shoes's feet.

"Stomp it out," I yelled.

"Not a chance. These are new shoes," he answered.

I was wearing flip flops, so I dove onto the skyrocket that was on the ground. The flame on the fuse went out. I stood up again feeling victorious.

"Payton, your shirt is on fire," shouted Lisa.

I quickly peeled it off and threw it on the ground next to me. The Singe poured the rest of his Mountain Dew on the smoldering holes.

"Perfect," I said before realizing I was now standing out in public in my Victoria's Secret sports bra. I bent over and picked up my slightly soaked and sticky shirt that had a big hole burned into the front.

"You've been 'Singed'," said Lisa.

"Sadly, not the first time." I said while shaking the excess liquid from my shirt. "I'll find another one down the beach at one of the shops." I threw it in a nearby dumpster by the back door.

The Singe picked the rocket off the ground. "Why won't you let us light it?"

"Yeah," agreed Shoes with a mystified expression.

I took the rocket away from The Singe. "Because we need to look it over for clues."

"Maybe it's one of those locator rockets," suggested The Singe. "It might lead us right to Brad."

"Highly unlikely," I said back.

"Look," said Lisa, "there's a small smiley face on the sticker."

"Right next to the name of the business who made it," I finished. "Celestial Fireworks."

"I know that place," said The Singe. "I bought a mega blaster from them yesterday."

"Do you still have it?" asked Shoes enthusiastically. "Let's spark that bad boy up."

"It was on the bus." He paused. All of us raised our eyebrows in anticipation. "I lost it in the fire." His face turned red.

"Maybe it was the fire," Lisa suggested.

"That could be too," he agreed with a guilty smirk.

I rolled my eyes. "Where is this fireworks shack located exactly?"

"It's down by the docks. You better find a shirt first. It's kind of in a sketchy neighborhood."

I sighed, "Of course it is."

***

I am not alive, but I grow. I don't have lungs, but I need air. I don't have a mouth, but water kills me. What am I?

***

We made a quick stop at a beach clothing store before heading towards the docks. My attire suggested I was a cheerful local with my neon orange and white Port Christabel T-shirt. Nineteen ninety-five later, I was good to go.

"I'm going to get an Uber," I said.

"Really?" said Lisa. "It's like five blocks. We're all young and healthy. I say we walk."

"I say we don't." I was trying to stand my ground.

"Let's walk," said Shoes. "I'm willing to burn off a layer of tread on these Christian Valenflashbek's."

"How much did those awesome, jet-black, bedazzled, foot rags set you back?" asked The Singe.

"I don't like to shop and tell, but it was probably more chicken wings than you could eat."

"Dude, holy crap, that's a lot."

Lisa and I looked at each other. What the heck is happening here?

"So, we're walking," said Lisa, who was wearing something athletic with good arch support on her feet. My flip flops would have to do. Five blocks was manageable, right?

We followed The Singe in the direction of the beach. He seemed to be confident for the first few blocks as we passed by familiar landmarks and shops. We took a right by the candle shops and a left just past the fire station. I was starting to sense a pattern here.

All was well until we stood at the entrance to a narrow alley between two old stone buildings. With nighttime approaching, the shadows gave it an ominous feel.

I pointed down the alley. "You want us to go through there?" I asked, not sure if I really wanted an answer.

"Yeah, we are starting to get into the sketchy neighborhood I was telling you about," said The Singe.

"Maybe we should go around," suggested Lisa.

My feet were starting to hurt, so my better judgement went out the window. "It really doesn't look that bad. We can do it," I said with false confidence.

The Singe led the way through the overflowing dumpsters and rat-infested bags of garbage. We tiptoed past a few make-shift cardboard houses. Luckily for us, the occupants were sleeping or elsewhere.

At the end of the narrow alley, there was a sharp turn to the right that opened to a wider space between the buildings; a space that was wide enough to conduct business, street business.

We stopped abruptly. "I changed my mind. I want to go back," I whispered, staring down at what I could only assume the locals called Death Alley. Hookers and their pimps lined the walls on the left. Dealers of stolen goods lined the walls on the right. If you were looking to lose your virginity and buy a fake Rolex, this was the place.

I turned to The Singe. "You went through here?" I asked with a semi-squeaky, terrified voice. "You didn't lose anything, did you?" I was referring to his virginity.

"That was during the day. I just had to deal with the rats."

"Let's turn around … now," said Lisa.

"I'm afraid for my Valenflashbek's," said Shoes, hiding behind us girls.

"What do we have here?" asked one of the big, burly pimps with dark, curly hair.

"I see fresh meat," said an extremely thin, horrifying little man.

"Okay, I've seen enough," I said. "We can run now."

The four of us turned around and headed back down the narrow rat-infested alley. We knocked over garbage cans and threw bags of garbage behind us as we ran, trying to slow down the two scary men who were chasing us.

When we hit the end of the alley, we ran around the corner and dashed into the nearest store. The four of us hid behind shelves in Smoky Joe's Smoke Shop. I saw The Singe's eyes light up when he realized we were surrounded by glass containers of cannabis, weed-spiked candy, bongs, pipes, and cannabis oil.

"This is way better than the fireworks store," said The Singe.

"They should sell chocolate-covered donuts in here," added Shoes.

I looked at them both and said, "No. Just. No."

"Cannabis oil has been proven to help with pain, cancer, anxiety, seizures, and more," stated Lisa, my health-conscious friend.

"Can I help you kids?" said a man in his fifties wearing a tie-dye T-shirt.

There was no sign of the creeps who were following us, so I stood up. "You must be Joe?" I asked.

"Yes, I am," he said slowly in a stoner-way.

"We're lost," I added. "Can you tell us how to get to Celestial Fireworks from here?"

Joe stayed behind his glass counter. "I'm glad to hear you're lost, 'cause weed and fireworks don't mix. Believe me, I've tried. Didn't end pretty," he said. "That's how I lost my pinky finger." He held it up for us to see.

"Whoa," said Shoes, walking closer to take a look.

"Gnarly," said The Singe in amazement.

"How do we get to the fireworks store?" I asked again.

"Oh … yeah … I forgot. From the front door here, go up one block, take a right, then go down two blocks. You can't miss the big, red building."

"Thanks," said Lisa.

"A word of warning, stay away from the alleys around here," said Joe. "Those people are crazy."

"Don't worry, we got it." I said before heading out the door.

***

"This is the place," said The Singe, excited to be back at the fireworks store.

We climbed up the two wooden steps, walked across the porch, and went inside the shop. The owner greeted us right inside the door. He was a pleasant-looking man in his thirties dressed in jeans and a Celestial Fireworks shirt.

"Hi, I'm Bernie Blastoff. This is my shop. Hey, I remember you," he said, directing his attention towards The Singe. "How was that Mega Blaster I sold you?"

"It took out a bus," I added before The Singe could say anything.

"Those things can happen if you're not careful." He laughed.

"My bad,' said The Singe. "Next time I—"

"Maybe there shouldn't be a 'next time'," suggested Lisa.

The Singe made a dispirited face and crossed his arms over his chest.

"What can you tell me about this skyrocket?" I asked Bernie, showing him the six-inch firework.

"That is definitely one of mine," he confirmed. He took it from me and examined it further. This is one of my special message fireworks."

"What's the message?" asked Lisa.

"You have to light it to find out," said Bernie. "They are very popular."

"See, I told you," said The Singe.

"Let's spark it up," said Shoes, taking out his lighter.

"Not in here, boys. My whole inventory will go up like the Fourth of July."

I rolled my eyes and breathed a sigh of relief that Bernie had a brain.

"Do you remember who might have ordered it?" I asked, trying to get any information I could.

"Sorry, I don't keep records of that. No reason to," said Bernie. He was about to hand the rocket back to me when he said, "Hey, what is this?" He pulled a small, rolled-up piece of paper from the bottom of the rocket. He opened it up. "Is one of you Payton?"

"That would be me," I said, raising my hand.

Bernie handed the note over to me with an inquiring eye. "You kids in trouble?"

I read the note: "Payton, give me those earrings."

"Not any more than normal," I replied. "Is there somewhere we can light the rocket?"

"We can light it out back in the parking lot because it's small," instructed Bernie.

To get to the backdoor, we had to pass by the larger fireworks. The Singe had to stop and salute the big pile of Salutes on the way outside.

"Those will kill you if you get too close," said Bernie.

"Cool," said The Singe in admiration.

"Decent," said Shoes. He stopped to touch one just so he could say that he did.

Outside, we gathered in a circle around Bernie who agreed to light it for us. I was okay with him doing that under the circumstances.

"This could be dangerous," I warned him.

"Relax, I've done this thousands of times," said Bernie.

He flicked his own lighter and touched it to what was left of the fuse. I plugged my ears and took two steps back. What can I say? Shit happens, mostly to me.

We all watched the flame work its way up the fuse and ignite the rocket. It flew thirty feet in the air, made a semi-loud bang, and burst into red, white, and blue letters: U, S, S.

"They spelled it wrong," said The Singe, looking up in the air. "It's missing the 'A'."

"A, S, S," said Shoes. "What's that supposed to mean?"

"No, I meant, USA," said The Singe, laughing at his friend.

"Oh," he said, feeling embarrassed.

"No worries," I told him, "we should probably go, guys. Thanks for your help, Bernie."

"Good luck, kids," he said before we left.

The four of us stopped on the front porch of the fireworks shop to figure out our next move.

"The first thing I need to do is get into the country club and get those earrings away from my mother," I said.

"Payton, you can't get in there dressed like that," said Lisa. "Or without a date."

"I have an idea," I said. "Follow me."

***

The answer to the riddle: Fire. Be careful, Payton, you might get burned.

CHAPTER SIXTEEN

GROUP FOUR: THE BLUE GHOST

"You suck, you doorknob," said Blond Ambition. "No, I've changed my mind. You're a doormat. I can't believe you killed me with a stupid grenade launcher." Blond Ambition threw his video game controller down on the couch.

"Such harsh words," said Wolfman. "You fight and talk like a girl."

"Do Not!" Blond Ambition stormed off to the kitchen to find more pizza.

"Finally, my turn," said Chameleon. "Prepare to die."

"Eat shit and this grenade," said Wolfman. There was a loud explosion noise that came out of the TV.

"Damn it, you are a doorknob," joked Chameleon when he realized Wolfman had just blown him to bits. Chameleon leaned over so he could see down the hall that led to the kitchen. "Blond Ambition is still busy looking for food. I'm taking another turn."

"Suit yourself. I have no problem blowing your ass into a thousand pieces again," said Wolfman.

"Thanks, buddy. I knew I could count on you."

"Let the battle begin," said Wolfman.

Chameleon looked down the hallway again. "Hey, where did that Julie girl go?" He asked.

"I think she went to the bathroom, but that was like a half hour ago."

"Girls?" commented Chameleon. He paused the game.

"Dude, WTF?" asked Wolfman. "I was just about to blow you to smithereens." He set the controller down and looked at his friend.

"Do you think that Julie girl would go out with me?" asked Chameleon.

"I don't know, man. She's engaged to that missing guy."

"So as far as I'm concerned, she's available," laughed Chameleon.

"You disturb me sometimes." Wolfman gave Chameleon a shove.

"We should probably try to figure out what that Blue Ghost sticker means, huh?"

"After one more game," suggested Wolfman.

"Fine by me," agreed Chameleon.

***

Ten minutes later, Blond Ambition came back with a fully cooked microwave dinner and a beer. Wolfman and Chameleon looked at him with disbelief.

"What?" asked Blond Ambition. "Payton's parents aren't going to miss a beer. There's like a case in the fridge."

"Go get me a beer," demanded Chameleon, pointing in the direction of the kitchen.

"Screw you, go get it yourself," said Blond Ambition. "It's my turn anyway. I heard you die like a little bitch."

"You're a little bitch," insisted Chameleon.

"Guys, knock it off," said Wolfman. He was looking at his two friends who were about to get physical.

It was too late. It was time to settle it like men.

Chameleon paused the game and set his controller down on the coffee table.

"So, we're gonna duke it out now?" asked Blond Ambition as he set his food and beer down on the end table.

"Hell no," said Chameleon. "We're going to wrestle." He rushed at Blond Ambition, knocking him to the carpet. In about two seconds, Chameleon had Blond Ambition in an armbar. "Say it. Say it," yelled Chameleon. "Say you're a little bitch." He was bending Blond Ambition's arm into unnatural positions.

"Never," screamed Blond Ambition. It was obvious he was in a great deal of pain.

"Stop it. You'll break his arm," shouted Wolfman.

Chameleon flipped Blond Ambition around, pulling him into a headlock with his knees. "How does that feel?" He squeezed his knees tighter together.

"What is going on here?" asked Julie in a groggy voice.

"I'm teaching Blond Ambition a lesson," answered Chameleon.

"Where were you?" Wolfman asked Julie.

"I fell asleep in Payton's room. What time is it?"

"Around 8:00," said Wolfman.

"Guys, knock it off. We need to work on the puzzle."

The boys ignored her. "Let me go, or I'll tell Julie what your tattoo means," said Blond Ambition. He was clearly grimacing in pain.

"You wouldn't dare."

"Try me." Blond Ambition was wincing and laughing at the same time. "It stands for un—"

Chameleon grabbed the Blue Ghost sticker from the nearby coffee table, peeled the backing off and—

"No. Don't. We need that," Julie yelled at Chameleon.

Chameleon stuck the sticker over Blond Ambition's mouth. He wasn't able to hold a squirming Blond Ambition between his knees any longer. He broke free and jumped to his feet. Blond Ambition peeled it off his mouth, crumbled it in a ball, and threw it on the carpet.

Julie ran over and grabbed the rolled-up sticker off the floor. "You assholes, that was our only clue to find Brad." She started to cry.

Chameleon was laughing and pointing at Blond Ambition. "You've been ghosted."

"Dude, your lips are blue," said Wolfman.

Blond Ambition ran over to a mirror in the hallway. "Oh crap." He wiped at it with his hand. It didn't come off. "What if it's poison?" He ran towards the kitchen.

"What if it's a clue," said Wolfman. The group followed Blond Ambition into the kitchen.

"Stop," they yelled as they ran after him.

"Don't you dare wash that off," yelled Julie when she saw Blond Ambition at the sink. "I think there might be something written on the back side of the sticker. She held up the crumpled sticker. There was visible blue ink.

Blond Ambition held still while the other three closely examined his face under the light.

"Is that the letter 'N'," asked Julie. She pointed to the corner of his mouth.

"I think so," said Wolfman. "That looks like the letter 'T' next to it."

"Yep, I see it," said Julie, touching Blond Ambition's face.

"Don't move your lips," ordered Wolfman. "It looks like MOUNT."

"I see it too," said Julie.

"Does anyone want to hear a funny fact about ghosts?" asked Chameleon.

"Not really," said Julie. She was focused on Blond Ambition's face.

"Good," said Chameleon. "Spirits tend to be more concentrated in places where there has been a lot of births and deaths."

They all got quiet and looked at him.

"You weirdo," said Blond Ambition with a laugh.

"Hold still," insisted Julie. "It looks like there are letters before MOUNT, but I can't tell what they are."

"Dang it, me neither," said Wolfman.

Julie sighed and started to cry again. "We're never going to find Brad in time." Julie walked over to the kitchen table and took a seat. She put her head down on the wooden surface.

Chameleon followed her over there. "Maybe this will cheer you up," said Chameleon. "Ghosts are ghosts, but demons are rare."

"Not as rare as this," said Blond Ambition checking his phone. He showed it to Wolfman first, then Chameleon and Julie.

"We need to go … now," said Julie. She got up from the table. The boys followed her out of the front door of the penthouse.

***

Ticktock goes the clock. Time is running out. Cinderella to the rescue. Will her plan workout?

CHAPTER SEVENTEEN

"Payton, are you seriously going to do this?" asked Lisa.

"Yes, The Singe and I are going in the store to borrow what we need. You and Shoes stay out here in the alley and be our lookouts."

Lisa gave me a troubled look. I did weird things with my eyebrows trying to lighten the mood. I don't think it helped.

"Fine. I'll leave them cash, okay?" I asked. "It'll be a quick in and out. What could go wrong?" I looked around the group for an agreeable face.

"I'm with Lisa on this," said Shoes. "This is a bad idea."

"It's not my fault that the bridal shop is closed," I said, defending my plan. "We'll sneak in the back window or something."

"Or something?" asked The Singe. "That sounds like a solid plan."

"That sounds like you are doubting me. Fine, I'll just go by myself then," I said trying to guilt trip someone into helping me. There was a long awkward pause of silence.

"If I do this, I want another Mega Blaster," The Singe demanded.

"Consider it done," I said knowing that it would somehow come back to bite me in the ass. "Now, help me pull that wooden crate over to the window."

The four of us carried it over to the window and placed it next to the wall. I looked around on the ground for an object to break the window. Where was a random brick or a rock when you needed one?

"Maybe it's unlocked," suggested The Singe.

"I doubt it," I said. "I've seen the bitch that runs this place. I'm surprised there aren't guard dogs."

I crawled up on top of the crate and tried the window. Yep, it was locked. "Scalpel," I demanded, holding out my hand. The Singe handed me a crowbar. I gave him a raised eyebrow. "Where did you find that?"

"Over there by the back door. It's almost like someone wants us to break in here."

That was a troublesome thought. "Almost," I said back, right before I broke the glass of the window. I carefully reached inside to unlock it. The windowpane slid up with ease. Before I attempted to climb inside, I turned to Lisa. "Watch Shoes and watch for the police."

"Sure thing," she said. She walked over to the edge of the building to check out the alley.

"We need a cool signal," proposed The Singe. "You know like a lion or an elephant noise."

"Can either of you guys whistle?" I asked Shoes and Lisa. The Singe made a sad face. Ugh! "Can either of you meow like a cat or bark like a dog?"

"I can pull off a pretty convincing guard dog," said Shoes.

"You're hired. C'mon, Singe, let's go." I signaled him to follow me inside the building. We both crawled through the window and dropped down to the floor without cat-like reflexes.

"Ow! That was my foot," I said, rubbing the top of it to make sure nothing was broken.

"Sorry, my bad. That was my knee."

The backroom was dark, narrow, and overcrowded with gowns and tuxedos all covered in long plastic bags.

"Hey, I think I found the light switch," said The Singe.

"Noooo," I whispered really loud.

It was too late, the lights flicked on. I dove for the light switch and shut it off.

"No lights," I said repeating myself. "Use the light of your phone to find your way around."

"Okay," he agreed. "You don't have to be such a lightbulb Nazi."

I rolled my eyes at him, but he couldn't see me in the dark. "The tuxedos are over there by the door, find your size and try it on to make sure it fits." I found a dark purple dress in my size. "I'm going to the dressing room to try this on. Behave yourself."

"I always do," was his reply.

You have no idea how much I wanted to believe him. I left him alone looking through the rack of tuxedos. The dressing rooms were on the other side of the store. I had to pass by the front lobby and desk area to get there. In the dark, the store had more of a creepy vibe than I had remembered. I tried my best not to think about how easy it would be to hide amongst the dress racks like a killer would in a horror movie. The dress shop scene from *I Know What You Did Last Summer* and basically anything from *Scream* came to mind. My feet moved a bit faster down the hall until I was safely behind a locked dressing room door.

After I hung my dress up, I turned on the flashlight app on my phone. I sat my phone and my periwinkle Prada purse down on the chair in the corner. My clothes quickly hit the floor. I couldn't wait to try on the gorgeous gown. The image I saw of myself wasn't half bad. The lighting was a little harsh, but all in all, I was happy with my selection. Why couldn't this have been my bridesmaid's dress? Because I'm Payton Marie Richardson, that's why.

The strapless sweetheart top had purple sequins that shimmered in the light. The poofy, three quarter length, tulle skirt had a pretty, iridescent sheen to it. Actually, I've changed my mind. I look fabulous. I admired myself for a few more minutes in the mirror. Now, it was time to accessorize with some fancy shoes. I looked down at the time on my phone. On second thought, my flip flops would have to do. There was no time for shoe shopping. I grabbed my phone and purse, ready to exit the dressing room. My hand was on the doorknob when I started to get that uneasy feeling again. Be brave, I told myself. It's just like ripping off a band-aid and running for your life. Just do it.

I twisted the knob and jerked the door open. There was a flash of light that temporarily blinded me. A scream left my body as I found myself inches away from a tall figure in the dark. My purse made contact with his face. He yelped and flew backwards into the wall.

"Dang, nice follow through, Payton," he said, pulling himself back to his feet.

My nose suddenly got that "oh so familiar" whiff.

"Payton, funny story," started The Singe.

I looked down the hall towards the lobby; there was a faint glow of light that was getting brighter.

"You didn't?" I asked.

"I did."

I grabbed him by the collar of his borrowed tuxedo, yanking him towards the light. The lobby was quickly filling with smoke from the burning unity candles and the dresses that were now on fire.

"You lit candles, why? Why would you do that?" I asked out of curiosity.

"I needed to see, and you said no lights so …"

I took a long cleansing breath and coughed. "We need to get out of here, pronto." My plan was to leave money on the counter to cover the damages for our borrowed stuff. Needless to say, I no longer had enough cash to cover the actual damages. Leaving my debit card wasn't happening. It was time to vacate the premises. I was going straight to hell for this.

The Singe grabbed the fire extinguisher from the wall behind the desk. He turned the nozzle towards the fire. I was admiring his tenacity to right his wrong, when I heard the sound of an attack dog and a loud alley cat's hiss and growl.

"Seriously, we need to go, NOW!" I yelled at The Singe.

He dropped the extinguisher on the floor. Most of the fire was put out by his effort. We both ran to the backroom to escape. The Singe tried to pull boxes over to the window for us to climb out. The room was foggy with smoke.

"Use the door," I insisted.

We unlocked it and ran out into the alley. There was a car waiting for us. Lisa and Shoes were already inside.

"I got us an Uber," said Lisa, waving us over.

"Good thinking," I answered back.

We squeezed in the backseat with them. The car sped away with the sound of sirens in the distance. The Singe's phone started dinging with alerts like crazy. His phone was blowing up, and not in the usual way for him.

I looked at him with a sour look on my face. "What did you do?"

***

A near escape topped off with an embarrassing moment. Glorious. You look like a princess in your gown, Payton, a social media queen ready for the ball. Get me those earrings, or someone is going to pay the price.

CHAPTER EIGHTEEN

"Funny story," started The Singe. "After I got dressed in my tuxedo, I was pumped about looking all dapper and shit. So … I wanted to savor the moment with some epic photography. While trying to use some mood lighting, I might have accidentally knocked over a candle or two. Hence, the flamage you witnessed."

His phone continued to blow up with alerts. "Give that to me." I wasn't taking no for an answer. His phone was already open to one of the social media sites. There was one picture of The Singe in his tuxedo with flames behind him. The second picture was of me, wide eyed in my dress, right after I opened my dressing room door. The caption read: "Too hot to handle. Hitting it at The Country Club Prom. #Singerella"

"Oh no!" I pointed my shaking index finger at him. "You take that down immediately." I started to hyperventilate. "Those pictures are from the crime scene," I said from between clenched teeth, hoping that our mid-thirty-something, male driver couldn't hear me.

"Aw, okay," said The Singe. His mood was completely deflated. "I had five hundred likes already."

We all turned around to look out the back window. With that kind of publicity, we were bound to be on somebody's radar. Honestly, I was expecting sirens and red lights. So far, so good. We weren't being followed by the police. I sat back in my seat to relax. The intense feeling of fear floated away.

"Um, Payton," said Shoes to get my attention. He was looking out the back window. "I think we are being followed by that dark colored SUV. It's still behind us after our last two turns."

There was nothing stealthy about the way we all turned around to peer out the back window at the same time. We looked like a bunch of dogs on out first car ride.

"Who do you think it is?" asked Lisa.

"I'm thinking it's the kidnapper or the FBI," said The Singe being as logical as he could.

"I could see it being the kidnapper. They are always watching," I said, giving my honest opinion. Whoever it was, they better not try to stop me from getting the earrings away from my mother. Brad's life depended on my success.

The Uber driver pulled into the long driveway of the Country Club complex. The car that was behind us continued to drive past the entrance. That was a relief, but they still knew exactly where we were.

"You can drop us off at the main entrance," I informed the driver. The four of us got out of the Uber. "Any chance you can hang around? We will need another ride in a bit."

"Sorry," he said. "I'm completely booked all night. Spring Break is one of our busiest weeks on the island."

"That's okay. Thanks anyway," I said to him before he drove away.

"Now what?" asked Lisa, looking for a plan from me.

"You and Shoes stay out here. The Singe and I will go in and mingle until I can find my parents."

"Okay," said Shoes. "We'll try to look inconspicuous."

"Dude, when in doubt," said The Singe, "act like a tree. It works for me."

"C'mon, Singerella, our kingdom awaits," I said to him.

We opened the door and went inside. The front lobby showed a lot of old-world charm. Its dark woodwork on the walls and ceiling, Persian rugs in dark reddish tones, and plush velvet armchairs screamed money. A uniformed gatekeeper with a large, pointed nose guarded the entrance to the grand ballroom to keep out the riff raff. Yes, we were the sort of riff raff they were trying to keep out.

"Hello," I said to be cordial and act like I was an invited guest. "Payton Richardson and guest."

"Do you have your tickets?" inquired the guard.

Drat, foiled again. "I forgot them, but my parents, Stan and Janna are already inside," I said with my best convincing smile.

He answered my smile with a blank emotionless stare. "Sorry. No tickets. No entrance." He was standing firm.

"But it's a matter of life and death that we go inside," insisted The Singe.

His statement did nothing to inspire him to let us in. He seemed even more annoyed. The guard took one look at our shoes: my flip flops and The Singe's worn-out sneakers. Then he looked us both in the eye and said, "Now, shoo, off you go." He pointed at the front door.

We had a line forming behind us. This was embarrassing. There were far too many witnesses to bean the man on the head and run inside. I grabbed The Singe's coat sleeve, pulling him towards the front door. It was time for a new plan.

"Are we giving up?" asked The Singe as we exited the building.

"No," I whispered back, "We are sneaking in. I have no idea how yet but that has never stopped me before."

"Sweet! A secret undercover mission. I'm in."

"Let's look for a side door." We walked down the front steps and into the parking lot. It didn't take us long to find Shoes and Lisa.

"We got the boot," said The Singe to answer their unspoken question.

"I think I saw a side door over here," said Lisa. She pointed to the left side of the building. Lisa led the way in the dark parking lot. We were passing by a group of bushes on the side of the building, when Julie jumped out of nowhere, scaring the crap out of us.

"Seriously, you need to stop doing that to me." The look I gave her was not friendly at first. "Why are you here? How did you find us?"

She laughed before answering me. "The boys saw The Singe's social media post. It was obvious that you guys needed our help."

"Where are Chameleon, Wolfman, and Blond Ambition?" I asked, looking around in the bushes.

Julie pointed into the darkness. "They are further down the way behind the second set of bushes. The boys are trying to pick the lock on the side door," explained Julie.

"Chameleon?"

"Yeah," she said.

"I'm sure glad he is on our team." We both laughed. "He has been really helpful through this whole mess."

"I'm sorry I have to ask you this, Payton, but why are you here?" asked Julie.

"It's all part of the scavenger hunt. We found a note in the mini rocket. I have to get a pair of earrings that my mother is wearing and bring them with us to wherever Brad is."

"Any idea where Brad is yet?"

"No, I figured we would all meet up and brainstorm the clues and figure it out. I feel that the four clues are all related. Once we make the connection, it will point us to one location."

"That makes sense," said Julie. "I feel better now that we might actually find him."

Lisa, The Singe, and Shoes nodded their heads in agreement. "We'll figure it out," said Lisa. She gave Julie a hug.

"Let's go check on the boys to see if they are making any progress," said Julie. We followed her around the bushes. She led us to the side door with a big "Employees Only" sign painted on it.

"Yes, we're in," said Chameleon, pumping his fist in the air in a celebratory motion. He looked in our direction. "Well, if it isn't the prom court," he joked.

"Not funny," I said in protest. I pushed Chameleon's hand off the doorknob. "You guys stay out here. The Singe and I will be out in a minute."

"Not happening," said Chameleon. "We are all in this together."

"Yeah," said Julie, standing her ground.

"We are all going in, Payton," said a voice from the dark parking lot. It was Crystal. She was not alone. Her group and Amber's group were with her.

"Oh, for Crissake. How did you all find me?"

The group came into the light from the side door. "Ask James Bond," said Crystal, gesturing with her head in The Singe's direction.

I sighed. "Of course." I completely understood. I had been Singed again. "Okay, you can all come, but you have to be quiet. I don't feel like talking my way out of a jail cell tonight."

The group slinked in the door. It closed behind us with a metal-on-metal clank. We crept down the dimly lit hall by phone light. At the end of the hall was a heavy metal door. I pressed on the horizontal bar. The metal bar depressed with ease. It wasn't locked. We all breathed a sigh of relief.

I poked my head inside the room. The light was on. It appeared to be an employee lounge/locker room. The group filed into the room after me. The door closed behind us as the last person stepped inside.

"Look, waiter and waitress uniforms," said Chameleon. "I have an idea. Julie and I will put on uniforms and go upstairs and blend in with the waitstaff."

"We can distract your parents, or something while you grab the earrings," suggested Julie.

"Guys," interrupted Luke. "that plan will never work. My mom saw you all in our kitchen tonight before she left."

"She didn't see me," said Crystal, offering her services.

"That's true," said Lily. "She is our only option."

"Fine." I decided to agree. "Grab a uniform and a tray up in the kitchen. Try to blend in. Hopefully, no one will recognize you from the news."

"What is going on down here?" boomed an elderly woman's voice.

We all turned in her direction. A well-dressed woman in her sixties was standing at the bottom of the stairs.

"Sorry, we got lost trying to find a bathroom." Sure, that seemed like a logical lie.

She walked up to the group. "And them?" She pointed to the fourteen others who were extremely underdressed for the affair that was going on upstairs.

There was an awkward pause until Crystal jumped in to help. "Hi, I'm Paylula Sommers, reporter for Channel Five News. I'm here to cover the ball. This is my crew. And you are? I want to make sure I spell your name correctly." Crystal stepped forward to shake her hand.

Oh, she's good. Really good.

"Oh, how lovely. I'm Emily Vandersloot, of the Palm Beach Vandersloots," she said proudly. They shook hands, then Blond Ambition hit her in the head with a nine iron. She fell to the floor in an unconscious state.

"What the hell is wrong with you," asked Crystal. "My story was working."

"Unless you were planning on pulling a news camera out of your ass," said Blond Ambition, "that story was never working."

I had to agree with Blond Ambition. The kid made a good point. "She is going to wake up soon, hopefully," I said. I looked at Blond Ambition and then, over at Emily Vandersloot. She was wearing a fabulous pair of dangly diamond earrings and a pair of silver sandals with her black and silver ball gown.

"Quick, give me her earrings and her shoes. I have a plan."

Lily, the queen of borrowing things, grabbed her shoes and her earrings and handed them to me.

"Watch her," I told the group.

"Can we tie her up?" asked Max with a grin.

"That probably wouldn't be a bad idea under the circumstances. She may be old, but she looks feisty."

"Gag her too," said Lily. "I can't stand arrogant, rich bitches."

"Then everyone go outside and wait for me," I said. "This has to be a quick in and out before sleeping beauty here wakes up and starts making noise."

"What about me?" asked The Singe. "I'm not missing out on the party after all of this."

"Okay, you can come too." I agreed. "You might have to run recon with my dad while I get the earrings from my mother." I held out my hand. "Give me your phone and your lighter." I wasn't taking any chances.

***

Solving the puzzles and saving Brad are not Payton's only problems. She is wracking her brain trying to figure out who I am. Thoughts of me are constantly running through the back of her mind. Why is that? Am I that unforgettable or is there something more sinister going on?

CHAPTER NINETEEN

The Singe sang the theme to *Mission Impossible* all the way up the back stairs. Right before I opened the door, I said, "No funny stuff. I mean it. As soon as I get my hands on those earrings, we are bailing out of here."

"Got it. Operation Snatch-n-Grab will be a success. Nothing will catch on fire." His words oozed confidence.

We slipped out of the door that was conveniently placed back by the kitchen without being noticed. The grand ballroom was decorated with beautiful flower bouquets, soft white twinkling lights everywhere, and lit candles on every table. It was a breathtaking romantic fire hazard waiting to happen.

"Shall we schmingle?" asked The Singe, holding out his elbow for me to wrap my arm around.

The guard from the front door was heading in our direction. He hadn't seen us, but maybe his large, pointy nose was leading him in the right direction. He was hot on our scent. We needed to hide in the crowd before he saw us.

"Let's dance," I said, pulling him into the crowd on the dance floor. We worked our way across the floor, dancing our way through the other couples in search of my parents. It wasn't exactly graceful. We stepped on each other's feet a lot. The two of us bumped into annoyed guests while we twirled in slow circles. I searched all the tables as we danced, but I didn't see my parents. "Where the heck are they?"

"Isn't that your dad over by the bar?"

"Great. Go keep him company at the bar while I look for my mother."

"Will do," he said. He walked immediately over to the bar, leaving me standing on the dancefloor like a wallflower. The Singe, my dad, and cocktails, what could possibly go wrong?

I didn't want to think about it. This was the perfect time for a quick bathroom stop to check my face and my fluid levels. I cut across the dance floor to the side hallway to find the nearest bathroom. The second I stepped inside the door, I found myself face-to-face with my mother at the mirror.

"Payton, I'm surprised to see you here," said my mother.

I could tell that she had a few cocktails in her. She was in a "happy" mood. "You know me, I love to play dress up," was my response, which wasn't a total lie.

"That's a lovely new dress. Where did you get it?" My mother was making idle chit chat.

There was no sense lying about it at this point. "At the bridal shop where I got the dress for Brad and Julie's wedding." That was still weird to say out loud.

"That dress is a better fit for you than the one Julie picked out. You look ravishing, my dear." She took a sip of her Old Fashioned that was on the counter.

I know. My mother brought her booze in the bathroom. How much "happy" juice did the woman have tonight? I looked at myself in the mirror. "Thanks, I do look pretty darn good in purple." I laughed. My mother gave me a one-armed hug.

"These earrings I borrowed from you are beautiful, but they are pinching my earlobes." She started to take them off.

Great. This was going to be easier than I thought.

"Trade with me," she demanded, holding the winged shaped diamond earrings in her hand for me to take.

I took the earrings from her. "I can't," I said. "I borrowed these." That was also the total truth.

"I'm not going to lose them. Hand them over," she said in a stern motherly tone.

"Seriously, Mom. They are NOT mine. I can't." I was doing my best to keep us both out of jail.

"Well, whose are they?" She demanded an answer.

I paused to think of a convincing answer to her question. Nothing popped into my head. My entire body started to sweat profusely under the pressure. There was no choice but to give in. None of my friends were an option. I didn't have a rich boyfriend. It was too late to tell her they were mine. It was going to take a miracle to get me out of this. I started taking off the earrings when my wish was granted. It was almost like magic.

All of a sudden, the bathroom lights went out. I assumed it was the whole building that short circuited or something accidental because I could hear screams beyond the bathroom. This was my chance to bolt out the door with both sets of earrings … so I did. I was going to hell for leaving my mother stranded in the dark, calling my name. That was a problem for another time. We needed to save Brad first.

Now, to find The Singe in the dark. My panicked state had my brain synapsing at record speed. I ran towards the bar area. It was rough in my borrowed heels that were a size too large for me. I did my best to not stumble and fall on my face.

"Payton." I heard someone utter my name in the dark. It was The Singe by the front door. When I got there, he opened the door for us both to escape. We ran right into the guard in the lobby. He fell backwards onto the floor because we kind of ran him over. I didn't feel too bad about it because he had been so rude to us when he kicked us out. We ran through the double doors and out into the parking lot. We nervously walked around looking for our friends.

"Did you get them?" The Singe anxiously asked me.

"I did," I said with a huge smile. I held them up.

"Sweet. You're welcome," he said with a shy, sneaky grin.

"What? I'm confused." I said, hoping for an explanation.

He stopped walking and turned towards me. "Okay, so get this. I went up to your dad at the bar. We chatted briefly. He told me that your mom was in the bathroom. I saw you head in there. I borrowed your dad's phone and texted Chameleon to cut the power on my signal. When the lights were out, I figured you could grab the earrings and run. How is that for a secret mission?"

"It didn't go quite that smoothly but thank you."

The Singe smiled back, feeling much like a secret agent.

We found the group on a grassy knoll on the other side of the building.

"Operation Snatch-n-Grab was a success," The Singe announced to the group. He and Chameleon exchanged an enthusiastic high-five.

"Now what?" asked Julie. "We are running out of time." She still showed honest concern for Brad in her voice.

"We need to compare notes on the puzzles," suggested Luke.

"Sixteen heads are better than four," said Lily. "We can figure this out if we all work together."

Group One with the letter tiles, what did you come up with?" I asked to get the discussion rolling.

"I solved the puzzle," said Teagan proudly.

"Yeah, right before you threw up from consuming too much alcohol," jabbed Crystal.

"It was my suggestion to go into the bar in the first place," Teagan sassed back.

"Guys, please. Just the facts. We don't have time for bickering," I said.

"Allow me," said Lily. She decided to take over. "The letter tiles spelled out 'Blue Marlin'. In the Blue Marlin Bar, we found a note inside their stuffed blue marlin that was hanging on the wall."

Max pulled the note out of his pocket. "Row, row, row your boat, gently down the stream. They're all tied up. You better hurry. Brad's about to scream."

"That's sick," said Lisa.

Julie started to cry again.

"Don't worry," I said to console her. "We'll find him."

"It says 'they'," said Max.

"Who's 'they'?" asked Luke, raising another big question.

"We don't know that yet," said Max.

This was pushing my stress to a new level.

"Group Two, with the death card, what did you figure out?" I directed my attention to the next puzzle.

"The card was a treasure trove of symbolism," said Amber. "It had everything: The Grim Reaper, the purity of the white horse, stealing souls, a sailing ship, a rising or setting sun, two towers, a dead king, a priest, and a woman with a child."

"Show the card to Lily," said Luke. "She's good with creepy gothic stuff."

"Thanks, honey," replied Lily. She took the card from Amber so she could look at it.

"Before we headed over here," said Feed Bag, "Thirteen figured out that we needed to head north by a clue we learned from Sadie the Sorceress. It has to do with the meaning of the sun on the card."

I raised my eyebrow at this Sadie character. "She sounds interesting."

"She was right about Thirteen having great insight and potential," remarked Feed Bag.

"Well, she was wrong about the other stuff," Amber said in a huffy tone. "I don't like cats. I'm a dog person."

"Lily?" I asked. "Do you have anything yet?"

Lily stared at the card in front of her. "Nope. I'm still percolating."

"Okay, let's go on to the third group, my group, with the skyrocket," I said.

"First of all," I started, "we traced the skyrocket back to Celestial Fireworks. Bernie Blastoff was a huge help. He actually found the note on the rocket demanding we bring the earrings with us. Showing up without them could have been disastrous."

"When we finally got to spark it, it displayed three red, white, and blue letters: U, S, S," said The Singe.

"It was spelled wrong," said Shoes. "It should have spelled 'USA'."

"Maybe it's not wrong," said Lisa, trying to convince the others.

"Fourth group, the Blue Ghost Sticker, what did you learn?" I asked.

"That Chameleon has a crush on Julie," said Blond Ambition, laughing.

Chameleon's face turned red. "I'm going to permanently ghost you," he said, moving in Blond Ambition's direction.

"Boys, knock it off," said Julie. She blushed a little when she said it. In my opinion, Julie seemed to be flattered with all of the attention.

"Before the sticker was destroyed in a ridiculous accident," said Julie, looking at the two boys, "we were able to read part of the word."

"The part of the word we could make out was 'mount'," said Wolfman. "Put on your thinking caps. We have a mystery to solve."

"All these clues have to lead us to one place," I said.

Everyone agreed with my conclusion.

"I got it," said Lily. She had our complete attention. "The Death Card represents the earth, the Blue Marlin represents water, the Skyrocket represents fire, and the Blue Ghost represents air."

"That's great," I said, "but where are we going?"

The group was gathered around the clues trying to put it all together. "Ugh! We are so close," I said, pacing around. I think better when I'm moving. If I had a cocktail in my hand, the riddle would be as good as solved already.

Chameleon got on his phone. "Don't mind me, I'm Googling."

"What does a picture card, a fish, USS, and a Blue Ghost have in common?" asked Julie in a desperate tone.

Thirteen started pointing at the card, then the note, then back and forth between the two. He was excited. "There's a boat on the card and a boat mentioned in the note," he said, beaming with joy.

"USS?" asked Crystal.

"A ship maybe?" suggested Wolfman.

"Not a ship," said Chameleon, holding up his phone. We all rubber necked it to get a better look at the picture.

"Earth, fire, water, aircraft carrier," said Lily with a satisfied look on her face. She was pleased with her Gothic sense of humor.

"But which one?" asked Julie. It was obvious that she was still frustrated.

"The Paramount," said Chameleon proudly, "also known as the Blue Ghost."

We all cheered with joy, then realized that was a bad idea, just in case we were all wanted felons. We quickly quieted down.

"What time is it?" asked Julie frantically. "Can we still get there from here in time?"

Chameleon looked at his phone. "It's 9:28. We have time to get there, but not much."

"How are we going to get there?" asked The Singe. "We need something big enough for all of us." That was an ironic twist since he was the one that blew up the bus.

I looked over by the front door and had a grand idea.

Lily saw it too. "If you're up for borrowing a limo, raise your hand," Lily said with a smirk. It was unanimous.

***

Who will solve the puzzle and open Pandora's Box?

CHAPTER TWENTY

Our mob of sixteen did their best to slink across the parking lot in the dark without getting noticed. We all approached the stretch limo with caution. Our main concern: was it occupied? Chameleon opened the driver's door. The driver's seat was empty. Next, he knocked on the back-passenger window to see if anyone was inside behind the blacked-out glass. No one answered. Chameleon opened the door and looked inside. The u-shaped, smooth, black leather bench seating was completely empty. A twelve-person limit sign was posted above the comfy couch seating area.

"Everyone inside, quick," said Chameleon.

One-by-one fourteen of us ducked our heads and climbed inside.

"I'm not sitting on the floor," said Teagan. "I want the full limo experience."

"Shut up and sit down," said Crystal, who was just "done" with Teagan and her whining ways.

"You can sit on my lap," said Max with a smile. That seemed to do the trick. Teagan squeezed herself over and onto Max's lap.

Chameleon and The Singe were the only ones left standing outside the car on the passenger side. They were fighting over who was going to drive.

"But I'm wearing the tuxedo," said The Singe, pleading his case. "Therefore, I should get to drive the beast. I look more like a limo driver.

"Not gonna happen," said Chameleon. "You don't have the experience of driving a large vehicle like this in heavy traffic. I drove the bus down here. Therefore, I am more qualified."

Blond Ambition hopped out of the limo. "Guys, we don't have time for this shit."

The front door of the country club opened. A man in his thirties, wearing a black suit and hat stepped outside with a set of keys in his hand.

"Hey, what are you doing with Miss Vandersloot's limousine?" He rushed down the steps. He confronted the three boys. Chameleon grabbed the keys from the driver's hand before he knew what was going on. The three strong, high school boys grabbed the driver and forced him inside the passenger compartment.

"Oh, I'm driving," said Chameleon, dangling the keys in Singe's face. "Finders keepers, losers … ride in the back." He laughed and ran around to the driver's side of the car. Blond Ambition shoved The Singe into the back of the limo. He then climbed in and closed the door before the limo driver tried to escape.

Chameleon pulled away from the curb. As soon as we were out of the parking lot and headed down the driveway, Chameleon rolled down the screen that divided the two compartments.

"How's our guest?" asked Chameleon. He was referring to the driver we just kidnapped.

"You can have the limo," said the driver, "just don't kill me. I'm not dying for that horrible Vandersloot woman."

Max laughed. "Tell us how you really feel about her," he commented and snickered again.

"Seriously," said the driver, "that evil woman ran over my foot with her golf cart on purpose and then refused to pay for my medical bills."

We all nodded in agreement that she was a vile human being after seeing her in action in the basement of the clubhouse.

I looked over at the driver. "Don't worry, whatever your name is—"

"It's Roberto," he said timidly.

"Don't worry, Roberto," I repeated. "We are just borrowing the limo to save our friend. We only need it for a ride to where we are going. You can have it back after that."

"Dude, you need to relax and have a drink," said Blond Ambition. He grabbed a bottle of brown liquid that was near his seat and took a drink straight from the bottle.

"A drink sounds good," said Teagan. She reached for a bottle of booze that was behind the sliding glass door of the liquor cabinet. It was located directly across from the leather seats. She took a swig of the bottle and passed it around the circle of people.

"Pass one of those bottles back to me," requested Roberto. "Miss Vandersloot keeps her top shelf liquor in that cabinet. Give me some of her caviar too. That bitch and her bloody caviar."

Teagan grabbed a jar of caviar and passed it on to Roberto. After that, she reached for another bottle to pass back to him. This is when she saw the box on the shelf. "Um, Payton, I think we have another puzzle to solve." She held up a four-inch by four-inch wooden box with a red smiley face painted on the front. It also had seven dials on the top of the box, one for each letter of the puzzle.

"Oh, that is definitely meant for us," I said. I grabbed one of the liquor bottles that was floating around the group and took a long drink. We still had brainstorming to do. I needed to recharge my battery.

After hearing about another puzzle, Chameleon slammed on the brakes. Everyone inside the car flew forward.

"No, keep going," shouted Julie. "Don't stop until we find the ship. Brad is depending on us."

Chameleon immediately put the limo back in drive. We could feel the engine change gears as the car's speed quickly increased.

"What ship?" asked Roberto. "Maybe I can help."

"We are looking for the Paramount," said Wolfman. "Do you know where it is?"

"I just moved here last month, but I think that is the ship that has daily tours."

"I'm already heading to the address given on their website," stated Chameleon.

"Chameleon, how close did you look at the website?" asked Luke. He held his phone in his hand. "It says that it's closed for repairs."

"That's not good," said Amber. "It could have been moved inland to one of the shipyards or to a private boat company."

"Hey, there's a note on the bottom of the box," said Teagan. She took it upon herself to read the puzzle riddle: "Where do you take a sick boat?"

"See. We're probably going the wrong way," said Max. His statement made Julie start crying again.

"Whoa, how do you move a metal fortress like that?" asked Shoes.

A blanket of silence hushed the chatter in the car. No one had a clue how to answer the clue or Shoes's question.

"Guys, where are we going, the beach or the shipyard?" asked a hurried Chameleon. "If I need to turn around, I have to do it now."

A mix of shouts came from the passenger compartment. It was a split decision.

"Julie," said Chameleon. She lifted her head when she heard her name. "Where do you want me to go?"

"The shipyard. Head to the shipyard," she said with confidence.

Chameleon Googled the nearest shipyard. "We should be there in ten minutes." This seemed to make Julie feel better.

"We still need to solve the puzzle," said Teagan. She passed the bottle and the box around the circle. Everyone took a swig of the bottle and a try at solving the puzzle. When it was my turn, I took another long drink. Don't judge me. I feel like I have been behaving myself much better today than in the past. The group needed me. Brad needed me, right? Am I behaving myself for Brad? No time to dwell on that now, that thought scared me more than anything.

I stared at the puzzle box on my lap. I tried moving the seven dials of letters to form a logical word. The only words that popped into my head were: convict, mugshot, illegal, lawless, and crooked. Well, you get the picture of where my head was at. I gave up and passed it to Thirteen, who was sitting next to me.

Needless to say, it was getting a little stuffy and rank in the limo with all of us crammed on top of each other. "Can someone please open a window?" I asked. "It's hot in here." I was feeling claustrophobic.

"Let's get some air in here," said The Singe, flapping his tuxedo jacket open and closed like a fan. He reached up and hit a button on the ceiling. The sunroof opened. "All right, that is more like it." He stood up with a bottle of booze in his hand. Before we could stop her, Teagan joined him. This had jail time written all over it.

"Get them down," shouted Chameleon from the front seat. "There's a cop car up ahead."

Max tackled The Singe. Amber, who was the closest, grabbed Teagan to pull her back inside. I closed the sunroof. We all did our best to portray a "nothing to see here" motif as we passed by the police car that was headed in the opposite direction. The entire group exhaled after the police car was out of sight.

Thirteen was completely engrossed in the puzzle. His fingers switched from dial to dial, trying different letter combinations. I looked past Thirteen and noticed that there was something wrong with Roberto. He looked a little green to me. "Are you okay?" I asked him.

"I don't think so. I think I am allergic to this caviar. That bitch and her imported caviar." He winced in pain and grabbed his stomach. He stood up quickly and moved to the nearest window in the back. He pushed the window down button and stuck his head outside the car. The expensive brandy and caviar were coming back up. I hoped it wasn't going to be contagious.

Lisa picked up the caviar container. "It expired last month." She took a whiff and made a disgusted face that wrinkled up her nose.

"He should change his name from Roberto to Ralph," said Blond Ambition. He laughed at his own joke. He was the only one.

"That's not funny," said Amber the pre-med student. "He's sick. We might have to take him to the doctor."

Roberto pulled his head back inside the car. "I feel better now. Pass me that bottle of brandy."

So glad that was just a false alarm. In the back of my head, I was worried that he might have been poisoned.

Thirteen started moving his feet around in a nervous way, which got my attention. He continued turning the dials on the box with his fingers rapidly.

"What's wrong, Thirteen?" I asked. He was clearly getting wound up.

The box made a click sound.

"I got it. I freaking got it," shouted Thirteen. "Where do you take a sick boat?" he asked in a calmer voice. He paused. "You take them to THE DOCK. Thanks, Amber, for your inspiration."

"We are going the wrong way," I shouted at Chameleon. "Head to the docks."

"Got it," said Chameleon. He cranked the wheel to the left. The limo went down through the median. It came out the other side of the longer grass headed in the opposite direction. After that, no one was in their original seat except for Chameleon. He continued to drive at an increased rate of speed.

Julie started to cry. "If he's dead, it's all my fault. I picked the wrong way to go." She leaned over with her head in her hands.

"No, it's not," I said to her. I was trying my best to make her feel better. "Chameleon will get us there in time." On the inside, I was blaming her a little. She was making stupid choices.

"I know how to get to the docks from here," said Roberto. "My cousin showed me a shortcut last week."

I waved Roberto up to the front of the passenger compartment. "Tell Chameleon how to get us there." He took a seat by the divider.

"Take the next right at the lights," instructed Roberto. "Then hit the first side road."

"What else did the box say?" asked Crystal. "Are we done with the puzzle?"

Thirteen found the box on the floor under his feet. He opened it up. Inside was a three-inch model of an aircraft carrier with the number thirty-three painted on one of its sides.

Chameleon stopped at a T-intersection. Straight ahead was a sign that said: "Docks." There was an arrow that pointed to the right, which was the north. There was another arrow that pointed to the left, which was south. "Which way do I go?" he asked.

Wolfman looked down at his phone to check the time. "We only have five minutes."

"Julie?" asked Chameleon. He didn't want to make the choice of which way to go.

She shook her head. "I'm not deciding."

"The north," said Thirteen. "Head north, just like the setting sun on the Death Card suggested."

That little voice in the back of my head was hoping that going north didn't mean death to Brad. I didn't share my fear with the group. I pushed the bad thought out of my head like I always do.

Chameleon turned to the right. After a couple of blocks there were ships docked everywhere.

"For Crissake, how the hell are we supposed to find the Paramount in time?" asked Lily. She was clearly saying what we were all thinking.

"Find slip thirty-three," said Roberto. We all looked at him. "My cousin works down here on the docks," he said to explain. "All the slips are numbered."

We did a quick deductive reasoning on which way to go by the numbers we saw nearby. The limo came to a screeching halt in front of slip thirty-three. It was the Paramount. Everyone climbed out of limo and did a victory dance. Julie actually hugged Chameleon, Roberto, and Thirteen.

I turned to Roberto, who was standing next to me. "So … are we good?"

"I didn't see anything," he said with a wink.

"Any chance you would want to stick around to see where this goes?"

"Nah, I should probably ditch Milton and Emily Vandersloot's car in the water and report it stolen." He smirked. "Good luck, Payton." He took the keys back from Chameleon. Roberto hopped back into the driver's seat of the limo. He burned a layer of rubber off the tires as he sped away in the borrowed limousine.

I really need to stop dragging other people into my web of lies, I thought as he drove away. It could be bad karma. I turned back to the group. "All aboard that's going aboard." We ran up the gangplank to get on the ship before our time ran out.

***

FYI: The number thirty-three means "the end" according to certain cultures. We will find out soon if it is true.

CHAPTER TWENTY-ONE

The Paramount was a massive aircraft carrier that stood around twenty stories high and roughly one thousand feet long. We stood at the top of the gangplank and took it all in. The flat, vast, wide-open flight deck stood before us like a sea of blacktop. A bridge jutted up out of the blacktop and towered above us to the right. Everything else was below deck. This definitely wasn't a fancy cruise ship. There were no lounge chairs or umbrella drinks. It was set up for war. Like it or not, my friends and I just enlisted for battle. I had a bad feeling that a battle to the death was about to begin.

At the top of the gangplank, there was a heavy, metal chain across the entrance to keep out unwanted visitors. There was also a note and a cardboard box meant for us. The card on the box was addressed to "Payton and friends." The note read: "Congratulations, you made it in the nick of time. Welcome to Paramount Island. Ring the bell to get your next clue. Place all phones, backpacks, and purses in the box before entering or suffer the consequences."

One-by-one, we climbed over the metal chain and placed our belongings in the box.

"I feel like we're being watched," said Julie.

"I'm sure we are," I replied, leaving my periwinkle purse in the box. I mentally said goodbye, knowing I probably wouldn't see her ever again.

Once we were all on the flight deck, we looked around for the bell. There were acres of hard, black, tarmac under our feet. This seemed like an impossible task.

"Give Brad back, you asshole!" yelled Julie. "I know you can hear me."

Somewhere in the bowels of the ship, we all heard a faint scream. It was Brad.

I ran to her side to stop her from doing something stupid. I knew what she was thinking, I was thinking it too. I wanted to run in the direction of his voice and help him.

My hand was holding onto her arm to stop her. "We can't. We have to play the game. Trust me. I know how this jackass's mind works. Do as you are told. Brad will be okay."

She nodded her head in agreement. I let go of her arm.

"Has anyone figured out why the note said, 'Welcome to Paramount Island' instead of 'Welcome to the Blue Ghost'?" asked Chameleon, questioning the group.

"Probably so you couldn't bore us to death with facts about ghosts," joked Blond Ambition. Blond Ambition and Wolfman high-fived.

"Fine," said Chameleon in a sour tone. "Figure it out yourself." He walked away and sat down on the tarmac with his back to the group.

"Blond Ambition, go apologize." I said in a lower tone so Chameleon couldn't hear me.

"No, he's being a jerk," said Blond Ambition.

"We need him to help us," I said to encourage him to change his mind.

"Good luck with that," said The Singe. "We can't do anything with him when he gets like this."

"By the way," said Chameleon, interrupting our conversation. "The ghost's name is Charlie. He lives in one of the engine rooms ... if anyone cares."

"You boys have to do something," said Julie. "We don't have time for his hissy fit."

"He's being a big baby," said Luke. "Do something."

"He won't listen to us," said Feed Bag. "We've been through this before."

"Maybe Julie should try," added Max. "He seems to like her."

I looked at Julie. "He's not going to listen to me either. Go talk to him." I urged her with a hand motion to go over to where he was sitting.

A horn blew from somewhere on the ship. The sound cut through the still of the night, startling us all.

"Hurry up," I said to Julie, nudging her in Chameleon's direction. "I think that was a warning."

Julie walked over to Chameleon. She sat down on the tarmac in front of him. They started talking. Julie reached for his hand. We couldn't hear what she said to him. To me, it looked like she was pleading for Brad's life. I just hoped that strategy would work on him. He seemed very despondent.

Chameleon nodded his head. They both stood up. She hugged him, which seemed a little out of character for her. Obviously, she was desperate for his help. They started making their way back over to the group.

***

I am just playing with you.

***

"Don't make a big deal out of this," I said to the boys before the two rejoined the group. Without wasting any time, I decided to ask Chameleon about his theory. "Why do you think 'Welcome to Paramount Island' is significant?"

The group gathered around us to listen to him. "First of all," Chameleon started, "when you've put together as many model ships as I have, you learn what the parts of a ship are called. What we are standing on is called what? Anyone?"

"The deck," said The Singe proudly.

"Correct," said Chameleon. "To be more specific, it's called the flight deck."

"Can you get to the point?" asked Crystal. Her hands were on her hips, showing her disgruntled mood.

"I can," said Chameleon, holding up his hand to mean wait. "For instance, this tower behind us has several names, one being the command center and the other? Anyone?"

We all looked at him dumbfounded.

"We give up," said Teagan. "Just tell us. I have to pee."

Chameleon's mouth formed into a huge smile before he spoke. "Its other name is 'the Island'. I think the bell is up there."

"Why didn't you just say that?" said Lily angrily.

"What a douche." I heard Luke mutter under his breath.

I elbowed my brother in the ribs. "Behave. We need this kid to figure this stuff out."

"Thank you," said Julie. She gave Chameleon a huge smile.

"What are we waiting for?" asked Max. "Let's go." He was the first one of us to head towards the Island to find the door.

"The base of the Island is generally around twenty feet across, so it doesn't take up too much room on the flight deck," explained Chameleon.

"Hey, was that light on up in the tower before?" asked Crystal.

"It must mean we're on the right track," I said to answer her back.

"That's known as vulture's row," said Chameleon. "It's a balcony for observing the flight deck."

Max found the door on the far side of the Island. He was brave enough to open the heavy, metal door first and stepped inside. We all followed.

Once we were all inside the big question was asked by Amber: "Where's the elevator?"

"Who cares," said Teagan. "I found the bathroom." She quickly disappeared behind the closed door.

"Sorry, Amber," said Chameleon. "The only elevators on the ship are to put the airplanes in the hangars below deck."

She shook her head and sighed. "Fine, let's get this over with."

After Teagan came out of the bathroom, everyone headed up the steps.

***

The rhyming was not my idea. Amateurs.

***

"We're here," said Chameleon, pointing at the sign on the wall that read: "Vultures Row." He opened the door to the staircase that led to the observation room. We all followed him like lemmings, never questioning his ability.

A small table lamp in the waiting area had been turned on, perhaps to guide the way. We were absolutely in the right place. There was an antique brass bell on the table next to an envelope.

Max grabbed the bell, opened the door to Vulture's Row, and rang it multiple times as loud as he could. "We found it!" he yelled into the brisk night air.

"Can you see anything out there?" asked Crystal.

"Just a bunch of sitting ducks in here," said Luke, laughing at his own joke.

"No. Nothing. It's pitch black." Max stepped back inside.

I picked up the envelope and opened it. Julie grabbed the clue away from me and began to read it out loud. "The Fortress of Secrets and Lies awaits. Don't tell the truth and learn your fate. Lying to me will cost a fee. Baring your soul will set you free."

"I don't think I want to play this game anymore," said Feed Bag.

"Me neither," said Teagan.

"Anyone else need a cocktail?" said Max.

"Quiet. Let me finish," said Julie, raising her voice. She continued: "Go down to the deck just above the sea. That's where you will find Brad plus three."

We all looked at each other with dismay and mouth the word "three."

Julie put her hand over her mouth in terror as she read the words on the page: "Read the questions in order to shake the tree. Who will fall out? Just wait and see. When you hear a bell ring, remove the next hood. Do as you're told; you better be good. I will be watching until the end of the game. Don't leave early or you'll be to blame. The stage is set in a room called the galley. There's only ten minutes until the grand finale. If you're late, there will be no debate. The people in the stands will have blood on their hands."

"Hurry, we have to go," said Julie.

The group followed Julie out of the room. I held on to Crystal's arm. I whispered, "This wasn't part of the plan. Did you do this?"

She whispered back, "No, someone has completely taken over the game."

"That's what I was afraid of." I had a really bad feeling that something really bad was about to happen. This is my life we are talking about, so it's a given.

Crystal and I followed the frantic group down the steps. When we all reached the base of the Island, the group stopped briefly to figure out a plan. Next to the stairwell that led down into the ship, we found a poster behind plexiglass that showed the layout of the vessel.

Chameleon pointed to a room on the second deck. "This is the galley and mess hall just above sea level."

"If there's a kitchen on this ship, I'll find it," said Feed Bag. He led the way down all four levels of steps.

Feed Bag was like a dog on the hunt for a bone. Without making one wrong turn, we ended up in front of the double doors to the mess hall and galley. We knew we were at the right place when we saw the note on the door.

After what happened last time, I let Julie open it. She stepped forward out of the group and pulled down the envelope that was taped to the door. Julie took one look at it, then she shoved it into my hands in an agitated way.

"Apparently, it's The Payton Show," she said.

I read the note: "Payton, you are the moderator. Only you are allowed on the stage. Give envelope number one to Julie. Pass the rest of the numbered enveloped out by name to each player. Have them take a seat in the front row. Follow the rules, or else."

"Or else, what?" asked Max.

"You don't want to find out. Trust me," I told him.

After the last envelope was handed out, I turned to address the group. "Everybody ready for this?" My answer was fifteen blank stares.

"It's showtime," I said. With a metal door handle in each hand, I flung the doors open and stepped inside.

***

Is everyone ready for the plot twist of the century? I want you to think about everything I have ever said from the very beginning. I will refresh your memory for those slackers sniffing paint fumes.

1. "What am I? Some say monster, others say master. Does that make me the sick, twisted individual who walks among you freely, day or night? Or the genius who thrives on being the last person you would ever expect?" That is the end all and be all of questions. The Answer: All of the above.

2. "Most of these people can keep secrets, deep dark secrets except for this one bitch. She has been poking around asking too many questions lately. This leaves me with no choice. I have to make a public example out of Payton Richardson. This time it will not look like an accident. It will be a creative masterpiece." I worded this very carefully. I never said that the bitch was Payton. You just assumed it was her. I said that I had to make a public example out of her. I would say that task has been managed well. Could someone else be the bitch asking too many questions?

3. "When Vivian showed up, I was in your bedroom with you, Payton. Right now, you are scared of her, Payton. You should be scared of me. I am going to do despicable things. You can count on it. You got lucky when you went out the window. You could have hid with me in the closet." Was I really in the closet? I never said I was in there. I just made an inference.

4. "For now, just know that I am watching. I am always watching." How could I be watching her every move?

5. *"I am the monster in your head. Can you feel me under your skin? Can you feel me creeping into your every thought? Soon, I will consume you." This one just slaps you right across the face.*

6. *"I am here in the bathroom with you, Payton. The steam is thick. You cannot see me, but you know I am here with you. You can feel me. I know that you can. The floor creaks outside the shower door. You pause briefly. What a rush. This game keeps getting better. I am going to disappear for now with the steam." I did not say that I was making the floor creak outside the shower. You are all so gullible.*

7. *"Rough morning, Payton? Could you look any guiltier? One anonymous call from me, and the police could link you to the other crime scene. Your fingerprints are all over the faucet handle. Your DNA is on that chip and the smiley face carved into the tree. Your footprints concealed mine perfectly. It is as if I was never there, only you. But if they lock you up now, my game and my fun will be over. We cannot have that. The game must continue." Just think about the phrase, "It is as if I was never there, only you." That one could go either way.*

8. *"I rode to work with you today. You should always check your back seat." This one is classic. I never said I was in the backseat. I just suggested you should look there. Another ingenious play on words. I am sure you all fell for that one too.*

9. *"Everything in your life happens for a reason, Payton. I am that reason." Payton controls her own destiny.*

10. *"Just out of curiosity, do you think I want Payton for her mind or her body?" Oh, that is a good one. Just let that one bounce around in your brain for a bit. I am sure the answer will come to you.*

11. *"The foursome and I are pushing you to step up your game. Are you going to pick up the pace, or do you mind if I play through?" I am basically asking Payton if I should take over for her. It is probably not the first or the last time I will use the game of golf to my advantage.*

12. *"I hear everything that is going on, Payton, so watch yourself." I feel like I am beating a dead horse. Think people!*

13. *"There is nowhere you can hide from me." This is getting exhausting. Have you figured it out yet?*

14. "Congratulations! You fell for the oldest magic trick in the book—misdirection. Can I get that standing ovation now? I am the master." This phrase should have set off red flags and had you questioning everything I have ever said.

Now that I have refreshed your memory, I will ask you again. Are you ready for the plot twist of the century?

The jaw dropping moment … the drum roll … could I be Payton? I will let that sink in. Curtain please.

CHAPTER TWENTY-TWO

The large expansive mess hall was filled with brown cafeteria-style tables. The left side of the room held the dark galley. The right side of the room was where the restrooms were located. On the far end of the room, a small, dark stage with a black fabric skirt was set up for entertainment or possibly a church service. Today, it was the scene of someone's sick, twisted game.

The crew walked behind me as we made our way up to the table closest to the stage. They all took their seats and sat quietly. I walked around to the steps on the left side of the stage. I took a deep breath. Soon, game show host will be added to my resume.

The lights on the stage flicked on when I walked up the steps. Four hooded figures in metal chairs faced the audience. Large, black velvet hoods covered each person from the chest up. The head coverings made it impossible to tell who they were. A few initial gasps escaped from the crowd, but the rest of them were silent, probably in shock from the weird scene that stood before them.

The bell rang, signaling Round One. I walked over to the first chair on the left and slowly removed the hood, stepping out of the way so everyone could see who it was.

Julie cried out in relief, "Brad!" She stood up, wanting to go to him.

The bell rang repeatedly, almost in a violent manner.

I motioned with a hand gesture for her to sit back down. The bell ringing stopped.

A smile formed as my eyes met Brad's. It was a mutual understanding of relief. For now, we were all safe. Brad's appearance was a bit disheveled: his dress shirt and pants were wrinkled, his hair was a mess, and the crack on his swollen lip was now scabbed over. His stay at Casa Paramount had not been enjoyable.

It was Julie's turn to ask the first question. I could tell she wanted to stand again but chose to stay seated. From my spot on the stage, I noticed four cables running across the stage floor, one attached to each chair. I feared what these would be used for. Deep down, I knew the answer.

Julie opened her envelope: "Brad, do you still want to marry me?"

Brad looked back at her with a loving gaze. "Yes, I would be honored if you would be my wife."

Julie seemed relieved with his answer.

"It's my turn," said Chameleon, eager to play. He opened his card and began to read: "You seem to have a lot of extra money lately. You have remodeled your home, bought a new truck, and recently took a trip to Mexico. How do you explain this on a cop's salary? Were you in cahoots with Rod Huntly and Kurt Meriwether?" Chameleon sat in his chair with his arms crossed in a confrontational manner.

"Look," said Brad in a defensive tone, "I had nothing to do with those two degenerates. Some of the money came from my investments. My great aunt left me a substantial amount when she passed away last year and my fiancé, Julie, was kind enough to help pay for the kitchen remodel for the home we were about to share." He nodded his head in a "take that" fashion.

Chameleon leaned back in his chair, signaling that he wanted more information. He didn't buy Brad's answer.

"I'm not a dirty cop and I resent the accusation, you little prick."

Brad immediately shook and winced with pain. It was obvious to me that he had just been given a few volts of electricity. The shock treatment was meant to keep the contestants in line.

Chameleon smirked ever so slightly. Brad and I saw it, but no one else seemed to notice.

"Hey, I'm just the messenger, dude," said Chameleon.

Teagan was contestant number three. She opened her card and giggled. This was not going to be good for Brad, I could tell.

Teagan cleared her throat. She was ready to drop the bomb. Her expression was downright giddy as she began: "Why did I find Payton's thong in the kitchen?"

"What?" Julie looked at Brad with daggers in her eyes. She immediately threw a knifey look my way too.

"It was before we were engaged," said Brad in his defense. "We just made out. We didn't have sex, I swear."

Julie was giving him the cold shoulder by turning away from him in her chair and refused to make eye contact with either of us.

"That's no way to treat your lady," said Chameleon.

"You stay out of this," said Brad, who was obviously upset by Julie's reaction.

"What about the time I caught you and my sister in your truck?" stated Luke.

Brad rolled his eyes. He was in big trouble now.

Julie swung around in her chair to face him again. "When was this? Were we engaged?"

"Look, Jules," said Brad, trying to smooth things over. "It was a long time ago. Tim had just died, we were emotional."

"When?" Julie demanded a better answer.

"You remember the night you called me about the toilet overflowing, and I had to go deal with the hole in the—"

His body twitched from being shocked.

"For Crissake, we didn't have sex," he blurted out quickly before he could be zapped again.

Julie turned to me for a reply.

"What he said. We never had sex."

Julie looked away from us again. Brad looked at me and managed to say thank you with his eyes without getting a jolt of electricity.

It was Lisa's turn now. She opened her envelope, read it, and looked over at me. I held my breath, waiting for the explosion.

Lisa stood up to read her card: "Do you still have feelings for Payton?" she asked in a shaky voice. She knew this was going to be bad no matter what he said.

My eyes looked over to meet Brad's before he could speak. Julie spun around in her chair again to hear him answer. I gave him a quick nod of my head to signal him that it was okay to say what he needed to, regardless of my feelings. Lisa sat back down awaiting his answer.

"No, I don't have feelings for Payton." He was immediately zapped hard. Brad clenched his teeth and rode out the pain with utter defiance. Brad started again after he caught his breath. "Once upon a time," Brad paused to look at me, "Payton was the love of my life." He turned to look at Julie. "When I met Julie, we connected in a new, exciting way." He looked back at me. "Part of me will always love Payton, but…" He paused again and took a deep breath. "My future is with Julie, that's if she will still have me."

Well, that stung a bit. Part of me held out hope for some sort of reconciliation.

Chameleon seemed equally disappointed by the unhappy expression on his face.

Julie took a second to think before she answered. This caused a great deal of tension in the room.

"Yes, yes, I will still marry you," she said finally.

Brad had a ginormous smile of relief on his face until Crystal interjected her own question.

"Did you kill Streak?" she asked out of turn.

All of the boys sat up straight in their chairs, waiting for his answer.

Brad looked around the crowd as he spoke. "No, I never killed that boy."

Everyone seemed okay with his answer, even the person running the game believed him.

The bell dinged, starting the next round. I was trying to pinpoint where the sound was coming from. It came from somewhere overhead. Most likely the intercom system, which wasn't good news for us finding the game's creator. They could be anywhere on the ship.

I walked over behind the second chair and slowly pulled the hood off. As soon as I saw his shoulders and wavy brown locks, I knew who it was. I was happy to see him but horrified that he had to hear what Brad had to say. It was my hotter-than-hot, still smoldering ex-flame Dylan.

It was my turn to start the round. I walked around Brad's chair, so I could see Dylan's face.

"Hey," I said to him as we made eye contact. "Sorry, I—"

Dylan's teeth clenched. He was getting a shock. I immediately flipped my envelope open so it would stop. It did. I looked over the question. It was a good one; one I had wanted to ask him for a while now.

I stood before Dylan and did my best to make eye contact while I read my question: "The night Stephani came into the restaurant and stole your recipe book; you claimed you had to drive her car back from her place because she took the keys to your truck. How did the lot get half-plowed if you didn't have your truck?" I stared at him with raised eyebrows hoping to finally get an honest answer to one whooper of a question.

"It was Stephani. She did it. She plowed the lot."

"Why would she do that?" I asked. It didn't make any sense.

"At her place, when we were fighting over my keys, I told her I needed my truck to plow the parking lot. She just laughed at me through the bathroom door and said, 'good luck with that.' That is when I left. She reported her car stolen and then plowed the lot sometime the next morning to wreck my alibi.

That sounded like something that evil exercise freak would do to get back at him. "Thank you for your honesty, Dylan." Everyone seemed satisfied with his answer.

I motioned to the next person to ask their question. Blond Ambition stood up. The game creator allowed it. He opened his envelope in a very straight-to-business way. I was almost expecting him to say "hear-ye, hear-ye."

Blond Ambition held the card out in front of him with both hands: "Why are you helping Stephani?" he asked in an official manner. After he was finished reading his question, he took his seat.

"We have a long history together. We've known each other since we were kids. When she gets into trouble, I feel like I need to help her out of it."

"Even if it's something criminal?" I asked him. It just slipped out.

"I've never seen Stephani do anything criminal. She always has this way of getting me to believe her and help her."

"Yeah, it's called tits and ass," said my brother in a mocking tone. The boys all laughed, even Brad.

Dylan looked at me. "I'll try to be better in the future, I promise." He seemed honest and sincere.

Feed Bag stood up. "It's my turn." He read over the question. "Good one," he said to himself before he started: "What is the secret ingredient in your chicken wing recipe?"

The boys all sat up at attention again. This was riveting stuff for them.

"I can't tell you that. It's my secret recipe."

Dylan got a huge shock.

"I won't," he said again, being defiant.

They jolted him again. Dylan fought through the pain. Why was he being so stubborn over a recipe?

"It belongs to me," proclaimed Dylan. He was fighting for what he cared about.

Zaaaaap!

As soon as he could unclench his teeth, he muttered the words: "Cajun seasoning."

"I could see that," said Feed Bag. "Thank you, Dylan." Feed Bag took his seat.

Dylan gave him an exasperated look.

Crystal stood up out of turn. "Where is the recipe book now?"

"It is in a safe place," Dylan answered. He did not let on that I knew where it was. He was trusting me that it was still safe.

This answer did not make Crystal happy. "C'mon, zap him! I want more information."

No further harm came to Dylan at this moment. The game's creator was happy with his answer.

Thirteen stayed seated when he read his question: "How and why is your step-mother Vivian involved?"

"That's easy. Vivian works for the Richardson's as their housekeeper. She got me my job at the restaurant. I really appreciate them giving me a chance to hone my cooking skills."

"Anything else?" I asked Dylan.

"Vivian is just looking out for me. She's trying to keep me safe."

"Did Vivian attack Payton with a knife?" asked Amber out of turn.

"No, absolutely not," said Dylan without hesitation.

To me, he looked like he was telling the truth.

Lily stood up. It appeared to now be a free-for-all. "How were you the only one to survive. Why didn't you drown like the others? Why didn't you die in Larson Park?"

"First of all, I don't remember how I got there." He paused before continuing. "Apparently, I somehow drove the car to the gate and climbed over it. I passed out on the shore of the lake where you and Payton found me. I'm sure I'm still alive because the lake was still frozen. Then there's the fact that you gave me some sort of herbal supplement to jumpstart my heart."

"You're welcome," Lily said before sitting down.

"I'm still confused on why I was wearing different pants. And where did the black cord I found in my pocket come from?" added Dylan.

"Okay, I'm done," announced Lily, trying to signal the next round.

"Can anyone answer that?" Dylan stared at the crowd of stunned faces. No one said a word. The entire group was dead quiet.

I could see his urgency on the matter. There were still unanswered questions for him. I had a few of my own. I really wanted to ask him about us. What did we mean to each other? That wasn't anything I wanted to discuss in front of the crew. The thought of being rejected twice was unbearable. Maybe we could have a private moment. I hated that we had unresolved issues.

***

Round three is about to explode. I cannot wait for you to see this.

CHAPTER TWENTY-THREE

The bell rang again starting the third round. That was my cue to remove another hood. This time, I stood in front of the person wearing the hood before pulling it off.

The hood slid away from his slender frame, revealing his identity. I backed up slowly in shock, almost falling off the stage. Gasps from the crowd brought me back into a more coherent reality. I found myself looking at the face of a friend I lost yesterday. It was Brent Biggerton. He was alive.

"But we all saw your body…" I said bewildered.

"Your mom and my dad are gonna kick your ass," said Brad. He was immediately shocked for interrupting. Brad shook from an oversized jolt. After the electricity subsided, he glared at Brent for making his life more difficult than it needed to be.

Lily stood up right away with her numbered card in her hand. She ripped into it like a kid on Christmas. Her Gothic darkness melted away for just a second: "How are you still alive?" she asked with honest concern. She was genuinely happy to see her friend.

Julie stood up out of turn. "You jackass, you wrecked my wedding."

Brad took the brunt of her defiance by taking a jolt for her outburst.

Julie seemed horrified that she had caused Brad pain. She found her seat and remained silent. Her bottom lip trembled, and a slow-moving tear rolled down her cheek as she sat perfectly still.

"How are you still alive?" Lily repeated.

"Don't anyone else get mad," he started. "After Lily and Payton visited me the night Payton left town, I felt like I was being followed. I figured it had something to do with the LoJack we found in Payton's purse. Even after I arrived down here in Texas to put our plan into motion, I noticed a car following me. The best thing for me was to be dead and hunt them from the shadows."

"Where did the body come from?" asked Wolfman.

"It came from the morgue. I didn't kill anyone," he explained in a pleading tone.

"What happened to his head?" asked Chameleon, looking for some gruesome details.

"Unfortunately, his head and hands had to be sawed off to make mortification embalming look believable." The crowd turned different shades of green at the thought of what he had to do to pull off his illusion.

"Dude, that's cold," said Chameleon.

"He was wearing your clothes," stated Lily.

"Yeah, my bad," said Brent. "The only reason I did it was to save myself."

"You could have given us a 'heads up'," I said to him. I was upset he didn't trust us enough to let us in on his plan.

"I gave Jeremy the notes to give to each of you. Were you able to figure out the puzzle?"

"Yes," said Lily, "but how about next time you just text me that you're not dead."

"Who is Jeremy?" I asked. "How do you know him?"

"I came down here early to get a job and scope out the place. I worked with him at the beach bar. How is Jeremy?"

"Dead," I said. "Eaten by an alligator right in front of me."

"You should have seen her. She was a mess. There was blood everywhere," said Max.

"Sorry to hear that," said Brent.

Luke stood up. "My turn," he said in the pissy mood of a jealous boyfriend. He ripped apart his envelope and seemed very satisfied with his question: "What is your relationship with Lily?" My brother stood with his arms across his chest, waiting for an answer.

"Does it really say that?" I asked.

"It says, 'How do you know Lily?' I put my own spin on it," he said in a cocky tone.

Brent cleared his throat. "I'm her friend." He immediately received a jolt of electricity. "I'm her tattoo artist." He received a second jolt. "Both are true," Brent said without getting zapped.

"Where did you meet?" asked Luke.

"C'mon, Luke, leave him alone. He answered your question. We're just friends," pleaded Lily.

"We met on one of those chat rooms," Brent confessed.

"Do you two go on dates?" asked Luke, prying for more details.

"Honestly, Luke, we're just friends. The answer to your question is no," said Brent.

This seemed to pacify my brother. He sat down. It still left the big question of why Lily had been sneaking off. I was going to ask her that soon. She was hiding something important. I could feel it.

The Singe stood up. "I think I lost my envelope." He felt his pockets. "Never mind, I found it." He did a drum roll on the table with his index and middle fingers. "I request the answer to this question: 'Brent, do you know who put the LoJack in Payton's purse?' " The Singe chuckled at his own witty attempt at humor.

That was a good question. I looked at Brent hoping to get a straight answer.

"No, I have no idea, but I have my suspicions." Brent added. He was just about to open his mouth when Lily spoke up.

"It was me," she said reluctantly. All eyes were on Lily.

"You?" I was shocked. "I thought it was Brad."

"Hey," said Brad in protest, but I ignored him.

"Why?" I asked Lily. I walked across the stage, so I was closer to her.

"Because you wouldn't include me or tell me where you were going. I actually thought you might be the one everyone was looking for."

"Me? That's crazy." This just took an interesting turn.

"Anyways, that's why I tried to throw your purse away. I actually did put it in the dumpster behind Brent's shop because I was afraid my fingerprints were on it."

"It's okay, Lily, I forgive you."

I walked back over by Brent, waiting for the bell.

Shoes stood up. I must have miscounted. He opened his envelope. "Did you figure out what the ruins on the back of the Key to Immortality means?"

I could tell Brent didn't want to say anything, even if he knew. It was the answer to eternal life after all. It was also the words Brent tattooed between the triangles on my tramp stamp.

"I haven't figured that out yet," he replied.

He was zapped right away. Even I knew he had figured it out by his expression.

"It's a riddle. I don't know the answer," he explained. He was zapped again, hard. He let out a guttural cry. "Aaaaaah!" As soon as the electricity stopped, Brent spilled his guts. "Okay, here's the riddle: 'Conceived in water, born in air.' I swear I don't know what it means."

Brent braced himself for another shock. He didn't get one. Odd, maybe the creator of the game already knows the answer.

I looked over at Chameleon. The wheels in his brain were humming along. If anyone could figure it out, he could.

Crystal stood up. It was her turn. I felt sorry for Brent. She opened her envelope in a smug, reporter-out-for-blood way: "Do you know where the Key to Immortality is?" She asked in a firm voice.

Brent looked her in the eye. "No, I do not." He stared back at her in a purely loathing way.

"You're not going to zap him?" she said, directing it at the game's creator. "He's lying. He has to know." Crystal walked past the boys on her way to the stage. She grabbed the can of pop out of The Singe's hand just as he was about to take a drink.

"Hey, that was my last Dew," he blurted with anger in his voice.

Crystal suddenly threw the can at Brent's head. He doubled over in pain.

"You bitch," screamed Brent. "I'm telling you the truth. I don't know where it is."

"Sit down, Crystal, before you get us all killed," demanded Brad.

"Make me," said Crystal with a smirk. "Good luck tied to that chair."

The lights in the mess hall instantly went out. I heard Teagan, Lisa, Julie, and The Singe, who sounded like a twelve-year-old girl, scream in the pitch blackness. The lights flicked back on.

"Is everyone okay?" I asked instinctively.

Crystal took her seat with a rebellious thud. "I'm not done," she said being obstinate.

The bell rang four times, signaling the fourth and final round.

I stepped over to the last hooded figure. After the shock of seeing Brent, I braced myself for another doozy.

The soft, velvet of the hood felt oddly comforting in my hand. The black fabric slowly slid off the head of the fourth player. The room started to spin. It was hard to breathe. I could feel the darkness closing in. The aperture of light narrowed and just like that, it disappeared.

"Payton. Payton." I could hear my name. All I had to do was open my eyes. I didn't want to. My dream state was safe. I liked it here. Just five more minutes…

"Payton." It was louder this time. I opened my eyes to see my friends crowded by the edge of the stage. They were staring at me. And staring at him.

"You fainted," said Julie just in case I hadn't figured that out.

I sat up in time to see Brad leaning forward in his chair to talk to him. "Nice to see you, buddy. So, are you FBI or CIA?"

"CIA," Tim said proudly.

Brad was talking to Tim Kline. Officer Tim Kline. My police friend that died of a blood clot after being shot. Oh. My. God. It was Tim!

"How? What? This is impossible." My brain was on emotional overload.

"It's nice to see you too, Payton." Tim laughed at my amazement. "Thanks for the black eye, by the way. Did you and Lily think I was a shark wearing goggles?" He laughed until he was shocked for the first time.

Lily stood up. "That was you?"

"Yes, I was doing surveillance on the Chaos party."

"In the water?" said Lily.

"I'm a retired Navy Seal."

"Cool," said The Singe. "He's a badass."

It was time to resume the game. I got back to my feet and cued Max that it was his turn. Max opened his envelope: "How are you still alive?"

That was the question of the day. We all gawked at Tim, waiting for his story.

"I'm assuming you want to know more than 'I faked my own death.' After I was shot, it was clear that I didn't know who I could trust. My best option was to have Dr. VonHoberg help me with the paperwork and cause of death that would seem believable. Apparently, you all bought it by the look on your faces."

"So, let me get this straight," I said to Tim. "All those times I called Dr. Parks because I thought I saw you; you were actually there?"

"Yes, I was trying to let you know that first night when Nick showed up. I figured it was better to stay completely undercover after that."

I took a deep cleansing breath. I'm not crazy. Good to know. "Do you have any lab reports for me?" I asked Tim.

"You're okay with me telling everyone?" he asked.

"Go for it." I told him. I had nothing to hide.

"The DNA on the cord found in Dylan's pants belongs to a Lillian Boman."

"Liar," shouted Lily. "It was planted." She said to defend herself.

I looked at Lily. I wanted to believe her. Dylan gave Lily a look of hatred.

"There's no way," said Luke, sticking up for Lily. "She's no killer."

"Thanks, honey," said Lily. Lily patted Luke's thigh in a romantic way.

"Maybe you should try less eyeliner goth girl," said Crystal.

"I said it's not me, Crystal."

"Like I trust anything you say, you bitch," she directed her comment back at Lily.

"Hey," I said. "I think we can still be civil here."

"I'm just reporting what I found," stated Tim. He paused, waiting to see if he was about to be zapped again.

"What about the urine samples I gave you," I asked, hoping it would shed some new light on the case.

"Both you and Dylan had traces of GHB in your urine. Streak's hair sample also showed trace amounts of GHB."

"I told you it was GHB, Payton. Remember?" asked Chameleon.

"He did tell me that," I said, confirming our conversation. I should have listened to him back then.

"The lab also discovered something extra in Payton's urine sample," said Tim.

"What did they find?" I was more than anxious to hear his answer.

"They found a member of the nightshade family. The lab couldn't narrow it down any further than that."

"What's that?" I asked. "I've never heard of such a thing."

"It's an ancient herb," said Chameleon. "Often used in shamanistic rituals and witchcraft. It was most likely Belladonna. Whoever gave it to you was probably trying to extract information, not kill you."

"That's good and bad to know." What do I know that anyone would want?

"I concur with his deduction," said Brent, "but I am leaning more towards Datura or Mandrake."

Tim looked at both boys with inquiring eyes.

"Relax, Special Agent Tim, I'm a science geek," said Chameleon. "I read a lot. I'm not some grand warlock."

"And I have a degree in medieval history," said Brent.

The bell rang for us to continue the game.

Amber stood up, ready to move on. She opened her envelope: "Who shot me?" Amber was clearly upset by this question. She was visibly shaking.

We all looked to Tim for an answer.

"It was Kurt Meriwether," said Tim. The crowd nodded in agreement with his answer.

"Ballistics didn't confirm that," said Brad. "We just assumed."

"I just heard the shots," said Tim. "Kurt shot me, why not Amber too?"

Wolfman stood up. It was his turn to ask the last official question. He opened his envelope: "Who else was there the night Tim and Amber were shot?"

"Amber and I were there, obviously," said Tim. "I saw Rod and Kurt before I was shot."

"I can probably answer that question better," I stated, taking over the conversation. "I found Lily unconscious on the floor, Julie in a box in the storeroom, and the Bald-headed Man aka Agent Smith outside the patio door. Oh yeah, the police were outside in the driveway by a squad car. I saw Brad, Rex, The Chief, and Matt. I also saw Lisa and Teagan in the woods outside.

"We were looking for you," said Lisa. She was upset about the possible implication. "We didn't shoot anyone."

"It's okay, I know," I said to reassure her.

"Wait a minute," said Crystal. "I didn't know those two were on the property. We need to re-examine this fact."

"Crystal, you were there too," I said, confronting her. "Your purse and your shoe were found in the bathroom with Amber. Were you there with Agent Smith? I've been wanting to ask you that for like … ever."

The whole group leered at Crystal, waiting for her to answer. She approached the stage.

"I wasn't there. They were planted. The night I met Agent Smith, I was looking around behind the college, someone stole my purse and my shoes out of my car."

"You never told me that," I said back to her response.

"Ask Smith, he knows all about it. He'll answer all your questions."

"Where is Smith?" I asked her.

"I don't know. He's not answering my texts or calls."

"I haven't seen him since this afternoon at the Dinosaur Sand Box."

Crystal came right up to the stage. "Well, I haven't seen him since this morning. You were probably the last person to have seen—" She looked down at the floor. "I'm stepping on something."

Teagan, who was sitting the closest, started screaming. "Is that a hand?"

Everyone that was seated around Teagan jumped up. I went to the edge of the stage to look over the side. "Someone lift up the stage skirt!" I yelled. I jumped down off the stage. Everyone except Crystal moved back.

Before I could grab the fabric myself, Crystal pulled the pleated skirt up enough to expose the body beneath. His gray, fixed eyes stared back at us.

I looked up at Brad and Tim. "It's Agent Smith. He's been stabbed."

Crystal and I stepped away from each other. I climbed back up on the stage and stood by Tim.

"Crystal, what did you do?" I was actually accusing her of murder.

"I didn't do this. What did you do, Payton?" asked Crystal.

Now she was accusing me … me of all people. I needed to explain before things got out of hand. "Look everybody, the plan that Crystal, Agent Smith, and myself came up with was supposed to be to get us all together to catch someone in a lie. It was supposed to get us closer to the truth. No one was supposed to get hurt or killed. Clearly someone else is in charge of this shit show. I'm sorry. The killer should be behind bars, not tormenting us."

"You guys did this?" asked Tim.

"Not this," I said, looking at Brad, Dylan, Brent, and Tim. "Someone took over the game in the beginning. I should have gone to the police right away, but they said no cops."

"I would like to bring an important fact in this case to everyone's attention," said Crystal. "During my research, I discovered an interesting fact about the first victim from Twin Valley. His name was Andrew Thompson. He was originally from River Bend. Guess who went to junior prom with him?"

"I didn't go to prom with him," I said in my defense. I looked around the room at all the suspicious glares.

"I saw the yearbook pictures from the dance," said Crystal, trying to make her point.

I looked over at my brother. "Help me out here, Luke, would ya?"

"My sister didn't go with Andrew," said Luke. "She went with his twin brother Adam."

"Are you guys sure?" Crystal was skeptical.

"I think I would know who I was dancing and making out with," I said.

"Maybe that's your alibi," said Crystal. Crystal raised her eyebrows, waiting for my answer.

I could tell by the look on her face that she didn't believe me. "My alibi? What's that supposed to mean?" I stood on the stage and put my hands on my hips in a confrontational manner.

" 'It couldn't be me, I would know the difference'," said Crystal. "It's all very *Basic Instinct* of you, Payton."

"Hey," said Max, "this would all make a great movie. Who wants to work on the screenplay with me?" He looked at his friends for encouragement. They all raised their hands. "We could shoot the movie and YouTube it."

Crystal immediately became enraged. "This is my story, damn it! Mine! These murders are the crime of the century. No one is stealing this from me. NO ONE! Understand?" Crystal was looking guiltier with each spoken word. Her eyes bulged. Her nostrils flared.

"Crystal…you need to calm down." I'm sure I had a terrified look on my face. I was trying my best to keep my cool.

"Untie me, Payton," said Tim, sensing that something bad was coming.

"Me too," said Brad, who was also on the same page as Tim.

I had Tim almost untied when Crystal suddenly pulled a gun from her purse. "Stop what you're doing."

I froze in place next to Tim. I looked over at Julie to get her attention. I did my best to nonchalantly show her my thumb and index finger like a gun.

She shook her head no. "Sorry Payton, I thought I was going on my honeymoon." Julie had left her gun at home.

"Shut up," yelled Crystal. She was pacing around in front of the stage.

She pointed the gun at me. "It has to be you, Payton. It's the only thing that makes sense. You are connected to all four crime scenes. You were the last one to see Smith."

I put my hands up out of instinct. "Crystal, don't do this. It's not me."

"Give me the earrings," demanded Crystal. I carefully pulled my right hand out of the air. I reached in my dress and took them out of my bra. Next, I slowly set them down on the stage floor. She grabbed them and put them in her pocket.

"I'm going to be a hero. I might even win a Pulitzer out of this," Crystal's eyes went soulless like no one was inside her head. Her index finger moved by the trigger.

"Oh my god, she's gonna do it!" I screamed. There was no time to duck out of the way.

The first shot whizzed by my ear, hitting something in the kitchen. A loud noise boomed behind me. She must have hit a gas line.

Everything that was happening in the room went into slow motion. Pandemonium filled the space around me. People were hiding under the tables or running for cover.

One of the boys, I think it was The Singe, yelled, "The kitchen's on fire!"

Just as Crystal's next shot left her gun, Tim stood up in front of me. We both fell over backwards with his chair landing between us. From the floor of the stage, I saw Crystal grab Amber's arm.

"Not me again, pick someone else," said Amber. "I don't want to die."

"Shut up," said Crystal. She put the gun to Amber's head and led her to the double doors.

Julie ran to Brad's side to untie him. I managed to get to my feet. Crystal and Amber went through the double doors. I ran over to the doors and pushed on them. Something was wedged in the handles, not allowing it to open. The room was starting to fill with smoke. We needed to get out of here, fast.

"Payton! Payton!" Brad was calling my name.

When I turned around, I saw Brent and Dylan standing next to Brad and Julie on the stage. Tim laid motionless on his side next to his chair.

***

If you want cake, you need to break a few eggs.

CHAPTER TWENYY-FOUR

Trying to pry the door open was no longer the most important thing in my life—Tim was. I ran frantically back to the stage. I stopped at the edge of the fabric skirt directly in front of where Tim laid motionless. His eyes were open and fixed. The t-shirt he was wearing was stained with blood in the center of the chest.

My instincts told me to climb up on the stage and try to help him. I had one knee up on the stage when I felt a hand on my shoulder. I looked up to see Brad standing over me. He had a hopeless look on his face. "Payton, I'm sorry. He's gone. We need to get out of here," said Brad.

"Come on, Payton," said Dylan. He knelt and touching my hand. "I'm with Brad. We're all going to die if we don't get off the ship."

I hated to admit it, they were both right. "Okay," I said. I took one last look at Tim before I pulled my leg off the stage. There was only a split second to mentally thank my friend for saving my life. When I turned back around, Lily had approached our group.

"Have you seen Luke?" She inquired. "I can't find him anywhere." She had a petrified look about her. "I thought he was under one of the tables, he's not."

I looked around the smoky room. "Luke. Luke, where are you?" I called to my brother.

"I'm over here by the door," he answered back through the smoke.

The door that Crystal had jammed shut, opened suddenly. A hooded figure stepped inside the doorway.

"Luke, look out," I screamed. I pointed at the figure that was a few feet behind him. The figure grabbed Luke and pulled him through the door. It slammed shut. Lily and I ran over to the door. We both reefed on the handles with all our might. It wouldn't open more than an inch or so.

"They must have jammed something back into the handles," said Lily. She rattled the door out of frustration. "Shit."

Brad waved everyone over to the group. "Guys, over here. Hurry!"

"There must be another way out of this room," suggested Brent.

"Let's try down here," I said, pointing down to the other end of the mess hall.

The smoke was getting thicker by the minute. We pulled our shirts up over our noses and mouths to protect us from the smoke. The group moved in unison across the room. At the end of the mess hall, we found a single door.

"This has to be the way out," said Brad. I could hear the optimism in his voice. He grabbed the handle and twisted. "It's locked." The optimism was gone. He looked deflated.

"Lily, can you pick the lock?" I asked.

"No, I left my tools out in the box like a good girl."

"Back to the other door," said Chameleon. "We can use our combined weight like a battling ram to break through whatever Crystal used to block the door." It was an epic free-for-all scramble for survival until then. When we got to the double doors, no one hesitated. We all ran at it at full speed. "Lean into it with your shoulder," he shouted.

"C'mon, show me the money," was Max's battle cry right before we all made contact with the door.

The doors burst open on the first try. "Jackpot," shouted Chameleon. A few of us stumbled when the doors gave way, but no one fell. We removed our face coverings and continued to run up four flights of stairs. I coughed several times to clear my lungs of any residual smoke. A few other people did also. It was a mad dash to the surface to save ourselves.

When we all reached the flight deck, we headed to the nearest railing to see if we could find Crystal and Amber, or Luke and the hooded villain. From the railing, we could see Crystal and Amber below. There was no sign of Luke or his kidnapper.

Crystal laid on her back on the blacktop. Amber sat near her with her knees pulled up to her chest. She was rhythmically rocking back and forth.

"Luke," I called out desperately to find my brother.

Lily joined in. "Luke, where are you?"

There was no reply. We all looked around the flight deck for him. There was no sign of him anywhere. Luke was gone.

"I'm worried, Payton. Where is your brother?" asked Lily. She was visibly shaken but more than the rest of us. I could tell that she had great concern for my brother's safety.

I grabbed her arm. "We'll find him. I promise." This was a promise I intended to keep.

The group headed down the gangplank to find out what happened with Amber and Crystal. We ran up to them until we got a closer look at the extent of Crystal's injuries. The girls in the group slowed down while the boys all rushed over to see the carnage. Crystal's normal pristine clothing was askew and covered with dirt, blood, and road debris. Her right leg was broken and twisted to one side. Crystal's neck and chest area had a clear tire print running across it. Her windpipe was crushed. She had died a gruesome death, most likely choking on her own blood.

Shoes took off his zippered sweatshirt and placed it over Crystal's face and torso. He did it to spare anyone else from seeing her gray fixed eyes staring into the heavens. "I used to watch her every night on the news while I ate my supper," he said like he had just lost a friend.

I turned my attention to Amber who was still rocking back and forth. Her arms were wrapped around her legs. She had an expressionless stare like she was deep in thought or in another dimension in time. Teagan and Lisa were kneeling next to her. They were trying to coax her out of her trance.

"Amber, what happened to you and Crystal?" asked Lisa in a soft comforting voice. She didn't answer Lisa. She was still in a state of shock.

Brad walked over to her. He grabbed her under the arms and stood her up. He held onto her shoulders while he interrogated her. "Amber, snap out of it," he said. She returned a blank stare. He shook her firm but not too aggressively. "What the hell happened to you two?"

This seemed to do the trick. She recovered quickly after Brad got a little rough with her. "They killed her. They purposely missed me and hit her with the car." She burst into tears. She pointed at Crystal's dead body. "Crystal flew over the hood of the dark blue sedan and landed there on the blacktop. Then they purposely backed over her to make sure she was dead. I'm lucky to be alive." Tears continued to flow down her cheeks.

"Who is they?" asked Brad in a stern but calmer tone. He let go of her. She was alert enough to stand on her own now.

"I don't know. I'm sorry. I couldn't see their face because he or she was wearing a black hooded robe." She turned towards me. "Payton, they have Luke. I saw the hooded person shove him into the back seat of the car before the car ran her over. Crystal shot at the car several times before the car hit her. I don't know if anyone in the car was injured."

"Brad, we have to go after my brother." I was determined to find Luke. He was counting on us to save him. "Amber, which way did they go?" She pointed to the entrance of the shipyard. Lisa and Teagan put their arms around Amber, giving her a long hug. I turned back to Brad. "We need a plan to save my brother?"

Julie walked over to Brad and gave him a big hug. She was interrupting our much-needed conversation. Lily, who was near me, wasn't being shy about her disapproval. She pulled the two of them apart. "You can do that later. We need to go after Luke." Lily was direct and adamant. Her message was received loud and clear.

"We don't even know where they went," added Brad. "It's damn near impossible without any way to contact the police. And I have no idea how I would explain what happened here tonight. I don't know if you guys noticed, but we are in deep shit. People are dead, and the ship is on fire."

Dylan and Chameleon approached us. "We found my backpack over there," said Chameleon. He pointed past Crystal's body. "The bad guys must have dropped it."

"Is everything still inside?" I asked. "Maybe there is something in there we can use."

"We checked the box on the gangplank," said Chameleon. "They took all the cellphones and the purses. I can't believe they left my bag." He opened the zipper and looked inside. "Apparently, they didn't want my spare pair of underwear, my clothes, or my body spray."

"Great, they left us without phones, identification, or money," I said.

"Those clever bastards," said Chameleon. We all looked at him with disgust. "Sorry, I didn't mean it the way it sounded."

"It's okay," I told him. "You're forgiven." We needed his brain to help us find Luke.

Dylan got my attention by whispering my name with his velvety voice. He held out his hand palm up. "I found the earrings Crystal took from you. They were by her body."

I took the earrings from his outstretched hand. When I looked down at them, I could feel the blood flow out of my face. I was sure that I was as white as a ghost. I had given Crystal the wrong earrings. These were Miss Vandersloot's earrings. Is that why she was dead? Was she killed for my error? I felt awful. The only good thing out of this: We still had a bargaining chip that could save Luke.

I looked into Dylan's eyes. I was immediately sucked into the vortex of his green pools of emerald yumminess. I sighed. He started to chuckle at me. I was busted. My bad. To cover, I jumped in with meaningful heartfelt banter. "I'm sorry you got sucked into my wake of destruction … again." I said to him.

"It's nice to see you … again." He smiled.

"It's really nice to see you too." I smiled back. The warmth between us was still there and heating up by the second.

Lily pointed her finger at us. "Now you two knock it off," she protested. Lily put herself between us. "We need to find Luke. Remember?"

"You're right," I told her. "I'm sorry." Dang it though, that boy has some badass pheromones.

"I have some good news and some bad news," said Chameleon, getting our attention. "The bad news: after searching my bag again, I realized my laser tag stuff is gone." We all looked at him dumbfounded. "Wait," he said. "I have good news: They didn't take my mini walkie talkies or my shark repellent that was in my hidden pocket of my bag." He held up his hand to signal that he had more to say. "This could be good news or bad news." He reached in his bag and pulled out a white envelope. "I found this in one of the pockets." He presented me with the envelope. It was just like the others from the game. "They left this for you, Payton."

I took the envelope from him. It was addressed to me with the number seventeen on it.

"Hurry up and open it," Lily said to me. "This could be about Luke." She grabbed the envelope out of my hand.

"Hey, what the heck?" I was angry with her. I could see her urgency, but her rudeness needed to stop.

Lily read the first line to herself and handed it back to me. She had a frightened look on her face. Lily nervously scanned the area around us and stared up at the aircraft carrier.

I opened the card. The note read: "Give this note back to Payton, or else. Remember, I am always watching." I looked up from the note and looked around as well. The game's creator knew my friends almost as well as I did. The rest of the note read: "If you want to see Luke again, use the three to find me. I know you still have the earrings. Naughty girl. For that, you had to pay a price. You are also a smart girl, Payton; you will figure out what the other two things are. I know you know where to find them, use them to find us. When and if you do, you must surrender them all to me. Those are the rules. Good luck, Payton. You have until 3:00 p.m. tomorrow. Race you home."

"I think I know where they are taking Luke. They are headed back to River Bend." I gave the group my opinion.

"We need to get to the airport," said Lily. She started to walk towards the entrance.

"How are we supposed to do that without a car?" said Julie. "We can't walk there."

Lily turned around. "I have an idea," she said, "but Brad can't get all butthurt if I/we borrow those dirt bikes over there." Lily pointed over her shoulder to the two motorcycles sitting by the next boat slip. "Let's go check them out." We all followed her.

"Who's going to ride those exactly?" asked Brad. His brow was filled with serious apprehensive wrinkles.

"Lily and I are going. It makes the most sense." I said this, not wanting any debate.

"You two are not going anywhere without me," stated Brad. He had a not-open-for-discussion tone to his voice. "I'm going to catch this jackass and end this game."

"Fine," I said, agreeing with him. "Let's go, we are wasting time."

Lily was checking out the motorcycles. "The keys are missing. I'll have to hotwire the bikes." She looked at Brad for his approval.

"This just keeps getting better," said Brad sarcastically. "Just do it."

"Yeah, it does," said Max. "You guys are tons more fun than my other friends back home."

Julie grabbed Brad's arm. "I'm going too," she insisted.

Brad turned towards her. He put his hands on her shoulders. "Jules, this could be dangerous. You are staying here, honey."

Julie whispered something in Brad's ear.

"What?" asked Brad. "Really?" He looked over at Dylan. "You're up, Romeo. I hope you don't get squeamish on the back of a bike." Dylan stepped forward accepting the challenge.

"They're all set," said Lily. Both motors were idling, almost begging to be ridden. Lily hopped on one bike. I hopped on the other.

"Boys?" I asked, "Are you coming?" Dylan jumped on behind me. He put his hands around my waist. I was a happy camper.

"No," said Brad. "This isn't happening." He didn't want to ride behind Lily.

"Stop being such a pansy," said Lily. "My brother taught me how to ride. Get on if you're still coming."

"I taught Luke how to ride," I said, finding weird humor in the face of tragedy.

"Get off, Lily," said Brad. He wasn't backing down.

"Get on, Brad," Lily inched the bike forward. She was prepared to leave without him. She could care less if he came, or not. "I'm not joking, Brad." This time she moved forward about five feet.

Brad jogged up to the bike and climbed on. "Just don't get me killed," his comment directed towards Lily.

"No guarantees," Lily joked. She twisted the throttle. The engine purred.

Brad looked over his shoulder. "Chameleon," Brad said to get his attention. "See if you can get ahold of the fire department on one of those walkie talkies."

"Sure thing," he answered back. "Do you want us to stick around until they get here?"

"It's probably better if you don't," suggested Brad. "They will ask too many questions. Keep an eye on my fiancé. If anything happens to her, I'll break your legs."

"You can count on me, sir." He saluted Brad out of respect, I think. It's hard to tell with him sometimes. The Chameleon tossed a walkie talkie to me. I caught it and passed it back to

Dylan. He tucked it into the front pocket of his dark green sweatshirt.

We pulled away on the motorcycles, heading for the airport. Lily and Brad were in the lead. Dylan and I were close behind. Note to self: Riding a motorcycle in a prom dress and heels is never a good idea. I did my best to tuck it in around me, so it didn't fly up in my face.

***

Magic keys open doors to opportunity. Old metal keys are the best. They will unlock many doors before finding their way to you. These keys are sacred and will protect you from evil. But will they protect you from me?

CHAPTER TWENTY-FIVE

There was no doubt in my mind that Lily was driving like a maniac to get under Brad's skin. Dylan and I were doing our best to keep up. She and Brad were darting through traffic, passing huge semitrucks and barely squeezing between cars and buses. Brad must have been shitting his pants.

Dylan and I had a close call with a semitruck on the four-lane highway. It was changing lanes and didn't see us. The truck pushed us over onto the side of the road. Good thing we were riding a dirt bike with deep treads that held steady on the shoulder in the rocks and dirt. Dylan held onto me a little bit tighter after that, so it wasn't all bad.

"Payton. Payton. Come in, Payton," squawked on the walkie talkie in Dylan's pocket. He held on tight with one arm and held the walkie talkie to the right side of my head with the other.

"I'm here," I answered back to Blond Ambition.

"You busy?"

"Yeah, kind of … What's up?"

"We just wanted to let you know that the fire trucks made it to the ship just after we left."

"Left to where?" I asked. He had me curious.

"We'll meet you at the airport. We figured out a shortcut.

Don't leave without us."

"You guys better hurry. We just took the airport exit."

"Don't worry. We will be there."

"We are going to check the parking ramp first. We'll meet you at the terminal." I instructed.

"Got it," he said. "Over and out."

"Roger that." Who knew I was fluent in walkie talkie lingo?

Dylan put the walkie talkie back in his pocket. "Do you think we should split up to search the ramp faster?" he asked.

"We'll talk to Brad and Lily at the next stop sign to see what they think."

As we approached the airport grounds, Lily was driving closer to the speed limit. It was easier to keep up with her. When they pulled up to the stop sign, Dylan and I pulled up next to them. Lily looked normal. Brad looked a little bug-eyed.

I put my feet on the ground to steady the bike. "Lily, what's the plan? I asked. "Should we check out the parking ramp for the dark blue sedan? Dylan thought we should split up so we can cover more ground."

"The parking ramp is a waste of time," said Brad taking charge. "They won't be flying commercial with your brother. We need to look for a private plane."

"That makes sense. We will follow you guys," I said.

Lily and Brad hung a right. We followed them past the parking ramp. There was a sign that directed traffic to the left for the private terminals.

"Let the group know that we are headed to the private terminals," I said to Dylan.

"Will do," said Dylan. "Guys, do you read me? This is Dylan."

"We gotcha, good buddy. What's going on?" asked Chameleon.

"We are headed to the private terminals instead of the parking ramp."

"Okay, we just disembarked. See you in a few. Over and out."

Lily pulled over before we arrived at the private hangars and terminals. We pulled over next to them. "Brad, why are we stopping here?" I asked.

"We need to be stealthy if we are going to catch them off guard," said Brad. "We can't roar up into the terminal area doing wheelies. This is real life, not The Action Channel."

"I beg to differ," said Lily. "But we can try it your way first."

Lily and I shut off the engines. All four of us climbed off the motorcycles and walked them over to the side of one of the closest terminal buildings. We stood in the dark shadows of the building trying to come up with a plan.

I looked at Dylan. He was dreamy. I sighed on the inside. "What did the boys say about their estimated time of arrival?"

"Chameleon said that they just disembarked. Whatever that is supposed to mean. They should be here soon."

"Disembarked?" Brad rubbed his hands over his face. He was clearly stressed by their comment. "What kind of shortcut did they take?" Brad asked. I had a feeling he didn't really want to know.

Dylan and I shrugged. "They didn't say," I added.

"Those little bastards didn't steal a battleship to get across the bay, did they?" Brad had a raised eyebrow and noticeable lines on his forehead.

"Let's hope not," I said to ease his pain. Anything was possible though with this group of boys and their intellect. Nothing was out of bounds or off limits.

"I'll have to turn in my badge and gun when I get home if this keeps up," said Brad. He paced around in a circle. "How many freaking laws are we going to break today?" Brad seemed like he was ready to scream or punch something.

"As many as it takes to get Luke back." That was Lily's answer. I had to agree with her.

"Maybe we can leave a note on the bikes to return them to the shipyard slip number thirty-two," suggested Dylan.

"Is your boy scout for real, Payton?" asked Brad.

"Hey," Dylan interjected. "I'm just trying to do the right thing here."

"Then stop helping that Stephani girl," said Lily. "That

would be a huge start to get me to trust you."

"If it makes you feel any better, I don't trust her either. I think she's been lying to me."

"It really doesn't," said Lily in a smug tone. Her Gothic bitch self was showing. "Now, enough of this babble. It's time to sneak around and not get caught or killed." Lily was ready to step out of the darkness and play spy.

I grabbed her arm. "Wait a second," I said to her. "I need to ask Brad a question." I turned to Brad. "You don't happen to have your badge with you by chance? It might come in handy if we need to interrogate someone or shake down a witness … or not get arrested."

"Sorry, Nancy Drew. I left my badge in my other tuxedo."

His answer did not instill confidence in our plan. "So, it's going to be the hard way. Terrific."

The four of us peered around the corner of the terminal building like something out of a spy cartoon. Brad, who was the tallest, was on the top. Dylan was second. I was squeezed in under him, which I wasn't complaining about. Lily, who was the shortest, was crouching on the ground.

"Is that the dark blue sedan parked by the far terminal?" Lily asked the group for our opinion.

"Could be," said Brad. "It's hard to tell from here."

"Maybe we should go take a closer look. I'm ready to storm the castle. I want my brother back."

"Ditto," said Lily. "I'm ready to die to save him from those goons."

"Whoa, whoa, whoa," said Brad, looking down at Lily. "Slow down. No one is dying."

"What exactly is our plan besides not dying?" asked Dylan. "Maybe we should think about this."

"See, the kid gets it," said Brad about Dylan and his sensibility. "A well thought out plan is the smart way to handle this."

"Dude, stop acting like a geezer," urged Dylan. "You're like four years older than me."

I had a feeling that this argument would have gone on

longer if a motorcade of seven airport golf carts didn't go roaring past us.

"Was that? … " asked Brad, hanging his head.

"It was," I said, agreeing with him. "Quick, we have to catch them."

We left our stealthy hiding spot to chase after the missing ten members of our crew. The four of us tried waving our arms in the air and shouting at them. So much for being stealthy. Lily even threw one of her shoes at the last golf cart. It bounced off and landed on the blacktop. The Singe and Feed Bag were oblivious to the fact that Lily had hit their cart.

We continued to chase after them. In the lead was Chameleon and Julie. Close behind them was Wolfman and Blond Ambition. Next, was Lisa and Amber. After them was Brent riding solo, followed by Shoes and Thirteen. In second to last place was Max and Teagan, who were sitting entirely too close to each other. Feed Bag and The Singe were still bringing up the rear.

In the distance, we could see a small plane leaving the hangar. It was taxiing to the runway.

"There's the plane," said Lily, pointing at it. "How do we stop it?"

***

I do love a good game of cat and mouse. Come and get me. Meow.

***

Dylan pulled out the walkie talkie without missing a step. "Guys, this is Dylan. Do you think you could stop that plane from taking off?"

Chameleon answered. "The calvary is on it. Prepare to be amazed."

"God, I hate that cocky little bastard," said Brad. We continued to run in their direction.

"You can't hate him. He's on our team," I said back to him in a joking manner.

We were all doing our best to keep up. Needless to say, it

was a struggle for me in Vandersloot's heels. I was falling behind. Dylan looked back and noticed that I was having a hard time. The adrenaline was helping, but I could still feel every strap digging into my skin.

Dylan came back to help me. "Jump on my back. I'll give you a piggyback ride."

Who was I to say no to that? I jumped up on his back and wrapped my arms around his neck. Dylan sprinted up to Brad and Lily with me wrapped around him like a boa constrictor. The boy had skills. That is all I will say on that. We tried our best to keep up, but the golf carts were pulling away from us. It wasn't all bad, they were closing in on the plane.

Suddenly, the six carts split into a horizontal row to cover both paths of the runway. One of the carts had orange handheld lights. It looked like Chameleon of all people. He was waving them at the plane. It looked like he was asking them to pull over. The plane seemed to be slowing down. By the time we caught up, the six carts had the plane surrounded.

"The little bastards might actually pull this off," said Brad with hope in his voice.

"It was Dylan's idea," I added proudly to give him credit.

Dylan put me back down on the ground as soon as we were close enough to the plane. I gave him a big thank-you hug. It was warm and inviting just like I remembered. I hung on a bit longer than he did. All right, back to reality.

Brad signaled the kids to leave their golf carts and to stay back. He approached the eight-seat, twin-engine aircraft with caution. This was far from over. I doubted they would surrender and give up without a fight. Brad pounded on the door of the aircraft. "This is the police. You are completely surrounded. Come out with your hands up," he said with every ounce of conviction he had left. I could tell he wanted this jerk as bad as I did.

"Don't try anything funny. You are outnumbered," added Chameleon.

"Send the boy out first," added Max, joining in on the testosterone fest.

Brad motioned with his hand to be quiet, that was enough. "This is your last chance. We are coming in," said Brad in his professional police tone.

Brad was enjoying this. I could tell. Who was I kidding? This was great.

The airlock on the plane's door disengaged. I held my breath. The boys disobeyed Brad's order. They all moved towards the plane ready to pounce on whoever came out.

The door opened. A voice I didn't recognize said, "Don't shoot. I'm unarmed."

"That's bullshit," I told Brad. "They have Crystal's gun."

"Come out slowly," said Brad. He was standing near the door of the plane. The boys were about ten feet behind him. There was no sense telling them otherwise. They wanted justice for Streak.

"Do you still want the boy to come out first?" said the same man as before.

"Yes, said Brad in a clear cadence. "Slow and easy. No one has to get hurt."

A figure emerged in the dimly lit hole of the doorway. He walked down the first stair. Lily and I couldn't contain ourselves. We rushed over to greet Luke. After three or four more steps, I realized there was something wrong.

"Okay, I'm coming out too," said the man.

They both stepped off the plane and into the light for us all to see.

"What the hell is this?" asked Lily. She turned to look at Brad.

Brad ran onboard the plane to search it quick. I followed him. There was no one else on board. We went back outside. This was bad. We screwed up.

"Sorry, sir," I said in my best apologetic voice. "We thought you were someone else."

He got an angry look on his face. He put his arm around his frightened seven-year-old son.

"Did you happen to see a creepy person in a black hooded robe traveling with a twenty-two-year-old man?" asked Lily to get as much information as we could out of him before he pressed charges.

With fire in his eyes, he said, "No, and you will be talking to my lawyer if you don't get those damn golf carts out of my way."

Brad signaled the boys to move them with a nod of his head. The rest of us turned around to slink away with our tails between our legs. That's when we saw another plane zooming down the other runway. There was a black hooded figure in the window waving or giving us the finger as the wheels of the plane left the pavement.

"There they are," I screamed. I turned around to the owner of the plane. "We need to commandeer your plane," I told the man.

"Over my dead body," he said. He pulled his phone out of his jacket pocket. The man was either calling his lawyer or the police. Neither option worked for me. I backed away from him. I wasn't up for a battle.

"Quick," I said to my friends. "We need to go to the terminal and rent a plane."

***

That was fun, Payton. You make me laugh. Everyone fell for my magic trick again. I do love the art of misdirection. When are you going to learn that you cannot outsmart me?

CHAPTER TWENTY-SIX

The crew parked the glorified golf carts next to the borrowed dirt bikes. Chameleon pulled a pen and a piece of paper out of his backpack. He wrote a note explaining that it was an emergency and to please return the dirt bikes to their rightful owners at slip thirty-two at the shipyard, and to please return the golf carts to terminal two at the airport. It seemed like overkill but at least we would be able to sleep at night … eventually.

"By the way, how did you guys get here so fast?" I had to ask. Not knowing was killing me. "What did you disembark?"

"Funny story," started The Singe.

"Funny, but true story," added Chameleon.

I was already regretting asking the question.

"Stop," said Blond Ambition. "I'm going to tell the story. Since we needed to vanish like a fart in the wind, we needed to get creative. We found this fishing trolly with the engine running. Get this, the captain was shitfaced and passed out on the deck."

Chameleon jumped back in. "The polite thing to do was to ask him for a ride. He didn't answer us. So then we asked if we could borrow it. He didn't say no …"

"Got it," said Brad. He'd heard enough. He was mumbling something not good under his breath.

"The captain let us borrow some of his rum too," added Blond Ambition.

"I'm going to pretend I didn't hear that," said Brad. He rubbed his face with his hands. "I'm on vacation. I'm not on duty. It's none of my damn business what these little maniacs do. I'm not their damn babysitter," he muttered under his breath. His face was turning red.

"Brad, calm down," I told him. "You're going to give yourself an aneurysm." I turned my attention back to the boys and their story. "Did you at least drop the anchor and shut off the guy's engine?" I had to know more.

"Of course," said Max. "We have manners and shit. Captain Stew will be none the wiser. We added water to his bottle of rum and covered him up with a blanket."

I put my head in my hands and rubbed my temples. There was a headache in there just dying to come out.

***

Outside the private terminal, Brad came over to me with an idea. After he explained it to me, I knew it would never fly. He thought we should pretend to be a married couple, all an elaborate scheme to try to rent a plane.

"Julie will never go for this," I told Brad.

"She's a good sport. This is for your brother." He had on his "trust me" face.

I looked over at Julie who was chatting with Chameleon. "You go break the news to her. She is not going to take it well."

Brad walked over to her. Chameleon saw him coming and rejoined his friends. Brad did his best to plead his case. It was like watching a volcano erupt. The blast of hot lava was inevitable. Brad proposed the idea that he and I were a married couple to make our cover story more believable. He was about to ask Julie if I could borrow her engagement ring.

Just in case you forgot, her ring was once mine. After I left him at the altar, I was kind enough to give it back. A little over a month ago, he proposed and gave the ring to her. It's all a weird mess. I was cringing on the inside and the outside watching this unfold.

The hot lava landed on Brad's face with a slap from Julie. Thawack! "What?" exclaimed Julie. "No way! You are out of your mind to ask me such a thing." She put both hands on his chest and shoved him backwards.

Brad looked at me, shaking his head no. That was a big fat no.

We rolled into the private terminal like a hot mess. Before we went inside, we thought it was best for Brad and me to go in first, our entourage to follow later. With Brad in his tuxedo and I in my prom dress, we kind of looked the part of jet setting celebrities. Stop laughing. I was prepared to totally commit to the part I was about to play.

Brad and I walked in the double glass doors of the terminal first. We strolled in arm-in-arm to set the stage, so-to-speak. It was probably better if my friends stayed outside and never heard the ridiculous lies that I was about to tell. I was not proud that I was getting pretty good at it.

We walked past the rows of empty chairs and approached the counter. The only person in the whole place was a younger guy in his twenties. He was thin with dark hair. Not to be mean, but this guy reeked of computer nerd. He was staring at his computer screen when we walked up. This was a good thing for us. A young mind could be easily manipulated.

He looked up from his computer. "Hi, my name is Brian. Can I help you folks?" he asked in a pleasant yet sleepy voice.

"You sure can," said Brad. He put his arm around me in an affectionate manner. "We need a flight out of Port Cristibel immediately. Probably something larger than the single engine plane that just took off. How big was that one exactly?" Brad was fishing for information.

"That is a four-seater. It holds a pilot and three guests."

"So, there were four people on that plane?" I asked without thinking. Dang it.

Brian gave me a weird look.

"Sorry, none of my business." I did the best I could to cover for my screw up. "How could you ever fit four people in a teeny tiny plane like that? We are looking for something bigger, a lot bigger." I extended my arms out for added affect.

Brad tried to redirect the questioning. "You know, honey, that looked a lot like my Uncle Milton's plane. Good ole Uncle Milton V."

I could see where Brad was going with this. He was struggling to remember their last name. "Yes, good ole Uncle Vandersloot," I added to help Brad out. "He's a peach. He and Emily are the best. They were so kind to let us borrow their limo to get to the country club gala tonight. Their driver, Roberto, is a hoot. We just love him, right, honey?" I affectionately rubbed Brad's arm.

Brad looked at me with wide eyes as I spun my semi-truth tale of white lies. I pinched Brad in the arm to get him to snap out of his state of shock.

"Yes, Snookums, Roberto is top drawer," Brad added a snobbish shade to his voice.

Holding in a laugh was almost painful. Brad was better at this than I thought he would be. I affectionately rubbed his shoulder. I caught myself doing it and stopped. Why did it come so naturally to rub my ex-boyfriend? Just for the record, I knew why. But why was I enjoying it?

"Just out of curiosity ... was that my uncle's plane?" asked Brad.

"Sorry, Mr. Vandersloot," said Brian. "The FDA regulations forbid me from disclosing that information."

"Surely you can tell me what he looked like," said Brad. "Was he a tall, thin, man with gray hair?"

"No, he was a nervous twenty-year-old guy," said Brian.

"Was his name Luke?" I blurted out without thinking. I bet they made him come in here to avoid witnesses.

Brian got another weird look on his face. "I don't know. What is going on here? I think I need to involve the police."

It was time to level with Brian. "I am the police," said Brad in an assertive cop tone.

"I'm gonna need to see your badge," said Brian. He obviously didn't believe a word after our performance.

"Look, Brian, you seem like a reasonable guy. I would show it to you, but I don't have it on me."

Brian sighed and did a pretty significant eye roll to show his disgust. He reached for the phone.

I panicked. My bad. Both of my fists had ahold of the collar of his shirt before my brain could weigh out my options. "Look, Brian, this is how this is going to go. We can do this the easy way or the hard way." So far, this was my best badass attempt of my lifetime.

Brian was getting my vibe by the shocked look on his face. "Take the money," he shouted. "I don't care. Just don't kill me," he shrieked in terror.

Our missing crew of fifteen just happened to pick this very moment to forcibly open the door and burst inside. Talk about a dramatic entrance. They had just witnessed his last statement and froze in their spots just inside the door.

Brian looked over my shoulder to see who had entered the terminal. "Help!" cried Brian. He was looking for assistance from the wrong crew.

"They're with us," I said. "Look at me, Brian." He did. I still had ahold of his collar. "They are not going to help you," I said in a slow, creepy tone that made the hair on the back of everyone's neck stand at attention. "Understand?" I added for a dramatic finish.

He nodded. Brian and the rest of the crew looked at me like I was a freak. Maybe I was. Clearly, my dark side was showing.

Chameleon broke the ice by doing a slow clap of applause. The rest of the boys, except Brad and Dylan joined in. "And the award for best supporting actress in a scary movie goes to …" Chameleon laughed at his clever joke.

I let go of Brian's collar. Then I straightened out the wrinkles in his shirt like an overprotective mother or a crazy person. You can pick which one. I'm not sure which one I was at the moment. I took a deep, cleansing breath and removed my hands from his shirt. "Here's the deal, Brian. No bullshit this time. My brother Luke, that guy who paid you earlier, has been kidnapped by a maniac and taken on that plane. You are going to tell me who scheduled that flight and where it is going."

Brad stepped in to intervene. "I really am a police officer. Can you help out my friend, or not?"

"And I'm really his fiancé," Julie said, holding up my/her ring for Brian to see.

My stomach and eyes rolled at her comment. "Seriously, Brian, we need your help. I'm worried about my brother. They might kill him if we don't find him in time."

The rest of the group gathered around us to show their support.

"It's the truth," said Chameleon, trying to help.

"I saw them throw her brother in the dark sedan that is parked outside," Amber said to help collaborate my story.

"Luke is my boyfriend," started Lily. She got in Brian's face with her Gothic persuasion. "You will help us find him." She smiled at Brian. It was creepier than the shit I did to him.

"Okay, everyone back off," said Brian. He took two steps back to distance himself. "I will help you out if you can keep your mouths shut."

"Deal," I said instantly. "Give us what you've got."

Brian started clicking keys on his computer. "The flight was scheduled last night by a Payton Richardson."

"I'm Payton Richardson. I didn't schedule this. This has to be a joke."

"Afraid not. Your credit card information is in my system." Brian swung the computer screen around for me to see.

"But that's impossible. I had my purse until … oh …"

"That's why they had us leave all of our purses, bags, and phones," said Chameleon. "They didn't need mine because it was no use to them … other than using it to transport the final envelope."

Lily snapped her fingers to get Brian's attention. "Where is the flight headed?" She asked impatiently.

Brian checked his computer again. "It's headed to River Bend, Wisconsin."

"Are we really going home?" asked Teagan. She looked at Max. "We were having so much fun together."

Brad butted in between Lily and me at the counter. "We need a plane fast, Brian. One big enough for all of us or two smaller planes. What's available?"

"Let me check the commercial flights first." He typed on his keyboard. "There is a flight this morning to the Twin Valley airport. It arrives in Twin Valley at 11:00 a.m."

I looked at Brad. "That's not enough time to hunt down what I need."

"That's the earliest flight I could find," said Brian.

"Try the private flights," I told him. It was going to cost more, but we were desperate.

"The small planes are all booked." He noticed my sad look. "All I have left are larger planes. I know the pilot. He could probably be here in an hour or so."

I looked up at the clock on the wall. It was 12:30 a.m. We had a little more than fourteen hours to find my brother before it was game over. "How big of an aircraft are we talking?"

"It seats forty-six, comfortably," said Brian. His fingers were on the keyboard waiting for my answer.

"Party in the sky," said Max. He and Teagan high-fived each other.

"Holy crap, that's huge," I replied. "Expensive?"

"It's twelve thousand dollars," stated Brian.

"Not horrible," I said, sounding a bit like a spoiled brat.

"An hour," added Brian. "It's twelve grand an hour."

"Oh …" I turned to the group for their thoughts. Their expressions were a mixed bag of emotions. The boys were obviously pumped. Brad was shaking his head no. Lily was crying. The girls shrugged their shoulders with indecision. "Do you have anything smaller?" I just had to ask one more time.

"I have a thirteen-seater for sixty-five hundred an hour, but then you take the risk of crashing because of the extra weight on board."

I took my credit card out of my bra and laid it out on the counter. "We'll take the forty-sixer."

"Your bra, really?" asked Brad.

"You know my bad luck history with my purses. I've learned to adapt for my own good." I was making a joke, but the trials and tribulations of my life really weren't that funny. They were more tragic than I cared to admit.

Brian ran my credit card. "Um … It's not going through."

I slapped the counter, showing my hissy fit. "It has to be Stan and Jana cutting me off. Maybe the Vandersloots got to them."

"Or it's the dude in the robe messing with you," said Blond Ambition.

"That's true. This could be part of the game. Now what? We're screwed." I put my head down on the counter. I felt defeated.

Max reached down in his sock and pulled out something. I could see him out of the corner of my eye. I lifted my head. He placed a platinum credit card on the counter. "I've got it," said Max with a smile.

"You've got it?" asked Brad, giving him the suspicious cop look.

I gave Max a huge hug, so did Lily. "I swear I will pay you back." I said to him.

"No worries, my parents are loaded. Did I forget to mention that?"

"You did," I said with a smile. He was truly coming to our rescue. Max was new to the group. I had no idea that we traveled in the same so-called social circles.

The boys gave him high fives. They were so happy, they lifted him off the ground.

"By the way," said Chameleon. "I want a boat for my birthday." They all laughed, but I was sure he was serious.

Brian interrupted our celebration. "I forgot to tell you that the pilot's fee is extra."

We all looked at Max. There was a brief moment of silence. "Add it to the bill," Max said, without sounding too full of himself.

Ah, now I get why he was the way he was, all Gluteus Maximus. It was most likely the money that made him act like a real butthead.

"I think I'm in love," said Teagan. She threw her arms around his neck and planted a kiss on his lips.

After Max came up for air he said, "I've never been happier that I started kindergarten when I was six."

That was a relief to all of us wondering if we needed to intervene on the behalf of the law. Max was eighteen. The boys gave him high fives. Teagan twirled her hair. Oh brother.

***

Ready for my next magic trick? This will feel like me sticking a dagger into your brain and giving it a good twist. Am I the misdirection? Am I the one helping Payton? I put on a robe and appear in public. Next, I do a disappearing act right in front of you. The chase is on. Let that sink in. Or… is Payton helping me? This game just keeps getting better. I am going to pull that dagger out now and walk away. Everyone try to keep their bodily fluids to themselves while I prepare for my next trick.

CHAPTER TWENTY-SEVEN

Without drawing too much attention to myself, I slipped into the bathroom at the terminal. It was time to let some of the emotional steam out before we boarded the plane. I went into one of the stalls and locked the door. Now that I was all alone, I could open the flood gates.

I tried to cry for fifteen minutes, but nothing happened. What the hell was wrong with me? Tim, Crystal, and Smith were dead. My brother was just kidnapped, and I was an emotionless robot. Was my sanity teetering on the brink of madness? Had all the tragedy turned me into a psychopathic ice queen? Had I flipped the switch and turned off my humanity? It certainly appeared that way.

The pilot didn't arrive until 3:30 a.m. Honestly, I should have been upset. I was just happy Brian could accommodate us at all. We all boarded the plane. There was plenty of room to spread out. On one side of the aisle, there were two cream colored, side-by-side, leather seats facing another set of cream-colored, side-by-side, leather seats. Between each set of four seats was a shiny wood-grained retractable tabletop.

On the other side of the aisle, there were matching cream-colored couches, large enough to seat four people comfortably. The floor was covered in a beige-colored carpet. Compartment dividers were constructed of the same wood grain as the tabletops. It was extremely sleek and elegant. Welcome to the friendly skies.

We had a three-and-a-half-hour flight ahead of us. The gang settled into their seats. I found a seat in the middle of the plane near Lily. We were both obviously upset about Luke and needed to talk. I was also going to use this opportunity to get answers to some very important questions that were still flapping in the wind.

Dylan tried to sit by me. I told him I needed some time alone with Lily to talk. He found a seat by my friends. I'm sure I looked guilty to some of my friends on board. This was my chance to clear things up before we landed.

After taking a two-and-a-half-hour nap in the terminal waiting for the pilot, the group was slightly reenergized. Once we were safely in the air at cruising altitude, the pilot gave us the okay to move around and hunt for food and beverages.

"I'm playing stewardess," announced Teagan. She came around to each group and took our orders. Teagan approached us with a beer in her hand. "We have turkey clubs or ham and swiss sandwiches." Teagan was in her element taking our drink and food orders. Perhaps this was a good career move for her to pursue.

"I'll take the ham-and-swiss," said Lily. She seemed to be handling this well.

Teagan looked at me for my order. "I'll have the same and a bottle of wine. Make it two if they're the little ones."

"Sure thing. I'll be right back," said Teagan. She sauntered her way to the galley.

Teagan came back in a few minutes with our prewrapped sandwiches and two regular-sized bottles of wine. "I grabbed you a Riesling and a Red Blend." She set them down on the table. She didn't bother to bring me a glass, just a bottle opener. The girl knew me too well.

I opened the Riesling first. I took a long drink. Lily reached for the bottle. "Payton, slow down. We need to keep our brains sharp and focused."

I pulled the bottle out of her reach. "I prefer my brain to be a bit fuzzy."

"Luke needs us," she pleaded.

"I'll be okay. I promise. Just let me decompress for a few minutes." I took another long swig from the bottle. I stared off into space, trying my darndest to clear my mind of everything stressful and bad. Let's face it, my brain would be empty if that were true. All of these unanswered questions popped up and ran across the movie screen in my head. How could I possibly ask her what I needed to ask her without tearing apart our friendship? Trust was everything right now.

"Payton, I have to tell you something important," said Lily, bringing me back to reality.

I turned to face her and took another drink of wine for good measure. It was strictly for medicinal purposes. "Okay, I'm listening."

Before speaking again, Lily looked around to see if anyone was paying attention to us. Lisa, Dylan, Shoes, Teagan, and Max were lost in their own conversation. Blond Ambition was sprawled out, more like passed out, and snoring on the couch across from us. Brad and Julie were kitty-corner from us, one section up. Brent and Chameleon were a few aisles up. They were having a good-spirited scientific discussion as far as I could tell. The rest of the boys were sprawled out in the back of the plane by the galley. I could see Feedbag's shoes hanging over the arm of the seat and food trays in the aisle. Amber came out of the bathroom. She took a seat by Lisa. Everyone was in their own little world. I figured it was safe for her to start talking.

Lily took a deep breath. "I have a confession to make," she whispered.

I leaned in. My eyes widened and my eyebrows stood at attention. I didn't have to pry information out of her after all. She was about to spill her guts.

"First of all, you have to promise you won't get mad," she whispered with a serious expression.

My brow suddenly fell into a furrow. "Okay, I'll try," I whispered back. It was the best I could tell her.

"I'm sorry that I put that tracking device in your purse. I should have explained everything the night you met Brent." Now, she had a sad look on her face.

"Why track me?" I asked her. I was insulted and a bit salty about it.

"You stopped telling me things. I thought you were hiding something from me."

"Lily, you were acting suspicious, and I was mad at you for thinking that Dylan was involved."

"I get that, I do." She leaned in closer. "I need to tell you a secret."

Here we go. This is what I had been waiting for.

"Five years ago, before I met Luke, my life was turned upside down. You know I have an older brother, right?"

"Yeah, you mentioned that you used to go to the park with him when you were a happy kid," I said, remembering what she had told me in the past. "How come I have never met him yet?"

"Payton, he died five years ago. My brother Matt drowned in the river. He was one of the victims. The police wouldn't help us investigate, so I started doing my own research."

"Wow! I am so sorry, Lily. I had no idea." Holy shit, mind blown.

"No one does. I invented this whole dark, Goth girl persona to go undercover. It was easy to get sucked into it. The dark web is full of chat rooms and other sites."

"Is that how you met Brent?" I asked her. I was beyond curious about all of this. It surely showed on my face. Brent's trustworthiness was still on the fence for me.

"Payton, I know what you are thinking. You can totally trust Brent. He has been helping me with my research. He is really smart and knows his shit. Anyway, my research led me to the dark arts and witchcraft. Brent and I figured out something really disturbing."

Lily paused like she wasn't going to tell me. "C'mon, you have to spill it now." I looked at her.

"All right," she said, finally. "Did you know that you can draw a pentagram on the map of Wisconsin, Minnesota, Iowa, and Illinois and hit the major cities where these drownings have occurred?"

"That's crazy. Did you tell anyone?" I was stunned.

"No, who would believe it. The police are still treating the cases as accidental drownings. Besides, I was trying to go undercover and join a few covens. We were trying to figure out which group or groups are doing this."

"Holy crap, Lily. That is so dangerous. Oh … is that where you have been sneaking off to? My brother mentioned something about it."

"Yes, that is where I have been going. I've been trying to keep it from everyone. What did your brother say about it?"

I chuckled first. Lily gave me a weird look. "Thanks to Brad, my brother thought you were sneaking around and having an affair with Brent."

"I would never do that. I love Luke. He is my whole life."

"He loves you too," I said to reassure her.

"I just hope he will still love me without all the eyeliner and black hair dye."

"I wouldn't worry about it. I'm sure my parents will be ecstatic."

We both laughed. Lily actually hugged me. Her hard-candy, Goth shell was melting.

"So, we're good?" she asked, with a new twinkle in her eye. A huge weight had been lifted.

"Yeah, we're good." I smiled back. This was such a relief. Now, I had to fix some other bridges. "I'll be right back. I need to have a conversation with Brad."

"Good luck," she said with a smirk.

"Thanks." I grabbed the bottle of Riesling and brought it with me. This might not go well.

Julie and Brad were sitting together in a set of the side-by-side chairs ahead of us in the cabin. They looked cozy. I took a seat in one of the leather chairs across from them. I set my wine on the tabletop. They gave me one of those "you're interrupting us" looks. It was early in the morning. I had quit giving a shit about manners hours ago. They were just going to have to deal with me.

"This is important. I need to talk to Brad." This was supposed to be Julie's cue to leave.

"So, talk," she said. "I'm not moving." Julie crossed her arms across her chest in a defensive manner. I hated that manner.

She had her chance to leave. "Okay, where do I start? Um … Brad, when were you actually kidnapped?"

"It was the night before the wedding. I was trying on my tuxedo in my room to make sure it fit, when there was a knock on the door."

Julie interrupted the rest of his story. "What do you mean by actually?" she asked with a not-too-happy look on her face.

Brad ignored her question. "I thought it was Julie or my dad, so I didn't look through the peep hole. I just opened the door. A hooded figure zapped me with a taser. I woke up in a locked room on the ship."

"What do you mean by actually?" Julie raised her voice and stood up.

I took a long drink from the bottle. I knew what was coming.

"Tell me right now," she insisted. Julie was now looking at me too for an answer.

Everyone around us noticed the scene she was making. They stopped what they were doing and came closer to hear and see what was going on. Lily pretended to eat popcorn like a smartass. I looked at Brad for guidance on how to explain it. He was doing his best to try to keep her calm.

I decided to go for it. "I called Brad a month ago and asked him if he would help Crystal, Agent Smith, and I with our plan to catch the killer. Brad was supposed to fake getting kidnapped the morning of the wedding, not the night before.

Someone found out about our game and changed it. I didn't realize anything was wrong at first."

Julie looked extremely angry. I don't think I had ever seen her this mad before. "Let me get this straight. We came all the way down to Texas to help Payton with her game. If you were kidnapped the morning of the wedding, were we even getting married?"

And there it was. The big freaking elephant in the room.

Brad stood up. "Jules, it was for a good cause. It is my job to uphold the law."

By the look on Julie's face, he was only making things worse.

Julie tugged at her engagement ring.

I stood up too. "I'm sorry," I said to her in an attempt to calm her down.

Once the ring came off her finger, she threw it at Brad. It bounced off his chest and landed somewhere on the floor. Instinctively, I bent over and tried to grab it. The ring rolled under one of the chairs. I grabbed it quick and stood back up.

"And you!" Julie said to me. "You just couldn't stay away from him." She slapped me across the face before she stormed off with Brad on her heels.

"Ow!" Damn that hurt. I picked up the bottle of wine and held it on my cheek. Maybe it would help with the swelling. Since my dress didn't have pockets and my bra was full of earrings, I stuck the ring on my finger for safe keeping. I wasn't going anywhere near Julie until she calmed the F down. The ring seemed smaller than I remembered. I tried to pull it off. It was stuck. "Shit! I can't believe he had my ring re-sized."

I looked around the group that had gathered to watch. They all still had a look of shock and awe on their faces. I picked up on the judgmental vibe too. "Hey, it seemed like a good idea at the time." I paused. "I'm sorry I couldn't tell any of you about our plan." I swear I heard crickets.

I looked over at Brent and Dylan. "I'm sorry you guys got mixed up in this whole thing. I'm thankful that nothing happened to you two."

"I'm okay," said Dylan. "I feel bad that I couldn't be more helpful."

"Actually, you can both help me," I explained to them. "First, I need more information. When were you kidnapped?"

Dylan started. "I was kidnapped shortly after I left the restaurant. It happened in the alley. They put a bag over my head and threw me in the trunk."

"Did they keep you on the ship?" I asked him.

"Yes, I was locked in a room."

"So was I," said Brent. "They grabbed me at the beach in the middle of the night, right after I put the body in the water."

"Why is that important?" asked Dylan.

"I was just looking at a timeline. No big deal. You guys never saw each other while you were being held captive, right?"

"Not until we were on the stage," said Brent.

Dylan nodded in agreement. "Yeah, that's right."

After the scene with Julie and Brad was over, everyone around us was about to fall asleep or were asleep. "You guys can have a seat. You look exhausted."

They sat across from me. I pulled the silver winged shaped earrings out of my bra and set them on the table. "The killer said in the note that I needed these and two other things to trade for my brother. I'm sure one of those is the Key to Immortality."

"I agree," said Brent. "What is the other thing the killer wants or needs?"

"Good question." I looked at Dylan. "Do you have anything you want to tell me?" Dylan looked back at me with his dreamy green eyes. Yowzah, they were intoxicating. I almost forgot I was trying to interrogate him. "Dylan, tell me more about this recipe book of yours."

"It's my collection of family recipes passed down from generations—"

"Dylan," I said, cutting him off. "If it is just an old recipe book, I wouldn't have had to stash it for you." I gave him the

"Payton the private investigator" stink eye. I'm sure it was hideous and horrifying in the predawn hours. "Spill it." I continued to stare at him. Brent stared at him too.

"Okay," he said reluctantly. "I really didn't want anyone to get their hands on it because it's an ancient cookbook for witches. It's called a—"

"Gramarye," said Brent, finishing Dylan's sentence. "Fascinating. I would love to see it."

"And I would love to burn it." Dylan was angry. "No one should have that evil book."

"But it holds ancient secrets," said Brent. He was trying to reason with Dylan. "The book probably holds answers to the necklace … to immortality."

"That is an even better reason to destroy it," said Dylan. Things between the two boys were getting heated.

I reached across the table and grabbed Dylan's hand. "I'm sorry, you can't destroy it. I have to trade it for my brother. Luke is counting on us to figure this out and find him." I gazed deep into Dylan's eyes. "I promise to do everything in my power to hang onto the book and not give it to them."

"That is not good enough." Dylan was upset. He pulled his hand away. Dylan ignored Brent and me by staring out the window at the dark morning sky.

Brent picked up one of the earrings. "Where did you get these?"

"Believe it, or not, I traded the Key to Immortality for them." I laughed at the irony.

Brent could tell that was all I was going to say on the matter. He held the earring up to the overhead light. As he twirled it around under the spotlight, we saw patterns flash on the light-colored walls.

"Did you see that?" he asked. I could tell he was excited. "Quick, find a piece of paper and a pen.

I dug around in one of the end tables next to the couch. Bingo! I found what I was looking for. I ran back to the table. When I got there, I noticed that Dylan was slumped over. He must have fallen asleep. I scanned the seats around me. Brent and I were the only ones still awake.

He held up each earring to the light. I did my best to trace what I saw on the piece of paper. Each earring was a different piece of a map. The part of the map where the X marks the spot was missing. "I wonder if the necklace has the final piece," I said.

"Yes, the third piece of the map is undoubtably hidden in the necklace, in my opinion," said Brent with a smile. "What a grand adventure this has turned out to be."

"Seriously, you need to get out of your basement more," I told him.

He laughed. "That will have to wait until I am no longer grounded. When my mom finds out I'm still alive, there will be hell to pay."

I laughed with him. "When the Chief finds out, he is going to kick your ass." I added.

"Truth," he said, totally agreeing with me. Brent was in big trouble.

"So, what is our plan going to be? Should I go get the book and the necklace and meet you guys wherever this map starts?"

"We'll need some time to figure that out, but I think we can handle that end of it," he said with confidence.

I looked out the window to see the sun peeking over the horizon. "We must be getting close. I'll go check with the pilot." I walked to the front of the plane. I knocked on the cockpit door.

"Come in," said the fifty-something pilot. When he turned around, I noticed the gold bar on his shirt said, "Captain Roger Stevenson."

I stepped just inside the doorway of the cockpit. "Hi, I just wanted to know how much longer until we land?"

Captain Stevenson checked his gauges. "In less than an hour, we will start our decent into the Twin Valley Airport."

"No. No. No. We need to land in River Bend." I was apoplectic.

"Miss Richardson, you need to calm down. This plane is too large to land in River Bend. Their runway isn't long enough to accommodate a plane of this size."

"That's not what Brian told me." I was frantic and got louder by the second. "What about Clearwater Falls or anything closer? This is an emergency."

"What's going on?" asked Brent. He came running to my rescue as soon as he heard me losing my shit. Lily, Chameleon, Max, and Teagan appeared in the doorway also. They had heard the commotion.

I turned to my friends. "We can't land in River Bend. The plane is too large." I turned my attention back to Captain Stevenson. "Where are we right now?"

"We are just south of River Bend," he commented.

"Do you have any parachutes?" asked Lily.

"There is one in the closet behind the door," said Captain Stevenson.

Lily pushed her way into the cockpit to dig through the closet. "Found it," she said. Lily handed it to me. "Get us low enough over River Bend for Payton to jump."

The Captain nodded but seemed skeptical on Lily's plan.

"I don't know about this," I said. Everything was happening too fast.

"Chameleon," said Lily. "Give Payton one of your walkie talkies. Do you have any clothes in your backpack she can borrow?"

My brain was saying, *wait a second.* My mouth wasn't saying anything at all.

"I have a sweatshirt and a pair of sweatpants she can borrow," said Chameleon.

The group started moving towards the rear of the plane. I was getting escorted with them.

"Great," said Lily. "Give her your shoes too. She'll break her ankle in those heels."

We stopped at Chameleon's backpack. Lily put the sweatshirt over my head, had me step into the sweatpants, and put on his shoes. She looked at me. I knew I looked ridiculous with

Chameleon's clothes over the purple dress. "Okay, what else?" She looked around the group, who were all awake at this point. "Shoes, give me your stocking hat. It's going to be colder than you know what out there." Lily put it on my head. I felt like a two-year-old getting dressed to go play in the snow for the first time. Lily and Chameleon fastened the straps of the parachute on my body.

"I need a knife," I said, having a moment of clarity.

Chameleon handed me his favorite knife. This was quite the honor. He pulled his laser tag goggles and the walkie talkie out of his backpack. "Better safe than sorry," he said to me. "It's weird that they took my laser tag guns but not the goggles." Chameleon put the goggles on my face. I stuck the walkie talkie in the front pocket of the sweatshirt. "Payton, now remember, it's just like the parasail. You can use the wind, just lean to change your direction. After you jump, count to ten and pull the cord."

I nodded. My life was flashing before my eyes.

Brent held up the earrings. "I have these. I'll take a closer look at the map and tell you where to meet us."

I nodded again. The world was spinning around me. I wanted to get off this crazy ride, but that wasn't an option.

Captain Stevenson came to the backend of the plane. "The autopilot is set. Everyone strap yourselves in your seats. Payton, hold onto something while I open the door. If the oxygen masks drop, put them on."

Lily and the group pushed me towards the back door of the plane. I grabbed onto the last chair to steady myself. The Captain opened the door. The wind howled through the cabin of the plane. I heard the girls scream in the background. I must be freaking out of my mind.

"I can do this. I can do this. I can do this," I muttered to myself as a gallant pep talk. I inched forward enough to see how high up we still were. "I can't do this. This is freaking impossible."

"I'm sorry, Payton," said Lily.

“For what?” I was turning around to look at her. Before I could, she shoved me out of the door.

“Lily, you b i i i i i i t c h!”

***

Never turn your back on a friend. It can be detrimental to your health.

CHAPTER TWENTY-EIGHT

"Aaaah! I'm alive. I'm alive. I'm alive. Aaaah!" I was falling at an incredible rate of speed. The wind whipped around my body as gravity hurled me towards the ground below. My current adrenaline rush might be easier to handle if my stolen dress wasn't over my head and slapping me in the face. Okay, get a grip or you're going to die. I pushed the dress down and took a look at my surroundings. The freezing wind bit my face. The view through my goggles wasn't pleasant. The ground continued to rush up at me. Aaaah! I let go of the dress. It covered my face again. Maybe I shouldn't see my impending doom. Next stop, Payton the pancake. Aaaah!

Okay, no more screaming. Calm down, you need to think. What did Chameleon say? Count to ten and pull the cord. Cord. Cord. Cord. Where is the freaking cord? I felt around the pack on my back. "One … two … three … four … screw it." My right hand yanked on the tightly braided, red, nylon cord.

At first, I heard the whoosh of the chute as it opened. I grabbed the straps on either side of my head with both hands, preparing for what was to come next. Without warning, I was jerked upward as the chute opened and captured the air. This temporarily solved the dress over my head problem, which was a good thing. As my current rate of speed quickly changed into a casual float, I felt a tiny wave of relief. Maybe I wasn't going to die after all. I decided it was safe to look down now. "Holy crap! Hello, River Bend." I could see the whole blasted town from up here. The view was astounding.

While the initial shock was wearing off, I noticed I was shaking uncontrollably from the cold. My heart was also still beating like a racehorse from the adrenaline surge. The best thing I could do for myself was to calm down before I passed out or had one of my panic attacks. I did my best to breathe in and out slowly. It seemed to help. Now that the worst was behind me, I felt a wave of triumph rise from within. I raised my hands in the air to celebrate. "Woo Hoo! Yeah! Take that, you scumbags," I screamed into the sky like a cocky badass. It was time for my Double O status mode. Payton the private eye was back.

I felt the front pocket of the sweatshirt looking for the walkie talkie. What a relief that I hadn't lost it after getting shoved out of a perfectly good airplane.

I put the walkie talkie up to my mouth. "Come in, Chameleon. Anyone read me up there?"

"Gotcha, Payton," he answered back. I could hear cheering in the background from the group. They were happy that I had survived. I was pretty darn ecstatic about it too.

"My chute is open. All is good. When you land, have Max buy a cell phone. Have him call the spare Richardson cell phone, so I know the number. I will grab it from my parents' house. I'll call him back when I get there. The number is 711-741-1846. Oh, and tell Lily she is in big trouble."

"Roger that," he said back. "Over and out."

I tucked the walkie talkie back into the front pocket. My attention went immediately to the ground below. Where was the dang hospital? It couldn't be that hard to find one of the largest buildings in town. Bingo! There it was to the right. I did my best to steer myself in that direction.

It would be great if I could "spy movie" land on the roof like a pro. At this point, I'll be lucky to find anything to break my fall that wouldn't kill me. Wind and gravity were about to foil my plan. Perfect. I was headed for a large grove of trees about a quarter mile from the hospital. Wish me luck on a safe crash landing. Oh my god! Aaaah!

***

The good news: I was freaking alive. The bad news: My feet hadn't actually touched the ground yet because my parachute was tangled in an enormous oak tree. I was dangling roughly ten feet in the air like a sitting duck. Fortunately, this was not my first solo mission and saving my own butt on a daily basis was now the norm. Today, I was feeling epically heroic. My current superhero status just nudged forward from pathetic wimp to pathetic badass. I realized that calling myself a badass at this point was a stretch, but I desperately needed a confidence booster to get myself out of this damn tree.

I reached for Chameleon's knife and cut the cords of the parachute. This didn't go exactly as planned. I landed on the ground kind of hard, rolling over my right ankle in Chameleon's oversized shoes. My injured ankle wasn't enough to slow me down. I was determined and focused on completing my mission. Getting to the hospital and retrieving the necklace from Rose was all I could think about. I tucked my hands up into the sleeves of the oversized sweatshirt and continued my jog in the brisk morning air.

The path I took to the hospital brought me to the back of the building. Maybe there was an employee's entrance where I could sneak inside undetected. I would walk in the front door and sneak up to the fifth floor like I had done many times before if my outfit wasn't so ridiculous. There was a good chance that I would be committed on sight and locked up indefinitely in this getup. *Ace Ventura* and his tutu popped into my head.

There was a garbage shed back here. I opened the wooden shed door and went inside. This was a great place to hide and watch the back doors, except for the smell. Wow! It really cleared out my sinuses.

After a few minutes, I got lucky. A delivery truck for the kitchen showed up. The driver propped the back door open to bring in multiple loads of produce and meats. I waited for him to disappear down the hallway, then I made my move.

Once I was safely inside the building, I headed for the Laundry Department to look for a set of scrubs or a lab coat to borrow. Outside the door to the Laundry Department, I discovered a rack of freshly starched white lab coats. I also just realized I was still wearing the laser tag goggles. I sighed. Well, if I was going to be an idiot, I might as well be a complete idiot. Good grief. The goggles went right into the front pocket of the sweatshirt before anyone saw me wearing them. Chameleon was going to want them back. I planned on doing my best to return all of my borrowed things. It was just good karma.

The door to the Laundry Department cracked open. Someone was coming. I grabbed the nearest lab coat off the hanger and ran around the corner. My arms slid into each arm hole as I ran.

As soon as I spotted the first stairwell door, I ducked inside. The stairwell was painted off-white. It was generic and sterile looking. Nothing to inspire me on my journey to Rose's room. I climbed the flights of stairs. I was exhausted to say the very least. I was running on limited sleep and limited brain power. This combination had never worked out well for me in the past. But I needed to stay focused. Just a few more hours and my brother would be safely home. I could do this.

When I reached the fifth floor, I cracked open the door to check the Nurses Station. It was unoccupied this time of the morning due to breakfast delivery and bath time. The staff had their hands full. It was the perfect time for me to go unnoticed. I slipped through the door and headed for Rose's room down the hall.

On the way to her room, I spotted an unattended food cart. I spelled bacon and maple syrup. One of my favorite morning meals. I grabbed one of the trays and walked into Rose's room like I was delivering her breakfast. Just so we're all on the same page, we all know that I am going to eat this, right?

When I walked into Rose's room, I discovered that she was still sleeping. This wasn't like her. The Rose I remembered was an early riser that loved to roam the halls all day. Maybe she was up late.

There was movement outside of Rose's room. I grabbed the tray and slid under her bed quick. This was a great opportunity to stuff my face before I retrieved the necklace from her secret stash spot. I was busy dunking rolled up pancakes into the plastic syrup cup when Rose's door opened. Someone peeked in and then closed the door. That was close.

Now that I finished my borrowed breakfast, it was time to grab the necklace and get the heck out of here. I felt bad about taking the necklace without talking to Rose about it first. Previously, we had made a friendly trade; her wing-shaped diamond earrings for the necklace. I would do my best to bring them back to her another day when we no longer needed them.

I stuck my hand in the hole of her box spring and pulled out Rose's secret stash box. A wave of relief came over me. My mission was almost complete. When I opened the box, the necklace wasn't there. A pearl necklace was in its spot. This necklace looked familiar to me. Crap, I think this was my grandmother's pearl necklace.

A memory from the night Nick escorted Rose out of my house popped into my head. As Rose walked by me, she held out a pearl necklace she was wearing. I didn't make the connection until now. If this necklace was my grandmother's, maybe Rose did another friendly trade, which meant the Key to Immortality was probably somewhere in my parents' bedroom.

I sighed and put my head down on the cold tile floor to think for just a second. What a waste of time this was. I didn't even need to come here after all, but how could I have known that.

The door to Rose's room opened again. This time, two sets of feet came inside. I did my best to stay still and quiet as they moved around the bed.

"She's still asleep," said a male voice.

It was Paul, one of the male orderlies. I knew this from my previous stay on the fifth floor.

"Dr. Parks wants us to keep her sedated, so she doesn't wander off again," said Dave, the other orderly.

"Let's give Rose her bed bath and if she wakes up, we will give her another pill," said Paul.

"That works for me," said Dave.

Great, now I was stuck here for a while.

***

It was cold outside, colder than I remembered. But I didn't seem to mind. It was refreshing.

The sky was winter white, like before a storm. There was ice and snow everywhere … and penguins … lots of penguins. Where was I? Antarctica? Greenland? Or maybe I was just at the zoo.

Nah, it was a faraway place in another dimension where people and animals coexisted in harmony. The weird thing that I couldn't quite figure out: why was I on my belly, on the cold ice, sliding backwards?

Dave and Paul had me by the ankles. They were pulling me out from underneath Rose's bed. How rude of them to wake me up from such a wonderful dream.

"I told you I heard snoring," said Paul.

They let go of my feet. I rolled over and looked up at the two orderlies. "So … how are we going to play this?"

The two orderlies threw me back a mystified look.

"Okay," I said, getting back to my feet. "I'll just go back to my room. Rose clearly isn't up for playing Prom this morning."

Rose unexpectedly shrieked as loud as she could to cause a diversion. She rolled out of bed and threw me the keys to the Maintenance Department's truck. I recognized the *Hello Kitty* keychain from when Lily and I had borrowed the truck previously. Rose tripped the orderlies that were headed in my direction. Paul and Dave fell to the floor. Rose winked at me. She signaled with a wave of her hand to go. Once again, Rose surprised me with her not so feeble actions. I headed out the door towards the elevator because it was my closest escape route. No one was in the hallway. The coast was clear. This was too easy. By the way, easy never ends well for me.

The elevator door was starting to open as I approached. It was Dr. Parks. The one person I did not want to see dressed like this. It would be grounds for an immediate psych evaluation. And she would call my mother. Dr Parks had her head down, reading someone's chart. The door to the next room was open. I quickly ducked inside before she saw me. About two seconds later, I saw Paul and Dave running in Dr. Parks' direction looking for me. Without missing a beat, I bolted out of the room I was in. The stairway was my only hope.

They were in hot pursuit. I didn't look back at the commotion behind me. It was better if they didn't get a clear shot at my face again. Of course, I knew Rose would never rat me out.

At the stairway door, I stepped inside and never hesitated for a second. My feet barely touched each step down to the next level. In my attempt to lose Dave and Paul, I left the stairway. I ran down the hall and got into the elevator on the fourth floor. The Maintenance Department was on the ground level with its own doorway to the outside. It was my best bet to get to the maintenance truck and hightail it out of the parking lot.

On my way through the Maintenance Department, I snagged, I mean borrowed, someone's winter coat from a hook on the wall. In the hallway by the backdoor, I came around the corner and ran into Rose.

"Rose, what the heck? You startled me."

She grabbed my arm. "Let's go outside before they catch us down here," she said.

I got in the truck. Rose nervously paced around, mumbling to herself.

"Rose, what is it? It's okay, you can tell me."

"Witches are sacrificing people around here," she said in a matter-of-fact way.

"Yes, I know," I said to reassure her it was safe to talk to me. "I need to find them, Rose. Help me, please! They have my brother."

"Follow the necklace. It will show you the way. But beware of the Horseman." She was getting extremely nervous and more agitated.

"Where am I going?" I pleaded with her for more information.

She approached the truck window. "The Pinelands of Darkness," she said. "Let the light reveal the way."

"Oh, brother. Thanks, Rose." I was about to hug her when the back door flew open. They had found us. The orderlies spotted Rose. Dave pointed at her. She started to run away from me so they would chase her. I took this as my chance to head out of the parking lot.

I did my best to drive home cool, calm, and levelheaded. There might have been no-signal lane changes, speeding, and rolling stop signs, but no tickets to speak of. I pulled up to my parents' white two-story Victorian mansion bought and paid for by their lottery winnings. It was a sight for these sore and tired eyes. It was nice to be home.

I found the spare key and went inside. "Hello house, did you miss me?" No one answered me which was a good thing. The first thing I needed to do was to find our spare cell phone. I found it in my dad's office. I plugged it in to let it charge while I went about my other tasks.

Second, I used our landline to call my mother. This was going to be an awkward conversation. The phone rang twice before my mother answered. "Hello?" said my mother, wondering who could be calling her from the house landline.

"Hi, Mom," I said in a breezy voice, waiting for the shit storm.

"Payton, what are you doing in River Bend?"

It was time to throw someone under the proverbial bus to save myself and my brother. I looked down at the diamond ring that was still on my finger. "Brad and Julie had a huge fight over the whole wedding thing, so a bunch of us took an earlier flight home." I held my breath waiting for some blow back.

"That poor girl. How awful for her. What was Brad's excuse?"

I could tell that she was about to demand some sort of an answer. "It just wasn't part of his plan." That was still part of the truth. Maybe I wouldn't go straight to hell when this was over.

"What a jerk," said my mother, without grasping the irony of me doing the same thing to Brad. "Have you talked to Luke or Lily?" asked my mother. "They aren't answering their cell phones."

"Yes, they are back here too," I said to avoid lying to her again.

"Well, you kids got out of here just in time. Did you hear that a bunch of crazy drunken Spring Break hooligans set fire to the bridal shop, blew up a ship down at the docks, and attacked Mrs. Vandersloot?"

"Wow! Those darn kids. You can't take them anywhere," I said before changing the subject. "Mom, the reason I called, is that I'm looking for grandma's pearl necklace. Where do you keep it?" I was hoping for a simple answer.

"In my bottom dresser drawer. Why?"

And there it was, the opportunity to lie like nobody's business. "We are taking Julie out on the town to cheer her up. I thought it would go nice with my blue dress."

"That is nice of you, dear. You are such a great friend to her."

I looked down at the ring stuck on my finger. "I'm trying to be," I said and sighed on the inside. I needed to try harder. Nice just wasn't on the top of my list at the moment. "See you, Mom. Say 'hi' to Dad for me." I hung up.

The necklace box was right where my mother/Rose had left it. Sweet. The Key to Immortality was safely tucked inside. I took it out of the box and put it around my neck for safe keeping. And I wanted to see if I felt any magical powers. Sadly, I did not. Maybe I needed to say, "Hocus Pocus" or "Blessed be." Still nothing. What a crock.

After stopping in my room to find some proper attire, jeans and a sweatshirt, I grabbed the charged cell phone from the office. There was still one more stop in the kitchen for the flashlight that was under the sink and maybe a chocolate pudding if I could find one.

It was time to test my theory. I had to know for sure if the necklace was the missing piece of the puzzle. I took the necklace off and shined the flashlight through the large, clear diamond in the middle. I tilted the necklace towards the kitchen wall. There was a clear outline of a map that shown on the light gray walls. That was all I need to know before I headed to find the rest of the gang.

Before leaving the house, I gobbled down two chocolate puddings, hoping they were not my last meal. I ran upstairs to grab a winter jacket and Chameleon clothes. When I was in the truck, I called the number Max had left for me. He answered. "I have the key in my possession."

"Great, I will relay the message to the group," he said.

"I'm on my way to retrieve the book. Where should I meet you?"

"We are on the edge of Clearwater Falls at the intersection of Big Math Lane and Pine Road."

"The Pinelands of Darkness?" I asked as I turned the key in the truck's ignition.

"Yeah, how'd you know that?" he asked in a surprised tone.

"Believe it or not, a crazy old lady told me."

"She doesn't sound so crazy," he joked.

"I think you may be right about that. See you soon."

Before hitting the highway to meet the gang, I drove out to my parents' restaurant, The Barbecue Shack. The cookbook/Gramarye was hidden in the secret floor safe in the office. My dad had it put in during the remodel. No one was supposed to know about it. It was a secret. Oh well. Let's just keep it between us, shall we?

I pulled up by the front door and ran inside. In the office, I moved the desk out of the way to expose the safe underneath. My fingers punched in the six-digit combination. The internal mechanism clunked releasing the lock. The door to the safe opened. I exhaled. I didn't even realize that I was holding my breath. I blew out a huge sigh of relief. The book was still in there. With the book in one hand and a beer in the other, I jumped back into the truck headed for the Pinelands of Darkness. Yikes. What could possibly go wrong?

***

Beware! The Pinelands of Darkness can be a scary place. Good luck getting past the gatekeeper.

CHAPTER TWENTY-NINE

FYI: The Pinelands of Darkness did not show up on a GPS search. I had to enter Big Math Lane and Pine Road into my phone to find my way. When I arrived at the site, I found a white Econoline van parked near the intersection. Lily must have recognized the Maintenance Department's truck I was driving. She slid the door of the van open and climbed out. I parked the truck on the side of the road. I immediately jumped out and headed over to the van.

"What took you so long?" Lily asked in a smartass tone. She stood next to the van in a confrontational manner with her hands on her hips.

Really? Popped into my head.

"What's the matter, you couldn't borrow anything nicer than that? I'm surprised you didn't commandeer a luxury SUV."

That's it! "What took me so long?" I gave her the stink of all stink eyes. I was no longer an emotionless robot. Lily had struck a nerve. My anger quickly manifested itself into rage. Before Lily knew what hit her, I jumped on top of her. Don't get me wrong, Lily was no Gothic pushover. I had my work cut out for me if I was going to win this fight. I did have the element of surprise on my side though.

Lily and I were rolling around on the ground like a middle school cat fight. We punched and clawed at each other until Brad stepped in and pulled us apart. Obviously, I was winning, that was my story anyway. I had landed a fairly solid right hook when I first attacked her. Lily would certainly have a black eye to remind her not to mess with me ever again.

One thing was for sure, my strength amazed me today. I was capable of more than I would have ever anticipated. Payton Richardson was a force to be reckoned with. She was a badass, afraid of no one. Yes, I just referred to myself in the third person. Badasses do that.

Brad had his arms out on each side of his body trying to keep Lily and I apart. I reached up with both hands to try to push Brad's outstretched arm away. He looked down at my hand when he saw the flash. "I see you found the ring," he said to distract me from trying to take Lily's head off. Brad stopping my fight, the diamond ring, me feeling embarrassed for losing my temper, this had déjà vu written all over it.

"Yeah, the dumb thing is stuck on my finger," I replied in a not-so-nice way.

"Sure, it is," Brad quibbled back.

I gave him a sour look.

"Enough already," said Lily. "We need to find Luke."

She was right. It was time to give up on this fight and concentrate on finding my brother. Brad dropped his arms to his sides as soon as he saw that we were giving up. Lily and I did our best to straighten our hair and clothing.

Brad looked at the both of us. "Can you two control yourselves for Crissake?"

"I can, if she can," said Lily.

"Lily, you could have killed me," I said in protest.

"But you're fine. You have more lives than a cat." Lily was pleading her case.

"Well, this cat had to cut herself out of a tree because of you." I put my hands on my hips. It was "go time" again.

The door of the van slid open, stopping Lily and I from starting round two of our cat fight. Brent stepped out of the van. "Payton, you're alive," he said joyously. "So nice to see your smiling face."

Just for the record, I wasn't smiling. Lily had me all worked up.

"Did you get the treasures?" Brent continued. "Can I see them?" He was being as transparent and as forward as I expected him to be.

"Yes, Brent, I have them." I reached beneath the collar of my sweatshirt to show him the chain of the necklace. I could tell by his eager expression that he would not be satisfied until I took it off and handed it to him. I was in the process of doing so when we were interrupted. The door of the van opened again. This time, Chameleon and Blond Ambition stepped out.

"Hi, guys," I said with a small wave of my left hand.

"Hey, Payton," they said in unison.

Just then, I had an idea that would make my life easier. "Can you guys do me a favor and ditch the truck down the road? Make sure you grab Chameleon's stuff out of the truck before you leave it. There is a bag behind the seat. Oh, and leave the winter coat in the backseat. It has to go back to the hospital with the truck."

"Anything for you, Payton," said Blond Ambition. I reached in my coat pocket and threw him the keys.

"Don't leave without us," said Chameleon as the two boys walked to the truck.

"Try to hurry. We're burning daylight," I said back.

Brad gave me one of his sideways glances. "What?" I asked him. "They needed some busy work." He seemed okay with my comment.

I took off the necklace and handed it to Brent. He held it up by the heavy, metal chain to admire its beauty. The rays of sunlight glinted off the shiny silver of the key and made the round, colored gemstones sparkle. The clear diamond stone in the head of the key's center seemed to be Brent's focus. When he held the key up to the direct sunlight, a beam of light passed through the stone and shined on the front of Brent's shirt. He became almost giddy when he looked down and saw the outline of the map on his chest.

"That's pretty cool," said Brad.

"Will it lead us to Luke?" asked Lily.

"That's the plan," I answered back. "We need to hurry and figure this out in time."

"This is excellent," said Brent, obviously excited to get started. He pulled a piece of paper and a small pencil out of his pocket with his left hand. "Payton, find where this new part of the map fits into the old part we drew on the plane, then trace it with this pencil."

I placed the piece of paper on Brent's chest. Lily helped hold it in place. For now, we were calling a truce for Luke. Once we lined up the new map with the old, I traced the lines onto the paper. Just as I finished, Chameleon and Blond Ambition walked up to the van.

"We parked the truck down one of the side roads," said Chameleon.

"The cops shouldn't find it for a day or two," said Blond Ambition.

"We have the rest of the map, guys," said Lily. "Let's go." Lily grabbed the shotgun spot next to the driver's seat. The six of us got back in the van. I climbed in the back next to Amber and Lisa. I sat on the floor in the back corner. On the other side in the back, Teagan and Max were still acting chummy. They sat next to each other, closer than need be in my opinion. Brent found a spot in the back by me. There seemed to be obvious tension between Brad and Julie. When Chameleon and Blond Ambition got back in the van, Chameleon sat next to Julie in the back while Brad was our esteemed chauffer. Was there possibly serious trouble in paradise?

I waved at Dylan, who was having a food conversation with Shoes in the back of the van. They were discussing a possible variation to the chicken wing recipe. Feedbag and Wolfman hung on every word, almost drooling at the prospect of tender, juicy, marinated meat. The Singe and his brother, Thirteen, were rubbing sticks together to see who could start a fire first.

It was business as usual. The gang was all accounted for, except for Crystal and Luke. I blew out a sad breath. I looked around the group. Who else were we going to lose along the way?

"Where to?" asked Brad, who was now behind the wheel of our mystery machine.

Brent looked down at the map. "We're close. Head north for about a mile and take a right."

Blond Ambition looked out one of the windows. "All I see is farms and more farms. Hey, maybe that Clip-clop Theory is true."

We all whipped our heads around and stared at him simultaneously.

"You know ... for their gene pool, like a—"

"For the love of all humanity, stop talking," I said to him. "Leave those sweet people out of this."

"Sorry," he said, "I was just thinking out loud."

"Think inside your head from now on," said Wolfman, shaking his head at his friend's comment.

After Brad took the right turn, we passed by a cemetery and more farms. "Now, what does the map say?" asked Brad, not wanting to get lost.

"Pull over," yelled Brent from the back of the van.

Brad slammed on the brakes. We all smashed together briefly, sharing our DNA with each other.

"Why did we stop?" asked Chameleon. He crawled over to Brent on all fours to look at the map.

"The map ended," said Brent scratching his head. "Turn around and go back. We must have missed something."

Chameleon looked at the map in Brent's hand. "Brent is right, go back."

"There is nothing out here but farms and a damn cemetery," stated Max. "Go back to what?"

The sudden jarring of my brain brought back a memory of something Rose had said to me. When I asked her where she was going, she had said, "the cemetery."

"Did you guys see that?" asked Max. He pointed out the window.

Brad slammed on the brakes again. We all braced ourselves better this time.

"Over there in the cemetery," said Max in an anxious tone. "There's a guy with duffle bags."

"Sweet!" said The Singe. "We have ourselves a body snatcher." He was beaming with excitement.

"Pardon me?" said Amber. "I'm not happy with this."

"Yeah, I didn't sign up for no Crypt Keeper nonsense," said Teagan. "I came on this adventure for booze and boys and I'm getting thirsty."

"Jinkies, Velma," said Max. "You and Scooby Doo can stay in the van."

Teagan gave Max a shove and flipped her hair to seal her message of disapproval. Max didn't seem too upset. He just laughed at Teagan's childish reaction.

"Pull over up here," said Brent. "We'll sneak back and ambush the creep."

"Screw that," said Brad. "We're coming in hot. When I slam on the brakes, everyone jump out and grab him if he tries to run." Brad was ready to show off his cop driving skills.

"That sounds like a solid plan," said Lisa in a higher pitched voice. She was obviously doubting any of this working out in our favor.

"Light the fire and streak the tires," said The Singe. "Yee haw!"

"Everyone hold on," said Brad. He stomped on the gas pedal. Our heads whipped backwards. I closed my eyes, crossed my fingers, and said a quick prayer. "Amen," I said out loud.

"Amen," said the rest of the van in unison. We were all praying for our survival.

I decided it was best to open my eyes. The van jumped the curb and headed down the narrow cemetery road like a bullet. We startled the tall slender man. He instinctively turned his body towards the ruckus that was headed his way. As our speeding van came closer to him, I got a better look at his outer garb. He wore a long brown jacket and a dark-colored ratty cowboy hat pulled down over his ears. His beady eyes were barely noticeable. I saw them for a split second before he turned to run away. He took off in the snow carrying two full navy-blue duffle bags.

Brad drove off the narrow road to the right, trying to cut him off. Everyone in the van was oddly quiet. I think we were all holding our breath. I looked out the passenger side window, trying to see what was happening. All was good. We were closing in on him.

"Come back here, you freak," said Brad, like the guy could hear him. He pressed down hard on the gas. Tombstones were flying by the window. I changed my mind. All was not good. This was the first time I actually felt afraid. What if we hit one of those stones? None of us were wearing seat belts.

Lily leaned over and honked the horn repeatedly to startle and fluster the man. It worked. He tripped over one of the smaller tombstones. The guy faceplanted in the snow.

"Ouch!" said Max, who was now watching the action from between the front seats.

"Hang on!" yelled Brad. He slammed on the brakes and cranked the wheel to avoid hitting the man. The van skidded to a stop in the snow. Max threw the door open. We all piled out like we were attacking a beach during wartime. Our precision was outstanding.

Feedbag, Shoes, and Wolfman got to him first. They jumped on top of him. The boys pulled him to his feet. Brad was playing his role of lead detective a bit too well. He walked up slowly, ready to interrogate and intimidate the suspect. The rest of us formed a circle around him to prevent his escape.

Brad looked him up and down. "What's your name?" asked Brad in a serious cop manner.

"I didn't see anything," said the man.

Brad got in his face. "That's not what I asked you."

The man trembled. "My name is Duffy, Duffy the Digger. That's what my friends call me. I won't say anything. I never do."

Lily walked up closer to the man. "Who do you think we are?"

"So … you're not the serial killer cult in the white van with the black hoods?" asked Duffy with apprehension.

"No," said Brad, "we are the good guys."

"Yeah, we are," said Max to ensure Duffy's trust.

"You can see why I would be confused," said Duffy in his defense. He sneered at us.

"Duffy, did you see the people that kidnapped my brother?" I asked, hoping to get an honest answer.

"I generally mind my own business," he said.

Duffy's answer was short and sweet. It was not what I was hoping for.

Lily walked up to him and got her Goth attitude on. She got in his face, then tilted her head to one side. "Not today, you're not. What are you doing here?" Lily gave him the death stare. Well, that was what I was calling it.

Duffy put his arms out to his sides. "I'm Duffy the Digger." His index fingers pointed at himself. "I rob graves, just in case you didn't notice. Those guys that you are looking for, they come and go. We peacefully coexist here in the graveyard. They do their thing and I do mine." Duffy stared back at Lily. "You don't scare me, Girlie."

Brad bent down and opened one of Duffy's bags. He looked inside. "Be afraid of me then. I'm a police officer. I'm about to haul your ass to jail. You better start talking."

"What happens in the cemetery, stays in the cemetery," was Duffy's inconvenient answer.

Brad reached into one of the bags and grabbed a handful of jewelry. "Do you know what this is?" asked Brad.

"My livelihood," said Duffy, mocking Brad.

"No, it's five-to-ten years in jail," Brad was turning up his bad cop demeanor.

I looked at the jewelry in Brad's hand. "Hey, let me see that cross necklace." I stepped closer. He handed it over to me. "This is my brother's. Where did you find this?"

Duffy was silent.

I looked around the group. "Can somebody bribe him with something, please?"

"Don't look at me," said Teagan, "I'm reformed."

I face-palmed myself. We could have used Teagan and her slutty ways right now.

Lily looked over at the necklace. I could tell that she recognized it too by the look I saw in her eyes. This guy was in big trouble. Without saying a word, Lily grabbed his left nipple. He yelped, even though she was twisting his coat fabric too. We all winced, knowing that she was inflicting serious pain with her purple nurple.

"Start talking and I'll let go," she said. Duffy was silent. She twisted it a little further.

Duffy let out another yelp. "Okay. Okay. Check out the footprints over there."

"And?" said Lily, twisting even further.

"Yow!" he screamed. "Sometimes they go in, but they don't come back out. That's all I know."

Lily let go. She seemed satisfied with his answer. "Show us where," she demanded.

The whole group followed Duffy over to the tracks in the snow. The tracks led us to a ten-foot by ten-foot concrete and marble mausoleum.

"Show us where you found it," instructed Brad. He grabbed Duffy by the sleeve of his coat.

Duffy pointed to the entrance of the mausoleum. "I found it right there next to the marble pillar."

"Luke left us a clue," said Lily. She seemed relieved. "Luke is still alive."

I looked up at the name on the front of the mausoleum. The word "Horsman" was chiseled into the stone. "We are in the right place," I informed everyone. "Rose told me to 'beware of the horseman.' I had no idea that it would end up being a building."

"How are we going to get inside?" asked Chameleon. "There aren't any windows."

"Let's ram the door like we did on the ship," said Wolfman. "We can use our brute strength."

"No good. It's steel reinforced," said Brad feeling the hinges. "Someone is definitely trying to keep people out."

"Or people in," said Max.

"Luke, are you in there?" shouted Lily. She pounded on the door. "Can you hear me?"

"On second thought, maybe we don't want to go in there," said Chameleon. "Have any of you ever heard of exploding casket syndrome? A decomposing body in a sealed casket acts like a pressure cooker until BLAMO! Smelly gas and body fluids everywhere."

"Oh man, I think I'm nauseous," said Dylan. He suddenly turned visibly green.

"Dude, you really need to keep some of your knowledge to yourself," said Max.

"Payton, try the key," said Brent. He smiled, feeling far superior with the use of his brain power.

***

Enter at your own risk.

CHAPTER THIRTY

The boys started chanting, "Key. Key. Key. Key. Key. Key. Key."

I held out my hand for Brent to give me the key back. He did. I slowly slid the three flat teeth of the key into the keyhole cover. The key fit, but when I tried to turn it counterclockwise to unlock the door, it wouldn't turn. "Something is stopping the key from turning," I said.

"Maybe it's another puzzle," suggested Max.

"Brent, Chameleon, you're up," I said. "You two are smarter than the rest of us combined. See if you can figure this out. I'm brain dead."

Brent and Chameleon stepped up to examine the lock. Chameleon was first up to bat. "First of all, it is clearly a custom lock to be able to house this antique key and be functional."

"And at this point," said Brent, "we are assuming it is functional."

We all nodded in agreement.

Chameleon touched the circular, gray metal plate behind the doorknob. The plate was made up of three separate circular disks of metal. The front disk was the smallest of the three, with each disk being slightly larger than the one before it. The largest of the metal disks was next to the metal door. The smallest disk had four creatures spread out evenly around the circle: an eagle, a man, a fish, and a bull. The middle disk had twelve symbols spread evenly out around the edge of the plate. The largest of the circular disks had numbers, one through thirty-one etched into the metal.

"This looks like a combination lock," said Chameleon.

"Check to see if they spin," suggested Lily.

Chameleon put his fingers on the three metal disks and tried to move them. "We have a spinner, folks," he laughed at his own joke.

"A combination lock with three levels," stated Brent. He smiled.

"I know what you're doing," said Lily. "Stop it. I am in no mood for your number crap."

Brent sighed with disappointment. "Let's start with the middle ring with the twelve symbols."

I looked around the group. "Does anyone know what they are?" Brent and Chameleon were the only ones raising their hands. I pointed at Chameleon. "Chameleon, give it a go, fascinate us."

"The twelve symbols are the signs of the Zodiac, one for each month," explained Chameleon.

"The answer is easy," said Max. "Which symbol is for March?"

"Slow down your roll," said Chameleon, "The signs of the Zodiac are based on the visible constellations in the sky, not by the exact calendar month."

Brent jumped in to show off his knowledge. "The concept of the signs of the Zodiac goes back even further than the Middle Ages. It goes back to the ancient Egyptian period, in the third millennium BC." Brent looked over at Lily for her reaction to squeezing the number three into the conversation again. He smiled. She glared.

"Everyone, cut the crap and get to the point," said Brad, in a tone that reminded me of his father. "We're all freezing off valuable body parts."

I let out a small giggle that did not go unnoticed. I looked around the group. "Hey, Duffy is gone," I said.

"He will be back," said Brad. "We interrupted his pillage and plunder."

Brent cleared his throat, which I have deducted from our history together, meant he was getting back to business.

"Let's go with Max's suggestion," I said to help things get back on track.

Brent started back in. "If we went by today's date, we would be under the Zodiac sign for Pisces, which is February 19-March 20." He put his fingers on the middle disk and started to turn it. "The glyph for Pisces is the one that looks like a curvy capital letter 'H'. Is everyone with me so far?"

We all nodded in agreement.

"The smallest disk has an eagle, a man, a fish, and a bull," Brent said to remind everyone.

"I am a Pisces," said Lily. "The symbol is a fish."

"Okay," said Brent. He turned the smallest disk to the fish. "Now for the last disk with the numbers."

"It has to be the days of the month," Max interjected.

"Set the disk to today's date, the sixteenth," said Chameleon.

Brent turned the plate to the sixteen. "If this is correct, the door should open," he said with a smile. He tried to turn the key. It wouldn't turn.

Brad blew out a discussed breath. "I thought you guys were smart. Find me something to beat this damn door down."

"I don't get it," said Brent. "Setting the rose should have worked."

"What did you just say?" I asked Brent.

"Setting the rose, the metal plate behind the doorknob is called the rose," said Brent to reiterate.

"Maybe we need to look at the key for the answers," I suggested. "It has a rose. I'm sure it's not a coincidence."

"Brilliant," said Brent. He took the key out of the lock. "Ideas anyone?"

"What month has a clear stone?" asked Blond Ambition.

"April is the diamond," said Julie.

I put my left hand in my pocket to avoid anyone noticing the diamond that was on my finger.

"Change the disk to either Aries, March 21-April 19, or Taurus, April 20-May 20," said Brent.

"Try Aries," I said, following a hunch.

Brent moved the plate to the correct symbol. "Ah, the ram," he said. "Aries represents the singular spirit of 'every person for themselves' philosophy. The symbol even looks like the horns of a ram." Brent turned and looked at me with a raised eyebrow. "Which date?"

"The first of April," I blurted out.

"April Fools' Day. Classic," said Chameleon.

"Why not? said Lily. "This game has been one big practical joke so far."

Brent moved the plate to the number one.

"What about the first disk," asked Lily. "Which of the FOUR is it?" Lily was smirking as she looked at Brent. It was more of their number nonsense. I rolled my eyes.

"Try them all," said Max. Most of the group nodded yes in agreement.

"Wait!" yelled Brad before Brent could spin the disk. "What if it's booby trapped. We need to think about this."

"He's right," I said. I rubbed my temples. "Think. Think. Think," I said under my breath to myself.

"Maybe it's part of a riddle," said The Singe.

"Yeah, look around for a clue or a piece of paper," said Amber.

The entire group started searching around the mausoleum. "Stop," I said to my friends. "I think I've got it. There is a riddle on the back of the key. Brent, what does it say again?"

Brent turned the key over to read it word for word. "Conceived in water; born in air."

The group was silent. The hamster jumped on the wheel in everyone's brain. I swear I could hear the squeaky wheels turning.

"There should be a frog or a tadpole on the wheel," said Chameleon. "A tadpole in the water transforms into a frog on land." He was visibly frustrated. His theory did make sense.

I'm not sure if I actually had a brainstorm or if it was just the fact that I had to pee when the following thought popped into my head: "What if the answer is 'man'?" I said and waited for the blowback.

The group was flat-out staring at me now without saying anything. It was unsettling.

"You know, like an embryo developing in the amniotic fluid which is also known as 'the water.' Then the baby is born into the air and breathes."

"Wow, Payton," said Brent. "I am impressed with your logic."

"I'd buy the 'Aquaman' answer," said Chameleon. "Let's try it."

Brent had his hand on the small, metal disk ready to turn it.

"Wait," said Julie, jumping into the conversation after being quiet this whole time. "It could be the bull too."

"I think we should stick to the answer of the man," said Lily in a firm voice. "It makes sense. Man's spirit is the fifth element and jives with the pentacle."

"I think it's Taurus and the bull," said Julie, not backing down.

"We'll try Payton's logic first and then Julie's," said Brent taking charge.

Everyone agreed except Julie. She looked at Brad. He pointed at Payton and shrugged. Julie crossed her arms across her chest and pouted big-time.

After my obnoxious eye roll, Brent started to turn the smallest metal disk to the stick figure of a man. He carefully inserted the key and turned it counterclockwise. "It's turning!" he shouted with joy. There was a distinct metal clunk of the lock being released.

"Try the doorknob," said Lily, eager to finally get inside and search for Luke.

Brent turned the silver-colored knob with ease. The door swung inside. Brent stepped inside the mausoleum and pulled the key out of the lock.

Everyone walked up to the entrance and peeked inside, except for Dylan. "I'm not going in there. I'll stay out here with the van."

"Are you sure?" I asked, touching his arm. When my hand touched him, those darn invisible sparks flew everywhere. The law of attraction was hard at work.

He looked at me with his emerald pools of joy. "Yeah, I'll be fine out here. Sorry, all the talk about exploding caskets has my stomach upset. Besides, I'm claustrophobic."

"Okay," I told him. "You've been through a lot lately. Do you want someone to stay out here with you?"

"I'll be fine out here in the van alone. If anyone comes, I'll honk. Don't worry about me."

I didn't like leaving him out here by himself, but I couldn't force him to go in there if he didn't want to. "Okay, do what you are comfortable with." Dylan walked over to the van and climbed into the driver's seat. I turned my attention back to the creepy cement box for dead people that I was about to enter.

I joined the group that was already inside. It was a tad crowded. Someone had found the light switch on the wall for the overhead light. The walls had been sheet-rocked, textured, and painted a light gray color that fit the small space. A red velvet wingback chair sat in the left corner for visitors. On the right side of the room was a closed, solid oak casket on a cart. The cart was covered by a black fabric skirt.

"Why doesn't it stink like dead bodies in here?" asked Feedbag. "Chameleon got my hopes up."

We all gave him a weird look.

"Bodies placed in a crypt like this usually dehydrate and become like leather," said Brent.

"Except for the rare ones that decompose and explode," said Chameleon. "I'm sure it is okay to open the casket since there is no smell." Chameleon reached for the lid. The rest of us moved back as far as we could in the confined space. He opened the lid with one swift motion. I held my breath. We all leaned forward to observe the possible car wreck inside.

"Where's the body?" asked Amber.

"Maybe Duffy took it," said Blond Ambition in a joking manner. Lily cuffed him in the back of the head for his stupid comment.

Chameleon opened the foot end of the casket. "Look, there's a bag inside." He opened the bag. "It's our cellphones and purses." He took his own cellphone out and passed the canvas bag around the room.

"So … the killer definitely brought Luke in here," said Lily.

"But where did they go? This is hopeless," I said, feeling defeated by a dead end. I took a seat on the floor.

"Didn't Duffy say that sometimes they go in, but they don't come out," said Brad. He was on to something. Brad walked over to the casket and started to feel around on the wooden surface.

"What are you looking for?" asked Julie.

"I'm looking for a latch," answered Brad. "I think there is a tunnel under this building."

I placed my hands palm-side down on the cement floor. It was warm to the touch. I looked up at Brad. "The floor is warm. I think you're right." I pulled myself to my feet and joined in on the search for the entrance to the tunnel. I was feeling around the legs of the cart under the casket. Brent and Chameleon were feeling around on the casket's wooden surface. Teagan, Lisa, and Amber were pulling on all the gold metal handles. Brad and Julie were feeling around on the inside satin lining of the casket. The rest of the group stood by and watched our failed attempt at finding anything at all.

"This is dumb … and taking too long," said The Singe. "Maybe I should go outside and start a fire so we can keep warm."

I pointed my finger at him. "Don't you dare go anywhere or even think about fire," I said in protest.

The Singe stepped backward and tripped over Max's outstretched foot. He fell backwards into the red velvet chair in the corner. His weight made the chair rock backward on its hind legs. We all heard the floor under the casket move.

"Singe, you're an accidental genius," said Brent.

Brad, Wolfman, and Lily pushed the casket and cart out of the way. A trapdoor was now visible in the spot where the casket once stood.

"Everyone stand back for your own safety," demanded Brad with an outstretched arm.

My guess, he was assuming that someone could be on the other side of the trapdoor. Of course, I didn't listen to him. Before Brad could stop me, I grabbed the edge of the trapdoor and slid it back. I stuck my head in the dark opening. "Luke. Luke."

Brad grabbed me by the shoulders and pulled me back. "Are you out of your mind? Have you ever heard of the element of surprise?" He had a disgusted look on his face.

I knew he was right. I was also lucky to be alive. There could have been a trap to the trapdoor. "Yes, I've heard of it," I said, being lippy. "It's right next to the element of stupidity on the periodic table." I made a sassy face at him.

"Good one," said Chameleon, digging my science humor.

Brad rolled his eyes at me, then he pointed his authority-figure finger in my direction. "Just don't," he said. I pulled out my flashlight. Brad grabbed it out of my hand. "I'm leading the descent into the tunnel. Stay behind me and stay quiet." He looked around the group. We all nodded that we understood. Brad was in charge. By the tone in his voice, he had never been more serious.

"Okay," I finally said out loud so that he knew for sure I was submitting.

He shined the flashlight into the dark hole. "I see a ladder," he whispered. He got down on his hands and knees. Brad carefully put his head into the hole and looked both ways to make sure it was safe before climbing down. He scooted to the edge of the opening and climbed down the ladder. As soon as he was at the bottom, a beam of light shined up from the hole.

Brent moved next to the opening and peered inside. He turned to the group. "Brad found a light switch. It should be safe for the rest of us to enter."

Before getting in line to make my way down the hole, I peeked out the doorway to check on Dylan. He was okay. He was sitting in the van. This made me feel better. "I'm next," I said. I butted in the line right behind Lily. Teagan gave me a mean look at first that morphed into a smile after I stared at her.

After Lily climbed down, I was eager to check it out. I didn't want to miss out on anything. The vertical metal ladder was a piece of cake. I nearly slid down it because I was so jacked up to see the killer's lair and look for Luke. Once I set foot down on solid ground, it was clear that this was a sophisticated tunnel system with heat and electricity. The warmth of the heating system took the chill off my face. Torch-style lighting sconces lit the medieval-looking stone covered walls. At the end of the short hallway, we all stopped at the locked gray, metal door. Brent stepped forward and used the ancient silver key to gain entry to the next tunnel. This time there wasn't a puzzle to solve. It was a bit too easy. This was making my stomach nervous waiting for something bad to happen.

After Brent unlocked the door, Brad stepped in and slowly opened the door out of caution. He stuck his right hand around the corner of the door jam, looking for a light switch. Brad flicked on the light.

"Three doors. Interesting ..." said Brent. He was intrigued by another chance to push the superiority of the number three on Lily.

"Stuff it," said Lily in response. "I'm in no mood for this." She walked over to the first door on the left and turned the knob. It was locked. I could tell by her extra-large sigh. "A little help, key master," she said.

Brent happily walked over to the door Lily was standing at and used the key to unlock it. After he unlocked the first door, he did the same to the other two. "What's behind door number one, Lily?" Brent asked like a game show host.

Lily pushed the door open. She stood in the doorway and didn't move. She said nothing. Her silence told me everything. It wasn't good.

"Lily, what is it?" Everyone could hear the dread in my voice. Without hesitating, I ran over and turned on the light to see what she was staring at. The roughly fifteen-foot by fifteen-foot space was a ceremony room. All four walls were covered in beige colored stones. Dark stained wooden beams covered the ceiling and were probably part of its support structure. The dark red tiled floor was covered with a large, circular area rug in dark red and black tones. A life-sized ancient statue stood in the right corner. Most of the far back wall was covered in a woven tapestry.

The shock finally wore off. Lily entered the room. "Brent, this is better than your dungeon." Lily felt the real stone walls with her hand. Brent's walls were painted to look like stone.

"Excuse me?" said Brad.

"Relax, Brad. He has a cool man cave is all." I said in Brent's defense. I turned my attention back to Lily who was now snooping around.

She bent down next to the edge of the rug. She pulled the rug back to expose the floor underneath. "Just what I thought," she said. "There's a pentagram painted on the floor."

Brent walked over to the tapestry on the back wall. "Nice Theosophische Darstellung Zur Alchemie," commented Brent.

Lily and I walked over to it. "It looks like the wheel of death," I said, staring at the creepy goat face in the middle.

"It is more like the wheel of life," said Brent, correcting me.

Brent pointed at the words that ran around the circle. "Vista, Interiora, Terra, Rectificando, Inuenies, Occultum, Lapidem."

Each word had a section on the wheel. "Is that Latin?" I asked.

"Yes, the first letter of each word spells out Vitriol, which is an old name for hydrochloric acid."

"What does it mean?" asked Lily.

Brent smiled because he knew the answer. "It roughly translates to visit the interior of the earth and by rectifying you will find the hidden stone."

We looked at him with blank faces.

Brent pointed to the last two sections on the tapestry. "Just concentrate on these two sections: Occultum and Lapidem. The first word means secret and the second means stone, as in the Philosopher's Stone."

"So this is how to find the stone?" asked Lily.

"What does this have to do with us?" I asked.

Brent pointed to the tapestry again. "See how the left foot at the bottom of the wheel is in the grass, and the right foot is in the water with the ice cubes?" Lily and I nodded on impulse. "It is probably no coincidence that the foot on the right is next to the word corpus."

"As in corpse? As in 'I see dead people'?" I asked. "Ish! No thank you. I've heard enough."

Brent laughed at me. "It could symbolize a corpse in cold water like the boys that are found."

Chameleon poked his head in the room. "Cool, is that a statue of Anubis?"

"Yes, it is," said Brent. "Anubis is—"

"—the Egyptian god of mummification and the afterlife," said Chameleon, stealing the words out of Brent's mouth. "He is the patron god of lost souls. Anubis was known for standing by the gods in the afterlife to assist with their resurrection."

"Creepy much," said Teagan as she walked by the doorway.

"Guys!" yelled Blond Ambition. "You need to see this." His voice was coming from the room next door.

Brent, Chameleon, Lily and I ran to the next room to see what was up. The room was long and narrow. The walls and the floor were covered with the same stone as the ritual room. Blond Ambition, Max, and Teagan stood next to a large, oval tub in the center of the room.

"That's not good," said Brent when he noticed that the tub was still full of water.

Max stuck his hand in the water. "It's still lukewarm."

"Lukewarm?" My heart sank. Was this tub filled for Luke?

"Why would they have a large party tub in a place like this?" asked Blond Ambition.

Chameleon reached up and cuffed him in the back of the head for all of us.

"Oh. Sorry, Payton," he said in a deflated voice once he figured out what he had said.

"It's okay," I told him. "This dark religion shit is a mystery to all of us."

"Hopefully, it means we are just a few steps behind them," said Lily to make herself and the rest of us feel better.

Brad poked his head in the room. "Payton, we found something else." He had a grim look on his face.

The last room was about the same size as the ritual room. Its décor was scaled back to gray, cement block walls and a gray tile floor. The room was divided into four cell rooms constructed for privacy. Each cell had a solid metal door with a smaller hinged door that opened to the hallway. The smaller hinged door appeared to be for passing food and water. Inside each cell, there was a small cot and a toilet. These rooms were not for entertaining. These rooms were for holding someone against their will.

Brad walked me inside the first cell. He picked up the light-colored jean jacket that I had seen my brother wear many times. "This is Luke's, isn't it?" Brad asked, already knowing the answer.

I nodded yes. "We are so close to rescuing him, I can feel it," I said.

Brad had the same grim look as before. "Payton, there is one more room I need to show you." He walked down the short hallway between the cells. I followed. He turned the doorknob on the mystery room door. Before he even opened it, I could hear the hum of large electrical appliances. I could also hear a metal-on-metal clank inside the room.

"Payton," said Amber, "maybe you shouldn't go in there."

I pushed the door open. I needed to know. Directly in front of me was an upright kitchen refrigerator. I felt a momentary relief. It was probably for keeping food, water, ect. No big deal. When I walked further into the room, I found Lily and Lisa each beating on the locks of two separate white, commercial chest freezers.

"Is Luke?" was all I could say.

Lily turned to face me. Her expression was a mix of grave determination and tears. "I don't know," she muttered.

Wolfman came into the room carrying a crowbar. "Look out. Stand back," he said. He pushed Lily out of his way. With his brawny brute force, he wedged the metal crowbar between the lid of the freezer and its base. He let his body weight and muscle do the rest to pop the lid open. After four or five tries, the lid of the freezer gave way. Wolfman urgently lifted the lid. The entire crew simultaneously moved as close as they could to find out who or what was inside.

Lily pushed her way back up to the front of the crowd. "It's empty," she said with a relieved sigh. She wiped the tears from her cheeks with the sleeve of her shirt.

Wolfman turned around. The crew got out his way. He approached the second freezer with the same determination as the first. Wolfman wedged the crowbar inside the crack between the lid and the base. This time, Brad stepped in to lend a hand. After only two attempts, the lid flew open. Everyone in the room craned their necks to get a good look inside. The room was dead silent.

"It's empty too," declared Wolfman.

"Freaking hell that was intense," said Chameleon. "I thought for sure he was—" He stopped himself, realizing that what he was about to say was in poor taste.

The tension of the whole group subsided.

"This is good news, right?" I asked. "This means Luke is still alive." I was positive and hopeful.

"We are right on their heels. I can feel it," said Lily.

"I bet we chased them away," said Brad. "Brent, Lily, you guys are in charge until I get back." Brad left the room suddenly.

The profound scene was too much for me to handle. The small room had me feeling claustrophobic to say the least. I ran out into the entryway to be alone and calm down. When I got out there, all the emotions hit me like an extra-large Winnebago. I slid down the wall until I was sitting on the floor. With my eyes closed, I concentrated on my deep breathing exercises.

Once I had my breathing under control, I opened my eyes and looked up to say a prayer, thanking the heavens for hope in my hopeless situation. This was when that pesky, little, tenacious hamster jumped back on the wheel in my brain. If we were right on the killer's heels, how did they get out of here without us seeing them? When I glanced up again, I noticed wires running along the ceiling. I got back up on my feet and followed the wires from the hall into the ritual room. The wires ran around the edge of the room. They were nearly concealed by the stone on the walls. I couldn't believe none of us noticed them before. The wires continued around the room to the wheel-of-death tapestry on the back wall. All this electricity and warmth was coming from somewhere and I was determined to find it.

I stared at the tapestry. It rippled like air was blowing on it. I grabbed the edge of the tapestry to pull it back to see what was behind it. Before I could do anything else, a hand reached out and grabbed my arm, pulling me behind the cloth curtain.

***

I repeat, enter at your own risk.

CHAPTER THIRTY-ONE

The space I was in was dark, narrow, and smelled oddly of wet dog. The person who grabbed me put their hand over my mouth to keep me quiet. I didn't try to scream after hearing his annoying voice whisper in my ear.

"Hello, Sweet Cheeks."

It was Brad. "What are you doing back here?" I asked him. "You scared the crap out of me." I punched him in the dark. I'm not sure where my punch landed, but I was satisfied when I heard, "Geez!" spring out of his mouth.

"Fine, you can come with," he answered back with his usual smug attitude.

"How did you find the tunnel?" I asked. "Did you follow the wires on the ceiling too?"

"No, but kudos to you. It was something Duffy said about sometimes they go in and don't come out. I figured there had to be another way in and out of this place."

"How did you get the door to unlock?"

"You know that statue of the golden dog man in the corner?"

"That's Anubis," I said, feeling smart.

Brad ignored my comment. "After the chair in the mausoleum opened the trap door, I pushed on parts of the statue to see if it would open the door behind the tapestry. Finally, when I twisted its left arm, the door unlocked."

"Great work, Detective Thomas,"

"Are you flirting with me in a dark tunnel?"

I couldn't see his face in the dark. I knew he was smirking from my past experience with him. I paused briefly before answering him. "No. Don't be dumb. Why would I do that?"

Brad started laughing because I had paused. "Said the girl still wearing my engagement ring."

"I told you, it's stuck. Hey, why didn't you tell Julie that I have it and give it back to her?"

"In front of everyone … no way. I am in no mood for that much drama."

"Trouble in paradise?" I was obviously probing for information.

"Shut up and help me look for the light switch."

Oh brother, that was a definite yes. I patted the walls with my hands trying to help find the switch. A warm, happy feeling crept into my subconscious. I didn't feel guilty about it. This was troublesome due to our history together.

"What about you and Mr. Smooth? Things seem a bit icy between you."

"There is no 'thing', just some lingering sparks that have fizzled out." The truth stung a bit to say out loud.

We both found the light switch at the same time. Our fingers touched and lingered. Brad pulled me close to him in the dark. History was about to repeat itself.

Brad nuzzled my ear and whispered, "God you smell good." His hot breath on my skin sent a warm glow through my body.

"I think it's called fear," I whispered back.

"Are you afraid of me?"

"I'm more afraid of myself and what I want to do to you," I said back.

"Well, then," he said pushing me away. "I supposed we better turn on the light and proceed down the creepy tunnel before I hold you to it."

Dang it, the attraction was real. "I guess that is one option," slipped out.

"Huh?"

I had thrown Brad off his game. There was awkward silence, sexual tension, and a lot of sweating. Maybe we were the wet dog smell. To make it stop, I threw myself at him and kissed him. The passion and heat were exhilarating as our warm lips and tongues met in a wave of desire. With Brad, our previous sex life was all or nothing. There was usually no stopping the train once it left the station. It was "all aboard, who's coming aboard." I was ready to blow that whistle.

Our lingering kiss was soon interrupted by voices on the other side of the tapestry. We stopped kissing to listen to their conversation.

"Where'd Brad and Payton go?" asked Chameleon.

"They just can't stay away from each other," said Julie in a disgusted, jealous tone.

"Does that mean you are free to move about the country?" asked Chameleon, laying on the charm. Holy crap! He wanted to know if he had a shot with her. He was finally going to get an answer.

Julie giggled in a flirty way. "Maybe it does," she said, trying to be coy.

I heard Brad grimace under his breath. He slowly and quietly pushed the door shut. "Good luck trying to follow us, you little weaseling bastard," said Brad. He was angry and being a hypocrite at the same time. I wasn't about to point out that fact.

Brad found the light switch again without my help. He flicked on the light, revealing a long gray cement block tunnel with a poured cement floor. Regular sixty-watt bulbs in small, white, ceramic ceiling fixtures lit the narrow passageway. There were no frills spent on this part of the tunnel. It appeared to be a simple escape route.

Brad took me by the hand. "C'mon, let's go find your brother."

I smiled back and touched his face in an adoring way. For a moment we had a deep bonding connection. We walked down the tunnel together shoulder-to-shoulder.

I turned toward him. "This creepy tunnel reminds me of the basement of the hospital where you hid under the sheet on the gurney to scare me."

"Payton, that was just a prank to get back at you for throwing up on my pants. You trust me, right?"

"Yeah, totally," I said back to assure him. Part of me was still a little unsure and uneasy. I turned and looked back down the long tunnel in front of us. "Is that a shoe?" I let go of his hand and ran towards it. As I got closer, I realized that it was Luke's tennis shoe.

"Payton, stop!" screamed Brad. "There is a tripwire in front of you."

I did my best to try to stop in time, I really did. My momentum carried me forward. I lost my balance and fell backward on my butt. My feet slid forward into the tripwire that was just inches off the floor. My head and torso simultaneously fell backward towards the hard, cement floor. A metal spear came out of the wall. It whooshed over my head, missing me by mere inches. The spear hit the other wall and stuck into the cement. From my perspective, I could read the words "Gate Keeper" engraved on the shaft of the spear. For once, my awkward clumsiness most likely saved my life. "Well, that was rude," I said with annoyance. I tried to get up.

"Don't move. Stay down," yelled Brad. "Let me check it out first." He slowly walked up behind me and carefully inspected the tripwire and the wall surrounding the spear.

I did as I was told. I stayed motionless on the cold, cement floor. "Tell me when I can move. I'm freezing down here."

"Okay, now slide backwards away from the tripwire," instructed Brad in a calm voice. Brad walked over to me and helped me get back to my feet.

I hugged him for saving my life. "Do you think the killer set a trap for me by leaving one of Luke's shoes as bait?" I asked.

"It appears so. That really makes me wonder what they are hiding on the other end of this tunnel."

"I feel like we are getting closer to the truth and the killer's identity," I added.

"Dangerously close," Brad commented back. "Give me your shoes. I want to try something."

I handed over my shoes for Brad's experiment. Brad threw the first shoe into the tripwire. This time, nothing happened. "Just as I expected, the trap is dead." He threw the second shoe over the tripwire to see if it was safe for us to cross over it. The shoe landed on the floor and rolled to a stop without setting off any more deadly weaponry.

"Follow right behind me," said Brad. "Go slow, there might be another trap." Brad maneuvered around the spear and stepped over the tripwire. Once he was over the tripwire, he held out his hand for me to grab. "Take my hand for balance. Don't touch anything."

"Got it," I answered back. His hand was warm and comforting. On the other side of the tripwire, I let go of his hand long enough to pick up my shoes and put them back on my feet. We went slow and steady another thirty feet or so until we hit the end of the tunnel. I looked at Brad. "There's no door. How in the hell do we get out of here?" I pounded on one of the gray blocks with my fist out of frustration. That was probably a stupid act. I could have broken my hand or set off a horrible chain reaction. Death by a thousand blades came to mind.

"Maybe there is a hidden door," suggested Brad. "I'll take the left side of the wall. You take the right."

We each worked on our section of the wall. I thought about the colored stones outside Brent's man cave to gain access. To unlock his secret door, the red stone needed to be depressed. Maybe this was something similar. My fingers pushed on random stones until I felt one move inward about an inch. "Hey, I found a loose stone." Brad came over to my side of the wall to help.

I worked my way across the row of stones that were at shoulder height. The next two stones to the right of the one that moved for me were solid. The next stone over moved inward like the first stone. Brad felt the stones of the next row down; all were cemented in solid, nothing budged. Brad and I migrated to the next row down. We each carefully pushed on the stones in the row. Brad found the third stone. It was directly below the first stone that I had found. From the third stone, I continued to press on stones to the right. The next two stones were solid. The next stone after that pushed inward. We checked the rest of the stones in this row, none of the other stones were loose.

"Onto the next row. I have a good feeling about this," I said.

"That makes one of us, Susie Sunshine, but I will let you be optimistic."

"Damn right you will," I said in a fun, snarky tone. "So far we have four stones in the pattern of a rectangle. It has to mean something." I stood back and looked at it. I shrugged my shoulders. Nothing was jumping out at me. I began pressing on the stones in the next row down. The stone right under the third stone didn't move. When I pressed on the next stone to the right, it moved. "Score." I put my arms in the air.

Brad looked at me. "Celebrating, really?" He pushed on the next stone to the right of the one I found. It depressed and made a clunk sound. "I raise your 'Score' and add a 'Sweeeeeet'. I just unlocked the door." He stood back to admire his work. "Well, sonovabitch! It's a smiley face."

I took a few steps back. He was right. It was a smiley face. Brad held his hand up to high-five me. I played along to celebrate our achievement. Brad pulled at the stones. A section of the blocks swung open to reveal a metal door that required a key to unlock it.

Brad sighed. "Now, what?" He tried the doorknob. It was a no-go.

I smiled at him. "I'm feeling optimistic." I reached under my shirt and pulled out the famous Key to Immortality. "I took it back from Brent when he wasn't looking. I kind of picked his pocket in the ritual room. He was too busy trying to explain the wheel-of-death to me to notice."

"Good girl. I am impressed." He said with honest appreciation.

"Hold that thought. We aren't out of the tunnel safely yet." The key slid into the lock without a hitch. I turned it slowly, waiting for something fiendish to happen. It didn't to our surprise.

"Wait here for a second," he said to me. Brad pushed the door open. He popped his head inside. "It looks like an old cellar."

"Any chance it's a wine cellar?" I snickered.

"I'm afraid not," said Brad. "Just your run-of-the-mill, creepy-ass, dark, damp, basement of a serial killer."

"By all means, after you then," I said to Brad to get him to lead the way.

A small amount of daylight streamed in from the small, ceiling-high windows, casting ominous shadows on the crumbling stone walls. The dirt floor was a nice touch. The perfect place to bury countless bodies. It really brought out the turn-of-the-century torture chamber vibe.

Most of the small rooms were completely empty. The dampness and the dirt made it a horrible place to store anything. Not even a potato would be happy down here. After searching around some more, we did find a furnace room that contained two furnaces. One furnace for the house or whatever was upstairs and one for the tunnel and ritual rooms. On the far side of the basement, we found a set of wooden steps that led upstairs. Brad started his ascent first. "Do you think anyone is home?" he asked with a smirk.

"Let's go find out," I whispered back.

"I wish I had my gun," he said.

"I wish I had my knife."

Brad turned around and looked at me with a raised eyebrow.

"What? A girl needs to be able to defend herself. On second thought, I wish I had a gun too."

"Honey, the world isn't ready for that and neither am I."

I wrinkled up my nose at him. "How do you know that I haven't been practicing during my sabbatical. I could be a lethal weapon."

"The lethal part I would believe."

"Talk like that is not going to get you anywhere near my pants, Officer Thomas." I punched him in the arm to make myself feel better. "No more wisecracks until after we find my brother."

"Okay," he put his hands up in an "I surrender" motion. He smiled back at me. "I'll do my best, but no guarantees."

This was a serious life-or-death situation, yet I found myself having fun with a man, my ex, that I've been known to despise in the past. Add in the engagement ring currently stuck on my finger, and I sensed a dangerous liaison where anything could happen next. The shit between us was getting real.

At the top of the stairs, we paused to listen for voices on the other side of the wooden door. Brad slowly twisted the knob and cracked the door open an inch to peer inside the room.

"What do you see?" I whispered anxiously.

"It looks like the kitchen. I see a small wooden table and a sink."

"Do you see anyone in the room?"

"No. The room is empty, and the lights are off. I don't think anyone is home." Brad pushed the door open enough for us both to enter. We walked into a farmhouse style kitchen. The room was decorated in blue and white. Chickens and roosters were on the towels and other kitchen décor. It was charming and not a bit psychotic.

Brad opened the lower cupboards looking for the garbage can. When he found it, the can was empty. "These guys are good. Not a single clue to who these bastards are."

I walked over to the refrigerator. I opened the door and peered inside. It had been a long time since my last meal.

"What the hell are you doing?" Brad asked angerly.

"I'm freaking starving, okay? Hey look, they have pudding." It was like they knew I was coming. I reached for it.

Brad slapped my hand away and closed the refrigerator door on me.

"Hey!"

"You almost got speared in the head by these assholes. You honestly think it is safe to eat their poisoned pudding?"

He had a point, a very good point. "They wouldn't?"

Brad grabbed me by the shoulders and looked me in the eye. "They would." He paused for effect. "Let's move on carefully to the living room, shall we?"

The room was fairly large. The furnishings were blue with beige tones this time. There was a comfy-looking blue cloth couch and love seat. The end tables and entertainment center were stained a dark oak. Outdoorsy pictures decorated the walls. They had a decent-sized TV. All in all, the room was warm and inviting, no pagan altars or medieval guillotines to speak of. I could have comfortably watched a movie here. What did that say about me?

We briefly poked our heads in the bathrooms and checked behind the shower curtain just in case. They were all clean. There were bottles of shampoo and conditioner on one of the shelves in the downstairs shower. Someone actually lived here.

Next, we headed upstairs to explore the bedrooms. There were three in this large farmhouse. They were all decorated in old country chic with homemade quilts and antique-looking furniture. Maybe the killer's grandmother lived here?

We were in the last bedroom, which seemed to be the master suite. It had a large queen-sized bed with loads of dresser drawers to snoop through. Brad and I were standing next to the bed, about to search through the nightstand, when something brushed against my leg. "Something touched my leg." I freaked out, knocking us both onto the bed.

Brad landed on top of me. He leaned over the side of the bed to see what had caused my calamity this time. "It's just a damn cat," he laughed.

"Sorry, I thought someone was under the bed or something," I felt stupid, but it was warranted after my previous under-the-bed scare and basically my life in general. The cat jumped up on the bed and stared at us. "Shoo," I said to the cat. It jumped down. "I'm more of a dog person."

"Me too," said Brad. "Maybe we should get a puppy."

"I'd be up for that."

"I'm also up for something else," he said with a sexy smirk. Brad kissed me.

This was not exactly the time or the place, but dang if he wasn't being charming. Of course, I kissed him back. Things were heating up and getting more passionate. His lips moved to my neck, one of my erogenous zones. I was reaching for his—well you all know what I was reaching for—when my hand brushed against the quilt. Instead of going for Brad's man parts, my curious brain took over. Why was I feeling a row of buttons on the quilt we were laying on?

I sat up abruptly. Our make out session came to a screeching halt.

"Oh, do you want to be on top?" Brad asked me.

I shook my head no and pointed at the square of fabric on the quilt next to us. Suddenly, it was hard to catch my breath. The walls were closing in on me.

"What?" he said, having no idea why I was freaking out.

"It's … it's … a piece of Streak's missing underwear," finally popped out of my mouth when my brain cleared. I pointed at the square of fabric. "You can see Amber's signature from the night Streak won the X-Box tournament and later drowned. She signed: 'Great job, Streak! Hugs and stuff Luv Amber.' "

"My dad thought the wolves ate his underwear after they chased him into the water."

"Nope. The killer made a trophy quilt out of the missing boys' clothes." I concluded.

Brad looked down at the quilt. "Is that white dog hair?"

Our eyeballs reached the end of their sockets at the same time. As soon as we realized WHAT we were sitting on, we both jumped off the bed. It might as well have been a quilt made out of skin. This was a whole other kind of deranged cootie I was going to have to scrub off. I couldn't have been any more creeped out if I had tried.

"Gross!" I screamed and ran out of the room.

***

Could I be under the bed right now? That nightmare never gets old.

***

I ran down the steps, across the kitchen, and out the side door that led into the yard. Brad was right behind me. It was clear to both of us that I was having one of my panic attacks. Brad caught up to me and grabbed my arm. He stopped me from running any further. Brad pulled me into him, trying to calm me down. His arms wrapped around me. I felt safe.

"You're okay. We're outside, just breathe," he said to comfort me.

"Why would they do that?" I asked with my face buried in Brad's chest.

"I don't know, Payton, but we've got them now. We have proof that they're not just accidental drownings. My dad has to listen to us after this."

I looked Brad in the eye. "But we haven't found Luke yet. What if they retaliate and kill him because we revealed their secrets?"

Brad rubbed my back. "We'll keep looking for clues. We'll find him first before we say anything to my dad. Are you okay with that? Can I let go of you now?"

"I'm fine. I'm not as fragile as everyone thinks I am." I said in my defense.

Brad put his hands up, signaling a truce. "I was just asking. Are you up for checking out that shed over there?"

"Always." I followed Brad over to the thirty-foot by thirty-foot, white, wooden shed. "Have you told your dad or Nancy that Brent is still alive yet?"

"Are you kidding? That is ALL Brent. I am not touching that conversation."

"But if your dad finds out that you knew about it, won't you get sucked into Brent's vortex of doom?"

"I'm willing to risk it. Besides, the killers said no cops. I am trying to help save your brother and catch these S.O.B.s."

I gave him a quick hug for putting my needs before his own. We stood in front of the side door of the shed. "What is the chance that the door is unlocked?" I asked.

Brad tried the doorknob. "I would say none. There must be something good inside."

I looked down at the door lock. It was newer. The Key to Immortality was not going to solve our predicament.

I walked over to the large garage door and tried to lift it. It didn't budge. "This is locked too. Any ideas?"

We walked over to a small window just to the right of the side door. The glass was filthy, we could barely see inside. I picked up one of the landscape bricks from the flower bed. "You might want to step around the corner while I break and enter."

"Just do it. Allegedly, we already set an aircraft carrier on fire, rode stolen motorcycles, and commandeered a man's fishing trolley. This is small potatoes."

"Well, look at you, bending the law for the greater good. I am proud of you. And by the way, that was Crystal who set the aircraft carrier on fire when she was trying to shoot me, so it doesn't count. We'll just add this brick to my long rap sheet that no one needs to know about," I said, just before launching the brick through the window.

Brad raised his eyebrow at me. "Am I consorting with a known felon? Wait, don't answer that."

"I prefer the term unknown conspirator," I replied with a smirk. "I do my best work undercover."

"You can explain that theory to me in detail later," Brad said with a sexy grin. He knocked the last bit of broken glass away from the windowpane. Brad held out his intertwined fingers with the palms of his hands up for me to step on. "I'll give you a boost."

My hands grabbed on to the outside and inside of the windowsill to steady myself. I stepped on his hands with my right foot and swung my left foot inside the window. I ducked my head inside the garage before I attempted to lower myself to the floor.

"Now, go unlock the door and let me in," Brad demanded.

My phone rang. I pulled it out of my pocket. It was Dr. Parks.

"Who is it?" asked Brad.

"It's my therapist," I answered back through the wall of the shed.

"You better talk to her or she will lock you up."

Brad was right. My phone continued to ring. She wasn't giving up. I needed to have my daily "I'm okay" chat with her. Last time we talked I wasn't exactly having a good day after watching Jeremy get eaten alive. "Hi, Dr. Parks. What's up?" I asked, trying to sound calm and breezy.

"Hello, Payton. I just wanted to check in on you with a quick phone consultation. Is now a good time?"

"Actually, it's not. I'm hanging out with my friends." Not a total lie. "How about I stop by your office tomorrow around 2:00?" I could see Brad anxiously pacing around outside the window.

"Oh, so you are back in River Bend?"

"Not yet, but I should be by tomorrow afternoon."

"A face-to-face consultation would probably be better, Payton. I am looking forward to seeing you, it has been a while."

Brad started knocking on the door to be a smartass. I ignored him. "Yes, it has been a long time. See you at 2:00," I said, trying to hurry the conversation along.

"You can tell me all about your wonderful trip."

"Did you get all the postcards I sent you?"

Brad stuck his head in the window and pointed at the door he wanted me to unlock. I waved him off.

"I did, Payton. Thank you so much for letting me know that you were all right while you were on your trip."

"No problem. Goodbye, Dr. Parks."

"Goodbye, Payton."

Brad stuck his head in the window again. "Are you going to let me in, or what?"

I walked over to the window. "The phone call interrupting us made me think back to the night Julie called and interrupted us."

Brad groaned in protest. "This is no time to walk down memory lane, Payton."

"Let me finish. It got me thinking. You never finished telling me about what happened when the station called you. I remember something about suspicious activity by the big hole in the ice near my parents' restaurant. What was that all about?"

"Let me in, and I'll tell you all about it."

"Tell me, and I'll let you in." I put my hands on my hips.

Brad rolled his eyes at me. "Fine. Have it your way. They sent a dive team out to the hole. The team pulled a vehicle and a deceased driver out of the water."

I went over to the door to open it. "Were they able to identify the body?"

"His name was Jimmy Sternhouse."

"Never heard of him." I unlocked the door.

Brad stepped inside the garage. "You and your drama." Brad looked around the garage. "There's not much to see in here. Less of a serial killer vibe though." He moved over to the shelving unit next to the wall. "How about I check out these boxes, and you check out what's under that tarp over there?"

"Sounds like a plan." The tarp was in the far corner near the garage door. While Brad pulled down boxes, I made my way across the shed.

"I'm surprised you don't remember Jimmy Sternhouse," he said while digging through a box of gardening supplies. He held up a small pair of hedge clippers and a watering can.

I peeked under the tarp. "Shut. Up," I whispered to myself. I pulled the tarp completely off, exposing the rest of the car.

As soon as Brad saw it, he walked over. "Well, shit. Isn't that Lily's car?" Underneath the tarp was a blue and white Volkswagen Bug.

I walked up to the back window. With my finger, I retraced the heart I drew in the dust that night outside Rod's house when Amber was kidnapped, and Tim tried to save her. "I don't think this bug is Lily's."

"Bug … that's his name," said Brad, not making any sense to me.

I opened the driver's door and climbed inside. "Whose name?"

"The person they pulled out of the water. Haven't you been listening to me?"

I peered over the backseat to check for anyone lurking, then I opened the glove box. "Yeah, yeah, Jimmy the Bug. I don't know him."

"No, Bug isn't right," said Brad, leaning on the driver's door. "It's something else."

"Uh-huh." I wasn't really listening at this point. I pulled out some papers, a set of keys, and a remote from the glove box. I pushed the button on the remote. The garage door lifted. "I would definitely say that this car belongs to the killers, not Lily."

"You are probably right. Maybe I should call it in?"

"Brad you can't," I pleaded. "They said no cops. What if there is a cop on their payroll?"

"Okay, for now I won't call," he agreed.

"Thank you." I started to look through the oil change slips and the other papers I found.

"Jimmy the Bug, that's not right," Brad continued. "Jimmy the Cockroach? Nah, that's not it either. Why can't I remember that kid's name?"

I put a folded piece of paper on my lap. "Kid?" I looked up at Brad.

Brad clapped his hands together. "I've got it. It's Cricket. Jimmy the Cricket."

"Cricket? The boys' little, quiet, gaming buddy?" I was shocked.

"Yeah, that's him," said Brad.

"Why wouldn't the boys mention that to me? Why would he be killed?" I thought back to the last time I had seen Cricket and what he said to me. "He said that he saw Rod and his buddy Kurt talking to the Bald-headed Man, AKA Agent Smith. He also said that he had seen you there too the night Streak died."

"So what, everyone saw me there that night. Big deal. It was probably just an accident, anyway. When we got out to the big hole in the ice, the 'open water' signs were gone. He probably drove right into the hole that night. The visibility was for shit with the snowstorm."

"This could be a really important clue." I was racking my brain trying to remember. I looked down at the piece of paper on my lap. I unfolded it. "Sonova—" I quickly put the key in the ignition and turned it. The engine purred. "I've gotta go."

"Is that the title?" asked Brad, pointing at the piece of paper on my lap. "Where the hell are you going?" He had his hand on the door handle.

I slammed the console shifter to "D" and pushed down hard on the gas pedal.

Brad yelped as I pulled out of the garage. "Dang it, Payton. You ran over my foot."

In the rear-view mirror, I could see Brad hopping around in pain.

That was going to cost me. "Sorry," I yelled back. "This is personal."

***

The thoughts that are running through your head must have you questioning your own sanity. I am brilliant.

CHAPTER THIRTY-TWO

My cell phone showed ten missed calls from Brad and one weird text from Dylan: "JOPETFVSA." OMG, Dylan. I smacked myself in the forehead with the palm of my hand. "I forgot about Dylan." Dang Brad and his distracting man parts. I tried calling Dylan back several times. He never answered. Hopefully, it was just an accidental butt text.

When I passed by the cemetery, the white van was gone and so were my friends. Crap. I was feeling guilty for abandoning them and leaving them all hanging. I also really needed to talk to them to get some answers. I looked down at my phone. It was at two percent. There was only enough battery life left for one quick call. This was a tough decision. I scrolled through my contact list until I found the right number. I hit dial. My phone beeped with a busy signal that immediately jumped to voicemail. A second later my phone died. I was S.O.L.

At this point, I was driving erratic: speeding, swerving, and running stop signs. Where was I going? My anxiety was out of control. The thoughts in my brain were scrambled. There was one very simple solution: Alcohol. Hey, no judgement. This was strictly for medicinal purposes … I swear.

I pulled into the first liquor store I could find. Five minutes later, I had a bottle of "getting it done" Gewurztraminer and a bag of salty, cheesy chips. I also picked up a spare bottle just in case I had to share somewhere along the way. This little present will make more sense in a bit. I was working on a plan. It wasn't a great plan, but a plan, nevertheless.

From the liquor store, I took Park Avenue to the highway. The roomy, double lanes and cruise control paired well with my strong, white wine in this borrowed VW Bug. The narrow, winding, backroads would have been a disaster in my jacked-up mental state. The random thoughts in my head were still all over the place. I needed to focus. The booze needed to kick in soon and calm me down so I could think straight. Luke needed me to figure this out.

My car ride was giving me time to figure out what Cricket's death meant. The conversation with him was on a continuous loop in my brain. It replayed over and over as I drove. There had to be a clue in there somewhere. Swigs of wine were helping me clear out some of the brain fog. I decided to turn on the radio to put myself in a better mood. Wine and song were my new, murky, inspirational concoction. Look out world, this rock-and-roll, hell on wheels, moving violation was on a mission.

After a few miles of wine and song, I decided my current plan was less than stellar. The missing piece of precious knowledge needed to be extracted from my brain. They weren't going to fall out of my head on their own. Since I couldn't ask my friends for help, I needed an alternative plan. I think I know just the person. I changed the radio to another rock station and continued my journey back home to River Bend. After forty-five minutes of blasting music and two-thirds of a bottle of wine, I was ready to put my plan into action. I took the first exit off the highway to make my first pit-stop.

I pulled up to the building and went inside. Dr. Parks was sitting at her desk. She was with another patient, who was sitting in my usual chair. When Dr. Parks saw me approach, she stood up. Her red pantsuit was striking against her long, silky, jet-black hair and bold, silver jewelry.

"Payton, I wasn't expecting you until tomorrow."

"I know. I'm kind of having an emergency. My phone died. I need to talk to you."

Dr. Parks looked at her patient. "Do you mind if we continue our session next week?"

"Not at all," said the female patient. "I'll call to set up another appointment." She picked up her purse and coat and left.

There was something about Dr. Parks' office that made me antsy. Maybe it was the thought of someone digging around in my subconscious that always put me on edge. The anxiety was coming back. It was hard to stand still. Slow, steady breaths were my best chance to calm down.

Dr. Parks sat back down at her desk. She watched me pace around the room. "Payton, tell me what has you so worked up." She extended her hand towards the chair, offering me a seat.

"I'm too upset to sit," I explained. "If it's okay, I want to walk around. I think better like this."

"Whatever makes you feel more comfortable, Payton." As Dr. Parks sat at her desk, her hands rested on the desktop. She waited patiently for me to unload my anxiety.

Everything was bubbling up to the surface. I felt like I was going to explode. "First of all, I just found out that one of the boys that hung out at the apartment above my parents' restaurant was murdered," flew out of my mouth.

"Payton you must be devastated."

I stopped at the fish tank to watch them swim around. This always seemed to calm me down in the past. There was something about water and bubbles that was so soothing. "I am, for sure," I answered back, still mesmerized by the swimming fish. "It really bothers me that I can't quite remember what the dead kid said to me the last time I saw him. I think I am having one of those depressed memories."

"I believe you mean repressed memories," she said to correct me.

"Yeah, that's what I meant. Duh, I feel stupid."

"No need to beat yourself up over it, Payton. You have been through a lot. Please go on with your story." Dr. Parks took a pad of paper out of her desk drawer.

While she did that, I wandered over to her trophy shelf. "Are you any good at recovering those repressed memories?" I asked her. "And if so, how does it work?"

"There are several methods, one being hypnosis. Most of the time just talking about it helps. Or seeing an object associated with that memory can trigger a response."

"That's interesting. Let's give it a try. All I can remember is Cricket telling me that Brad was there too, but I knew that. Even my friends saw him, everyone saw him that night. It is no big secret."

Dr. Parks was taking notes. She stopped and looked up from her notepad. "Do you recall anything else?"

"Cricket also told Tim and me that the Bald-headed Man was seen talking to Rod and Kurt. That is no big deal either. They are all dead so it doesn't matter. I don't get it. I'm stumped." I picked up Dr. Parks' golf trophy and turned towards her. "Highschool?" I asked.

"No, college," she answered back. "I am sure that whatever Cricket said to you will all make sense someday."

"I won't hold my breath," I joked.

Dr. Parks laughed. "Yes, that is never a good idea."

I put the trophy back down on the shelf. "I suppose not." I chucked slightly. "Unless you're drowning," I said under my breath.

"What was that, Payton?" asked Dr. Parks. "I couldn't hear you."

"Oh, it was nothing important."

"Is there anything else bothering you, Payton? I'm picking up something in your body language."

"Just some family drama." I leaned against a nearby high-backed chair. For some reason, I couldn't take my eyes off of the trophy shelf.

"It might help to talk about it," she suggested.

"Maybe. I guess we could try it, but I'm not really supposed to be talking about it." I pointed at the shelf. "What used to be here?"

"It was just some old photos. They were outdated, so I took them down."

"Oh, yeah, that's right. I remember now." I sat down in the chair I had been leaning against. Things were starting to click in my head big time. I pulled my opened bottle of wine out of my oversized purse.

"Payton, we have talked about the negativity of self-medication."

I popped the cork and took a drink right in front of her. "Do you want to hear about my family drama, or not?"

Dr. Parks cleared her throat. "If you must. Please continue."

"So, if I tell you this thing, it won't leave this room, right?" I gave Dr. Parks a serious look.

"Our sessions are confidential, Payton. I could lose my license."

I took a deep breath and let it fly. "My brother Luke is missing."

"Oh, dear. Does your mother know?" popped out of her mouth.

"I'm hoping to find him and spare her any drama. I would appreciate it if you wouldn't say anything to her."

"That is very considerate of you and completely understandable. But maybe the police should be informed on this matter. It is not like your brother to behave like this, correct?"

"No, it's not." I felt antsy again. The need to move around the room overwhelmed me. I popped up suddenly, startling Dr. Parks. She jumped slightly in her chair.

Dr. Parks was right. The littlest thing can bring back a memory. For me it was a combination of visual and verbal cues. I had come to the right place to get my answers.

I decided to repeat myself and expand on our conversation. I strolled around the room, drinking wine as I talked. "No, it is definitely not like my brother to disappear. While we are on the subject of brothers … I'm just wondering if yours is here? How is he, by the way?"

"Payton, you are not making any sense. What is this all about?" Dr. Parks stood up.

I pointed to the shelf with my free hand. "Those pictures you took down, one of them was a younger picture of you and a blonde-headed man. I never noticed the family resemblance until now. That guy in the picture is your brother, right?"

"Payton, I think you are having another delusional episode brought on by the stress of your missing brother. Maybe I should call your mother."

My temper flared. I approached her desk. I took the last swig of my wine and dropped the empty bottle on the rug. I pulled the extra bottle of wine out of my bag and set it down on her desk. "Here's a gift for you." Dr. Parks picked up the bottle and read the label. She laughed.

"It wasn't meant to be funny," I said in a sassy tone.

"Witch's Brew? I do enjoy a glass of Chardonnay from time to time. I don't think I have ever had this particular blend. Thank you, Payton. That was very thoughtful of you."

"Cut the crap. I found the VW Bug in the shed. The title was in the glovebox. It's registered to a Nicholas Flamel, one of the great alchemists of the 1300s. Oops. Nick is your brother, isn't he?"

"On second thought, perhaps I should have you admitted to the fifth floor. A rest and some new medication will do you wonders." Dr. Parks picked up the phone to call the hospital.

I rested both of my hands on her desktop in an aggressive manner. "Put down the phone and tell me where my brother is, or do I have to beat it out of you."

Dr. Parks took a few steps back. "Payton, calm down. I have never seen you like this."

"Well, buckle up, it's show time. I'm just getting started." I turned away from the desk and headed over to the trophy shelf. I picked up the golf trophy and turned back around.

Dr. Parks set the phone down. "Payton, what are you doing?"

I approached her desk again.

"Look, Payton, maybe you just need another vacation to dry out and get some perspective on life."

"I don't need a freaking vacation. I need to find my brother. If you don't start talking, I'm going to start working on my follow through." I held the trophy over my head. I was prepared to do some damage. "Tell me where my brother is," I demanded.

"Payton, what has gotten into you?" Dr. Parks was trying to stay calm, but I could tell I had her rattled. She reached for the phone again. I smashed it with the trophy. It fell to the floor.

"I couldn't put it all together until I realized that Cricket wasn't trying to tell me he had seen Brad at the restaurant that night. I just assumed when he whispered, 'the policeman was here too last night' that he was talking about Brad. I know now who he was talking about. And so do you, Dr. Parks. Admit it."

Her astonished, scared, little bird expression turned into a smirk. She knew she could no longer try to talk her way out of it. She started clapping her hands together, applauding me. "Well done, Payton, the FBI would be lucky to have you."

"Damn straight they will. Right after I bust your ass, I'm headed right over to the academy." I paused and tilted my head. "Come on out, Nick. I know you're here."

A door opened behind me. I swung around to watch him emerge. A figure of a man moved slowly out of the shadows. He was pushing my brother who was tied to an office chair on wheels. Luke also had a gag over his mouth to keep him quiet.

"Luke, thank god," I said when I saw that he was okay.

"Hello, Payton. We meet again," said the man as he approached.

"You have more lives than a cat," I told him. I was expecting Creepy Nick, not the person who was in front of me.

"I'm really more of a dog person," he said, being cocky. He walked to the center of the room where the lighting was better.

"You can call me Nick if you like, Officer Tim Kline is just my alias."

Well, that was a plot twist I didn't see coming. "Damn … you and Nick look a lot alike. What do you have to say for yourself?" I asked him.

"I suppose you want answers."

"That would be nice since you have put me and my family through hell." I took a seat in the high-backed chair to listen to his story.

He looked at Dr. Parks. "I'll start," said Tim. "First of all, Kurt and Rod made my life easier when they kidnapped Amber. What a couple of dumbasses. Then there was you, 'Hey, Tim, can you go over to Rod's house and check it out?' That was perfect for me to pull off my plan. I just had to show up at the right 'damsel in distress' time, and you did the rest."

I scowled at Tim. "I thought you were my friend."

"Sorry, it was all part of my misdirection. I tell you one thing and then I do another. It is classic."

"It's mean," I said, making another not-so-pleasant face at him. "So, who shot Amber? I'm assuming it wasn't Kurt."

"That was me," said Dr. Parks with an evil grin. I kidnaped Lily and Julie and brought them to Rod's house. I also put Kurt in your car. That was fun."

"Fun? You thought that was fun? It was horrifying. That bastard was going to rape me and kill me."

"Fun for just me, then," said Dr. Parks.

I gave her an evil glare. "You are supposed to be my doctor. You are supposed to help people."

"I do help people," said Dr. Parks. "I helped Tim out by shooting him to make his plan look believable."

"Thanks, sis. You can always count on family," said Tim. "By the way, Payton, just in case anyone checks, or you decide to blab, all the ballistics paperwork will prove that Kurt's gun shot Amber. I made sure of it. Remember what I said, you can get anything done if you have the right paperwork."

I rolled my eyes and sighed at his comment.

"I wouldn't dig too deep into what happened to Kurt if I were you, Payton. It was your knife sticking out of his chest cavity. You do have anger issues. Just ask your therapist. I'm sure it is clearly documented in your file." Dr. Parks and Tim laughed.

I pointed at them both. "I didn't do anything. You two are despicable." Then it hit me. "Oh. My. God. Is that why you gave me your knife? It wasn't to protect me; it was to incriminate me. Tim, you're an asshole."

They both laughed again.

"Shut up! Stop laughing!" I was beyond angry at this point. I wanted to grab my brother and storm out, but I needed more answers. "Why did you kill Crystal and Agent Smith? Was Crystal trying to buy her way into the group with the wrong pair of diamond earrings?" I just had to ask to make sure it wasn't my fault for giving her the wrong ones. I needed to be able to sleep at night.

"They were both collateral damage," Tim said in a nonchalant manner. "Agent Smith was getting too close to figuring out our identities. He had to die so I could take over the game. To answer your question: Crystal was never with us. Crystal was a scavenger hellbent on doing a huge story that would expose the drowning deaths. We couldn't have that."

"Did you kill Crystal because she shot you? Wait a minute, she shot you. We all saw her. How are you not dead?"

"Technically, Payton, Crystal was trying to shoot you," said Tim. "I stepped in front of that bullet."

"Thanks?" I didn't know what else to say. "You still didn't answer my question."

"Fine," said Tim. "Usually a magician doesn't reveal his secrets. I wore a bullet proof vest with exploding red dye like in the movies. All I had to do was get Crystal riled up and jump in front of you, dying a hero … again. No one would look for me. It was a perfect plan." Tim beamed proudly over his clever accomplishment.

"What if she shot you in the face?" I asked to burst his big bubble head.

"She didn't," he said through clenched teeth.

Dr. Parks stepped forward. "Just in case you were wondering, I was the person in the hood who ran the bitch over. I quite enjoyed it too." She laughed sadistically.

"You should really see someone about that laugh," I said to her. "You are the crazy one, not me."

Dr. Parks looked at me and scowled back.

"Payton, you really shouldn't say disparaging remarks about my sister." Tim grabbed ahold of Luke's shoulder and arm, bending it in an unnatural way. Luke winced in pain.

"You two are sick in the head. I'm going to turn you both in," I said without remorse.

"Not so fast, Payton. I have something for you to watch," said Tim. He walked over to the laptop on Dr. Parks' desk. Tim clicked on a few of the keys, then turned the screen around so I could see it. "You might want to get a closer look at this," he said. I got up from my chair and walked over to the desk.

"Who do you think the police are going to believe?" Dr. Parks said followed by another sadistic laugh.

I watched the video in horror. It was the video surveillance from inside the local grocery store. It showed Hoodrat, the boy found in the river behind our local college, leaving the store. I was right behind him carrying a bag of chips. "What is this?" I demanded an answer."

Tim had a sinister smile on his face. "Remember when I told you that the report showed a nightshade drug in your system?" asked Tim.

"Yeah?" I was afraid of where he was going with this. "I believe one of the boys mentioned that it was for extracting information out of people." I paused. "Oh god, what kind of information did you pull out of my head?"

Dr. Parks chimed in. "It is also used to put information in. You are a great hypnosis patient, Payton." She looked absolutely giddy. Dr. Parks snapped her fingers and smiled.

"You take suggestions very well," said Tim.

"I think I'm going to be sick," I replied. I was turning green. "You bitch. Take whatever you put into my head out right now." I walked towards Dr. Parks ready to bean her with her own trophy. From behind me I heard my brother yelp in pain. I stopped in my tracks and turned around. Tim removed Luke's gag. He had a knife at my brother's throat.

"Drop the trophy and step away from my sister," Tim demanded.

I let the trophy drop out of my hand. It hit the carpeted floor.

"Now give me my key and my book and I'll let Luke go. You keep your mouth shut, Payton, and I won't have to send this tape to the Chief," said Tim.

"I can't just let you leave," I said in protest.

Tim cut Luke's neck just enough to draw a few drops of blood. "My key and my book, Payton. I will not ask you again."

"Do it," blurted Luke. "Do whatever they want."

I could see the fear in my brother's eyes.

"Fine," I grimaced at them both. I pulled the key off from around my neck. I tossed it at Tim's feet. He bent down and picked it up. After that, I pulled up my shirt and took the novel sized book out of the waistband of my pants.

"Hand it over … slowly," said Tim.

I walked over halfway to Tim and my brother. "Untie my brother first," I demanded.

"Give me the diamond earrings and I will," said Tim.

I felt my pockets and my bra. "Oh crap, I don't have them." I did a quick brain search. Shit, Brent still had them.

Tim put the knife back up to Luke's throat.

"No, don't hurt my brother. I can get them for you, but why bother. We have all seen the secret tunnels, the ritual rooms, and the house. That place is no use to you anymore."

"That, you will pay for," said Tim. He untied my brother. "Stand up," he said to Luke.

I handed Tim his book at the same time he let go of my brother. I gave Luke a big hug. This was almost over.

Tim put the book up to his cheek. "It is still warm," he said.

I cringed. "Can we go now?" I asked.

"Not quite yet," said Dr. Parks. "We have one more surprise."

"You are going to loathe our very existence after this," said Tim with a smirk.

"Oh god, what did you bastards make me do?" I slowly let go of Luke and slid to the floor. "Did I kill someone?" I briefly rested my face in my hands to hide from my shame.

Tim and Dr. Parks looked at each other and laughed. That wasn't a yes or a no.

"Come on out so Payton can see you, Sweetheart," said Luke without emotion.

I looked up at my brother and then back at the doorway in the rear of the room.

"Lily, you bitch," I shouted. "Are you in this too?" My anger was running rampant.

A girl walked out of the backroom. Her raven hair bounced with each step. It wasn't Lily. It was Stephani.

"What the hell is going on here?" I asked. The Titanic hadn't struck the iceberg yet. I was extremely confused.

Stephani walked over to Luke. She laid a big, wet, juicy kiss on his lips. "Hi, Honey," she said.

I jumped to my feet. "Luke. No!" The room was spinning. I made it over to the chair to steady myself. "Lily is going to kick your ass," I said to my brother.

"Lily is a poser," said Luke. "I wanted a real Goth girl. It's hilarious that Lily was sneaking out and going to meetings behind my back trying to find … me." He laughed out loud.

"That's not funny," I said. "Is all this because of Mom and the money?"

"No. I just wanted to fit in, to belong to a cause."

"Luke, please. It's not too late for you. You haven't killed anyone yet. Come with me. We'll let them go."

"Sorry, Payton. Remember when you caught me outside the bathroom in Smiley's with Levi? I was trying to lure his drunken ass outside. Between your interference, Brad showing up, and Dylan showing up to stop us, we had to come up with a solid plan B."

"Plan D was more like it," said Stephani.

"That is why Stephani was there, to help you?" I asked my brother.

I stared at Stephani. "You twisted pile of crap. You corrupted my brother. I'm glad I chased you out that bathroom window, you skank."

"And I beat Dylan over the head and left him for dead in the alley because of you, you calamity-filled control freak," said Stephani. "Oh yeah, and I also had the pleasure of spiking your drink and watching things, heat up." She laughed at her own joke. "Speaking of Dylan." She turned to Tim. "How is he?"

Tim walked over and grabbed the laptop again. "Why don't we take a look."

"Why won't you bastards just leave him alone? Don't you dare hurt him."

Tim clicked on a few keys and showed me the screen.

Dylan was lying on a narrow cement walkway of a dam. There were no railings, just pooling water on one side and a rushing waterfall on the other. He appeared to be barely conscious. There was audio. I could hear Dylan mumbling my name over and over. It was gut-wrenching.

Dr. Parks walked over to me. "You shouldn't have left him alone in the van."

"Please don't kill him," I pleaded. "Let him go."

"He's probably going to kill himself," said Luke. "That's usually how it works."

"Shut up, Luke." I had heard enough of my brother's crap.

He chimed in again. "By the way, did you get a bizarre text from him?"

I gave my brother a strange look.

"That was my idea. If you add up all the letters in the text according to the Numerology guidelines it equals thirty-three. It means the end. J (1) + O (6) + P (7) + E (5) + T (2) + F (6) + V (4) + S (1) + A (1) = 33" He laughed uncontrollably.

"When did you get so demented?" I asked him.

"I don't know. I think I was born this way."

"Dylan's death will be ruled another tragic accident," said Stephani.

"Or maybe a suicide," said Dr. Parks.

"Seriously, what is wrong with you people?" I asked, throwing my hands in the air.

I turned to Stephani. "But he's your ex-boyfriend. How can you be so callous?"

"Ew! Dylan has never been my boyfriend." She laughed. "He is my pain-in-the-ass stepbrother."

"Oh, so it's complicated," I said, remembering how Dylan had explained their relationship. Why wouldn't he just tell me?"

"That do-gooder kept threatening to convert me or turn me in. I've had enough of his interference in my life. It is really up to him to save himself," said Stephani without remorse.

Tim addressed the group. "You guys ready to get out of here?"

They all nodded in agreement.

"It is really up to Payton," said Tim. "She can either try to stop us, or she can try to save Dylan. It's her choice."

"We'll even let you keep the VW Bug as a parting gift, just let us go," said Dr. Parks.

I turned to my brother. "Luke, please don't go with them," I begged.

"Sorry, sis, I'm one of them now. I have been for a while. I should probably let you in on a few of my own secrets. The knife you found on the roof is mine, not Vivian's. I put it out there in the rain gutter so no one, especially mom, wouldn't find it."

My mouth was hanging open.

"As for your landlord, Lyle, dying of a heart attack: that was me, not you. I came by your sorority house to grab the dead body we stashed in the basement freezer when Lyle caught me. Then you came home, messing up our plan. I suggested that we bring you into the group. Dr. Parks did the rest with her brain magic and Hocus Pocus. I recommended Dr. Parks to

Mom to help you with your panic attacks. It was the least I could do, under the circumstances."

I was frickin' speechless. All of my mental issues were caused by my brother and this group of miscreates.

"Now I have to ask you the big question: Which side are you on, Payton?" asked Luke.

My heart hit rock bottom. I looked them all in the eye. "I am on the side where you don't freaking kill other people."

They all laughed at me as they walked to the door.

"Stop!" I said. "Dr. Parks, you have to undo whatever you did to my brain."

"Maybe you should call me and set up an appointment." She laughed at me, then went out the door.

I looked at Luke. "Mom is going to kick your butt."

"Give her my best. Bye, Payton." He disappeared out the door arm-in-arm with Stephani.

Tim and I were the only ones left in the room. "Do you have anything you would like to say to me?" I asked him.

"Actually, I do. Do you remember Streak?"

"Yes," I said confidently. I was about to get some answers to what happened to him.

"You were there that night. You saw everything. You might not remember it yet ... but you will."

"I don't believe you." I was furious.

Tim smiled and continued. "Rod saw you too, Payton. I did us both a favor by framing him."

"I know in my heart that I didn't do anything." I was angry. They made me an accessory to murder. I bent down and picked up the golf trophy that was at my feet.

"You better get off your high, white horse, Payton. It could be the death of you."

"Kiss my ass." I threw the trophy at his head.

He ducked. The trophy bounced off the door jam. "It's been real, Payton. See you later."

"You can count on it," I said in a sassy tone. "Watch your back, Tim. I'll be coming for you."

“And what a marvelous game it will be.” He smiled and walked out the door.

CHAPTER THIRTY-THREE

This was all too much to handle. Part of me wanted to curl up in a ball and cry for days or drink a case of wine and feel sorry for myself. Honestly, I was completely justified in doing both. I don't think a person on this planet would give me grief about it after they took a glimpse into my life. The standard assessment has always been pathetically tragic. Of course, the badass old lady, my future self, showed up to my rescue me again. "Oh. Hell. No, she said. "Get your crap together and go save Dylan."

I did what the old lady told me to do. I grabbed the bottle of Witch's Brew off the desk, which I interpreted as me getting my crap together. Next, I went outside to see if they really left the VW Bug behind. It was still parked right where I'd left it. Who knew that Tim was going to be a man of his word? He turned out to be a serial killer with morals, talk about a mental stupor. Do I hate every fabric of his being, or do I give him tiny props for keeping a smidge of humanity? There was no correct answer or time to dwell on this conundrum. I jumped in the car and sped out of the parking lot. Please let me get there in time to save him. Whatever horrible things they had me involved in; I was going to do my best to redeem myself. Undoing all of it was the only option for me to ever sleep again.

***

I pulled up to the dam to search for Dylan. The property was completely fenced in, a chain-link fence ran around the entire perimeter. The top of the fence was covered in razor wire. How the hell was I supposed to get in there? As I walked along the fence line, I could tell I was in the right place. The dam looked the same as the video I had watched in Dr. Parks' office. The cement sidewalk between the water was identical. There was a pool of water on one side of the sidewalk and rushing water on the other. The only thing that was missing was Dylan.

"Dylan! Dylan!" I cried out hoping he could hear me. I wandered the fence line searching the rushing water for any sign of him. When I found the gate, it was padlocked. Shit. I intertwined my fingers in the metal links of the gate and shook it out of frustration. "Dyllllaaaan!" I screamed. "Where are youuuu?"

At this point, I feared the worst. Then another thought popped into my head. Was I actually too late, or was this a sick joke to get me here? Could this be a distraction so they could escape? I should have expected this kind of misdirection out of Tim and his crew. Nevertheless, my spirits were mixed on the matter. I wanted Dylan to be safe. On the other hand, what if he was all part of this evil joke? Ugh! This was horribly difficult to mentally maneuver. I decided to put the road map going on in my brain on hold and search for Dylan just in case my hunch was wrong.

I searched the area below the dam one more time. My fingers were crossed while I walked along the fence line. I said a little prayer that for once did not contain any swear words. "C'mon, Dylan, show me a sign. Give me something to keep me going." I closed my eyes and counted to ten. It was extremely scientific, I know. "10, 9, 8, 7, 6, 5, 4, 321." I peeked out of one eye. "No way." I slammed my eyelid closed. "Make it go away. Make it go away. Make it go away," I whispered under my breath.

I slowly inhaled and exhaled. When I opened both of my eyes this time, it was still there; a dark black object tumbled in the icy water below the dam. It looked like Dylan's black leather jacket. That was the last straw of the day. I was broken. My knees collapsed, hitting the hard ground. After a second or two of shock, the waterworks started to flow. Tears ran down both of my cheeks. I sobbed uncontrollably. So much for being a badass, I was reduced to a blubbering idiot.

"You bastards," I screamed as if they could hear me. "I'm going to kill all of you. Do you hear me?"

"Who are you talking to?"

I turned around to see Brad behind me, and the white van filled with my friends parked next to the VW Bug. The emotions took over. I jumped into Brad's arms. It felt warm and safe.

After a long hug. I looked at Brad. "I was talking to the killers. It was Dr. Parks and Tim. Tim is still alive."

Brad put his hands on either side of my face. "I know," he whispered to me. "I ran the plates on the VW Bug and the deed to the house. The car was registered to a Nicholas Flamel with Tim's Riverbend address. What an idiot. The house was listed to Dr. Parks. The local cops are out looking for them now."

"Wait. How did you find me?"

"We saw the video in Dr. Parks' office and came here. I knew you would try to save him, Payton. You have a good heart. You could never hurt anyone."

I started to cry again. No one knew why, but I knew. I pointed at the water. "Dylan is in there."

Brad gave me a hug. "I'm sorry, honey."

I hugged Brad harder. I needed him to be my rock.

"Don't freak out, but I called the dive team," said Brad. "The water's cold. If they can find him right away, there is a chance they can revive him. They should be here any minute." He stroked my hair and kissed the top of my head.

Lily was walking over to us from the van at the same time the dive team pulled up in their van. Brad and I moved out of their way. They cut the chain on the gate with a large pair of bolt cutters and headed to the river. Lily walked up to us. The rest of the gang slowly climbed out of the van.

"Where's Luke, Payton?" asked Lily. "Did you find him?"

My heart sank. My stomach was in knots. I stared at her, not knowing how to tell her the horrible truth.

Lily grabbed me by the shoulders. "Where is he, Payton?" She looked over at the water. "He's not …"

It was time to open my big, Bombay door of a mouth and drop the bomb on everyone. They could all share my grief. "He's not here, Lily. He's with them."

"Why is he still with them?" asked Brad. I could tell he was as confused as Lily.

Lily let go of me, but her eyes pierced my soul. "Didn't you give Tim and Dr. Parks the key and the book?" Lily asked me in a very accusing way.

By now, everyone was out of the van and crowded around us. I gazed at them all with a "don't make me say it" expression. They glared back. They wanted an answer. "Guys, this is so bad. Luke is with them because he is involved in all of it. He is one of them."

Brad and most of the group gave me the deer in the headlights astonished look. I looked over at Lily to see her reaction. She slapped me across the face. "Ow!" Instinctively, my hand covered my soon-to-be red cheek.

"Liar," yelled Lily. "Why would you say that?"

Brad stepped between us before round two of our previous fight started. "Ladies, now is not the time or the place to air out your laundry."

I lowered my voice. "Lily, I am as sorry about this as you are. If that stupid Stephani girl hadn't corrupted my brother, we wouldn't be having this conversation."

"So he's seriously with them … and her?" she asked.

I could see the truth settle in. Her face went expressionless with shock. I sighed. "Yes, it's all true." I looked over at Brad. "We have to get him back."

Brad hugged me. "We'll find them. We'll hunt them down, wherever they are, and make Luke come with us."

"And when we find them," said Lily, "I'm going to kick Luke's ass … and hers."

"That's exactly what I told him, Lily." My comment didn't seem to help her mood any. I found myself glancing over at the water as the divers searched for Dylan. I could feel the anxiety building up inside me. I took a deep breath and told myself to breathe through it just like Dr. Parks had taught me. Ugh! What a bitch.

Lily's phone beeped. She took it out of her pocket. "Are you kidding me? Payton, your bastard of a brother just broke up with me in a text."

"I'm sorry, Lily." I gave her a sympathetic look. My brother had taken the chicken shit way out all the way around.

"Brad, what's the plan to find them?" asked Lily. "I want revenge on these assholes."

The whole gang looked to Brad for our next move.

"I'm in," said Chameleon. "They killed my best friend."

"Yeah," said Blond Ambition. "We want revenge too."

Brad looked around the group. "Is everyone in?"

We all raised our hands, even the girls. The entire group was in this to the bitter end. Our unbreakable bond was solidified in the need for justice.

"Okay, then," I said. "As soon as we pinpoint their location, we are going after Tim, Dr. Parks, Luke, and Stephani."

"Hells yeah," said Max. "This will be the road trip of the century."

The dive team came out of the water and walked over to talk to Brad. The much-needed distraction from the inevitable was over. It was time to face the truth about Dylan. I wanted to run away. One of the divers was carrying Dylan's black leather jacket. I could feel my knees getting weak. They were about to give out. Brad must have sensed it. He put his arm around me to stop me from losing my balance.

"Sorry, Lieutenant, this was all we could find." He handed Brad the jacket. "We used the sonar. There is no sign of a body."

Brad had a grim look on his face. "Any chance the body could have floated down the river?"

"We don't believe so, sir. With the slow rate of the current today, the decedent's body should still be here on the bottom. It won't travel until it fills with gases during decomp and re-floats."

There went my knees again and now my stomach was nauseous. I bent over and let out a few dry heaves. It could have been the bottle of wine and the chips talking back. Either way, it wasn't pretty.

"Thanks, for coming out right away, guys. I owe you one," said Brad.

"We'll always have your back, Lieutenant," he said before the team left.

"You okay?" asked Brad.

I stood back up. "Yeah, I think so." My phone rang. It was my mother. Dang it if she didn't call me at the worst possible time. I didn't even have time to react to the news about Dylan. I figured I had better answer it just in case Luke had sent her a breakup text as well.

"Hi, Mom. What's up?" I did my best to sound cheery while tears ran down my cheeks. Her psychic ability to analyze my spoken words was uncanny. I had to hold it together. I decided to walk away from the group so I could lie my ass off without judgement.

"I just received a disturbing voicemail," said my mother.

Oh shit. This was bad. "Who from?" I played dumb.

"It was from Vivian. Apparently, I'm going to need another housekeeper and you are going to need a new chef at the restaurant. Vivian and her son are leaving town A.S.A.P."

"What was her explanation?" I asked frantically.

"Calm down, my dear. I was just wondering if Dylan had said anything to you. It was all so sudden." She sighed. "Good help is so hard to find."

"No, he didn't say anything to me about leaving town." For the first time, I looked out at the water with hope. I wiped away the tears with my mitten. Maybe they did fake his death so they could all get away without question. "Did Vivian happen to mention where they were going?" I asked my mother, hoping she slipped up and left us a clue.

"No, she didn't. Just a quick apology for the short notice."

"Oh, okay," I said with a clear, disappointed edge to my voice. It wasn't going to be an easy task to find them. I looked over at Brad. I could tell by the anxious look on his face that he urgently needed to talk to me. "I gotta go, Mom." I was about to hang up.

"Payton, wait. There is one more thing I need to tell you. When you see your brother, tell him he isn't the least bit funny."

Oh, no. "What did he say to you?" I was beyond curious under the circumstances.

"He sent me a text saying, 'to spend my money wisely and he'd see me in the next life.' You tell him he is not getting out of Easter dinner this year. He gets so darn dark and broody sometimes. I blame Lily for that. Maybe Luke should talk to Dr. Parks. She has really helped you."

I was speechless … again. I tried my best to not sound sarcastic. "Yes, she has out done herself with me."

"I'll let you go. I know how busy you young kids are. Remember to pick up after yourself and your friends. We no longer have a housekeeper. I don't want to come home to a big mess. Bye, my dear."

"Bye, Mom."

Brad walked over to me. "How's Mom?"

"Freaking clueless. She told me that she doesn't want to come home to a big mess."

Brad made a cringey face. "Understatement of the century."

"We need to find my brother, pronto."

Brad held up Dylan's coat. "Do you want this, or should I book it into evidence? I'm confused on what I should do with it."

"I'll take it. After talking to my mom, I don't think Dylan is dead. Vivian just left town in a big hurry."

"Interesting … the plot thickens," commented Brad.

"Like corn starch," I said. Brad handed me Dylan's jacket. "I'll hang onto it. I'll give it back to Dylan right before I bitch slap him." I felt my nostrils flare with anger.

"We have to find them first," said Brad.

"Have you ever known me to give up on anything I set my mind to?"

He shook his head no. He knew damn well how tenacious I could be. "They can run, but they can't hide. I will never stop looking." I said it and I meant it.

Julie walked up to us. "Payton, can I talk to you for a minute?"

Brad looked at Julie and me. "I'll give you two girls some space." Brad pointed at Lily. "I'll go check on her. Maybe Luke inadvertently said something to her about where they might be headed." He ran away like a coward.

It was best if he wasn't around for our conversation. This was going to be awkward and uncomfortable. Julie stared at me without saying anything, so I decided to take a stab at this and start. "Just gonna rip off the band-aid." That was supposed to stay in my head.

"What?"

"Uh, nothing. So … I found my … your … the ring," I started. This was not ouchless. This was horrendous. I sucked at this. Basically, I sucked at being a friend and a human being. I tried to pull the ring off my finger. It was stuck.

"That's okay, Payton. You can keep it," said Julie. "I discovered that there are other fish in the sea." She waved at Chameleon. He waved and smiled back.

"And sometimes you get schooled and an old fish swims back," I said, trying to make a joke to lighten the drama.

"That was lame, even for you, Payton," laughed Julie.

"Yeah, it was." I laughed with her. "Isn't Chameleon a little young for you?" I just had to ask.

"Not at all, you can teach the young ones stuff."

"Ew!" I said. "You've been hanging around Teagan too much."

Julie laughed again. "Payton, get your mind out of the gutter. And for your information, he will be nineteen in a few months. I was talking about stuff like taking out the garbage. Brad was horrible about that."

"Yeah, he is. I'll have to work on that." I cringed on the inside. I didn't mean to throw that in her face. "Sorry, it isn't going to be weird between us now, is it?"

"No, don't be silly. We can both be happy." She smiled and hugged me.

During our hug, I looked over at Brad. He gave us the two thumbs up approval for acting like adults. I'm thinking that it was mostly my fault when we didn't.

Before Julie walked away, she said, "Payton, don't worry, we will help you find your brother and bring him back home."

"Thank you, my friend." We smiled at each other.

Brad walked over as soon as the coast was clear. "That seemed to go well."

I gave Brad a loving gaze. I couldn't help it. It just came naturally. "Yes, it did. Julie told me to keep the ring." I looked at him for his response.

"It is yours to keep if you want it," said Brad.

"Are you saying what I think you are saying?"

Brad started to open his mouth.

"Wait, before you say anything. I need to make a confession."

Brad got a serious look on his face. He even furrowed his brow with anticipation.

"Just listen, okay? You know that I am a stubborn, tenacious, pain in the ass," I started.

"Yes, go on," he said with a smirk.

"This isn't funny. I think I may have done something unthinkable." I was on the verge of tears again.

"I don't believe you could." Brad seemed adamant.

"You don't understand. Dr. Parks and Tim said that they used those witchy drugs and put what they called 'suggestions' into my brain. I think they got me to do their evil bidding."

"Payton, honey, you don't have an evil bone in your body." Brad gave me a hug. "Those drugs can't change your personality. They can make suggestions, but they can't turn a good person bad."

"What about my brother? Whatever they did to him, he's not the same." I burst into tears.

"He's not you."

"But I saw the tape. I followed Hoodrat out of the store. What if I killed him?"

Brad pulled back and grabbed my hands in his. "Payton, you didn't watch the whole tape. I did when I was in Dr. Parks' office."

"Tim turned it off after I followed Hoodrat out the door."

"If you would have watched the rest of the tape, you would have seen Tim, who was wearing a disguise, leave the store right after you. He stopped in the entryway and tied his shoe before he left. He looked like he was trying to avoid the camera."

Relief washed over my entire body. "Are you sure I'm not a killer?"

"This is how sure I am." Brad got down on one knee.

Oh. My. God. This was really happening.

"Payton Marie Richardson, will you marry me?"

"Yes," I said and started to cry … again or was it still? My life went from a disaster to a dream come true.

Brad turned around to the white van filled with our friends. "She said 'yes.' We're celebrating. The burgers are on me."

Hoots and hollers left the van. Even Julie seemed happy for us.

Brad stood back up. "The Barbecue Shack?"

"Not on your life. I'm not cooking tonight, Sweetheart." I laughed.

"Story of my life now, I suppose," Brad said with a smirk and a wink.

I punched him in the arm because it was our thing.

We walked towards the van. "I think I know a place," said Brad. "They make a mean mushroom Swiss burger."

"Extra fries?" I asked.

"Of course. With some cherry pie for dessert?" Brad winked.

"Deal."

THREE MONTHS LATER AT THE BARBECUE SHACK

I was behind the bar doing what I do best, mixing a pitcher of margaritas for Lisa, Teagan, Amber, Lily, Julie, and myself when Brad walked through the door.

"Look what I found," Brad said, holding up a file folder.

"Am I supposed to be amazed, honey?" I answered back. I smiled at the love of my life.

"You should be." He smiled back and leaned over the bar to kiss me. "This file folder was taped under Tim's desk."

"You're kidding. What does it say?" After three months, there might be actual hope in finding my brother.

Brad opened the file folder and set it down on the bar.

"What are we looking at exactly?" asked Julie.

"It's Tim's personnel file," said Brad, answering her question. "Look at what it says here. He pointed to a typed sentence.

I read it out loud. "DNR- do not resuscitate. See medical file for further instructions." I looked at Brad and shrugged my shoulders. I was a bit confused. "I don't have to sneak into the hospital, do I? I always get caught."

"No," he laughed. "I already paid the Medical Records Department a visit today with my badge."

My eyes lit up. "So what did his medical file say?"

"If Tim died in the line of duty, he wanted his body sent to his family."

"Where is the son of a bitch?" asked Teagan.

We were interrupted by a stampede of gamers' feet running down the stairs and coming in the front door.

"We're back for more food," said Feedbag.

"And we came hungry this time," said Blond Ambition.

"I'm shocked," said Amber.

"Hey, we're good for business," said Max, throwing a hundred down on the bar top.

I couldn't argue with him there. "I'll put your order in with our cook in a minute, boys. Brad was just about to tell us where Tim and his coven have been hiding out."

Chameleon walked over and took a seat at the bar by Julie. "Where are the dark and demented?"

"Waukago Park," said Brad. "They are somewhere in the windy city."

"Well, that blows," said The Singe. "I was hoping to go somewhere warm."

"Everywhere is warm, Dumbass," said Wolfman. "It's June." We all laughed.

"What makes you think they're in Waukago?" asked Amber.

"They left a string of bodies across the Midwest this spring. The last three were in the Waukago Park area," said Brad.

"Why do you think it's them?" I asked.

"Where the bodies were found formed an equilateral triangle, an upside-down equilateral triangle," commented Brad.

"The sign for water," said Brent. "Oh, it's them. They are taunting us."

"Exactly," said Brad. "The bastard has come home to roost. It's the same area as where he wanted his body sent in his DNR request."

"How are we going to get there?" asked The Singe.

"Plane, train, automobile?" asked Lisa.

"Definitely a road trip," I answered back. "No more planes."

"I think I can get us another bus," said Chameleon.

"I'm thinking something a bit classier," said Max waving around his wallet.

"No worries," I said, "this trip is on Stan and Janna."

"Before we go anywhere, we need a plan," said Brad.

"I prefer to wing it." I laughed. Brad gave me a horrified look. "Obviously, I'm kidding. I have a better idea. Let's play a game."

Lily grinned. "I like it."

"Let's give Tim a dose of his own medicine," said Brent.

"Some good old-fashioned vigilante justice," said Max.

"Damn straight," said Thirteen.

"Is everyone in?" asked Brad. He held his hand out in a fist. We all put our fists in the circle, giving each other a fist bump.

"This will be our last hoorah before heading off to college in the fall," said Shoes.

"Summer vacation here we come," said Blond Ambition.

SNEAK PEEK INTO ULTIMATE REVENGE: END GAME

Red Rover, Red Rover, send Payton right over. It is time to start our new game, kitty cat. People knowing our identity is irrelevant. The show must go on. Before it does, here is a big unanswered question: Do I want Payton for her body or her mind? Answer: Her mind, of course. Payton is not my type. I prefer my conquests to be more impressionable. I must be in complete control. Payton is too obstinate for her own good. My prediction: It will kill her one day. However, it would be easy to wrap someone like Teagan or Julie around my little finger. Enough said.

Here is another big question running through your brains: Who is Warlock? Answer: Tim. Is Streak dead because he beat Tim at a video game? He is not that petty. There is another reason why that kid is dead. It is up to you to figure that out. I will not spoon feed you or hold your hand while you cross the street. Get your shit together and solve that mystery.

Next on the agenda: What evil deed will we make Payton do next? Tune back in to find out. You do not want to miss this; it will be priceless. What evil deed has she already done? I cannot wait to tell her. Payton's innocence will be lost forever. She will not handle this well. Payton will either rise to our challenge, or cave like a little bitch. Yes … I am a monster.

The list of my chosen victims is laminated. The wheel will soon be set into motion. I predict a bumpy ride for some of Payton's friends. What about Payton? Will we let her live? That is a good question. No one is off limits in Round Three. Anything can happen. Those are the rules. I told you that I am pure evil within. Why would you doubt me?

When I am done playing around, we will all watch The Chosen's light fade. I will tell all while you peer through your fingers in horror. That is what everyone wants, right? So, you will have it. You are all so annoyingly predictable. I loathe your existence, which says a lot coming from a serial killer like me. The demented and the morally corrupt will look down on your souls in the end. They will spit on your graves when they walk past your rotting corpses on judgement day. Am I being too harsh? Look in the mirror and then tell me again how and why you should be forgiven.

Why should you be let into the pearly gates when others are not? I thought so. You better work on your end game. Your dark side is showing. You do not have a snowball's chance in hell at redemption.

Speaking of redemption, what about everyone's favorite stud boy Dylan? Alive or dead? Just asking for a friend. I could go either way on this one. He means nothing to me, but I think Payton's feelings still run deep. I see another brutal test in the future.

Just out of curiosity, did I fool any of you brainiacs? If not, I have a few more tricks up my sleeve that you will not see coming. How many of you thought I was Payton? I must admit, that was a stroke of genius. I will be gloating about that for quite some time. God I am brilliant. I am the master. Can I get another standing ovation? No!? You will not deny me after this. I will let you wannabes in on a little secret: Only Dr. Parks and In The Mind of a Murderer spoke in proper English without contractions. Did anyone catch that? I thought not. I told you to pay closer attention this time around. Now get on your feet and give me the round of applause that I deserve.

Nice! That is more like it. Before we part ways, I will drag the dollar bill through the trailer park one last time. Someone Payton knows is related to me. Who is it? And there it is, your cliffhanger. And for extra credit: Who will die first? Someone close to Payton, or someone close to me? I dare you to chase us to find out the answer.

***

This is Payton Marie Richardson. I'm about to get even with a serial killer. Would you like to watch?

S.K. Lundberg started her career off in the medical field before switching gears later in life to follow her passion for writing. Currently, she enjoys a quiet, small town lifestyle that allows her time to spend on her favorite hobbies. Most of her spare time revolves around her family, the dogs, friends, fun foodie experiments, sports, staying fit, music, her love of all things creative, especially her tie-dye projects, and of course, a good book to read is always a must.

Made in the USA
Middletown, DE
18 March 2022

62762513R00198